A SPLENDID LITTLE WAR

THE WAR TO END ALL WARS people said in 1918. But by 1919, White Russians were fighting Bolshevik Reds for control of their country, and Winston Churchill wanted to see Communism 'strangled in its cradle'. So a volunteer R.A.F. squadron, flying Sopwith Camels and DH9 bombers, went there to duff up the Reds. 'There's a splendid little war going on,' a British staff officer told them. 'You'll like it.' But the war was neither splendid nor little. It was big and it was brutal. Before it ended, the squadron wished both sides would lose. If that was a joke, nobody was laughing.

For Shiela

A SPLENDID LITTLE WAR

A SPLENDID LITTLE WAR

by

Derek Robinson

Magna Large Print Books
Long Preston, North Yorkshire,
BD23 4ND, England.

British Library Cataloguing in Publication Data.

Robinson, Derek
A splendid little war.

A catalogue record of this book is
available from the British Library

ISBN 978-0-7505-3819-0

First published in Great Britain in 2013 by MacLehose Press
an imprint of Quercus

Magna Large Print is an imprint of Library Magna Books Ltd.

Printed and bound in Great Britain by
T.J. (International) Ltd., Cornwall, PL28 8RW

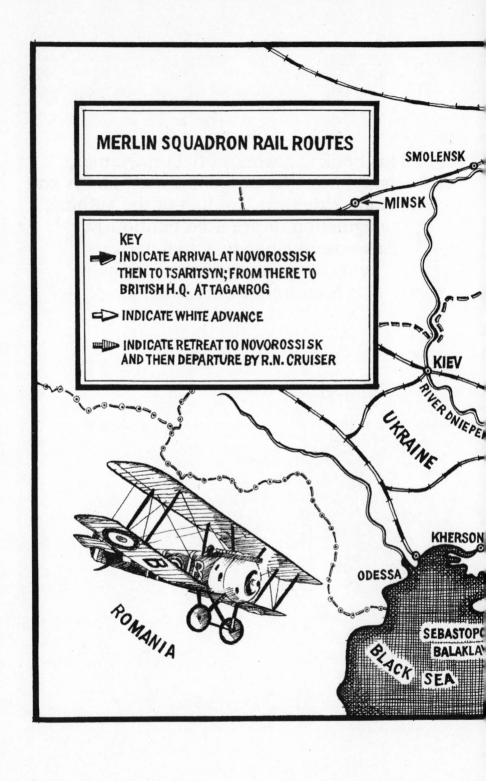

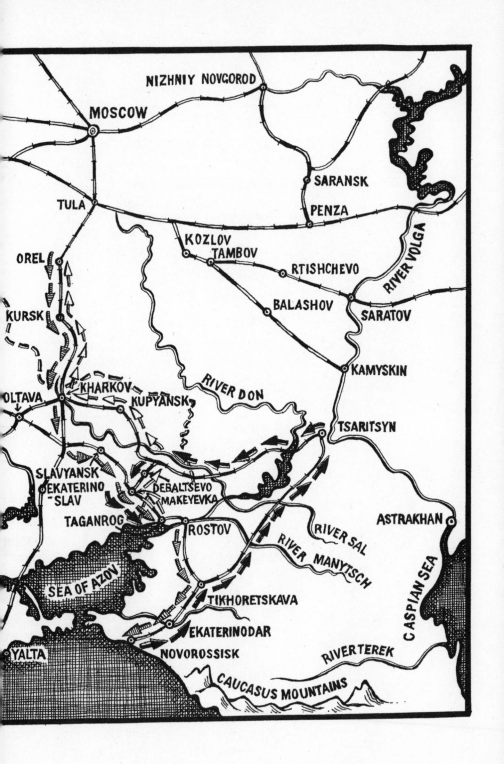

FOREWORD

A Splendid Little War is based on fact. In 1919 Britain sent forces from all three Armed Services to Russia, in support of the White armies in their civil war against the Bolshevik armies. Britain also sent military supplies to the value of more than a hundred million pounds – a billion pounds in modern money – to help the White cause. This policy was known as 'the Intervention'. It ended in failure. Many British personnel died in Russia or in Russian waters.

The Intervention was a complex affair. In the Baltic, the Royal Navy engaged in sea battles against the Soviet fleet and bombarded positions inland. In the far south, British units fought Bolshevik forces on the shores of the Caspian Sea, as they did in the far north, at Murmansk and Archangel. British troops were sent to Vladivostok, on the Pacific coast. Training units went to the heart of Siberia, to assist Admiral Kolchak's anti-Bolshevik campaign, and took part in the fighting. At various times, Canadian, American, French, Greek, Japanese and Czech forces were all involved in the conflict. But Britain was by far the biggest actor, and the biggest spender.

The crucial action centred on the White armies in south Russia, where they were hard pressed by the Red armies. In 1919 a couple of R.A.F. squadrons, manned by volunteer aircrews, arrived to help; this provided the theme for the novel. The story it tells is, I believe, true to the history of the Intervention. For greater detail about what is fact and what is fiction, see my Author's Note at the end of the book.

D.R.

CAST OF CHARACTERS

IN RUSSIA

Wing Commander Griffin, C.O. of Merlin Squadron

'A' FLIGHT (Sopwith Camels)	'B' FLIGHT (DH9 bombers)
James Hackett	Tusker Oliphant
Tiger Wragge	Gerry Pedlow
Jeremy Bellamy	Joe Duncan
Rex Dextry	Mickey Blythe
Junk Jessop	Douglas Gunning
Daddy Maynard	Michael Lowe
	Tommy Hopton

Russian Liaison: Count Pierre Borodin
Adjutant: Captain Brazier
Radio and Supplies: Lacey
Lacey's agent: Henry
Medical: Dr Susan Perry, Sergeant Stevens
Chief Air Mechanic: Flight Sergeant Patterson
Commandant at Beketofka aerodrome: Colonel Davenport
Visiting Officer: Colonel Guy Kenny
Contacts at British Military Mission H.Q.:
Captain Butcher
Captain Stokes
Daddy Maynard's rescuer: Major Edwardes

IN LONDON
David Lloyd George, Prime Minister
Jonathan Fitzroy, aide to P.M.
Advisory Committee:
Charles Delahaye (Treasury)
Sir Franklyn Fletcher (Foreign Office)
General Stattaford (War Office)
James Weatherby (Home Office)

COMPLETE CHANGE OF SCENERY

1

Bennett had lost the aerodrome.

Embarrassing. Damned embarrassing.

It couldn't be more than a mile or two away, but the Camel was shaking like a wet dog. Whatever was wrong with the engine resulted in this huge vibration. His compass was a blur. Smoke swirled into the cockpit and made him choke and cough. Something in the engine had probably broken, maybe a piston rod or a cylinder head, Bennett wasn't terribly *au fait* with the workings of a rotary engine. It stuttered and threatened to quit. It was throwing oil: his goggles were spattered with the muck. If he ducked his head to avoid the oil he couldn't see where the Camel was going, and he knew he had to find a field, any field would do. But when he raised his head and searched, the oil spatter got worse and he couldn't see through the smoke. He could switch off the engine and stop the spray of oil but he knew the Camel would glide like a brick and he hadn't much height anyway. What he didn't know was this Camel was old and tired. The squadron always gave a new boy the worst aeroplane. He glimpsed the top of a pine tree racing past. Crash meant fire, he knew that, knew he must be able to get out fast. He looked down to unfasten his seat belt and didn't see the next pine. It clipped his left wing. The Camel spun. Bennett got flung into a black and spiky forest at a speed that left his wits far behind him, which spared him the knowledge of what he hit and what it did to him. The Camel flew on, sideways, and met a tall oak tree. Birds panicked for half a mile around. Then silence again.

Butler's Farm aerodrome was three miles from Epping Forest. The airfield had been hastily built in 1917, when Germany began sending form-ations of Gotha bombers to raid England, and fighter squadrons were hurried back from France to reassure the frightened civilians. The Gothas couldn't guarantee to hit any target smaller than a town, and sometimes not even that; and the number they killed would have been less than a hiccup on the daily death toll in the Trenches. But the idea of total war was new and shocking to civilians, and so a squadron of the latest Camels came to Butler's Farm in Essex. The pilots liked it: London was just down the road. A few enemy machines got shot down in flames while Lon-doners applauded. The threat receded. The Camels returned to France for what, to every-one's surprise, turned out to be the last year of the war. Not everyone lived to be surprised: air combat killed several, and a few Camels went out of control and buried themselves and their pilots deep in the mud of the Western Front. It could be a lethal little fighter.

After the Armistice, the surviving pilots flew

back to Butler's Farm and the squadron set about rebuilding. Jeremy Bennett was one of the new boys. Eighteen, tall, captain of rugby and cricket at Lancing, he passed out top at Flying Training. The war was over, but his type was exactly what the new Royal Air Force was looking for.

Now the adjutant couldn't find him.

He'd taken off two hours ago, so he was probably out of fuel, and phone calls to all the local aerodromes drew a blank. The adjutant had asked a couple of pilots to go up, fly around, make a search. Nothing. It was early March, cold and grey. The day was wearing on. A mist was forming.

Then the adjutant's phone rang. The police had heard from a farmer who'd seen a plane go overhead, sounding wrong, making smoke. Heading? Sort of north, he'd said. When? Hour ago, maybe hour and a half. Why had he waited so long? Harrowing his field. Finished harrowing, went home, reported it. The adjutant pencilled a cross on a map.

It wasn't much of a search party – two officers and a sergeant mechanic – but then it wasn't much of a clue. They took the adjutant's car, got lost in the lanes but eventually found the farm, and the farmer. 'Seemed wrong,' he told them. What sort of wrong? 'Well, you know. Sounded bad.' He coughed harshly, to demonstrate. 'Worse than that. And I saw smoke, too.' Asked how high it was, he pointed to a flock of crows heading homewards. 'Twice as high as them.' They got in the car and drove on.

They were both pilots: Wragge, an Englishman,

and Hackett, an Australian. At twenty-two, they were hardened veterans of the air war. They had gone to France in the autumn of 1917 and were lucky enough to have joined a flight whose leader could count up to one. He held up his index finger. 'Look after Number One,' he told them. 'For Christ's sake, don't make the Supreme Sacrifice. That's not going to win this bloody stupid war. The clown who said it's noble and honourable to die for your country never knew what it's like to get a bellyful of incendiary bullets at ten thousand feet. Are you listening? Make the other silly bugger die for *his* country. Then whizz home, fast. Got it?' They got it. They learned more skills from others, and helped a number of German pilots make the Supreme Sacrifice. They were flight leaders when the war ended, with a reputation for quick and efficient killing. Instead of saying *damn and blast,* the squadron said *wragge and hackett!*

That was in France. Now they were sitting in the back of the adjutant's car, watching the Essex hedgerows go by while the afternoon slipped away; looking for a lost Camel that might be hiding behind that haystack for all they knew. 'This is bloody silly,' Hackett said. Just an idle remark. Not serious.

'What was he doing out here?' Wragge asked. It wasn't really a question. 'If it was him.'

'I told him to learn the landmarks. Stay in sight of the aerodrome. Bloody idiot.'

Rain speckled the windscreen. 'You get these nasty mists in Essex, sir,' the sergeant said. 'Bad for navigation. Fogs, too. Spring up out of

18

nowhere. Mists and fog.' He sucked his teeth.

'I hope you know where you're going,' Wragge said. 'I'm completely lost.'

'Remember that ginger-haired Irishman when we were on the Somme?' Hackett said. 'Kelly. Got lost in a fog, flew into a hill, lickety-split. Always in a tearing hurry, Kelly.'

'Not easy to find a hill in France.'

'Well, he was very lost. Why have you stopped, sergeant?'

'Epping Forest, sir. D'you want to go in? It's big.'

They got out and looked at the forest. Rain flickered through the headlights. Nothing was in leaf; the trees were black and gloomy. 'It would take a regiment a week to search that lot,' Wragge said.

Hackett put his chin up and sniffed. 'Funny smell.'

'Charcoal,' Wragge said. 'It's a wood. Charcoal burners.'

Hackett kept sniffing. 'Smells funny. We've come this far. Let's go and ask the natives. Maybe they saw something.'

The sergeant had an electric lantern. They followed Hackett's sense of smell, and after a hundred yards they found the oak tree with the Camel wrapped around a fistful of branches. A petrol tank was still dripping. Chunks of hot metal had dropped and started a small fire at the base of the tree and it still glowed, but amazingly the flames had not reached the Camel. It was shattered, but the bits were intact. The cockpit was empty.

19

They walked in increasing circles and soon found Bennett. He lay with every limb twisted so that they pointed the wrong way. They carried him back to the car. It had a rumble seat, and that seemed the obvious place to put him. It was open to the weather and the rain was hammering down but Bennett didn't care.

The car jolted up the lane and sent brown bow-waves flying into the dark. 'Take it steady,' Wragge told the sergeant. 'We don't want another accident.'

'Bloody awful climate,' Hackett muttered.

'Well, it's England,' Wragge said. 'It's what we English call a baking hot day in Essex.'

'It's rained like a bitch every day for a week. Where the hell does it come from?'

'We import it from the Atlantic, old boy. Been doing it for centuries. Steady, reliable, phlegmatic stuff. Very traditional. You Colonials wouldn't understand.'

The sergeant said, 'It's not like Australia, Mr Hackett. You planning on going back?'

'Back to what? Sheep and cricket? No thanks.'

'Get used to the rain, then,' Wragge said. 'Settle down here and breed goldfish. The fun's over.'

'It was the war to end all wars,' the sergeant said. 'Everyone says so.'

'By Christ, I hope not,' Hackett said. He sounded annoyed.

They delivered the body to the Medical Officer and gave the news to the adjutant, who thanked them. 'Don't thank us, Uncle,' Wragge said. 'He killed himself, poor bastard. We just got wet feet.'

20

The adjutant knew better than to argue. He was an ex-cavalry major, aged forty-five, felt like sixty-five in the company of these casual assassins. He reminded them that tonight was Dining-In Night in the Mess, distinguished guest present, look smart, be sharp; and he watched them go. *Younger than my sons,* he thought, *older than Methuselah.*

He phoned the Medical Officer and confirmed that Jeremy Meredith Tobias Bennett, aged eighteen, really was dead and not the makings of a practical joke. The Royal Flying Corps had become the Royal Air Force, but it retained its undergraduate humour. Only a week ago, the Egyptian ambassador in London had telephoned him to discuss the proposal by His Majesty King Mahomet to make the squadron honorary members of the Royal Camel Corps, in recognition of its pluck and courage. He was pretty sure that the voice belonged to Flying Officer Dextry. Bloody idiots. Problem was, they hadn't enough to do. Peace was boring.

The adjutant fished out some papers from his in-tray. Restaurant in Chelsea demanded payment for damages caused by horseplay leading to food-fight. That was 'B' Flight. They'd blamed it all on a crowd of American aviators. Self-defence, 'B' Flight said... Metropolitan Police were looking for the officers who hired some horses and raced them down Park Lane and up Piccadilly. Probably Hackett's doing. And somebody's Camel went and flour-bombed the Brighton Express as it left Waterloo, so now Air Ministry was furious. One flour-bomb actually hit the dining car. Few

21

pilots had that kind of skill. In the margin, the adjutant wrote: *Jessop?*

The last paper was the worst of all. The accounts for the Officers' Mess showed a loss of £483, a horribly huge amount. Flying Officer Bellamy was President of the Mess Committee, but he claimed that his predecessor, chap called Champion, must have pocketed the money, lost it at the races, spent it on floozies, who knew what? The trouble was, Champion was dead, got into a spin, made a hole in the heart of Essex. Left a hole in the Mess funds.

The adjutant tossed the papers back in his in-tray. Tomorrow was soon enough. Nothing would change, of course. He'd still be surrounded by bloody idiots.

The camp at Butler's Farm was built fast, mainly from Nissen huts. Luckily, part of the airfield had been a cricket field, and the pavilion became the Officers' Mess. Long yards of creamy linen covered trestle tables. There was much silverware, looted in the final advance when the squadron had occupied an aerodrome suddenly abandoned by the German air force.

Flying Officer Bellamy's disasters had not yet been made public and he had decided to go out with a bang, if not a cheer. There was a lot of wine. Bellamy knew what the chaps liked: game soup, baked stuffed haddock, roast rib of beef, jam roly-poly with custard, welsh rarebit. No fancy frog names, no mucky sauces. Plenty of mashed potato with the beef. He told the waiters to be ready with second helpings. Bellamy was no good at sums, but he knew the chaps.

Dinner went well.

The C.O. got them to their feet for the loyal toast, and then introduced their distinguished guest.

'A man,' he said, 'whose achievements in our recent difference of opinion with the Boche have become a thing of legend, both as a pilot and as a leader. He took air fighting to a new level, as the enemy soon discovered, because invariably he was above them, and shortly afterwards they were descending at a great rate of knots, usually without a tail or a wing.' (Laughter.) 'I'm sure everyone here knows his astonishing record. Gentlemen: our guest … Wing Commander J.E.B. Griffin.'

Few fighter pilots were tall. If your head stuck outside the cockpit, it was the equivalent of facing a gale on top of the Alps, which didn't help eyesight or breathing and exposed you to the enemy's guns. So nobody was surprised to see that Griffin was short, with broad shoulders. He didn't look like a hero; but then most heroes look like ploughboys or bricklayers: compact, strong, quiet. The squadron got ready for a few words about how we won and what an honour it had been to serve, and Griffin surprised them all.

'Gentlemen,' he said. 'We thought it was all over. But there is still a certain amount of what the infantry calls mopping-up to be done, and I have been asked to lead a new squadron. It seems that our Russian friends need a hand to help put their house in order.'

He took a sip of water and let the rumble of comments subside. Russia? Wore fur hats and had snow on their boots, didn't they? Russia. Crikey.

'For those of you who are looking for a complete change of scenery, I recommend northern Russia. We have bases at Murmansk and Archangel. They are on or about the Arctic Circle and both need pilots. If you relish a challenge, this is the place for you. The natives are treacherous, and the enemy – the Bolsheviks – are savages. The cold is brutal. Last month a general took his gloves off to pin a medal on a chap, got instant frostbite, and pinned his own fingers instead. Fact.'

They enjoyed that. Griffin allowed himself a small smile.

'You will live in hovels and share them with lice and fleas. No beer, and the vodka is foul. Nothing can stop your engine oil from freezing. Your pay is good but there is absolutely nothing to spend it on except funerals. Yes, north Russia is a challenge.'

They laughed, and applauded. 'What's he playing at?' Wragge asked Hackett, and got a shrug in reply.

So, if that's your meat, I can arrange it,' Griffin said. 'Meanwhile I shall be leading my squadron to south Russia, down on the shores of the Black Sea. Climate like the French Riviera. Rich farming country – melons as sweet as honey, cherries as big as plums, beefsteaks as thick as thieves. I don't care for caviare but maybe you do. You'll have to sing for your supper, of course. The White Army holds the south. The Red Army wants it. General Denikin leads the Whites. Brilliant commander, splendid patriot, and if Russia has any future, the saviour of his nation. Britain has sent him supplies worth millions of pounds. Our task is simple: we help him duff up the enemy, who are a complete rabble, and we escort his march on Moscow. Oh, and by the way: you'll get paid one grade higher than your rank for doing it.'

A storm of applause. The adjutant looked around and counted Dextry, Jessop, Bellamy, Wragge and Hackett on their feet, cheering. Good. That should thin out the bloody idiots and make his in-tray lighter.

Two-thirds of the squadron volunteered for south Russia. 'I'll take half,' Griffin told the C.O. 'You can keep the drunks and the sex maniacs and the ones who like pulling wings off butter-flies.'

'Oh, thanks enormously,' the C.O. said. He began going through the list with a red pencil.

'Is it really true that everyone will get paid above his rank?' the adjutant asked. Griffin nodded. 'The only reason I ask,' the adjutant said, 'is the squadron hasn't converted from R.F.C. to R.A.F. ranks. Not totally, that is. Some chaps are cap-tains, some flight lieutenants. What's the R.A.F. equivalent of a colonel?'

'Don't know. What matters is each chap gets a bucket of roubles every week.'

'Simpson,' the C.O. said. 'Isn't Simpson the one who wears a corset?' He didn't wait for an answer. The red pencil thudded through Simp-son.

'Roubles, you say,' the adjutant said. 'I don't think we can wait for troubles. Not if you want these officers *immediately.*' He frowned hard at a mental picture of complex problems. 'It's their Mess bills, you see. I fear they can't pay them now. In fact I know they can't.'

Griffin looked him in the eye. Neither man blinked. Each knew that R.A.F. Butler's Farm wouldn't have a hope in hell of getting money out of a pilot once he was on his way to south Russia. Each also knew that the red pencil had not yet finished its work. The C.O. became aware of their silence, and he looked up.

'The pity is,' the adjutant said, 'sometimes the best pilots owe the most money.'

'How much? To wipe the slate clean.'

The adjutant thought fast. 'Five hundred pounds.'

While Griffin wrote a cheque, the C.O. finished his list. 'Hackett,' he said. 'Australian. Tenacious bugger.' He twirled the red pencil.

'Oh, you'll like him,' the adjutant said quickly.

'Chuck him in,' Griffin said. 'I'll take him instead of a receipt.' He waved the cheque to dry the ink. 'This is War Office money. Cash it fast, before they change their minds about saving the Russian Empire from the Reds. By all reports, the Reds are winning hands down.' He saw the look on the C.O.'s face. 'Joke,' he said. 'I haven't the faintest idea who's winning. A pal of mine at the Foreign Office reckons the Reds are surrounded on all sides by White armies. He's guessing. Hoping, too, probably. All I know is this bloke Denikin's running the show in the south and he's been asking for British squadrons for months.'

'I hope you hammer the Bolsheviks good and

26

hard,' the C.O. said, 'After what they did to the Tsar.'

'Dirty work. Mind you, we can't talk,' Griffin said. 'We chopped off the king's head once. Be sure your chaps are at Air Ministry tomorrow, ten a.m. prompt, drunk or sober. Long journey ahead.'

2

Long, slow journey.

Griffin had collected about twenty pilots from the best squadrons. The first plan was to send them by train to somewhere in Greece, probably Salonika, and ship them the rest of the way. They got as far as Calais and were recalled. Nobody knew why. Next plan was to put them on a ship in London docks, a Swedish freighter unloading timber. It had no passenger accommodation. Griffin got on the phone to Air Ministry, who called the Ministry of Shipping, who called the War Office, by which time it was raining so hard the spray was knee-high, and everybody went back to their hotels and unpacked. The train plan was revived and this time they got as far as Paris. But several big avalanches in Austria had closed the line to Salonika and they went to Marseilles instead.

The city was pleasantly sunny in the early spring. Lots of bars, open all day and half the night, unlike the tight-laced pub hours in England. Wine was cheap. On the pilots' improved pay scales, very cheap. The Marine Landing Officer had his hands full with ships taking troops home to be demobilized, but he managed to find berths for Griffin's party on a small French liner, got them cheap at short notice. Griffin couldn't round up his pilots fast enough and the ship sailed. It took the M.L.O. a week to get them on board another vessel, an old Mediterranean ferry that called at Nice, Genoa, Naples and Palermo before it limped into Malta with engine trouble. The captain didn't trust the Maltese repairs. The ship crawled along the North African coast and finally quit at Alexandria. The captain was Egyptian. He felt at home here.

Griffin was due some luck. A Royal Navy cruiser was about to leave for – thankfully – the Black Sea. The pilots slept four to a cabin. The weather was fine; they lived on deck, playing poker, watching the Aegean Islands drift by, guessing their names, getting them wrong. Past Gallipoli (bloody steep, bloody rocky, you wouldn't want to attack up there, not with the Turks firing down, what a shambles) and the cruiser didn't stop at Constantinople, which was on the left while most of Turkey was on the right, very confusing.

After that, the Black Sea turned out to be not at all black. 'Red Sea isn't red, either,' Hackett said. 'And the Indian Ocean's green. I've seen it.' That started an argument. It was easy to argue with Hackett and difficult to stop. Prove him wrong, and he said: 'Yes, that's what most people think, but most people have brains fifteen per cent smaller than mine.' He went on, dodging and ducking, slipping and swerving. Angering some, amusing others. It passed the time. There was nothing to look at except the Black Sea. Very boring, the sea. All water. Nobody could understand why the Navy got so excited about it.

Nobody had much to say about Russia because nobody knew much about the Russians. Griffin said the Bolshies needed to be taught a lesson, and that was good enough. There were chaps from all over the British Empire in his squadron, and the Empire was good at keeping the natives in line. None better.

3

A major from the British Military Mission to Denikin (D.E.N.M.I.S.) climbed onto a broken packing case that was leaking puttees, khaki, infantry, for the use of, and raised his megaphone. The dockside at Novorossisk was loud with the bangs and whistles of unloading freighters.

'Keep together!' he shouted. 'Put your luggage on that wagon. It will be safe. It has an armed guard. Keep together and follow me! Do not speak to any civilians. Beware pickpockets. Do not buy, sell or exchange anything. Ignore all corpses, beggars, prostitutes, Frenchmen and mad dogs. Keep together! Follow me!' He climbed down.

The sky was gloomy grey to the horizon and it leaked bits of rain that stung like hail. The wind was from the north, fierce and cold as charity.

The pilots climbed onto two lorries. Bellamy found himself sitting next to the major. 'Somewhat chilly for the time of year, sir,' he said.

'About normal. Gets a damn sight colder. Sea

29

of Azov is still frozen.'

'My goodness.'

'You don't know where that is, do you?'

'Um ... to be brutally honest, no sir.'

'Offshoot of the Black Sea. Between us and the Crimea. Hundred and fifty miles across. Solid ice.'

'Heavens. We were led to expect something more like the French Riviera, sir.'

The major hadn't smiled since he came to Russia and he saw no reason to start now; but he looked at Bellamy and allowed his eyelids to sink a little. 'Russia has two seasons. Too bloody cold and too bloody hot. Who told you that French Riviera twaddle?'

'The C.O., sir. But I'm sure he was misinformed.'

'You're sure, are you? Congratulations. You're the only person in this bloody country who's sure of anything.' Already the major was tired of Bellamy. He looked away.

In the other lorry, Jessop and Wragge were trying to decide whether Novorossisk was a dump or a dead loss. 'Look at the *mud*,' Jessop said. 'The place is all mud. The streets are deep in mud. It's supposed to be the biggest port in these parts and everywhere you look it's mud.'

'But it's busy. Crowds of people.'

'All mud-coloured. Maybe that's what they export: mud.'

'Some of them are waving at us. And cheering. Holding flags. So it's not a dead loss, is it?'

They waved back. Nothing extravagant. A nod and a smile to the grateful natives.

30

'I've just seen a man eating a slice of mud,' Jessop said. 'If it wasn't that, it was a portion of rhubarb crumble, which seems unlikely, don't you think?'

The lorries splashed through potholes and delivered them to the Novorossisk headquarters of the British Military Mission, in a requisitioned girls' school. Servants took their caps and great-coats, brushed them down as if they were prize stallions, and showed them to the cloakrooms. The washbasins were small and low, but the water was hot and more servants stood by with towels, and bottles of hair lotion from Trumper of Bond Street, and boot-polishing requisites to offer a quick brush-up to such footwear as was less than officer-like. Then to lunch.

The dining-room walls were hung with group photographs of unsmiling girls, immaculately dressed in school uniform. So there had been a time when Novorossisk was not entirely made of mud. A portrait picture of the headmistress, with eyes that could penetrate sheet steel at fifty yards, looked down on the crowd of young men drinking sherry. They were many, and a lot of sherry was going down. Lunch at the Mission was clearly an important occasion.

The airmen joined in. A tall, hawk-nosed flight lieutenant called Oliphant, balding and therefore looking older than his twenty-three years, was sinking his second sherry and looking for a servant with more, when Griffin prodded his ribs. 'Spread the word, Olly. I've just got orders. We entrain to somewhere called Ekaterinodar this afternoon. Off to the wars! Bloody good, eh?'

31

Lunch was a leisurely affair and excellent. Nobody seemed in a hurry to get back to work. Each pilot had been seated among the hosts. 'We don't get many visitors,' a chubby captain said. His hair was dark blond, as sleek as beaten gold. He stopped a passing waiter. 'Rudyard, my dear fellow... Bring butter. *Quantities* of butter. And fresh mustard. This mustard is medieval. Now be off with you!' He clapped his hands.

Pilot Officer Maynard watched this. He was nineteen, looked seventeen, shaved twice a week whether he needed it or not. 'Is his name really Rudyard?' he asked. It was a safe question.

'It is now. He's what we call a *plenny*. We have lots of them. *Plennys* are Russian prisoners-of-war, deserters mainly, quite safe, they make jolly good servants. This one's Russian name sounds like someone knitting with barbed wire, so we call him Rudyard. He likes it, he's a happy man, didn't like fighting for the Bolos. Bolsheviks,' he said before Maynard could ask. 'We call them Bolos. What they call us I don't know. Never met one. Poisonous lot, by all reports. Eat with their mouths open, I expect. You know the sort.'

'You don't see much of the Front, I take it,' Hackett said.

The captain looked startled. 'Good grief, no. We're the Supplies Mission. The warriors are all up-country. We make sure the ship unloads its cargo. Once the goods are on the quay they belong to Denikin's lot. Russian responsibility, not ours. What brings you to Novo, may I ask?'

'We're Royal Air Force,' Maynard said.

'Pilots.' Hackett pointed to his wings. 'We fly.'

'Ah, yes. Balloons. Spotting for the guns.'

'Aeroplanes. Scouts, I hope.'

'Flying machines. How amusing. My advice is, do lots of stunts. The Russians will be tremendously impressed. They admire anything modern enormously. Looping the loop, and so on.'

Hackett breathed deeply and ripped a piece of bread in half. Maynard said: 'The docks were awfully busy. Is all that stuff for the Russian troops?'

'So my sergeant tells me. I stay away from there. Can't speak the language, for a start. I write reports.'

'How amusing,' Hackett said through a mouthful of bread.

'Keeps the general happy,' the captain said. 'Thing I learned in France, you can't have too many good reports. And if I say it myself, I'm jolly good at it. Ah ... butter. And mustard. Bully for you, Rudyard. Now be about your business, my boy.'

Griffin had been given a seat at the top table, next to the Mission Commandant, an amiable brigadier who told him he wouldn't have any trouble with the Russians provided he remembered his status. 'Training and maintenance, old chap, that's what we're here for. Help the White Russians fight, but stay out of the scrap. Advise but don't intervene. What's the name of your outfit?'

'Hasn't got a name, sir. Just an R.A.F. squadron. Should have a number, but...'

'Better off without one, in my opinion. Put a foot wrong, and some base-wallah in London

33

knows who to blame. Ah, soup.'

Griffin supped his soup. 'A squadron's like a club, sir. Pilots like to belong to something. I know numbers are out, but still… In France, there was an outfit called Hornet Squadron. Stung a lot of Huns.'

'A nickname,' the brigadier said. 'Let's see: bees, wasps, termites. No. You want something Russian. A bird? Charles is our resident bird-watcher. Charles! We need a good Russian bird. Something exciting. No sparrows, no pheasant.'

Charles, a tall, tanned lieutenant, didn't hesitate. 'Goshawks, sir. Goshawks are everywhere.'

'Goshawk has been taken already,' Griffin said.

'Oh. Well, I've seen larks, some tawny owls, magpie, and of course great tits in abundance. Very handsome.'

'Great Tit Squadron,' Griffin said. 'That's asking for trouble.'

'Bigger and tougher,' the brigadier told Charles.

'Um … let's see … golden eagles? They're all over Russia. No? What about the great bustard? Lots of them on the steppes, although I suppose the name is unfortunate. Might lead to jokes in bad taste.' Charles thought hard. 'Doesn't leave much, I'm afraid.' Then he brightened. 'Merlin. I've seen merlin. Bird of prey, small but dashing, chases and kills other birds.'

'Merlin Squadron,' Griffin said. 'Yes. Merlin Squadron.'

'Thank you, Charles,' the brigadier said. 'I'll put you in for a D.S.O.'

Griffin turned to Oliphant. 'The squadron's got a name. Merlin Squadron. Bird of prey. Like a

34

hawk. Merlin Squadron. Pass it on.'

'Certainly, sir. Good choice.' Oliphant was sitting next to an elderly lieutenant with a faded M.C. ribbon. 'We've got a name. Merlin Squadron,' he told him. 'We're going to somewhere called Ekaterinodar. Not far, I believe.'

'It's seventy miles, and it's over the mountains. Last time I went there the trip took fourteen hours. My advice is: eat hearty.' He signalled a waiter. 'More soup for this officer... No dining cars on your train. No heat, no lavatories, broken windows, first class means you might get a seat with springs to poke you in the rump. Plenty of bugs. And plenty of life in the bugs.'

'Seventy miles,' Oliphant said. 'Fourteen hours.'

'The mountains are steep, old boy. The locomotive has to take a little rest now and then. If you feel like a walk, get out, stretch your legs, have a pee, pick some flowers. Not yet, of course, too bloody cold for flowers. Travel in this frightful country is a far cry from taking tea on the *Brighton Belle*.' A waiter poured red wine. 'Everything's a far cry. Cheers.'

Oliphant drank, and finished his soup and got to work on the second bowl. 'Ekaterinodar,' he said. 'Near the fighting?'

'Hard to say. The war tends to wander about. Tell you one thing: the place is stiff with typhus, smallpox, enteric fever, malaria, influenza, you name it. I wouldn't linger there, if I were you.'

Oliphant thought the man might be slightly drunk, or perhaps he was inventing these horrors, feeding tall tales to the new boys. He ate a big lunch and he said nothing to Griffin. And then the squadron shook hands and thanked everyone and was trucked to the station, where their train was late and turned out to be even slower and dirtier and colder than the lieutenant had said. The mountains were magnificent but scenic splendour was no substitute for heat.

The pilots spent a bitterly cold and hungry night, and reached Ekaterinodar in time for breakfast. They assembled on the platform, yawning and stamping. Griffin sent Wragge to find the station canteen. He came back, shaking his head. 'Bloody awful language,' he said. 'Either the Russians don't eat breakfast, or they do and they've eaten it all. Take your pick.'

'Jessop,' Griffin said sharply. 'For Christ's sake stop scratching.'

'I'm being eaten for breakfast, sir,' Jessop said. 'The little Russian bastards think I'm bacon and eggs.'

Griffin looked around. All he could see was a wall with signs and posters in a garbled and incoherent alphabet, and a drifting crowd of civilians, rich and poor, carrying what mattered most to them, whether it was a live chicken or a sable overcoat; and bunches of soldiers with faces from a dozen races, all wearing a mix of tired uniforms and all bearing the shut-in defensive look of an army that has been given too many stupid orders and is wary of hearing more.

'No point in standing here looking stupid,' Griffin said. 'I'm going to find the H.Q.' He pointed at Hackett. 'You're in command.' They watched him disappear into the crowd. A minute passed.

'We could eat Maynard,' Dextry said. 'He's fresh.'

They looked at Maynard, who frowned hard.

'Not without roast potatoes,' Jessop said. 'I couldn't stomach Maynard without roast spuds.'

'Here's a funny joke,' Dextry said. 'What is a roast potato and six bottles of Guinness?' Nobody cared. 'A seven-course meal in Ireland,' he said. Nobody laughed. 'I can change the potato to boiled cabbage, if you like.' Nobody spoke. 'In that case, you can all go and piss in your hats,' he said.

'Salvation!' Hackett announced. He waved his cap. 'Here comes God Almighty.'

A captain wearing a brassard with the letters R.T.O. cut through the mob. He was the Railway Transport Officer. He knew all, commanded all, permitted this, denied that. 'Burridge,' he said. 'Are you Major Burridge?' He squinted at the unfamiliar badges of rank. 'You're not Burridge.' He made it sound like an accusation.

'Hackett, flight lieutenant. This is Merlin Squadron, R.A.F.'

'No.' He rapped his gloved knuckles on his clipboard. 'Got no authority for you. Don't exist here. What's your transit priority number?' Fifty yards away, another train was arriving with a screech of brakes and a gush of steam. People rushed towards it; hundreds of people.

Hackett heard the hoarseness in the captain's throat and saw the weariness in his eyes. This man had been on duty all night and few things had gone right for him. 'God knows our number,' Hackett said. 'But we're here, and we need your help.'

'So you say. Without authority...' The clipboard got another rap. 'Not my problem.' As he turned to leave, Hackett grabbed him above the elbow. Hackett's fingers could unscrew a rusty nut from a corroded bolt as if they were opening a jar of jam, and they found a nerve in the captain's arm. 'We'll go for a walk,' he said gently. 'You and me and Wragge.'

The R.T.O. could stand on his dignity as pain flowered down his arm, or he could walk. The pain reached his fingers and he dropped his clipboard. He walked.

The others watched them go. 'Fat chance,' Jessop said. 'We don't exist. Starve to death for all he cares.' All around, men were sitting down.

Hackett stopped when the squadron was out of sight. With his free hand he had unbuttoned his greatcoat and opened the flap of his holster and now he took out the revolver. As he released his grip on the R.T.O.'s arm, he raised the gun and tickled him under the chin with it, until the man looked him in the eyes. 'Mr Wragge will explain,' he said.

'These men are not soldiers,' Wragge said. 'They are intrepid aviators, cavalry of the clouds, knights of the sky. They don't understand the regulations that are meat and drink to you. They have spent all night in a freezing, stinking, crawling Russian train and now they want breakfast. If I tell them otherwise they will kill you, and then me. Is that reasonable?'

'You're mad. You're raving.'

'So we have three options. First, Hackett here could shoot himself. He's desperate enough.

38

Wouldn't let you off the hook, though. Second, he could shoot you. The boys would like that.' Now the muzzle was tickling the R.T.O.'s ear. 'Please them enormously, that would. Or third, we could shoot that squalid peasant.' He pointed. Hackett used the revolver to turn the R.T.O.'s head.

A family of four squatted on the stone floor. They were like a thousand others: scrawny legs, hopeless faces, barefoot, dressed in tattered sheepskins, everything permanently dirty.

'Go ahead.' The R.T.O's voice began to crack under the strain. 'Shoot his wife too. And the children, bloody orphans, get rid of them, won't you?'

'Ah! Talking sense at last!' Hackett said. 'Now do we get breakfast?' The R.T.O. nodded. 'And transport to the aerodrome?' Another nod. 'You tell the boys,' Hackett said. 'They'll love you for it.' He bent down and fired and shot the spur off the R.T.O.'s right boot. The bullet ricocheted off the station floor and sang its way to nowhere special. The R.T.O. stumbled, almost fell, recovered. 'That's bloody idiotic,' he said. Now his voice was stumbling too.

'Of course it is. In France an SE5 squadron near us had a C.O. who did the same thing to some fart just like you. Now you can ride on half a horse, and I can die happy. Lead on.'

Griffin was waiting for them. 'Found the H.Q. Locked. Empty.'

'The captain will oblige us,' Hackett said. 'Only too willing.'

The R.T.O. took the pilots to a military canteen

39

and stood watching as they drank hot coffee and ate fried-egg sandwiches.

'He changed his tune very smartly,' Oliphant said.

'We found that we went to the same school,' Wragge said. 'After that, he couldn't do enough.'

'We heard a shot. Thought maybe you decided to have him put down.'

'What? Shoot the best slow left-arm spin bowler that St Jennifer's ever produced. Not cricket, old chap.'

'St Jennifer's. I didn't know there was a Saint Jennifer.'

'Not many do. A small school, but with very high standards. You'd never have got in, Olly. Not a hope.'

The R.T.O. came over. 'Two lorries,' he said. 'Waiting outside. You haven't heard the last of this.'

'Well, you know where to find us,' Hackett said. 'Up in the clouds, duelling with death.' He took the last sandwich and bit into it.

'Have a word with the management,' Wragge told the R.T.O. 'Worcester Sauce is what this place needs. Otherwise ... well done. Bully for you.'

'My report will go directly to the general.'

'Of course it will. Worcester Sauce. Make a note of it.'

4

The Royal College of Embroidery had occupied a building in the centre of Grosvenor Crescent, Belgravia, since 1783. Few Londoners knew it

40

existed; nobody polished the small, discreet nameplate. But the house was only a short cab-ride from all the major offices of state, and on a bright but chilly afternoon in March 1919, men from most of those offices were standing in its Reading Room. They were watching the Prime Minister, the Right Honourable David Lloyd George, who was talking quietly to his chief adviser. As they watched, they were thinking their various thoughts.

Charles Delahaye from the Treasury was thinking about tax. Paying for the war had been relatively easy, you just borrowed from the Americans, who, God knows, were happy to lend. But how was the P.M. going to sell this painfully expensive peace to the people?

General Stattaford from the War Office, six feet two in his socks, was thinking how short the P.M. was. Midgets were taking over the world. Even the Grenadier Guards had lowered their height requirement. Tragic, really. How can you have a short Grenadier?

Sir Franklyn Fletcher, Permanent Private Secretary at the Foreign Office, was thinking the P.M. looked awfully tired. All this rushing back and forth to France for the Peace Conference. Suppose President Wilson had to go back to America, suppose the P.M. went down with this terrible flu which was spreading everywhere – that would leave Clemenceau running the show and then we're really *dans le potage*...

James Weatherby, from the Home Office, was thinking Lloyd George looked like a small greengrocer. What did women see in him? The

41

man had all the charm of a walrus and more sex than a goat. The British newspapers were squared, nothing to worry about there, but what if the truth appeared in the foreign Press? The old goat might sue for libel. Weatherby shuddered.

Lloyd George nodded goodbye to them all, and left.

His chief adviser, Jonathan Fitzroy, sixty, was built like a blacksmith, face like a turnip, mind like a razor, and morals of a stoat. Or so people said. He gestured at the armchairs, arranged in a wide circle. For himself he chose a large cane chair. It gave him a height advantage.

'Gentlemen: you probably know each other. However...' He quickly introduced everyone, ending with General Stattaford. 'I shouldn't be here,' the general said. 'Forgot my *petit-point*.' He smiled when they chuckled. One up to the Army.

'An unusual rendezvous, I agree,' Fitzroy said. 'We're here because, first, my sister runs the College, and secondly, it's completely private. Free from gossip. And that matters because our agenda has only one, very delicate, item: Russia. The Prime Minister feels the public needs to be reassured. Some aspects of our Russian involvement may be causing confusion. It's a matter of communications. Why are we in Russia? A simple and easily understood message is what the P.M. seeks. He looks to you for help.'

'Two words. Strategic necessity,' General Stattaford said. 'Bolsheviks pulled Russia out of the war in the east. Common knowledge. Obviously we had to go in and start it again, otherwise the

Boche would hammer us twice as hard in the west. Damn near did, too. Strategic necessity, gentlemen. Any fool can see that.'

'The Foreign Office looks uneasy,' Jonathan Fitzroy said.

'I can see what the general means, but...' Sir Franklyn frowned. 'We never actually got the war going again in the east, did we? And anyway, the Armistice changed all that.'

'I don't know anybody who believes we're still in Russia because of the German war,' James Weatherby said. 'That's ancient history. Frankly, the Home Office doesn't give a toss what their Bolsheviks did last year.'

'Doesn't it? I do,' the general said. 'Betrayed the Allies! Made peace with the Hun! Opened their doors, told him to help himself! I call that treachery. Despicable vermin. A lot of good men died on the Western Front, gentlemen, friends of mine, just because the Bolsheviks threw in the towel. If I'd been given my way, the minute the Boche surrendered I'd have ordered them to about-turn and march east and not come back until every Bolshevik was cold meat. You may smile, gentlemen, but if my strategy had been applied, Russia wouldn't be a problem for us today, would it?'

'I'm not saying the Bolsheviks don't matter,' Weatherby said patiently. 'Far from it. The Home Office is very concerned about Bolshevik inter-ference *here*. Rioting in Glasgow and Belfast was definitely provoked by Communists. Blood was shed, a few men died. Typical Bolshevik tactics. Destroy from within.'

Silence. Then Jonathan Fitzroy said: 'So ... is that our advice to the P.M.? We're in Russia because that's where the threat comes from?'

'No other country wants to get really involved,' Sir Franklyn said. 'Not on Britain's scale, anyway. Not Italy. France went in and pulled out. America thinks it's done enough. We're on our own. It's rather a lonely crusade, isn't it?'

'A crusade against an international conspiracy,' James Weatherby said. 'Lenin's own words. Communist world domination.'

'Red tentacles,' the general said helpfully.

'The man in the street wouldn't know a red tentacle from a black pudding,' Sir Franklyn said. 'Britain has fought a lot of foreign wars, some popular, some not, and I can tell you what the man in the street recognizes. It's victories. Success proves we must be doing right. The best message the P.M. could give the nation is a thumping victory in Russia. Unfortunately...' He raised an eyebrow at Fitzroy.

'A military victory would certainly help,' Fitzroy said. 'The pity is, the Bolsheviks seem to be doing rather well. People want to know why. And we don't need awkward questions asked in the House.'

'Easy,' Stattaford said. 'Tell the blighters it's not in our national interest to give such information.'

'We tried that. The House didn't like it.'

'Don't know why. Censorship worked jolly well in wartime.'

'War's over. In peacetime they want straight answers.'

'So says the *Manchester Guardian*,' Weatherby

44

said. 'Not to mention the *Daily Express*.'

'Radical rags,' the general muttered.

'You've been very silent, Charles,' Fitzroy said. 'Does the Treasury have an opinion?'

'The Treasury has seven hundred and fifty-seven million opinions,' Delahaye said. 'The Tsar's government borrowed seven hundred and fifty-seven million pounds from Britain to fight their side of the war. If our troops in Russia can persuade them to pay it back, I'm sure the British taxpayer will express a very heartfelt thank-you.'

'Prospects are poor, I'm afraid. Lenin and Trotsky say they won't cough up a kopek.'

'Then why are we in Russia?'

Another pause for thought.

'I remember reading a letter to *The Times*,' Sir Franklyn said. 'Something along these lines: If we withdraw our forces now, we should be letting down our loyal Russian friends. We came to their aid once. They need us more than ever now.' He looked around. 'Maybe it's the decent thing to do?'

'Honest broker,' Weatherby said. 'That's us. Hold the ring. Give the real Russians a fair chance. How does that sound?'

'Simple comradeship,' Stattaford said. 'Shoulder to shoulder. Guarantee a fair fight.'

Nobody could improve on that. 'So we're doing the decent thing,' Fitzroy said. 'I think the P.M. might like that. Thank you, gentlemen. Shall I ring for tea?'

45

FRIGHTFUL BRIGANDS

1

Seven Sopwith Camels hung in the sky. Suppose a peasant, half a mile below, straightened his back and saw the ragged arrowhead and heard their faraway drone, it would be as meaningless as luck, as irrelevant as flies on a wall. Long before they faded to a tiny blur, he would have gone back to his toil.

Griffin was at the point of the arrowhead. He had almost lost the sense of going somewhere. Nothing changed, nothing moved, except the Russian landscape which drifted backwards like a vast drab carpet being very slowly unrolled, and even that never really changed. Griffin was not a deep thinker. War had discouraged deep thought: waste of time and effort, why strain your brain when it might be dead tomorrow? But now he glanced down at the unrolling carpet, always the same old pattern, grey and brown, the bloody endless Russian steppe, as bleak as the sky, and he couldn't shake off the foolish thought that this journey could last forever.

It was their fifth hour in the air, and he knew he was dangerously cold. When the R.T.O.'s lorries had taken his squadron to the airfield at Ekaterinodar, he had found seven Camels and a brigadier with fresh orders for him. 'Fly your Camels to

Beketofka, which is the aerodrome for Tsaritsyn. You can't miss it. Go east and follow the railway line for six hundred kilometres. There's a splendid little war going on at Tsaritsyn, you'll like it.'

'And the rest of my squadron, sir?' Griffin asked.

'Seven Camels is all we have. Your other chaps remain here until we can arrange something. Don't worry, you'll get them all.'

Griffin chose six pilots and told them the plan. 'Get a good night's sleep. We're off tomorrow, after breakfast. Take a toothbrush, that's all. The lighter your load, the further she'll fly. So move your bowels too.'

'Six hundred kilometres, sir,' Hackett said. 'Camel's range is two hundred, two-fifty with a big tail wind. Have we got a big tail wind?'

'Full tanks, cruising speed, watch your throttle settings,' Griffin said. 'We'll refuel twice. There are petrol dumps beside the railway.'

'Does each dump have an airfield, sir?' Jessop asked.

'No need. The entire Russian steppe is one long landing ground. That's what I'm told.'

Nobody crashed, but the steppe was no bowling green, and the Camels bounced hard on landing and rocked like tightrope walkers. The pilots refilled their tanks, emptied their bladders, ate some chocolate, took off and did it all again two hours later.

Griffin checked his watch. Open cockpits were essential, they gave you a good all-round view, but by God you paid for it. Today's wintry blasts were no worse than usual but five hours of them sucked all the warmth from a man's body and the

47

cold numbed his mind. Cold could be a killer. After a while it made a pilot shrink inside himself and forget his surroundings, which might be a stalking enemy or a sudden snow-covered hill.

Griffin waggled his wings and they all climbed three hundred feet. Now he had their full attention. Stick forward, into a shallow dive. Nothing as exciting as this had happened since the second refuelling when Jessop took off and nearly hit a passing swan.

Griffin nudged the dive more steeply, and the wind in the wires stopped singing and started howling. A small Russian town drifted into his line of sight. Spectators! Good. The altimeter needle fell through a thousand feet and he let it sink to six hundred before he led the flight back up, stick held firmly against his stomach and his backside pressed into the seat as they soared into a loop. Briefly, he put his head back and looked down at little white faces clustered in the town centre. The Camel escaped from the loop and dived. The white faces scattered. 'Don't panic,' he said aloud. *Probably never seen a loop,* he thought. *Or a Camel.* The flight levelled out at three hundred feet and got back on course. Nobody was warm, but nobody was sleepy, either.

Half an hour later, Tsaritsyn came in sight. A spur line took the railway to Beketofka aerodrome. A long train stood in the sidings, with steam up. There were canvas hangars, a windsock, several huts and sheds, a tented encampment, three lines of aircraft. A field next to the aerodrome was full of a cavalry camp. The Camels re-formed in line astern and prepared to land, and some people

48

down there fired rifles at them and missed. Griffin cheered. After endless miles of empty steppe they had found the war again.

After the rough and bumpy fields where they had refuelled, Hackett was relieved to touch down smoothly on the turf at Beketofka, and he was pleased to see familiar faces in his ground crew. A sergeant fitter helped him down from the cockpit. 'What have you got in the engine, Mr Hackett?' he asked. 'Handful of marbles? Bag of rusty nails?'

'It's a dozen gold sovereigns, sergeant. If you can fish them out, you can keep them.'

A rigger was twanging a wire. He made a face. 'I know,' Hackett said. 'Wait till you see the rudder cables. Treat in store.'

Colonel Davenport was the camp commandant at Beketofka. His left sleeve was pinned up at the elbow, he wore the ribbon of a D.S.O. and his face was as lined as crumpled paper.

'I leave the flying to you,' he told Griffin. 'I look after good order and discipline. Got my hands full keeping out those thieving Russians in the next field. Steal the laces from your boots if you don't kick 'em in the teeth first. Cossacks, you see.'

'I think they shot at us when we came in to land, sir.'

'Yes, they shoot at anyone they fancy. At Jews, especially. But that's none of our business. Now: you're here to buck up the White Army, right? So you report to General Wrangel. He's the big chief in these parts.'

49

'I thought we were under General Denikin, sir.'

'Denikin's C-in-C for the whole South Russian front. Wrangel commands his right wing, what they call the Caucasus Army. Mainly Cossacks. God help the Bolos if Wrangel's army gets inside Tsaritsyn. God help Tsaritsyn, for that matter.'

Griffin's hearing had nearly cleared after more than six hours behind a roaring rotary. 'Do I hear artillery, sir?'

'After a fashion. Six out of ten shells don't explode. Dud fuses. But Russian infantry like to hear their guns going bang-bang... Come on, I'll walk you to your quarters.' These turned out to be the train. Half the coaches were Pullmans. 'Believe me, it's by far the best digs you'll find in this benighted country.' Colonel Davenport pointed at a thin column of white smoke rising like a prayer from the locomotive, climbing through the chilled air, finally bending to the breeze. 'Constant hot water. I wish I had that. I'm pigging it in a hovel.'

'Always welcome, sir. Merlin Squadron will be honoured.'

'Awfully kind. Here come two chaps you'll find essential.' Much saluting took place. Davenport said: 'May I present Count Borodin. He's your liaison officer with General Wrangel. Speaks better English than I do.'

Borodin was tall and slim, under thirty, clean-shaven, sleek, in a uniform of soft green and grey, free from decorations. He looked like the kind of officer who carries the maps for a general. He said, 'An honour, wing commander. General Wrangel sends his compliments. He looks forward to seeing your machines in action.'

'And I look forward to seeing his men biff the Bolos.' *Borodin, Borodin,* Griffin thought. *Where have I heard that before?*

'And Sergeant Major Lacey runs your Orderly Room,' Davenport said. 'With a certain flair not entirely found in King's Regulations.'

'Well, a Camel Squadron needs flair. Bags of flair.'

Griffin didn't like the looks of Lacey. Not tall enough for a sergeant major. Too young, and his uniform fitted him too well, he'd had it tailored, by God. There was something wrong with his eyes too. They looked calm and clever and a little bit amused. What in hell's name was there to be amused at? Nobody got to be a sergeant major by calmness and cleverness and laughing at things. 'I shall depend on you to uphold the traditions of the squadron, Mr Lacey,' he said. Whatever the hell that meant.

'Yes, of course. I am also your Signals Officer, sir. I operate the radio. Messages have arrived from General Holman at the Military Mission H.Q. in Ekaterinodar, marked Urgent and Most Important.' Now there was a hint of a smile. He didn't talk like a sergeant major, either. He sounded like a bishop announcing a winning hand at whist.

'Lead on,' Griffin said.

The C.O. took the largest compartment in the Pullman coaches. It even had a bath. A silent Russian with a Mongolian face and the build of a 15-year-old boy gave him a whisky-soda and ran the bath, helped him out of his sheepskin coat and flying boots and would have undressed him completely if Griffin had let him. He retired immediately to a corner and squatted on his heels.

Griffin slid into the bath and let the warmth drive out the cold from his stiff limbs. His mind looked back at the tedious hours of flying since Ekat. He'd heard people talk of the famous Russian steppes. Now he'd seen one. Flat and empty. And endless. Presumably somebody scratched a living down there. Dreary, dreary. He'd never understood what his father saw in agriculture, and he'd been happy to leave it to the old man.

His father, Henry Griffin, had inherited a corner of Leicestershire that was big enough to reach well into the counties of Rutland and Northamptonshire. His grandfather, Spencer Griffin had acquired this corner when he made an obscene amount of money out of guano, seagull droppings. He bought a small Atlantic island that was deep in the stuff, just when agriculture was booming and needed fertilizer. It was like shovelling up money. When the boom ended he bought land: farm after bankrupt farm. Farming didn't much interest him; in fact, compared with his triumphs in guano, nothing much interested him; so he lived in London, and had the decency to die at the age of forty-eight when he walked home in fog as thick as mushroom soup and caught pneumonia.

So his son got the farms. Now Henry *was* a good farmer, good enough to know eventually that his own son – John – had an incurably low threshold of boredom. Show him a field and it yawned like the prairie. So did young John.

He was a strong, cheerful lad but school was a

mystery to him and forget even the thought of college. He was good at foxhunting and he joined the Quorn and the Belvoir, and enjoyed it. When there was no hunt, he was a dashing point-to-point jockey. He was twenty-two when war broke out. That was serious, but not as damned serious as what happened when his horse abruptly refused and sent him flying arse-over-tit into a pile of rocks. He broke an arm and a leg and several ribs.

They took a long time to heal. By then, the war was bogged down in the Trenches, so he joined a cavalry regiment. Good chaps, but no action. The only action seemed to be in the sky. Aeroplanes looked fun.

In 1916 the Royal Flying Corps took him – good horsemen made good pilots, everyone knew that – and, amazingly, he found something useful that he was very good at. An appetite for the kill helped. A fat slice of luck did no harm. And for the lucky ones, promotion was rapid.

Major-General Trenchard headed the R.F.C. and he believed in aggressive patrolling far behind the enemy's lines. So did John Griffin. 'They started it,' he told his squadron, 'so let's get over there and finish it.' If that was costly, well, they were all volunteers, nobody said war was cheap. And the dead made no complaints. Decorations and further promotions proved that Griffin must be right.

Now he was a wing commander, with a whisky-soda, in a hot bath, and he had a bunch of young brigands to lead in a bright and breezy new war. What could be better?

He reached for the signals and read General Holman's orders. 'Get Borodin,' he told the Russian boy-servant.

As he soaked in the tub the count gave him an outline of Wrangel's plan to capture the south side of Tsaritsyn: bombard the trenches, infiltrate the outer defences, assault the city. 'We have tanks which—'

Griffin raised a hand. 'Enough. Something I learned in France was, get it on half a sheet of paper. More than that I'll forget anyway.' He looked at his fingers. The tops were wrinkled. He stood up and let the water drain from him. They made an interesting contrast: the polish of Imperial Russia, or what was left of it, and the intrepid aviator, naked and dripping, here to show them how the Allies duffed up the Hun. 'Who was that strange child I found in here?' Griffin asked.

'Your servant. A *plenny*. Each of your officers has a *plenny*, we find them loyal and eager to please. Yours is called Jack.'

'An ex-Bolo? You captured him?'

'The *plennys* were happy to change sides. The Red Army forced them to fight. Your chef, for example, was formerly with the Hotel St George in Moscow but the Bolsheviks put him in their infantry, a foolish move.'

'Our train has a chef?'

'You can have two, if you wish. They cost nothing.'

'We shall need another. Ekat is sending me six bombers and their crews right now. A dozen men.'

'Twelve more *plennys*, then. Of course. We have what you might call a plenitude.' He handed

54

Griffin a towel.

'Thanks.' What exactly did 'plenitude' mean? He let it pass. Borodin's English was too damn good to be true.

2

The *plennys* woke the pilots at seven, with glasses of Russian tea. It wasn't Earl Grey, but as they sipped it and enjoyed the comfort of clean sheets and sunshine, they began to think that the long, sometimes hard and dirty and often bitterly cold journey had been worthwhile if it helped to restore the good old days. You wouldn't get tea in bed under the Reds.

The *plennys* had brushed the uniforms, cleaned and polished the boots, made the buttons shine. The pilots met for breakfast in the bar, which doubled as a dining room. Griffin liked their smartness. 'This isn't France,' he said. 'People wandered into the Mess wearing rugger shirts and jodhpurs. Not our style. We're here to show the flag.'

'Which flag is that, sir?' Wragge asked. 'Hackett's an Aussie, Bellamy's Canadian and Dextry claims to be Irish.'

'Give the butter a shove,' Griffin grunted.

'Ireland's British,' Maynard said.

'Don't tell them that in Dublin,' Dextry warned. 'They'll blow your patriotic head off.'

'That's just the Fenians. Not like the royal Irish regiments in France. They were jolly decent chaps.'

Griffin pointed his fork at Dextry. 'Tell your Dublin friends to keep their little war going. When we've mended Russia we'll go back and sort out Ireland.'

'Yes, sir.'

'And let's drop the sir in the Mess. Makes me feel like my grandfather, and he's dead.'

At 9.30 they all walked to the aerodrome. The sky was bigger than they had ever seen in France or England and it was drenched in the kind of blue that gives atheists second thoughts. Maybe Russia had more sky because it had more distant horizons. Already the sun was pleasantly warm and the breeze made only an occasional ripple in the grass. Perhaps spring had arrived overnight.

Maynard looked at the vast expanse of grass and wondered if cricket was out of the question. He played an imaginary straight drive, knees bent, plenty of follow-through. Bellamy was looking at him. 'Bit stiff,' Maynard said. 'Loosening up.'

'Save the next dance for me'

They stopped near the C.O.'s Camel. The other machines were dotted about, just as their pilots had left them.

'Get lined up on me,' Griffin said. 'We'll make a mass take-off. I bet the natives have never seen one of those. Ten o'clock kick-off. That's when the White artillery will start raising holy hell. Make sure your tanks are full, your guns are loaded, your bladders are empty. Off you toddle.'

His mechanic was waiting for him.

'Didn't expect to see these Camels again, Mr Griffin. Not outside the knacker's yard.'

'Explain?'

'47 Squadron flew them at Salonika. That's where most of us mechanics were before this, and we watched them Camels sitting in the rain at Salonika, not getting any younger. Then they got flown to Ekat, those that still flew, that is, and it rains at Ekat too, rains like buggery, and here they are, sir, bloody soggy if you'll pardon my Bulgarian. The Bulgarians, that was the enemy at Salonika, nobody knew why, ancient history now, a bit like your Camel, especially the wings, because it was the wings that copped all the rain, sir.'

Griffin walked around the Camel, prodding the wings, twanging the wires. 'No holes,' he said. 'Ailerons work. See?' He made one move up and down.

'Fabric should be tight as a drum, sir.' The fitter rapped the skin with his knuckles. It didn't sound like a drum. 'Soft as shammy leather.'

'It flew me from Ekat.'

'Level flight, sir. Cruising speed. Not combat. Not chucking her about.'

Griffin said nothing about performing the loop over the small town. The aeroplane had certainly felt slow and heavy. Still, they survived. 'Will she fly?'

'You can take off, sir. After that...' He shrugged. 'It'll be like flying a wet dishcloth.'

'Thank you, sergeant. Take-off is in fifteen minutes.'

Griffin walked away, and watched the other machines being pushed into position. He liked the Camel. It was a small fighter, less than nineteen feet long. Full of fuel and ammo, it weighed little more than half a ton. If it was empty, two men could pick up its tail unit and easily tow it. He liked its chunky, compact shape, liked the way he could throw it into a tight right turn so fast that it tugged the blood from his brain and left the enemy flying straight and looking silly.

It would be good to get back into a war. The sweet smell of spilled petrol drifted into his nostrils. That's the stuff! Keep your Paris perfumes.

Three of the Camels had been lined up with his own. The other two hadn't moved. Somebody's backside needed kicking.

Hackett and Bellamy walked over to him. 'My fitter can't start the engine,' Bellamy said. 'It nearly started and then something went bang and caught fire. He wants to look inside the engine.'

'How long will that take?'

'Hard to say. He's waiting for it to cool down. He says a lot of petrol was sloshing about, so maybe a fuel line broke. And the extinguisher made a bit of a mess.'

'Broken fuel line wouldn't go bang.'

Bellamy could think of other possibilities but he saw the C.O's expression and he shut up. Griffin turned to Hackett. 'What's your excuse?'

'I've got woodworm. Also mildew. The cockpit has a nasty smell and my rigger's got piles. I don't feel very well today, sir, and I can't fly. But if you want one reason, here it is. The fitter reckons my Camel's dangerous. To me. Not to the enemy, because he says the aeroplane will collapse in the air as soon as I chuck it about. Or sooner, if the wind gets rough.' Hackett's tone was frank and conversational. He might have been discussing the selection for a football team.

Griffin's eyes were wide and unblinking. 'You refuse to fly.'

'Half the wing struts are cracked or split. Somebody bound them up with wire and now it's rusted through. Painted, but rusted. The struts are there to keep the wings apart, but in fact the wings are holding the struts in place.'

'Not any longer,' Bellamy said. 'Look. Your chaps have just taken off the top wing.'

'Sweet sodding suffering Christ on crutches!' Griffin shouted. 'We came five thousand miles for *this*? I'm down to five machines!'

'I don't think a monoplane Camel would fly,' Hackett said. 'Not fast, anyway. Might touch fifty going downhill.'

Griffin turned away and took a large step and kicked a small flower, light blue, a charming but fragile messenger of the coming spring, and sent its petals flying. 'We'll do it without you two slackers. I'm not going to fail General Wrangel. We'll fly all day if we have to.' He stopped because a man on a motorcycle was chugging and bouncing towards them. 'Wrangel's final orders,' Griffin decided. 'Targets and so on.'

It was Count Borodin. 'Good morning, wing commander,' he said. 'The assault is off. Postponed. No fighting today.'

Hackett and Bellamy sat on the grass. Griffin pushed his cap forward so that the peak shadowed his eyes and he had to tip his head back to stare at the count. 'Off,' he said. 'What's wrong? Weather not good enough?'

'No, it's the tanks, you see. The infantry were promised British tanks to lead the attack, and they've all broken down, so now the infantry won't advance. Perhaps tomorrow?' He offered a blue porcelain jar with a sealed lid. 'The general sends you this small gesture of welcome.'

Griffin accepted. It felt heavy. 'What is it?'

'Caviare, the very best.'

'Caviare *from* the general,' Bellamy said. 'Shakespeare never thought of that.'

'Shakespeare never thought of anything,' Hackett said. 'Bacon wrote it for him. I read it in the *Daily Mail.*'

'Shut up.' Griffin pointed at Hackett. 'You're in charge here. Get all these Camels repaired, serviced, made totally good, today. Come with me,' he told Borodin. 'We'll visit these bloody useless tanks. Is that straw?' He pointed to tufts sticking out from the edges of the motorcycle's tyres.

'Reeds. We find reeds are stronger. There are no spare tyres in Russia, so we pack the old tyres with reeds.' He kick-started the machine. It had no pannier. Griffin sat sideways on the petrol tank. They chugged away.

'He's not a complete idiot,' Bellamy said. 'He knows that if two Camels are duff, they all need looking at."

'Caviare,' Hackett said. 'Nobody ever gave us caviare in France. Omelettes, plenty of omelettes during the fighting. Here, they give us caviare for not fighting. Funny war.'

'Come on, let's spread the news.' They walked towards the waiting pilots.

The tanks were in a field where sunflowers had been grown. The blackened stalks stood thickly, two feet high, except where tank-tracks had made narrow paths. Borodin followed one of these, turning left or right as the tanks had turned, until it delivered them to a small tented encampment. The tanks were huddled there, grey and muddy and motionless. Borodin killed his engine.

'Elephants' graveyard,' Griffin said.

A British Army major came out of the largest tent. No hat, no tie, and his tunic was undone. 'Major Riley,' he said. He had a fading black eye and one front tooth was missing. 'Welcome to the Armoured Division, or as I call it, the Tank Trap.' A faint whiff of cordite came with him. Griffin knew at once to tread carefully. He introduced himself and the count. 'I'm Royal Air Force. Merlin Squadron. I was supposed to support the attack,' he said.

'You're new here? And you want to know the score. Come inside. There's coffee. Tastes like creosote, so I cut it with vodka, then it tastes like hot creosote.' They went into the tent and he waved them to a sofa that everywhere leaked stuffing. 'Cavalry of the clouds, isn't that what they call you? Well, I'm cavalry of the mud. Today the mud won.' He sounded cheerful.

'I see you've been in the wars.' Griffin touched his own eye.

'The shiner? Yes, I was instructing a Russian driver and he got carried away by the excitement. Lost control, hit a tree, my head smacked against his head.' He gave them tin mugs of steaming coffee.

'It's very quiet here. Where is everyone?'

'The Russian crews are in their tents, cooking lunch. My N.C.O.s are in *their* tents, probably playing pontoon.'

'Lunch?' Griffin looked at his watch. 'So early?'

'Well, they've been up since dawn.' Riley sat on an ammunition box. 'Time is different here. Breakfast doesn't count for much. Lunch at eleven, dinner at four. Otherwise they go all huffy.' He was cleaning his nails with a broken matchstick. 'You can't do anything with a huffy Russian. And he'll do bugger-all for you.'

Griffin glanced at the count, who gave one small, sad nod. 'But if they're not huffy today... This is none of my business, I know, but... What's the problem? With the attack, that is.'

'I'll show you. Bring your coffee.'

They walked to the tanks. 'This is a British Army Whippet,' he said. 'I've got four of them, and two Mark Fives. The Whippet's not much more than an armoured car on tank-tracks. Very simple. Almost foolproof.'

'Almost,' Griffin said.

Riley kicked the Whippet. 'A simple fault in the engine. Timing needed adjusting. Ten-minute job. Took my Russian an hour, made a hash of it, buggered up several other parts in the process, crippled the Whippet. Same sort of thing's happened to the others.'

Griffin took a sip of coffee. Smells like a bonfire, he thought. Tastes like one, too. 'Surely your N.C.O.s could...'

'They could, but their job is to supervise. And you have to make allowance for the Russian character, very proud, very arrogant, very brave, very stupid.' Riley remembered the count's presence. 'Not the nobility, of course.'

'Who are flawless,' Borodin murmured.

'Where's their loyalty?' Griffin asked. 'Don't they want their tanks to go into action?'

'Yes, of course, but... Look, it's not like France. Many of these chaps never saw a car or a lorry before Wrangel put them in uniform. A tank to them is a piece of magic. They're like schoolboys, you tell them to do something and if it's difficult then it's impossible. But put them in a tank that's in working order and they are fearless, brave as lions, fight anyone. Like a boy on his first bicycle, couldn't be happier. When it breaks down it's *our* fault, it's British junk so scrap it, get a new tank, like *that*.' He clicked his fingers. 'I say no, mend it, they resent that. Damn Britisher, thinks he knows better than a Russian. If you're not very careful...' He shrugged.

'They go all huffy.'

The count cleared his throat. 'Suppose your N.C.O.s got the tanks running,' he suggested, 'and you sent the Russian crews off to fight in them?'

'Not what we're here for. Our job is to teach them how to repair and service, so they can fight, and fight again. But you may be right.'

Riley walked with them to the motorcycle. The faint sound of an accordion reached them. On a sunny day, under a clear blue sky, Riley's Russians chose to stay in a tent and make sad music. British troops would be out, kicking a football about. 'Well, thank you,' Griffin said, 'It's been very..." What? Strange? Depressing?

'Illuminating,' Borodin suggested.

'No,' Griffin said sharply. 'Well, yes, but also valuable. Learned a lot.' Damned if he was going to be tutored by a bloody foreigner. Whose language was it, anyway?

'You're a wing commander,' Riley said. 'Never met one of those before. If I let you drive a Whippet, will you give me a ride in the sky?'

'Gladly. Duties permitting.'

Riley turned to go, and then turned back. 'Borodin,' he said. 'Borodin. Any relation?'

'I'm the illegitimate son. Father was also an illegitimate son, so you might say I carried on the family tradition.'

'And now you're Count Borodin.'

'Yes. My mother was a princess, a distant cousin of the Tsar, and said to be the most beautiful woman in Russia but not, alas, the cleverest. She was besotted by my father's genius. Their ambition was to create a child with her looks and his mind. It never occurred to them that the reverse might happen. But the Tsar took a fancy to me. When I was ten, he made me a count, a sentimental gesture, easy for an emperor, although he forgot to add an estate.'

'Ah. Pity. Just the title. And the name.'

'What I also didn't get was any genius. But that was a sort of blessing. It helped me blend in with the nobility. They dislike anyone with talent, it reflects badly on them.'

'You're young,' Riley said. 'Maybe there's a spark waiting to be fanned to a flame.'

'That's a kind thought, but... No. I've tried to

compose. Quite hopeless. One day I shall decompose.' Joke.

Riley glanced at the exquisitely tailored uniform, the tasselled lanyards. 'Still... It hasn't held you back.'

'I'm on General Denikin's staff. He likes having tall officers around him, it improves the tone. He sent me to Tsaritsyn to stimulate the war.'

Riley nodded. 'Tell Wrangel the tanks will be ready for action tomorrow.'

The motorcycle bumped and bounced back to the train, with Griffin hanging on to the handlebars. He got off and massaged his bruised buttocks. The ride had given him time to think.

'Look here,' he said. 'I don't like the way you treat this war. That remark about Denikin. Very flippant. I didn't bring my squadron thousands of miles to mock the leadership. We're here to help Denikin's Volunteer Army defeat the Bolsheviks and give your country the benefits of democracy. Understood?'

'Democracy,' Count Borodin said. 'Not a word the average Russian peasant would recognize. Or even admire. Still... If ordered to do so, let's say, by a modern Ivan the Terrible, I suppose he might–'

'Enough,' Griffin said. 'Tell Wrangel we're ready when he is.'

3

The pilots gave the C.O.'s orders to the ground crews, and the ground crews grumbled and got on with it. Ground crews always grumbled. It was part of the job. Tell them not to grumble and they turned sullen.

Nothing much else was happening on the aerodrome. On the far side a flight of biplane bombers stood silent. They wore the red, white and black roundels of the White air force.

'Should we stroll over and say hello?' Maynard suggested.

They shaded their eyes and looked.

'DH9s,' Wragge said. 'Worse than the DH6.'

'Bloody awful bus,' Bellamy said. 'War Office was glad to get rid of them, I expect.'

'Tell you what,' Hackett said to Maynard, 'you go and talk to them. Tell them it's a bloody awful bus.'

'I don't speak Russian.' Maynard felt that somehow he was being made answerable for the DH9s.

'Wave your arms. Shout. That always works.'

'Worked in France,' Jessop said. 'Made the frogs jump.'

'If you really want to make a frog jump, poke him in the ass with a sharp stick,' Hackett said. 'We had frog-jumping contests back home, I won a lot of money.' They had turned away from the DH9s and were walking back to the train.

The *plennys* were lined up outside the Pullman coaches, standing stiffly, as Sergeant Major Lacey inspected them. They had shaven heads and wore clean black coveralls, and each man held a pair of British Army boots in his left hand. Lacey was meticulous: he looked at teeth, fingernails and feet. The pilots watched. When Lacey reached the last *plenny*, Hackett strolled forward. Lacey saw

66

him coming and squared his shoulders slightly. This was as close as he came to standing to attention, a posture he regarded as unnatural and absurd. He saluted – it was more of a gesture – and Hackett returned the salute. Immediately all the *plennys* saluted too, Russian-style, palm down, and they held the salute.

'Hullo!' Hackett said. 'Do they want me to inspect them?'

'Certainly not. It's the way Russian troops do things. If I salute a senior officer, they must follow suit. They'll stay like that until you go away.'

'Good God.' The *plennys* were rigid. Some salutes quivered with tension. 'Tell them to stand easy.'

'I don't know the words. They're perfectly happy. If you want to make them happier, you could present this award to the best-turned-out man.' He gave Hackett a tin of corned beef. 'Third from the right.'

Hackett looked in Lacey's eyes. 'Where's the joke?'

'No joke. He'll be delighted. Russians will do anything for a tin of bully beef.'

Hackett made the award. The *plenny* dropped his boots, took the tin in his left hand and intensified his salute until his hand bounced off his forehead. A smile lit up his whole face.

'Crikey,' Hackett said. 'What will they do for two tins? Still... Smart-looking bunch.'

'Smart enough to escape from the Red Army, or they'd be dead by now. The squadron couldn't manage without them. We'd be peeling our own potatoes and washing our own socks.'

Hackett left. The *plenny* salutes ended. Lacey had forgotten the Russian for 'dismissed' and so he said *'Do svidanya!'* and fluttered his fingers. They understood.

He joined the pilots. 'Coffee in fifteen minutes, gentlemen. Lunch at one, dinner at eight. Tomorrow, breakfast will be at seven, because the assault starts at eight.'

'How d'you know that?' Jessop demanded. 'We haven't been told.'

'It was in the air,' Lacey said. 'I plucked it from the ether.' He reached up and made gentle plucking motions.

'Ah, yes. The radio.'

Hackett said: 'Don't tell me you talk to Wrangel's staff.'

'We are kindred spirits.' Lacey spread his arms until they aimed at the horizons and he slowly revolved. 'I talk to the world. I'll put a girdle round about the earth in forty minutes.'

They were puzzled. Sergeant majors didn't speak like that. What language was it, anyway?

'I go, I go,' Maynard said. 'Look how I go – swifter than arrow from the Tartar's bow.'

'You go bats, my lad,' Wragge said. 'That makes two of you.'

'Shakespeare. It's Puck in *Midsummer Night's Dream*,' Maynard explained. 'We did it at school. Put on the play. I was Puck.' He could tell they didn't think much of Shakespeare or Puck, or of Maynard as Puck. 'I was much smaller then. Years ago.' It was two years ago, when he was seventeen. 'I flew about the stage. Not a patch on the Camel.' He chuckled. Nobody else did.

'Bugger Puck,' Hackett said. 'We need some exercise. A gallop would be good. Where can we get some horses?'

'No stables around here, I'm afraid,' Lacey said. 'You might try those Cossacks over there.'

'Right. Maynard! Go and borrow a few rides. Bribe them with bully beef.'

'But I don't know Russian. *Any* Russian.'

Hackett pointed in the direction of the Cossack camp and scowled. Maynard knew he couldn't do it, but he couldn't stay there and stare back at Hackett either. He went.

For the first few steps, Lacey walked with him. 'Just keep saying *Nichevo*,' he said.

'Meaning what?'

'Who cares? Never mind, it doesn't matter.'

Maynard felt a surge of anger. 'Oh ... go to hell.'

'No, no. Really, it means all those, and more. *Nichevo* is the Russian answer to anything. It means all is well. Use it lavishly.' Lacey turned back.

4

The Cossack camp was huge and the air was rich with horse dung. The men all had ragged beards and moustaches and their uniforms – green blouse-type tunic, dark breeches, knee-length riding boots – were stained and patched and, frankly, dirty. Some wore fur hats; all carried a weapon on their belts.

Maynard marched between their tents as if he knew where he was going. Some Cossacks

69

shouted. Many of them laughed at him. He felt like a cowboy who had lost his horse and strayed into an Apache camp. He kept a slight smile and reminded himself that he was a commissioned officer of his Britannic Majesty and he must show it. Nevertheless he was deep inside their camp, he had no idea where he was heading and these frightful brigands could knife him in a second. Then one of the biggest brigands, with a chestful of cartridge belts and a scar that made one eyebrow hang low, stepped in his path and asked a long question in a voice that rumbled like distant thunder.

Maynard heard him out and said: *'Nichevo.'* He tried to make it sound friendly. It certainly impressed the man. He walked around Maynard, looking closely at his uniform. The pilot's wings got a long stare.

'English,' Maynard said. No effect. He experimented. 'Englishski.' Nothing. French might work. 'Angleterre?' No good. 'Angliski.' Bullseye! He said it again, this time with a big smile. The man embraced him and Maynard got Cossack beard up his nose and in his mouth.

The man took him into one of the bigger tents and shouted, 'Angliski!' at two other hairy brigands. They all talked, often simultaneously. Maynard smiled and nodded. He found himself holding a glass. A lengthy toast was proposed and they looked at him. Desperation made him try anything. 'Wrangel?' he suggested. Not what they had hoped for, but good enough. Glasses raised, down in one. Maynard got half down in one and felt as if he'd swallowed hot volcanic lava. They

70

pounded him on the back and laughed and found a chair for him. The lava dribbled into his gut. His eyes wept but tears couldn't put out the fire. At last he could speak. 'Vodka?' he whispered, and that was his funniest line yet. How they laughed!

He remembered his mission. He took out his pocket book and a pencil and drew a picture of a horse, an ugly horse whose legs were too long, tore off the page and gave it to them. He held up five fingers.

They talked among themselves, talked for so long that he finished his vodka in small, cautious sips. It seemed churlish not to. Then they took him to a bigger tent where a man in a noticeably cleaner uniform, so he must surely be an officer, was shown the picture. Maynard had a horrible thought: maybe they believed he wanted to *sell* them five horses. How to explain? But another toast was being made and this time he knew better than to swallow it whole.

This vodka was pepper-flavoured. Maynard got the strange impression that his head might fall off unless it was very carefully balanced. They took him out and showed him a horse with legs much shorter than on his picture. More of a pony, really. He didn't care. *'Nichevo,'* he said. They all drank to that and took him to a yet bigger tent, full of generals, they must be generals, their chests all clanked with medals. Quite soon there was another toast. Maynard drank it all, he was getting the hang of it, felt rather pleased with himself. It was the last thing he felt before the ground came rushing up at enormous speed. He didn't feel them pick him up, or lay him on a bed, or say *'Nichevo.'* Pity. He would have agreed with them wholeheartedly.

'I think we can expect spring lamb quite soon,' Lacey said. 'It's Chef's masterpiece. An occasion when strong men weep with joy.'

'Joy,' Griffin said. 'I knew a girl named Joy.'

'And he does the most memorable things with cucumber.' Lacey was sitting in the chair in the C.O.'s Pullman compartment. Griffin lay on the bed. 'In season, of course. Like mushrooms. Once you have seen him stuff a mushroom, fungi will never look the same to you.'

'So you say. You can't stuff Yorkshire pudding. Can he handle Yorkshire pud?'

'With ease. I've told him what the chaps like – the same as they liked in France, which was what they'd grown up on. Apple Crumble, Treacle Tart, Sherry Trifle, Spotted Dick. I've explained them all. Chef wasn't keen on Spotted Dick at first. He thought it must be a medical treatment, like mustard plasters. But he came round to it. The king of Bulgaria once asked him–'

'Crumpets. I'm partial to a crumpet for tea.'

'Ah. Well now. Crumpets. Crumpets are different. But...'

A distant clamour got Griffin off the bed and over to the window. He saw his pilots watching a bunch of mounted Cossacks approach. With them they brought half a dozen unmounted ponies. Sunlight flashed on the flourish of steel. 'Trouble,' he said. 'Know them?' He didn't wait, grabbed his cap and pistol and buttoned his tunic as he left.

The Cossacks galloped around the pilots and came to a halt in a flurry of dust and small stones and snorting horses. Their leader shouted: *'Zdravstvuite! Dobroye Utro!'* After that he made a statement full of fire and saliva.

'He's got Maynard,' Wragge said. 'I bet they want money.'

Maynard was propped in front of the leader. His chin was on his chest and he slumped so much that his hands were lost in the horse's mane. The leader gripped him by the collar.

'He looks dead,' Jessop said. 'Blood on his face. So it can't be ransom.'

The leader got to the point. *'Na Moskvu!'* he shouted. The rest shouted: *'Na Moskvu!'* He waved both arms and Maynard fell sideways. The leader grabbed him by the ankle before he could hit the ground, and said something very amusing; they all laughed and clapped their hands. Maynard's hair rested lightly in the dirt. He was suddenly and violently sick.

'D'you think he might choke?' Jessop asked.

'Hard to say. His colour's improving,' Hackett said.

'So would yours, if you were upside-down.'

'True.'

Griffin arrived. 'Bellamy, Jessop, go and get that officer. Wragge: find some *plennys* and a stretcher... Hackett, what's the story here?'

'Well, Maynard offered to...' That was when Count Borodin's motorcycle came clattering and backfiring. It spooked the ponies into a stampede, and the Cossacks went after them, shouting and steering them into a tight bend that became a slow and dusty circle. Their leader watched, smiling proudly. He made a short speech. Griffin looked at Borodin.

'He says we shall ride into Moscow, side by side, before Christmas.'

'What about Maynard?'

'Drunk as a lord.'

'Give him my compliments, and ask him to join me on the train for a drink. That seems to be the universal language in Russia, but you'd better come along too.' Maynard was being stretchered past. His eyes were half-open but unable to focus. 'Bloody fine effort, laddie,' Griffin told him. 'Damned good show. Best traditions of the squadron.'

Sergeant Major Lacey mixed up a hangover cure that tasted of mustard and toothpaste and caused Maynard to throw up twice more that afternoon. But by the evening he was in the bar, sipping soda water and discovering that he had become an accepted member of Merlin Squadron. They praised him for his Cossack adventure, and for the five ponies he had brought. It made the whole frightful episode seem almost worthwhile.

AN ABSOLUTE CAKEWALK

1

Griffin had the Flight in the air at fifteen minutes to eight. The servicing had been rushed, and the ground crews weren't happy, but Griffin believed that God didn't create war to make ground crews happy. The Camels formed up in the usual arrowhead. Within ten minutes Bellamy turned back with a leaky fuel tank. Petrol was sloshing around his boots. He landed very gently. Maybe his ground crew had been right to be unhappy. He left the cockpit in a hurry and ran. Nothing caught fire.

The rest of the Flight passed over the six tanks as they crawled towards Tsaritsyn. Not much punch there, Griffin thought. Wouldn't have dented the Hun front in France. He climbed to a thousand feet and circled, letting everyone take a good look at the Red trenches outside the town. Neat and straight with regular kinks: just like France. Little fountains of mud appeared, some next to the trenches, most not. Wrangel's artillery barrage had begun. Griffin gave it ten minutes to soften up the defence. Then the Flight fell in line behind him and he steered to attack the length of the trenches.

The long descent, even at a shallow angle, built up a healthy speed. Griffin was easing back the stick as he fired a short burst into the trenches less than a hundred feet below. His bullets went chasing among the soldiers until he climbed, and levelled, and dived again and fired again. Nobody fired back. It was easy.

The five Camels followed his example. Maynard, at the tail, was surprised to find what fun it was. Swoop, fire, climb: it had a feeling of fairground gaiety. A few troops got over their surprise and offered some ragged rifle fire, but nobody could catch him. It was simple. Just fire, and men fell down. What sport.

The Flight climbed away and Maynard climbed after it. Now the tanks had arrived. They began prowling alongside the trenches and shooting down into them. That was more than enough for the defenders. They scrambled out and fled. Griffin saw them running. The Camels went down and chased them until all the ammunition was spent. They turned for home.

Bellamy watched the Flight land. The pilots strolled over to him, their faces smudged with oil spatter, jubilant at a job well done, and told him what a hoot it had been.

Bellamy didn't care. He had breathed too many petrol fumes and his stomach hurt. He felt rotten. 'I blame the eggs at breakfast,' he said. Nobody listened. 'Huge hoot,' Wragge said. 'Not like France. More like skittles. Every bullet found its billet. That's Kipling.'

'No, it's not. It's bollocks,' Bellamy said. He felt cheated. Bloody eggs. Bloody leaky fuel tank. He'd missed the party.

'I personally wiped out a whole regiment of

Bolos,' Hackett said. 'That's worth a medal, isn't it?'

'It was a routine strafe,' Griffin said. 'We're off again in an hour.'

'I'll be ready,' Bellamy said.

'It really was a cakewalk,' Maynard told him. 'An absolute cakewalk. You should have seen it.'

'So everyone says,' Bellamy muttered. 'Everyone shot a regiment. Must be easy.'

'It's as easy as falling off a bicycle,' Jessop said. 'Do it once and you never forget how.'

'You haven't got that right,' Wragge said.

'No? Fetch me a bicycle and I'll prove it. Look – here comes a motorbike. I get double points for falling off one of those.'

Griffin said: 'You get double points for idiocy, Jessop. Now shut up while we find out what's next.'

Borodin gave his machine to an airman to hold, and said, 'General Wrangel compliments you on your performance at the enemy trenches, and says he now intends to capture Tsaritsyn on the way to Moscow.' He offered a large envelope. While Griffin was opening it, the count told the others, 'Actually, I made up that bit about Moscow. It's a thousand miles up the Volga to Moscow, and the river is full of Red gunboats.'

'So what's the best way to Moscow?' Dextry said.

'A good question. Perhaps Denikin has a Grand Plan to win the war.'

'We had all sorts of Grand Plans in France,' Hackett said. 'Neuve Chapelle, Loos, the Somme, Ypres, Passchendaele, and lots more. Ask the War

77

Office, Count. They've probably got some spare copies going cheap.'

'We Russians have a surplus of our own, thank you. Remember that there were more German divisions fighting us in the east than you in the west.'

'Must have been bloody noisy.'

'Yes, at times. And afterwards bloody quiet, for some.'

'Alright, shut up, gather round,' Griffin said. 'Here's the plan. Wrangel's men have the trenches. Stage two is the outer defences, south side. Houses are fortified strongpoints. Wrangel's guns will put up a short barrage to keep the Bolos' heads down. Then we go in and do a low-level strafe, all guns blazing, then the tanks go in, then the infantry make a hole for the cavalry. We'll take along some small bombs, twenty-pounders. Carry them in the cockpit. Toss them out if you see anything juicy.'

'Try and hit a chap called Trotsky,' Borodin said. 'The *Daily Telegraph* has been very hard on Trotsky lately.'

'How on earth do you get the *Telegraph?*' Wragge asked.

'Oh... Lacey gets it for me. The rugby reporting is excellent.'

'Take off in an hour,' Griffin said. 'Get something to eat. You two.' He pointed to Wragge and Hackett. 'Stay.'

'Bow-wow,' Wragge said. 'And I know I speak for Hackett too.'

The others left.

Griffin was frowning hard, and his left eye was

twitching. He took a deep breath and seemed about to speak, then turned away, stared hard at nothing worth looking at, turned back again. They watched with interest. He was in the grip of strong emotions. They had never seen him like this before.

'Look here...' Even his voice was different: tight, a bit hoarse. He cleared his throat. 'I don't like your attitude. Any of you. Too jokey. Too casual. We're here to do a job, not a music-hall act. It's not good enough.'

'Oh well,' Wragge said. 'You know what the boys are like.'

'Yes, I do. They treat war like a game.' Griffin's temper was rising. 'Like Eton against Harrow at cricket. And you're no better.'

'Not me. I hate the bloody game,' Hackett said.

'Cricket's more than a game,' Wragge insisted. 'I opened the bowling for Harrow and we were definitely... Here, I say...' He was looking into Griffin's revolver. It trembled with rage, only six inches away.

'The bullet in here cost a shilling,' Griffin whispered. 'You're not worth a shilling. You're not worth a slice of cold toast. I could shoot you now. No loss to anyone. You're an ex flight commander who's forgotten what war is about.' He used the gun's muzzle to raise Wragge's cap from his head and he fired a shot through it. Wragge staggered back. Ground crew stopped working and stared. The cap spun through the air and dropped and rolled in a small circle and flopped. 'What is war about?' Griffin demanded.

'Killing the other bastard,' Hackett said fast.

Griffin turned to him. 'And why are we fighting?'

Hackett thought, Buggered if I know and buggered if I care. But the smell of the revolver was sharp in his nostrils and Griffin's finger still curled around the trigger. 'Why do lions roar?' he asked. 'What makes eagles soar?' He frowned a little to look like he was making an effort.

Griffin sniffed. He resented the questions because he didn't see their point, and if he said so, he might look weak. 'End of message,' he said, and strode off, heading for the Camels.

Wragge found his cap. 'Half a guinea, that cost.' He poked his finger through the hole. 'Just because I opened the bowling for Harrow. I took three for twenty-seven. It wasn't a very good Eton side, but still... What sort of an idiot shoots a chap's cap?' They were walking to the train.

'I shot that R.T.O. in the spurs,' Hackett said.

'That was different. The man was a buffoon.'

'Well, the C.O.'s bonkers. And I'm hungry.'

Chef was serving a second breakfast in the dining-room car. Like most chefs, he had been well built – spend your working life sampling your own cooking and you put on a few pounds – but the Red Army diet had soon changed that. All the *plennys* were thin. Now Chef was starting to add a few ounces. His shaven head made his inky black moustache, thick and curling at the tips, dominate his face. He never smiled and he never spoke. He put a plate of eggs and bacon in front of Jessop, who said, 'Oh, thanks awfully, you are a prince among men, Chef, and a scholar with the skillet.' Chef stood erect, thumbs and forefingers gripping the seams of his trousers, until he was sure that Jessop had finished burbling. He collected a couple of dirty plates and went back to his kitchen.

'Can't we teach him to say something?' Bellamy said. *'Bon appetit,* or *Rule, Britannia.* Anything.'

'Not possible,' Lacey said. He was sitting in a corner, writing up the day's menu. 'Ever since he saw his entire family slaughtered. Wife, children, parents, grandmother. The Moscow Bolsheviks waded in blood to seize power. Chef was struck dumb, never spoke a word again. Devilled kidneys for lunch, by the way, with fluffy pancakes.'

Hackett and Wragge came in. 'Order up some grub, Lacey,' Hackett said. Chef appeared with two plates of bacon and eggs. 'Don't bother, you're too slow,' Hackett said. He took his place.

'What was all that, with the C.O.?' Jessop asked.

'He shot my hat,' Wragge said. 'Shot it dead.' He poked a finger through the hole and waggled it. 'See?'

'You must have done something.'

'We biffed the Bolos,' Hackett said. 'Sent 'em packing. But that's not good enough for him.' He was stirring an egg yolk with a piece of toast. 'We looked happy. We smiled.' He gave a twisted parody of a smile. 'And that spoiled everything.' He ate the toast.

Bellamy stopped sipping milk. 'I didn't smile at anyone,' he said.

'You didn't do any Bolo-biffing,' Wragge said. 'So you don't count.'

Lacey took Wragge's cap and looked inside it. 'Seven and one-eighth... I can replace it, if you

81

don't mind a hat last worn by a captain in the Royal Inniskilling Fusiliers. A trifle gaudy, but... You've no objection?'

'Won't he need it?' Wragge asked, and at once was sorry he'd spoken.

'Typhoid fever, Novorossisk. We keep a stock of replacement items of uniform. Thoroughly disinfected, of course.'

'I've always fancied myself in a kilt,' Jessop said. He poured coffee. 'Bit draughty in the cockpit, maybe.'

'Nobody else would fancy you,' Bellamy said. 'I've seen your legs. Very shabby.'

'What a bunch of queens,' Hackett said. He aimed his fork. 'He wants to wear a skirt, and *he* goes around looking at fellows' legs.' He spoke just as Griffin came in.

'Not serious,' Wragge told him. 'Just playing charades.'

'Yes,' Griffin said. 'That sums up the lot of you.'

2

Bellamy was sweating as he walked to his Camel for the second strafe of the day. His body felt cold but his face was hot. He mopped it with his handkerchief and told himself the air would be cool when he took off.

'We found the leak, sir,' his fitter said. 'Not in the fuel tank, strictly speaking. In a joint, where the pipe joins... Well, you don't want to know all that, do you?' He thought Bellamy looked a bit under the weather. A bit tenpence in the shilling.

'Anyway, it's repaired. Had to drain the tank first. Can't mess about with hot metalwork next to petrol. All it takes is a spark... Anyway, your tank's full again and we swabbed out your cockpit, got rid of the stink.'

Bellamy nodded. That milk hadn't been a good idea.

'We turned her over, sir, and she fired, first time of asking.' The fitter wiped a streak of oil from the fuselage, giving Bellamy time to say Well done or Thank you or any bloody thing. But the pilot just cleared his throat and spat, messily, and wiped his chin.

'Strictly speaking,' the fitter said, 'we should give her a test run, full revs, be sure that joint can take the strain, otherwise...' He screwed up his face. Didn't exactly shake his head, but he almost shrugged his shoulders.

Bellamy knew what was happening. They thought he didn't want to fly. Giving him a chance to back out and blame the mechanics. He was furious, and the fury brought some colour to his cheeks. 'Guns armed?' he snapped. 'Bombs on board? Right. Start her up. Sod the joint.'

But his guts rumbled. They sounded to him like someone moving heavy furniture. Felt like it, too. There was unfinished business down there and he wanted to lie down and let the two sides fight it out.

He climbed into the cockpit and was glad of the support the seat gave him. If he went sick now... They'd never believe him. Wouldn't say so. But he'd seen it happen, in France. Chap got a name for dodging the dangerous patrols and soon the whole squadron knew about it and nobody would drink with him, he was odd man out, you could tell from the way they gave him a sideways glance, nothing said. It was solitary confinement in the crowd. He wasn't going to risk that. He'd sooner die.

Ten minutes later, the Flight attacked Tsaritsyn from out of nowhere. 'We go in low,' Griffin had said. 'Low is ten feet. Line abreast, flat out, fire when I fire. Non-stop strafe.'

Bright sunlight sent shadows of the Camels racing ahead of them. The Gnome rotary engines flung back ribbons of burnt oil. The engines were past their best and flat out meant little more than a hundred miles an hour, but at ten feet up it felt a lot faster. Maynard enjoyed it. Speed was like brandy to him. Suppose he sneezed now, jolted the joystick an inch, he'd hit Russia with a bang like a howitzer. That would mean goodbye, Michael. Instant cremation. Well, who wants to linger? Uncle Stanley lingered for years and years, poor devil... Tracer rounds were streaking from the next Camel. Maynard had missed Griffin's signal. His thumbs squeezed the triggers and he felt the shudder of twin Vickers pumping bullets at the houses.

Bellamy didn't care whether or not his guns hit anything. His hands trembled and the houses were a wandering blur. The ground raced by, treacherously close. All he wanted was to finish. Get it over. Escape.

Griffin found himself singing. A hymn, *Guide me, Oh Thou Great Redeemer...* The Red defence got over its surprise and rifle fire flashed from windows. He hunched behind the solid shield of his engine. A Camel made a very thin silhouette when seen head-on. Only a lucky bullet would find him. Then it was time to escape, and his Camel vaulted the houses as if on springs.

Tsaritsyn was a seriously big city, and it was a mess. Half of it lay in ruins and the other half had been knocked about. This was not the first time that Wrangel's men had tried to capture it, and when Griffin took his Flight up to a safe height, they could see why he wanted it. Tsaritsyn sat beside the Volga and the river was a mile wide or more. There were ships on the river, with steam up. Whoever held Tsaritsyn blocked a supply line that reached deep into Russia, above and beyond Moscow. The Reds couldn't move south without it, and Wrangel couldn't move north. This would be a bloody battle.

Heavy machine-gun fire failed to reach the Camels. The shooting was wild, and artillery fire was worse: the shell bursts were too high. Spent bullets and shrapnel fell back on battered Tsaritsyn.

Griffin signalled his formation to spread out. It took both hands to unclip a 20-pound bomb and drop it over the side; and with the stick between the knees, the aircraft lurched about the sky. The pilots tried, and failed, to track the fall and see what they hit, but too many bangs were going flash down there. And a 20-pounder was only a firework.

They came together again in a loose arrowhead and flew back to the southern defences. During the strafe, the ground had been empty. Now it was seething. Wrangel's infantry, thousands of them, were running at strongpoints. Their banners made tiny splashes of red, green and white, and already their dead lay in hundreds. The Camels' strafe had been a gesture, a threat. Maybe they had killed a few Reds, maybe not. What mattered now was the enemy's machine guns and, further back, his artillery. As the pilots watched, Red shells were blowing holes in the White assault. But Wrangel had more infantry, more banners.

The Camels cruised up and down. Nobody bothered them. Who cares about toys in the sky when the real fighting is on the ground? After twenty minutes, they saw a sudden change. A strongpoint, maybe two, had fallen. The infantry stormed through the gap. Cossack cavalry followed at the gallop, steel glinting in the sunlight. Griffin turned the Flight for home.

3

'We're through the wall,' General Wrangel said. 'Now the hard work begins.' He gave his binoculars to Count Borodin.

'Let us pray we don't capture another vodka distillery, sir,' Borodin said.

'That's beyond our control.'

'Yes, like our troops. Drunk and incapable. And soon dead.'

They stood on top of a wooden tower on a small hill, south of Tsaritsyn. Men had cut trees from the banks of the Volga and built this skeletal lookout for the general. Its purpose was obvious, and occasionally a big Bolshevik gun lobbed a shell at it. Sometimes a near-miss sent bits of hot and jagged shrapnel flying through the open framework of logs. It was hard to destroy the look-out and impossible to disturb Wrangel. He was tall and wiry and had a face that someone said was like a hungry eagle. All eagles look more or less alike, hungry or not, but the description stuck. Count Borodin had served on the staff of many generals. None was thin and few stood within artillery range of a battle. Few stood anywhere, if there was an armchair available.

Borodin pointed at the sky. 'Late, as usual,' he said. The White Russian squadron of DH9s was arriving, very high, probably five thousand feet. Their formation was ragged. It changed direction and became more ragged. 'Just dots,' Wrangel said. 'They won't frighten anybody.'

'They fly high to avoid the artillery, sir,' Borodin said. 'It also permits them to see the Red aeroplanes a long way off and run away.'

'They suffer from delayed bravery,' Wrangel said. 'I have many officers like that, all seeking a new Tsar to die for. But not yet. Look: that must be the Red arsenal.' A flash of yellow erupted inside Tsaritsyn, and a rolling thunder followed. Black smoke pulsed upwards. 'Bang goes the Bolshevik ammunition. We can expect panic, retreat and large slaughter. Time for lunch.'

4

Wrangel was right about lunch but wrong about

the arsenal. White cavalry had been massing, preparing to charge down a street. Red defenders dynamited houses on both sides: that was the explosion. As the dust settled, the defenders climbed onto the barricade of rubble and shot down the White cavalry, still panicking from the dynamite blast. So there was no retreat, and the slaughter was of cavalry.

Wrangel sent Borodin to invite the Camels to return to Tsaritsyn.

'Preferably with many incendiaries,' Borodin told Griffin. 'Fire from the skies upsets the Bolsheviks.'

'Where exactly are the enemy positions? How shall we know where to make our attack?'

'If you bomb our troops, they will fire at you, whereas the enemy will fire at you whatever you do.'

Griffin called the Flight together. 'It's a bloody shambles,' he said. 'We're liable to get shot at by friend or foe.'

'Just like France,' Wragge said. 'Frog artillery always potted us.'

'Is that relevant?' Griffin said in a voice like sandpaper. 'Then shut up. Fuel tanks a quarter full. With the weight saved we'll take extra incendiaries. Attack the north side of the city. That's the Bolos' way out. Height, a thousand feet. Let them see the bombs coming.' He looked sideways at Bellamy. 'Are you fit?'

'I'll manage.' His face was bleached.

The weight of incendiaries in the cockpits upset the balance of the aircraft, and they bounced and lurched into the air. They kept clear of the west of the city but a few machine guns saw them coming and as the Camels turned to cross the northern side, a bright flicker of ground-fire could be seen. Griffin dropped a bomb and that was a signal for the rest.

The pilots were very widely spaced and they needed to be: using both hands to heave a bomb sent the machine dipping and skidding. Hackett threw a bomb too hard and his knees lost the stick and his Camel flipped onto its back. At once another bomb fell without his help, so he stayed inverted and punched and kicked at the rest until they dropped. 'Sheer bloody skill!' he shouted, and levelled out. Nobody had noticed. Too busy doing it the hard way. They flew home.

Lucky groundfire had made a mess of Bellamy's port wheel, but he didn't know this until he touched down and the Camel slewed so violently that his face whacked the gun butts and broke his nose. Wheel struts snapped; the fighter crabbed along on its belly, spraying chunks of propeller; the engine stalled; nothing caught fire. Bellamy, too weak to move, sat and swallowed the blood that ran into his mouth. Not a good day.

5

'Unforgivable,' Lacey said. He had prised the top off a tea chest and was sniffing the contents. 'This is Assam, and what's worse, it was picked from one of the inferior hills. Where is my Earl Grey?'

'Beats me, old chap,' Captain Brazier said. 'I'm not a bloody quartermaster, I just signed for the rations. I hope you've got plenty of hot water. Our plumbing died the death when we left Ekaterinodar.'

'I've been shaving in cold water for two days,' Oliphant said. 'My chops are chapped.'

The three men were in a railway wagon full of boxes of food and drink. They were on the train that had brought 'B' Flight, the other half of Griffin's squadron. Now it was in a siding next to Beketofka aerodrome. Six De Havilland DH9 bombers were strapped to flatbed trucks, with their wings lashed alongside. Oliphant was the flight leader.

'Assam,' Lacey said. 'Undrinkable. I shall have a strong word with our man in Ekat about this. Well, I suppose it's good enough for the troops.' He moved on. 'Pears soap, Cooper's Oxford marmalade, Gentleman's Relish... Good, good.' He ticked his list.

Guns rumbled in the distance, and Brazier cocked his head. 'Artillery. I'd like to see that. What I really want is a three-egg omelette.'

'And so you shall. What's in that barrel you're sitting on?' Brazier stood up, and Lacey levered off the lid. 'It's my Earl Grey!' he said. 'Praise be. Civilisation is saved.'

'It's only a cup of tea, for God's sake,' Oliphant said.

'Wrong. Or perhaps right. It is tea and it is for God's sake.' Lacey hammered down the lid. 'Now we can go. You shall both have hot baths and fresh eggs in abundance.'

He padlocked the wagon and they strolled towards the Pullman cars. 'You haven't changed,'

Brazier said. 'You were a mouthy chump then and you're a mouthy chump now.'

'Do you two know each other?' Oliphant asked.

'Like brothers,' Lacey said. Brazier gave a snort of derision. He was a large, square man with a hard, muscular face, and his snort was strong. 'Please,' Lacey said. 'You'll frighten the horses in the next field.'

'A year ago, I was adjutant to a bunch of ruffians called Hornet Squadron,' Brazier said. 'Lacey was my Orderly Room sergeant. He was spoiling the pilots with luxuries, it was all totally illegal, and his peculiar rackets got both of us sacked and sent to the Front Line.'

'Luxuries,' Oliphant said. 'What sort of luxuries?'

'I can't remember them all. English pork sausages were one. Also high-proof gin and rum. And coal, we were getting double our ration of coal. Honey. Cotton bedsheets. Lacey wanted silk, but I put my foot down. Canadian bacon. All wangled. Pinched. Fruits of fraud.'

'None of it was for profit,' Lacey said. 'I did it for fun. War can be awfully boring. And those pilots weren't with us very long, were they? While they survived, the least they deserved was soft toilet paper. The official issue was just like onionskin.'

'We ran out of coal on my squadron,' Oliphant said. 'Last winter of the war. Bloody cold, we were. We froze on patrol and we froze when we landed. One chap got frostbite. Who was that? Parker? Barker? Doesn't matter. He wasn't around for long.'

Brazier grunted. He didn't care about casualties. They were the small change of battle. 'Anyway, here we are again, Lacey and me, back where we began,' he said. 'And if you mention the fortunes of war, Lacey, I'll box your ears.'

'We're not exactly as we were, are we?' Lacey said. *'Carpe diem.* Opportunities came my way and I climbed the greasy pole of rank while you were hammering the Hun. I heard you got killed.'

'Lightly shot in several places.'

'Possibly by your own men.'

'Possibly. They wanted to retreat. I didn't. I shot a couple, the rest saw reason and I got a Military Cross out of it. Medals are cheap. But peacetime soldiering isn't for the likes of me. So I volunteered for this show instead.'

'Very wise. And we have wonderfully soft toilet paper.'

'Damnation. Almost forgot.' They halted. 'Mission commander asked me to tell you that you're commissioned. God help us. Acting Pilot Officer Lacey. How did you wangle that?'

'I have done some service to the State,' Lacey said. 'Did you hear of the unsavoury affair of the general's wife, the blond gigolo, and the gallon of gelatine?'

'No thanks.'

'Nor shall you. I wiped that particular slate very clean.' They walked on.

Griffin came out to meet them. 'When will your bombers be ready to operate?' he asked.

'Well, not before tea,' Oliphant said. It was a joke, but the C.O. stiffened and he stared as if Oliphant had belched at a royal wedding. 'As you can see, sir, our machines haven't been unloaded yet,' Oliphant said. 'If the mechanics work overnight, some might be flyable early tomorrow. Maybe breakfast-time. It depends.'

Griffin prodded him in the chest with his swagger-stick. 'Get this straight. We have a city to capture. You can forget tea and breakfast. We're fighting a war. First light tomorrow I want you bombed-up and ready for take-off. No excuses.'

Oliphant took half a pace back to escape the prods. 'Yes, of course, sir. This is Captain Brazier, by the way.'

Griffin ignored Brazier. 'Bomb the Reds. Bomb the bloody Reds. Bomb the blighters around the clock. No quarter, no mercy. Blow the Bolsheviks off the face of the earth.'

They watched him stride away. 'Quite keen, isn't he?' Oliphant said. 'Almost brisk, at times.'

'It's the smell of cordite,' Lacey explained. 'Highly intoxicating.'

'You wouldn't know cordite from custard,' Brazier said.

'Chef makes very explosive custard,' Lacey said. 'Put too much on your Spotted Dick and it'll blow your socks off.'

'More tosh. I wish I'd taken you with me to the Trenches. A month with the infantry would have knocked the tosh out of you.'

They walked on. What a funny war, Oliphant thought.

6

Oliphant's Flight had six bombers, but he had

brought ten pilots and ten gunners. Extra men had turned up at Ekat, and from what he had seen of action in France, he knew there would be wastage ahead. No point in having a machine without a crew.

The newcomers crowded into the Pullman bar-dining-room for tea, and were impressed to be offered hot buttered crumpets, even if these were square. 'Chef hasn't quite got the knack of it yet,' Lacey said. 'Have some strawberry jam.'

'We've been living on Russian bread and potato soup,' Oliphant said. 'Allegedly potato. Tasted like turnip to me.'

'Chef does a very acceptable Gratin Dauphinois. And his Gratin Pommes de Terre Provencale is improving rapidly.'

'He can't cook a cheese omelette,' Captain Brazier said. 'No cheese in it.'

Lacey shook his head. 'Russians. Hopeless. Square crumpets, and then a cheese failure. Chef shall be shot.'

Brazier sipped his tea and studied Lacey. 'You were never much of a soldier, were you? More of a grocer's assistant in uniform.' He was six inches taller than Lacey, and his voice had the hard edge of command. 'Now you're suddenly a pilot officer who can't fly an aeroplane. Promoted from grocer's assistant to grocer. Nothing to boast about, is it?'

Lacey had no answer and he was smart enough to keep quiet. Oliphant looked from one to another and told himself that this was not his quarrel. Then Count Borodin came in and said that he had brought a squad of *plennys* for the new Flight.

They all went out to see. 'Golly,' Oliphant said. 'Shaven heads. And not the glimmer of a smile. Are you sure they're on our side?'

'Treat them as batmen,' Hackett told him. 'Give one of them a tin of bully beef and he's happy as a pig in shit. Just don't salute. It makes them jump like nuts in May.'

'That's meaningless,' Wragge said. 'You don't find nuts in May. Nuts mature in autumn. Everyone knows that.'

'Not in Australia, chum. My best friends were nuts, and they were nutty as hell in May. You see an Aussie nut in May, stand aside.'

Brazier pointed at the biggest *plenny*. 'I'll have him. What's his name?'

'Rapotashnikov,' Borodin said. 'But you may call him Nigel.'

7

One by one, the DH9s took off and circled the airfield. The Camel pilots came to watch.

The bombers were single-engined biplanes, with a crew of two: nothing special about the design except that the machine was almost twice as big as a Camel. Its wingspan was forty-two feet; the Camel's was twenty-eight. In a Camel, the pilot could sit in the cockpit and talk to his mechanic, face to face. Not in a DH9, which stood more than eleven feet high to the upper wing. Fully loaded, it weighed over a ton and a quarter, including a pair of 230-pound bombs carried inside its bomb bay and smaller munitions hung under the wings. That was why the wings were so long: they provided the lift for this load. What the Camel pilots were most interested in was the engine that dragged this beast into the air.

The Camel had a Le Rhône rotary, a short-assed job where the cylinders spun in a ring and carried the propeller with them. It was as light as an engine could be, and very compact, so that the pilot sat close to the nose. There was barely enough room for the twin Vickers machine guns between him and the propeller. This arrangement made the Camel highly manoeuvrable. It could jink like a swallow and turn on a sixpence, all from 110 horsepower. But that pull would scarcely make a DH9 taxi, let alone get it off the ground. It needed the Siddeley Puma, which had six big cylinders arranged in line, like a truck engine. The Puma was so hefty that there wasn't enough room for all of it inside the body of the aircraft: its uppermost length poked out, exposed to the air.

This was good for cooling, but no help to a pilot who was trying to look ahead. Still, the engine made 230 horsepower, twice the little rotary's output, power that was needed to haul the bomb load through the sky. It made heat as well as heft, and the designers had added a novelty: a radiator placed just in front of the wheels, which the pilot could lower to catch the slipstream if the Puma began to overheat. So, alongside a Camel, a DH9 was a lot of aeroplane. It needed twice the take-off run before it came unstuck.

Griffin watched one as it slowly and grudgingly made height. 'Pumas,' he said. 'You couldn't get

Rolls-Royce Eagles?'

'We took what they gave us, sir,' Oliphant said. 'These Nines got flown in from Salonika, just as you see them.'

'Nines. Is that what you call them?'

Oliphant shrugged. 'Everyone does.'

'Sounds like you're selling shoes. Ladies' shoes.' They watched a bomber drift down and land. Its engine was misfiring and burning too much oil. 'That's Tommy Hopton,' Oliphant said. 'Good effort. He couldn't have seen much grass through that muck.'

'Pumas stink.' Griffin turned his back on them, 'Air Ministry's gone and dumped its duff junk on us. Surplus to requirements, send it to Russia. Quick way to lose a headache without spending money. Thoughtless bastards.'

'I'm sure the troops can make the Pumas work, sir.'

'Are you? I'm not. There's one way to find out. Tsaritsyn hasn't fallen yet. That's your target. Get bombs on target now. You can crash on the way home if you want.'

'Yes, sir.'

'And drop the sir. I'm not here to be buffed up like a brigadier's buttons. I'm here to win.'

Tommy Hopton taxied back to his ground crew, and Oliphant went to meet him. 'Sounded like a cracked cylinder head, Tommy,' he said.

'Felt like a burst valve spring. Smelt like grim death.'

'Bust exhaust pipe,' his gunner said, and coughed hard. 'Maybe both pipes,' he wheezed.

'Otherwise it's a good, strong bus. Does what

97

it's told,' Hopton said. 'Pity about the Puma.'

'We'll knock it into shape.' That was all balls. He knew it; they knew it. Move on, move on. 'See that smoke on the horizon? Tsaritsyn. We're going to bomb it if we have to crawl there on our hands and knees. Otherwise the C.O. will burst into flames.'

They turned and looked at Griffin, who was kicking at weeds. Hopton said, 'He's not a happy man, is he?'

Wragge had joined them. 'The skipper may not look happy on the outside,' he said, 'but I can assure you that deep down inside he's as miserable as sin.'

'What's the Red defence like?' the gunner asked. 'Are their fighters any good?'

'None. Frankly, it's not much of a war for us. Either the Bolos haven't got an air force or someone's lost the key to the hangar door. It's very dull up there. My advice to you,' he told the gunner, 'is to take a good book. That's what I do.'

He left. 'Camel drivers,' the gunner croaked. 'All piss and wind.' His throat still hurt from that godawful exhaust smoke.

A WASTE OF GOOD HORSES

1

It was midday before the Nines were ready to fly, and by then Tsaritsyn had fallen.

Count Borodin brought the news. He said that the remnants of the Red Army were in full retreat, flooding out through the northern gates of the city and fleeing panic-stricken by rail, boat and foot. 'Actually, Tsaritsyn has no gates,' he said, 'and the remnants are too tired to flee at any great pace. All the trains and the boats left yesterday, full of officers. Which leaves the poor bloody infantry on its poor bloody feet, as usual. But, for the purposes of Wrangel's bulletins, the remnants are fleeing panic-stricken through the gates etcetera.'

'Good. We'll bomb them,' Griffin said.

'Yes, he'd like that. D'you know, it makes a change for me to be on the winning side. The last time was three years ago, and the fleeing remnants were only Bulgarians, so they don't count. Is it possible for me to come along and watch?'

'Can you fire a Lewis gun?'

'I was a pilot in the Tsar's Imperial Air Service. I can hit a squirrel in the eye at one hundred yards.'

'Just shoot the fleeing Bolo remnants in their fleeing Bolo backs.' Griffin didn't smile. Carnage was a serious business.

The land north of Tsaritsyn was not steppe. It was broken by hills and ravines that appeared and ended for no apparent reason. The railway followed the easiest route along valley floors, and so did the retreating Red infantry. It was not an organized retreat. Clumps of men who had fought together now walked away from the defeat, too tired to run. Why run when the next town, Kamyshin, was a hundred miles away and the first real stronghold, Saratov, two hundred beyond that? Then the bombs began to fall.

All but one of the Nines had taken off. They circled the airfield, climbing to three thousand feet and making hard work of it, before they headed for Tsaritsyn, where a few of Wrangel's triumphant troops fired at them out of high spirits, and missed.

The Camels followed, high above, and watched. The bombers soon found the mass of the enemy trudging between hills, and Oliphant got his Flight into line astern. There wasn't much point in aiming. The whole valley was a target. When he knew he couldn't miss, he pulled a toggle and his pair of 230-pound bombs fell away. The aeroplane bounced, as expected, and he banked it a few degrees to give himself a better view.

He'd seen bombings before, many times, but he always enjoyed watching the creation, out of nothing, of a pure white explosion. The roaring Puma drowned the noise, and this made the spectacle seem silent. It reminded him of a conjuror producing a bunch of flowers from a hat. Then the creation slowly collapsed and left bodies strewn around it like petals. Bombs were blossoming all over the valley and men were running everywhere. Why run? Oliphant thought. You're just as likely to run into the next bomb as away from it.

The Flight left the valley, turned, lost height and flew back. It went down to a hundred feet, a comfortable height for a gunner with his Lewis to spray the survivors.

Count Borodin was Oliphant's observer and he fired intelligently: short bursts at visible groups. Nothing wasted. This time, nobody ran, which surprised Oliphant. They stood and let themselves be killed. Maybe they had had enough. Maybe they didn't care.

High above, Griffin led the Camels in lazy circles until the Nines turned for home. Just when he thought his escort duty was done, two enemy aircraft came out of the north, black specks that grew into a blue Spad and a grey Nieuport, each with a red star on the rudder. Before they arrived the Nines had gone, lost in the haze of smoke drifting from Tsaritsyn. Griffin felt the old kick of excitement, the familiar prickle of blood surging to his fingertips. The enemy were outnumbered, but that was their stupid affair. As soon as he could see the sheen of the Spad's propeller disc, he signalled *Scatter* and his formation went five different ways.

Hackett climbed. He opened the throttle and tucked the stick into his stomach and watched the land fall away. No looping. He'd seen bravos performing stunts like that over France and he knew where it got them: wrong speed, wrong attitude, easy meat. He made height, invaluable height, levelled out and found the blue Spad far below, flying in circles. It was steeply banked and tail-chasing a Camel. Small streaks of tracer stabbed at the space where the Camel had been. That was foolish. That was hope over experience. A new boy's mistake. Hackett pushed the nose down.

He slowed the dive by flying small S-bends to left and right, and timed his arrival so that he joined the circle, fully banked like the others, close behind the Spad. It didn't see him. Definitely a new boy. He had a good view of its tail unit. The rudder was unusually long: it reached forward an extra yard or more. Well, Spad knew best. He squeezed the triggers and the twin Vickers blasted the tail unit. Debris flashed by. Bits bounced off his wings. Hackett banked right so hard that his vision briefly went absent without leave. When it returned, the Spad was tumbling and its tail unit was elsewhere. In another part of the sky, the Nieuport was going down in a leisurely spin. It had lost a wing. 'Well, that was quick,' Hackett said aloud. He felt flat. It had all been too easy.

Griffin felt differently. He thought: First blood to us. Now we'll go and beat up some more bloody Bolos.

As soon as the Flight had assembled, they flew north. They saw retreating soldiers but the numbers were too few. Maybe the sound of bombing had driven the others to hide. The C.O. had no appetite for machine-gunning a poxy platoon of Reds, not after the victory in the valley, so he pressed on for five, ten miles, hoping for a juicy concentration of troops just waiting to be strafed. Nothing. He turned the Flight and flew south and there, tucked into a narrow ravine, maybe fifty yards wide, was the very thing. Not infantry but cavalry. Packed tight, everyone in the saddle, as if ready to charge.

The C.O. went first, swooped, began machine-gunning when he was a hundred feet up, kept his thumbs on the triggers until he was so low that his wheels were skimming the raised lances of a few riders, and as the ravine narrowed he climbed away, back into the clean blue sky. The others followed, one by one, and left a shambles of collapsed and dying horses, their legs thrashing, their riders dead or dying or trapped under the fallen animals. In three minutes the guns were empty. It was all over.

As the Flight regrouped, Wragge wondered about that attack. The cavalry had been in formation, as if they were ready for action. Why? Who did they expect to attack? There was nobody for miles and miles except retreating Red soldiers. And shouldn't we have seen a red banner? People said the Red Army always waved red flags. Maybe they were hiding. No, that didn't make sense. They weren't in any danger, nobody to hide from, not until Merlin Squadron showed up. All very puzzling. If they weren't Red cavalry, then who were they? So they had to be Bolos. Well, they learned a lesson. Never dawdle after you've lost a battle.

Killing horses wasn't much fun. Wragge had never killed a horse before. In France, he had never even seen the cavalry in action. Trench warfare was no place for horses. Machine-gunning cavalry seemed a great waste of good horses. Pity there wasn't some way of killing the cavalrymen and saving the horses. Damn it all, the horses hadn't done anyone any harm, had they? Oh well.

They cruised home, in nice time for tea. Chef had made more crumpets and some of them were almost round.

2

Next day Griffin woke, pulled aside a curtain and saw nothing but a thick grey mist. He opened the window and looked out. He could see one end of the next Pullman coach but not the other. 'Bugger,' he said. His *plenny* opened the door and stood ready for orders. 'Get Lacey,' Griffin said.

He was shaving when Lacey appeared, wearing a black dressing-gown of Oriental design featuring golden eagles. Underneath, he wore scarlet silk pyjamas. Griffin wore a plain white nightshirt. 'You look like the doorman in a Chinese brothel,' he said.

'I bow to your superior knowledge of that *milieu*,' Lacey said.

The *plenny* brought two cups of tea. The cups were generously breakfast-sized and carried someone's royal monogram. 'That will be all,' Griffin said. The *plenny* did not move. '*Spasibo*,' Lacey said and nodded at the door. The *plenny* left. Lacey sat in the armchair and sipped his tea. 'It's Fortnum's Number Seven Blend. A quiet introduction to the day. I think you'll like it.'

The C.O. finished shaving. As he towelled his face he examined his jowls and found them satisfactory. Ever since he rode point-to-point in England he had watched his weight. His cheeks were slightly hollow and his skin was like polished leather. In France, when he was a flight commander, he had seen a pilot eat a second helping of treacle pudding with custard, told the man he didn't like gluttons, and sacked him. Fat pilots were like fat jockeys: too greedy for their own good.

'What news on your radio, Lacey?' he asked.

'Wrankel's report to Denikin says his troops need a week to recover. He asks for reinforcements, so that he can advance northwards. Everything else is routine. We get a delivery of petrol here today or tomorrow. Ditto coal for the locomotives. There's some delicious spring lamb on the way too.'

Griffin was pleased. The British Mission in Ekat had warned him that he might have to badger the quartermaster-generals for the necessities of life. 'Nice to know the Russians appreciate us,' he said.

'You mean Wrangel? I don't deal with his lot. Russian staff officers will rob, cheat and swindle, and leave you starving at the roadside. I use my own sources.'

'Which are what, exactly?'

'Oh...' Lacey finished his tea. 'You really shouldn't concern yourself with petty details of housekeeping. That's my job. And the adjutant's, of course. He and I ... we understand each other.' Lacey looked Griffin in the eye and almost smiled.

He's challenging me, the C.O. thought. He's a streak of piss with an acting pilot officer's stripe, and I'm his wing commander, and he's telling me not to walk on his grass. But Griffin had served on squadrons in France where the C.O. had picked a fight with the quartermaster and everyone had suffered from that: no fires, bad food, precious little whisky. The Camels and the Nines couldn't fly without petrol and Lacey knew where to get it. Griffin suppressed his anger, postponed it to a better day.

'The squadron has a name,' he said. 'I want it painted on the side of every Pullman carriage. So big.' He held his hands far apart. 'Nothing jazzy. Strong, but...'

'Quietly understated,' Lacey said. 'British to the core. One of the *plennys* is bound to be good at that sort of thing. It shall be done.'

Immediate action: it made Griffin feel better. 'What sort of man is Captain Brazier?' he asked.

'He's a war-horse.' Lacey walked to the window and looked at the mist. 'Sound the bugle and he pricks his ears and snorts. He's a great snorter.'

'Brazier had a good war. His ribbons say so. But he's only a captain.'

'Well, he's been up and now he's down. A year ago, when the Huns made their last Big Push and nearly reached Paris, he rallied the ranks and became an acting major. He's awfully good at that sort of thing. He terrifies his men more than the enemy do. The ranks needed a lot more rallying, and he was briefly an acting lieutenant-colonel, but then the Huns gave up and the War Office had a big surplus of terrifying officers, so now he's a captain again. He's no fool. He has a weakness for gramophone records of regimental marches.'

Briefly, Griffin wondered if that was a joke. Probably. Not very funny. 'What's your weakness, Lacey?'

'Oh ... sometimes I succumb to Grieg. But

Rachmaninov is more bracing. And you?'

'Bashing the Bolos,' Griffin said. 'Bolo-bashing. Very noisy. You wouldn't like it.'

3

There was some dispute during breakfast as to whether this was mist or fog. Those who had known London pea-soupers voted for fog because it had a sulphurous smell. The pro-mist crowd argued that this stuff was the wrong colour and anyway the smell came from the fires of Tsaritsyn.

'I shot a wallaby once,' Hackett said. 'Terrible smell. They had to evacuate Adelaide.'

'Adelaide was his sister,' Wragge explained. 'She had a very distinctive aroma. It was an inherited trait. All families have them.'

'What's yours?' Jessop asked.

'Modesty.'

'You hide it well.'

'Nine centuries of breeding, old boy. One doesn't brag about it.'

'Alright, shut up,' Griffin said. 'We can't fly in this clag. We'll get the machines serviced and spruced up. Tomorrow's another day. If the Bolsheviks counter-attack we'll be ready. If they don't, we'll do some Deep Offensive Patrols, try and stir up the Red air force, if it exists. Where's Bellamy?'

'Ill in bed,' somebody said.

'I brought a medic from Ekat,' Oliphant said. 'Sergeant in the Medical Corps. The doctors won't travel, they say the whole of Russia is stiff with plague.'

Griffin and Oliphant stood in the corridor out-side Bellamy's Pullman car and heard the sergeant's opinion. 'Malaria,' he said. 'Either he'll recover in a week, or he won't.' They could see the *plenny* wiping Bellamy's face. Sweat reappeared at once. He lay under a single sheet, and it clung to his body. He shivered all the time, and the sheet copied the shivering.

The mist thinned but was reluctant to lift. Griffin hated to see officers standing around, tunics unbuttoned, ties loose, gossiping, so he found them jobs: inspecting the Other Ranks' quarters, checking the ammunition stores, supervising the digging of latrine pits (the Pullman lavatory system would soon need emptying), making sure the Cossack ponies were fed and watered.

Two bomber pilots, Gunning and Lowe, asked permission to visit Tsaritsyn. 'Why?' Griffin asked. Lowe had seen this coming. 'To inspect the effect of our bombing, sir,' he said.

'How?'

Lowe hadn't looked that far ahead. 'Um...'

'Two hundred pounds of Amatol,' Griffin said. 'It turns a Bolshevik into a pound of strawberry jam. Look closely or you won't find anything. Go and see Colonel Davenport, the aerodrome commandant. If he says yes, you can go.'

When Davenport saw them approach they re-minded him of his son. Well, many young officers made him think of Philip, dead in Flanders like thousands of other subalterns. Why him? Why not? Philip caught a packet in Flanders and now he was buried at St Margaret's in Chalfont St

Giles. Just look at these two: medium height, grey eyes, square chin, good teeth. Could be brothers. Twin memories, sent back to haunt him. He got rid of them quickly. 'I doubt you'll find much of interest,' he said. 'Ruins are ruins. God knows I've seen plenty. Sergeant!'

He gave his orders. 'I want these officers armed and horsed. You are their escort. Any threat, bring them out fast.' They left. But the memories lingered.

Armed meant holstered revolvers. The mounts were Cossack ponies. The sergeant carried a leather whip; its thong was so long that the tip bounced in the dust as they rode. 'You rather remind me of the American cowboys, sergeant,' Gunning said. 'Herding cattle and so on.'

The sergeant thought about that. 'This bleedin' country, if you'll pardon my French, sir. It's not like anywhere else.' That ended the conversation.

The city stank. The air was foul with the smell of unburied dead, both human and animal. This was not guesswork; Gunning and Lowe could see the carcases, mostly blackened and bloated. More bodies were hidden in the ruins, releasing a stench that was as sweet as sugar and as sour as vomit. The officers held handkerchiefs over mouth and nostrils. Useless. Even the ponies tossed their heads and blew noisily, hating the air.

There was nothing noble about the ruins. The walls that stood were black with smoke. Those that fell were hillocks of rubble. Some streets were still burning. The sergeant followed what might once have been a broad avenue. Soldiers watched them pass. Some were wounded, some were drunk, some were both. Their uniforms were far from being uniform: tattered, filthy, a mixture of colours. Most were barefoot. All looked underfed. 'Keep moving,' the sergeant said, and as he spoke a handful of women and children saw the visitors and ran towards them, shouting, pleading. Their rags were worse than the soldiers'. The sergeant cracked his whip at them, left and right, but they came on and the lash knocked a few to the ground. 'Go!' he bawled. 'Go, go!' Gunning and Lowe turned the ponies and whacked their heels against the ribs.

They stopped when they were outside the city, and let the ponies recover.

'The whip,' Gunning said. 'Was that absolutely necessary?'

'They're starving,' the sergeant said. 'If you'd given them a crust of bread, sir, ten thousand more of them would come out from nowhere and knock us all down. That's what hunger does, sir. Real hunger.'

They rode back to the aerodrome, thanked the sergeant and went to say goodbye to Colonel Davenport. They found him outside his office with Count Borodin, both men looking at five corpses laid out in a row, face up. All five wore the grimy, shapeless, sheepskin clothing of Russian peasants, with one small addition: red stars cut clumsily from cloth were pinned to their chests. 'The two on the end are far too old,' Borodin said. 'Even the Bolsheviks wouldn't conscript such grandfathers.'

'You're right,' Davenport said. 'And if those cut-throats killed these two, they probably murdered them all.' He turned and stared at a pair of

Russian men standing beside a farm cart.

'They want ten roubles per head,' Borodin said. 'Fifty roubles. Not bad for a night's work.'

Lowe could still taste the stink of Tsaritsyn and he cleared his throat. Davenport looked and saw two well-brought-up young Englishmen whose faces were utterly empty of understanding. 'Some idiot offered ten roubles for every Red Army soldier brought to us,' he told them. 'See the result. Civilians, all civilians. Russians kill their neighbours and pin a red star on them. If we pay, there will be more. If we don't there will be trouble.'

'Every Russian village has a feud,' Borodin said sadly. 'It's our national industry.'

Davenport squared his shoulders. 'Did you two find what you wanted in Tsaritsyn?'

'Yes, sir,' Gunning said.

'Interesting city, sir,' Lowe said.

'We ought to get back to our squadron, sir,' Gunning said. They saluted and marched away.

'Five roubles a head, no more,' Davenport decided. 'And I won't pay until those thugs have buried the bodies, here and now.' Borodin beckoned to the waiting pair. 'For two pins I'd bayonet them both,' Davenport said. 'That's what this country needs: a bloody good purge.'

'The Cossacks used to perform that duty for the Tsar,' Borodin said, 'but in the end their hearts weren't in it.'

4

The mist dissolved and a soft sun gave the remains

of the day an easy warmth. The steppe was changing colour: traces of red and yellow and blue could be seen in the distance. Wildflowers wasted no time here. Winter turned to summer with only a slight pause for spring.

Alongside the trains, some of the airmen were playing a casual game of football – the moustaches versus the clean-shaven. When the game began, Dominic Dextry had been exercising one of the Cossack ponies, riding bareback, and the animal enjoyed chasing the ball, so he declared himself referee. He was Irish, from County Cork, and he applied Irish rules to the game. The moustaches scored a goal but he disallowed it and penalized them for foul play. 'That's ludicrous,' a moustache said. 'Totally asinine.'

'Well, the ball was in an offside position, so it was.'

'Don't be absurd, Dominic. The ball *cannot* be offside.'

'It can in Ireland.'

'That's because there's too much Guinness taken, faith and begorra.'

'Nobody says begorra in Ireland, and I'll fight any man who says otherwise, begorra so I will, I will.'

'Your horse is eating our football, Dominic.'

'And after three hundred years of potatoes and English tyranny, can you blame the poor creature?' But the ball was too big for the pony's mouth and it lost interest. There was grass to be eaten. Football was amusing but grass was better.

Dextry slid off and lay on his back, looking at the sky. It was entirely a faded cornflower blue that wouldn't be allowed in Ireland, where there were always bully-boy clouds bustling in from the Atlantic. He snapped a stem of grass and chewed it. The pony moved its head and licked Dextry's ear, found it curious but tasteless, went back to real food.

Dextry missed Ireland, or some of it. He missed the talk in the Cork bars, always fast and funny and never two people agreeing on anything, so that an evening was better than a Dublin play. He missed the games, the Gaelic football that was something between havoc and homicide. And the sweet smack of a shinty stick. Shinty made English hockey look like badminton on the vicarage lawn. But his family had money and they had sent him to school in England, to Rugby school, where he was taught a more gentlemanly kind of football, even if his legs still had the scars to prove it. Every year he went home on holiday, and then one year he arrived to find the big old house in County Cork was a smoking ruin.

The English said the Irish liked a fight, and there were sixty thousand Irishmen in uniform in France, every one a volunteer, but Dominic discovered there was also a corrosive and undeclared war in Ireland which he had never suspected, and much of it was between Irishmen. He was sixteen. His family moved to Dublin and stayed with relatives. Dublin was a bleak and brooding place, not knowing whether to back the sixty thousand or to give the English a good kicking. Dominic left. He went to Wales and stayed with a friend from school, and tried to empty his mind of Irish bloody politics until the fight had burned itself out.

113

Another year at Rugby and soon he was eighteen, just. The Royal Flying Corps was glad to have him and he was glad to be in France. Should have been killed but beginner's luck, or the luck of the Irish, or some damn thing, saved him; and when all that careering a mile or two above the Trenches was over, he was glad to volunteer for Russia because it was a long way from the bad blood still being splashed about the Emerald Isle. Russia promised good fun, good pay, good grub.

He let his eyelids close and he watched tiny gold specks wander about a primrose sea.

Griffin sat beside him. 'Don't get up,' he said. 'I'm ready for a gallop, but I've never been one for bareback. That's for the Red Indians.'

'Awfully slippery. I fell off, going nowhere.'

'Saddles. Cossacks have saddles.'

'We could ask. Tell you what. My *plenny*, Gladys, speaks a little English. We could tell him what we want and send him over to their camp.'

Griffin scratched his jaw. 'Give him six tins of bully beef. Should buy six saddles.' He stood up. 'Gladys? You did say Gladys?'

'Oh ... I called him Jeremy at first, but it upset him. Very rude word where he comes from. He likes Gladys better.'

Griffin walked away and then came back. 'Don't get too friendly with your *plenny*, Dextry. They're all ex-Bolos. Not safe. They jumped once. Might jump again.'

Half an hour later, Gladys came back with a Cossack who was driving a farm cart loaded with six saddles and bridles. Griffin looked them over. 'Been in the wars,' he said. 'Only to be expected.

114

Saddle up three ponies. You, me and Gladys.'

They rode north, into the steppe. The saddles were small but so were the ponies, and the riders soon taught their legs and backsides to adjust. New and very green shoots of grass were already showing through the silvery-grey dead growth left by winter, and small flowers made spatters of brightness. It was easy riding: the land was never entirely flat, but its gradients were gentle. 'Good tank country,' Griffin said. Dextry agreed. After that there was nothing remarkable to comment on.

Once, they came upon a hare and sent it bounding off. Dextry gave chase; the hare ran in wide circles and made fools of them. Once, they scared some partridge, which took off so fast that they were a camouflaged blur against the grassland. Then there was quiet again. The steppe was peaceful. Nothing broke its solitude: not a hillock, not a river, not a tree. Just grassland to the horizon. Dextry wished he could see a tree. A dead tree would do. Just a stump. Then they saw smoke.

It was a cavalry camp. Small, only about a dozen men. 'Must be on our side,' Griffin said. 'The Reds wouldn't dare show their faces so far south.' He was right. The *plenny* went ahead and talked to their leader, and he came back and gave Dextry a smile. 'Yes, good,' he said brightly.

They were offered vodka, and took it. The *plenny* whispered to Dextry, who said: 'Really? Oh, jolly good.' He proposed a toast. *'Na Moskvu!'* Griffin said the same. Roars of applause. Big smiles. Much hand-shaking. All friends.

After that, things fell a bit flat. No more vodka,

and not a lot happening. Gladys the *plenny* seemed quite keen on leaving. He brought the officers' ponies to them, which was a pretty broad hint. 'Slow down, Gladys,' Dextry said. 'No need to rush.'

'They had casualties,' Griffin said. 'Over by the fire.'

They moved closer. The man on the ground was alive, but he was in a very bloody condition. Most of his face was damaged. Parts of his body were hurt; blood had soaked through his clothing and spread into the grass. His eyes were the only parts of him that were obviously alive. He watched the officers approach.

'Fresh wounds,' Griffin said. 'We didn't hear any fighting. My opinion, he's been knocked about.'

The *plenny* took Dextry's sleeve and whispered again.

'Commissar,' Dextry told the C.O. 'Apparently he's a commissar. Bolshevik politico attached to Red troops. I suppose these chaps captured him.'

'Is not your business.' A young cavalryman had come over and now he stood between them and the victim. 'Please go.'

'Good English,' Griffin said. 'That's a lucky break.'

'I was at school in Petersburg. We all learnt English. Listen when I say, this man is our business which you cannot understand.'

'Can't we?' Dextry said. 'He's a prisoner of war and you're beating him to death.'

'For intelligence. To make him tell us secret intelligence. To help us defeat the Reds.'

'That's not war, that's savagery,' Griffin said.

'You're supposed to be fighting for decency and you're acting like animals.'

'If the Red Army captures you,' the young cavalryman said, 'they will do things to you far worse than we do to him.' He spoke so calmly that they had no answer. 'All my family are dead. Father, mother, sisters, brothers, murdered when the Bolsheviks took power. Butchered. Thank you for your help, your guns, your money, but do not insult us by telling us how to fight our enemies. Russia is not a tennis court.'

Gladys the *plenny* was alongside with the ponies. They mounted and turned to go. 'At least, shoot the poor bastard dead and finish him,' Griffin said, and dug in his heels. They cantered away. They heard no shots.

After ten minutes, Griffin said: 'I don't believe what that man said. He was lying. All that stuff about school in Petersburg. Too smooth by half.'

'It did rather run off the tongue.'

'There's a lot of desperadoes about. Deserters, bandits, that sort. The fellow they caught was probably a horse thief.'

'Law of the jungle.'

'Not our funeral. Nothing happened back there.'

'Nothing at all,' Dextry said. 'Less than nothing. And that's an exaggeration.'

5

Count Borodin arrived alongside the Pullman trains in a Chevrolet ambulance hauled by two stolid oxen. His motorcycle was in the back. He honked the car horn and Lacey came out.

'We found this in Tsaritsyn,' Borodin said. 'The Reds must have captured it in another battle. Slightly soiled.'

'It's been full of blood,' Lacey said.

'Half-full. It had a lot of worse things in it yesterday, but we left it overnight and the dogs cleaned it out. Many wild dogs in the city. It's a gift from General Wrangel. If your mechanics can make it go, it might be useful for your business trips.'

'Very thoughtful.' Lacey kicked a tyre. 'Solid rubber.'

'Yes. No more annoying punctures. Go anywhere. Scoff at broken bottles, sharp nails, enemy bullets.'

'Scoff?' Lacey tugged an ear. 'Scoff... Sometimes you sound far more English than the English. How is that?'

'Well, I had a triple-hyphen tutor. Mr Rosedale-Frost-Forrest-Hungerford. Not many Englishmen can claim that. He used to cry if I split an infinitive. Happy days, schooldays.'

'I was sent down a mine as soon as I could walk. I toiled at the coalface from the age of three. What fun! How we laughed!'

'Goodness,' Borodin said. 'Was that a jibe? Do you envy me? Would you really rather be a bastard footnote to an imperial comic opera? Because that's all I am.' He was amused.

'Envy. We English aren't much good at envy.' That sounded feeble. The truth was that a small part of Lacey would very much like a share of Borodin's gloss. He tried self-mockery. 'We're good at hypocrisy. I could give you lessons.'

'No true Englishman would ever say that.' By now Borodin was almost laughing. 'But you're not typically English, are you? You're the joker in the pack.'

'What pack?' Lacey spread his arms. 'Look around you. It's just a war. Nothing but noise and confusion and...' He pointed to the Chevrolet. '...and a lot of blood. I take it that General Wrangel is pleased with us.'

'Yes, yes, he's very happy. Total triumph. One small anxiety. Your friends in the next field, the Cossacks. They sold you some ponies, I believe.'

'And saddles. Griffin wanted saddles.'

'Of course. Unhappily the saddles became available because of the small anxiety. Yesterday the Cossacks sent some of their cavalry, not many, to take care of the Red retreat.'

'Take care of? Food, blankets? Medical aid?'

'Medical aid would have been useful. The cavalry got strafed. Several aeroplanes found them in a little gorge. Escape was difficult. Half the men and the horses were killed. You couldn't call it a battle. More ... what's the word ... *mechanical* than a battle.'

'Noise, confusion and a lot of blood.' Lacey walked around the Chevrolet and kicked the tyres he hadn't already kicked, until he ended up where he began. 'Well, the Reds have an air force. So it's no great surprise, is it?'

'I spoke to the survivors. Some had never seen a train or a car until they came here, so aeroplanes are a mystery. Magic in the sky.'

Small pause.

'Look,' Lacey said. 'Stuffed mushrooms and

119

beef stroganoff tonight, with a decent claret. Can you stay for supper?'

'Afraid not.' Borodin heaved his motorcycle from the back of the car. He tried to kick-start it and failed. Tried again, failed again. 'There's something else, but keep it under your hat. Cossacks have a habit of packing up and going home after a battle. Perhaps that party in the gorge were deserters. It's a possibility.'

'Only a small anxiety, then,' Lacey said. 'What you chaps might call *nichevo*.'

'Yes, *nichevo*.' This time the motorcycle fired, and the count went bumping and bouncing across the grass.

The owner of the oxen uncoupled them and led them away, well satisfied to be paid with two tins of corned beef. By then, several off-duty ground crew had found the Chevrolet and were tinkering with it. That was when Griffin and Dextry rode in. Jack, the C.O.'s *plenny*, came running and took his pony. Griffin walked, slightly bowlegged, to his Pullman and looked at the name painted on it. 'Is this a joke?' he asked in a voice that cut humour off at the knees.

'Sweet blind O'Reilly,' Dextry murmured.

'I wrote it down for him,' Lacey said, 'but artistic licence seems to have won the day.' The R and the N had been Russified so that the name read MEЯLIИ SQUADЯOИ .

Brazier arrived. 'What's the problem? Ah, I see. Jolly japes. Well, that won't do. Typical Bolo trick. Bad for morale. Which one is he?'

'The poor chap's illiterate,' Lacey said. 'He paints shapes, not words.'

'Oh, leave the damn thing as it is,' Griffin said. 'It's special. And so are we.' He climbed into the Pullman.

The others looked at each other. 'What prompted that?' Brazier asked.

'We had rather an odd ride,' Dextry said. 'I think I need a drink.' He headed for the bar car.

6

Lacey went to his radio room and called up his contacts at Wrangel's H.Q. and the British Military Mission H.Q. and elsewhere. He was scribbling on a message pad when the adjutant opened the door and three *plennys* carried in pony saddles. He pointed to a corner. They put the saddles on the floor and went out.

'Left lying around,' he said. 'I don't like an untidy camp.'

Lacey nodded, and kept writing.

Brazier sat behind his desk. 'We're not damned cavalry,' he said. 'If people want to ride horses, they should have grooms to clear up behind them.'

Lacey's nod was very small.

Brazier stretched his legs and looked at the dust-motes wandering in the rays of the afternoon sun. He shared his office with the radio room, and it was a comfortable arrangement. He had worked in worse spots; much worse. He focused on the dust-motes. There were thousands of them and they never collided. How was that? He had no patience with questions to which there was no answer, and so he looked instead at the velvet curtains and the pictures on the wall, sketches of naked women done in charcoal. Where did Lacey get them? Same place as the carpet. Thick. Soft. Unsoldierly. Brazier breathed deeply and flared his nostrils. He had all he needed: a desk and a chair, a copy of *King's Regulations*, a bottle of whisky. He reached for the book and opened it at his favourite chapter: 'Discipline – Arrest and Custody'. He began reading. After a while he murmured, 'Conduct prejudicial to good order and discipline.' Useful catch-all offence, that one. He looked at the column headed 'Maximum Punishment (On Active Service).' 'Two years' imprisonment,' he said. Not much. Insubordinate Language got Penal Servitude. Mutiny got Death.

Lacey closed his message pad and took off his earphones. He leaned back and linked his hands behind his head. 'Very satisfying,' he said. 'A dozen British Army motorcycles were lying on the docks at Novorossisk, quietly rusting away because the Russians couldn't make them go. Faulty sparking plugs. But the army dump at Salonika has plugs galore. A word in Salonika's ear, now the motorcycles roar with life, and every general in Denikin's armies wants one as a toy.'

'Idiots.'

'Happy idiots. Also, a lot of the war supplies sent by London had the wrong labels. Nurses' underwear, for example, was labelled football boots.'

'Doesn't surprise me.'

'Russians don't play footer. So the crates were left to rot on the dockside. Luckily, our man in Novo spotted the mistake. Same thing happened with army band instruments, labelled disinfectant, while a crate of disinfectant was labelled swimming costumes, which the Russians didn't want because they always swim naked.'

'I suppose it's too much to hope that London sent a crate of nurses' knickers that was full of disinfected trombones,' Brazier said. 'No, I thought not. There's nothing new in your laundry list, Lacey. When I was in Palestine I took delivery of a railway truck full of left-hand boots. Never got the right-hand boots. The truck's probably still there. War is waste.'

'Not in this case. The motorcycles fetched a good price, and the nurses' lingerie was in hot demand. The Ekat opera company snapped up the band instruments – Bolos had destroyed their originals – and we made such a profit that we donated the disinfectant to the hospitals.'

'I don't care,' Brazier said. 'Sell your damned knick-knacks wherever. It doesn't matter to me.'

'Well, it should.' Lacey got up and straightened one of the charcoal nudes. 'Delightful creature... There was enough profit to buy a huge amount of Russian champagne. We traded half of it with the captain of an American cruiser in Novo harbour. He gave us a large box of gramophone records – the latest Broadway hits – and half a dozen enormous smoked hams, plus a barrel of salted herring and a case of rum. With the rest of the money I bought caviare, castor oil and soft toilet paper for the squadron.'

'The last two items,' Brazier said. 'Cause and effect, I suppose.'

'Heavens, no. The oil is for the aeroplane engines.'

123

Brazier put his head back and let his eyelids fall until he seemed to be looking at Lacey from a great distance. 'How sad,' he said, 'that the war has to intrude in your grocery affairs.'

'Ah, the war. Yes. I have a couple of military messages. Wrangel told Denikin that he must have another squadron of British fighters.'

'Bloody Russians. They think Britain's an open tap.'

'Wrangel says he needs them because his cavalry got strafed, badly, by the Red air force,' Lacey said. Brazier's grunt expressed his feelings about cavalry. 'Count Borodin told me what happened,' Lacey said. 'Apparently the Cossacks got trapped in a ravine.' Another grunt from Brazier. 'It happened very quickly,' Lacey said. 'Cossacks don't know much about aeroplanes.'

'And they didn't stop to look when they got strafed. Machine guns have that effect. Everyone gets his head down.'

Lacey looked at the saddles. 'Those came from the Cossacks.'

They went over and looked. Brazier squatted on his heels and fingered the holes in the leather. 'Fresh damage,' he said. 'You don't take much interest in battlefields, do you? I do.' He picked up a saddle and turned it over. 'See here. The round has emerged from the underside. Either the horse was standing on its head or the bullets were fired from above. High above.' He put down the saddle and opened a penknife and poked it in the most inviting hole and found nothing; tried another hole and found the remains of a bullet. He quickly found three more. 'Rather battered,' he said. 'Most are. I saw a lot of these in France. They're calibre 0.303 inches, the standard British ammunition.' He gave them to Lacey, and stood up.

'We supplied ammunition to Russia during the war,' Lacey said. 'The Reds might have captured it.'

'Our bullets wouldn't fit Red machine guns. They fire the standard Russian bullet, which is 7.62 millimetres. Not the same thing at all.'

Lacey squeezed a bullet between his fingers until the pain made him stop. 'Should I tell the C.O.?' he asked.

'He'll hate you for it. They'll all hate you. And it won't change anything.' He took the bent bit of metal from Lacey's hand and tucked it in a tunic pocket. 'Furthermore, they won't believe you. But go ahead, if you wish.' Brazier almost smiled. He was enjoying this.

'I don't wish.'

Brazier went back to his desk. 'Stick to groceries, Lacey. You won't get blood on your fingers.'

7

The nearest Red air force base was at a place called Urbàkb, fifty miles to the north. Perhaps seventy or eighty. The maps didn't always agree. Next morning, the White bomber squadron resident at Beketofka set off to raid it, and Griffin's squadron followed.

It was like following children going on a picnic. The White bombers did not bother with formation-keeping: they flew at whatever height they pleased, in any pattern, or none. There was a lot of low cloud, which did not help. Oliphant identified the leader's machine by the white streamer flying from its tail, and he kept his Nines far behind it. The Camels were high above, as usual, scouting for trouble.

There was none until they got in sight of Urbàkb. Then guns opened up and the White bombers flew into a sky that was blotted with black. It looked a lot worse than it was because the gunners miscalculated the height and so there was plenty of empty air. The cloud, too, provided patchy cover. Oliphant could see enemy machines parked down there. He wheeled his Nines away from the action and let the White bombers have first crack.

It was a full squadron, twelve aircraft, and their concerted attack should have made a mess of something, but already three White bombers had turned away from the target and were heading for home. They did not appear to be damaged. The remainder milled about. Soon, bomb bursts made small brown fountains, but Urbàkb was a big airfield and attacking the grass would do no lasting harm. And Red fighters were taking off.

Oliphant re-formed his Flight into line astern and flew towards the hangars. The flak gunners saw him coming and turned their fire on him, so he put his nose down and changed height before they could change the fuses in their shells. A heavy machine gun came looking for him and sent stitches of red tracer climbing and bending and whipping past. Then he was over the first hangar and he pulled the toggle that released the bombs. As he climbed away, the Lewis gun behind him was firing long bursts, probably at the man chucking up the red tracer. Oliphant hoped his observer had many more drums of ammunition. Fighters were still taking off, and it was a long haul back to Beketofka.

Griffin's plan was to engage the Red fighters over their own aerodrome. He felt sure they would defend it, and if his Camels couldn't knock them down they would enjoy a good, long scrap that would exhaust the enemy's ammunition and give the Nines a healthy start. But to his surprise, the Red fighters fled. They kept low, and they kept going, grey specks between empty steppe and a ragbag of clouds, until he lost them. Extraordinary behaviour. Pathetic, really. He waited another minute. Nothing.

He signalled his Flight into line abreast and they went down where the guns could not depress their barrels. They flew low across Urbàkb airfield and shot up everything with wings that they saw. Some burned, one exploded, none was airworthy as the Camels cleared the base and climbed, still chased by the red tracer. Griffin thought: Pity about the fighters. We came all this way and they couldn't even raise a team. He put his Flight into arrowhead, cruised around, looking for a juicy target, found none and headed for home.

It was fifteen minutes before the Camels caught up with the Nines, and when they did they flew straight into a messy battle with eight Red fighters. Hackett identified two Nieuports, an Albatros, a Fokker D9, a couple of Spads and maybe a Sopwith Pup before he was into the usual mad-

127

house, dodging one bomber to try to get a burst at a Red fighter chasing another bomber. Two wrecks burned on the steppe below, and a Nine had fallen out of formation with a dead engine.

Its pilot was Gerard Pedlow, and he knew that his best hope was to dive hard and pray that the wings would not fold like wet paper under the strain. He heard the chatter of the Lewis behind him. That meant an enemy was chasing, looking for the kill. Not a happy situation. His wings were shuddering, the cockpit instruments were a blur, the wind in the wires and struts screamed. The Nine had a big, heavy engine, now totally dead and hellbent on burying itself and its crew. The joystick in his hands felt as rigid as an iron bar. At this rate they were bound to crash. He used every muscle and heaved on the stick. Something moved. He thought he'd bent it. Then the nose came up by inches and if it hadn't been for the wheels he might have got away with it. But the wheels scraped against Russia and snapped off with a bang and the bomber bounced and fell on its belly and skidded through a mist of grass and dirt as if it had no wish to stop.

When it stopped, everything stopped.

No blind, suicidal skidding. No rackety shaking. No noise. Just a pain in the stomach. Pedlow undid his seat belt and the pain did not go away but his bruised stomach felt able to breathe more easily. He was dazed and his eyes kept going in and out of focus. He worried about his stomach. It shouldn't be breathing, that was the job of the lungs. Now his ears were singing. What was there to sing about? And he could taste something that might be bile. Bloody bile. 'Well, sod the lot of you,' he said aloud, and surprised himself. At least one bit of him worked properly. He tried to stand up but his legs were empty. Not a drop in them. Now that was strange. He fell asleep.

His observer, Joe Duncan, shook his shoulder. 'Wake up, old chap,' he said.

Pedlow was enormously refreshed. He felt he must have slept for hours. 'Did you get that Hun?' he asked.

'He wasn't a Hun, he was a Bolshie. I scared him off. They've all gone. You can't stay there.'

Pedlow got out. His empty legs were full again. That's what a night's rest did for a chap. Duncan held his elbow and made him walk until they were far from the wreck. There was nothing to rest against, so they sat back-to-back and leaned on one another.

'Jolly desolate,' Pedlow said. The steppe was empty apart from the remains of their Nine. Most of the wings had been torn off and the fuselage was ripped open.

'The chaps know where we are,' Duncan said. 'Someone will turn up.'

Nobody appeared for an hour or so, and then it was a man driving a farm cart. He stopped and stared at them and said something that meant nothing. He was dressed entirely in fleece. His hair and beard were thick and long.

'We've been captured by a dead sheep,' Duncan said.

'Angliski,' Pedlow called out. 'Angliski aeroplaneski.'

The man went over to the wreck and walked

around it. He climbed onto what was left of the starboard wing and looked into the cockpit. The wing broke under his weight, and the whole wreck lurched. 'That's not a good idea,' Duncan said, and before he could act, the Nine caught fire and the man ran for his life.

'There was petrol in the tanks,' Duncan said. 'I expect the sun turned it into vapour. All it took was a spark.' A small explosion blew the wreck apart and doubled the height of the flames. The man kept running until he was near the airmen.

He stopped and stared; came closer and studied their uniforms. He was especially interested in the pilot's wings on Pedlow's tunic, and he reached out a trembling hand and almost touched the badge. He fell to his knees and raised his hands in prayer, and made a long, husky statement that ended when tears washed away his voice.

'Hey, hey,' Pedlow said. 'Don't concern yourself. It's only an old Nine. We smashed it, not you.'

The man edged forward and bent and touched his forehead against the toe of Pedlow's flying boot.

'I may be wrong,' Duncan said, 'but I rather think he's praying to you.' The forehead moved to the other boot. 'He seems to have mistaken you for somebody wonderful. Charlie Chaplin, perhaps?'

'Tell him to stop.'

'Can't. He's adoring you.'

'I'm not bloody adorable. Christ, he smells.'

'Don't worry, Gerry. Nobody else adores you. To me you will always be a squalid bog-trotting Irishman with no scruples. Hullo, he's on his feet again.'

The man stood and unfastened the many fleeces that made up his clothes until a final flourish exposed his crotch, and he made it clear to them that there was little to see: he had been castrated.

'Charming,' Duncan said. 'You've got no scruples and he's got no goolies. We're being entertained by the village idiot.'

'He seems quite proud of himself,' Pedlow said. 'I think we should show our appreciation.'

They clapped their hands. He bowed, cried a little, went away and fetched the farm cart.

'Off to the madhouse,' Duncan said. 'Maybe they serve tea.' They climbed aboard.

8

The Rose Garden behind the Royal College of Embroidery was just coming into bloom. Jonathan Fitzroy and General Stattaford strolled the gravel paths between the flowerbeds. Sunshine had followed a shower, and raindrops glistened on the first brave blossoms.

'When I retire I shall be a gardener,' Fitzroy said. 'A garden never argues, never complains, never raises objections. Unlike the Cabinet, or the House of Commons, or Fleet Street, which are all permanently dissatisfied. That's why I thought it might help if you and I had a chat before the others arrive. I've always found that the best meetings are those where the decisions are agreed beforehand.'

'I take it the Prime Minister has turned down our suggestion' Stattaford said.

'Not entirely. He rather likes the idea of Britain holding the ring to let the Russians have a fair fight. But his question is, does it square with the facts?'

'Wouldn't work, anyway.' Stattaford paused to smell a rose the colour of buttermilk. 'Russians can't fight fair. Never could.'

'That's why I felt it would be helpful to look at the facts. The military facts. The overall picture.'

'Think of an elephant.' The general had a blackthorn stick and he sketched the outline of an elephant in the gravel path. 'Moscow's about *here*. Where the eye is. Bolshevik H.Q. Up here, on top of the elephant's head, is our North Russia Army, no great size. Murmansk and Archangel. Arctic Circle, dreadful place, ice or swamp, take your pick. Go further left, down among the tusks and the trunk, there you've got Finland, Poland, Baltic States, Ukraine. All anti-Bolshy. They got out of Russia when the Revolution blew up, now the Reds want them back. Very messy.' They walked on and reached a garden bench. Fitzroy spread a copy of *The Times* and they sat down. Stattaford tapped his left leg with the stick. 'Bit of Hun shrapnel wanders about. More rain coming, I shouldn't wonder. Not important.'

'Admiral Kolchak,' Jonathan said. 'The newspapers seem quite keen on Kolchak. Where d'you place him?'

'Deep in the belly of the beast. Siberia. Imagine the elephant's spine. That's the Trans-Siberian Railway. Kolchak's H.Q. is at Omsk. About as far from Moscow as we are, sitting here.'

'*The Times* says–'

'Kolchak wants Moscow. He probably does. He claims to be Supreme White Commander of all Russia.'

'You're not impressed.'

Stattaford shrugged. 'He's an admiral. The admiral of Omsk.'

'That leaves ... what? General Denikin?'

Stattaford chuckled. 'Put him on the elephant's left front foot, with his coat-tails in the Black Sea. Now Denikin is a soldier. Been fighting the Reds for the best part of two years, all the way from Petrograd. Won a few battles, lost a few. Good army, tough as old boots. We kit 'em out. New boots, khaki uniforms, field guns, everything. Money.'

'So ... the elephant's left foot has some kick in it.'

Stattaford examined his fingernails for signs of dereliction of duty. 'There's a song. "Ours is a nice house, ours is." Know it? Music-hall ditty. Has a line: "With a ladder and some glasses, you could see to Hackney Marshes, if it wasn't for the houses in between." Clever, isn't it? When I look at a map of Russia, it reminds me of the song.'

'Too deep for me, old chap.'

'Remember the elephant. Remember its tail. That's where the American troops are, and the Japanese, at Vladivostock. Quite a lot of them. Doing very little. They're six thousand miles from Moscow. Russia is an elephant so big, it can't even see its own tail. And vice versa.'

Jonathan stood up. 'I think the others are arriving. Well, thank you, general. Very helpful.'

'Missed out a few warlords,' Stattaford said. 'Just fleas on the elephant.'

They reached the library to find that the meeting

had begun without them. 'Four million men,' James Weatherby was saying. 'Nearly four. As near as dammit, four million. *That's* what the Home Office worries about.'

'Well, it doesn't worry the Treasury, I can assure you of that,' Charles Delahaye said. 'Most of your four million men are demobilized. Paid off. Happy civilians. That's a huge saving, and God knows we need it. The country should be grateful.'

'I don't want to seem dense,' Jonathan Fitzroy said, 'but is all this relevant to Russia?'

'Yes and no,' Weatherby said. 'Yes, we think it is and no, we can't be sure it isn't. The Army's demobilized. Happy civilians? Not necessarily. Home Office gets some worrying reports. Men who've been trained to kill by gun and bayonet for four years don't become model citizens when you give them a trilby hat and a rail warrant home.'

'Poppycock,' Stattaford said. 'Utter tosh. The British soldier is highly disciplined.'

'Then what were the mutinies about?'

'No mutinies. A few cases of insubordination. Regimental officers stepped in, the men saw sense.'

'Did they? They burnt down Luton Town Hall first. They seized Calais, and you had to send in two divisions of troops to get it back from them. There are Communists in the Army. They took control of that march from Victoria Station to Whitehall, three thousand soldiers, all armed, enough to fill Horse Guards' Parade! Of course, that wasn't a mutiny. It just took a battalion of Grenadiers with fixed bayonets and two troops of Household Cavalry to make them see sense.'

134

'All because some idiot at Victoria Station forgot to provide the men with tea.' Stattaford ground out the words like eating stale bread. 'It *wasn't* a mutiny. If you want to see mutinies, go to Russia. They shoot all their officers, rape their wives, and blow their noses on the tablecloth.'

'Moving on...' Jonathan said.

'We all know about the Bolsheviks,' Weatherby muttered.

'I wasn't talking about the Bolsheviks,' Stattaford said.

'Let me perhaps remind everyone why we are here,' Jonathan Fitzroy said, fast, before anyone could ask what the general meant. 'The P.M. seeks a formula to reassure public opinion. A satisfying reason why we're at war in Russia.'

'We're *not* at war in Russia,' Sir Franklyn said sharply.

'Exactly. Why we're *not* at war in Russia. Oblige us, if you would, with the view from the Foreign Office.'

Sir Franklyn Fletcher was tall and wiry, with a face like an intelligent gamekeeper, which was not a bad description of his job. He had been in the Foreign Office all his working life, and his goal was to leave his country no worse off when he retired. He walked over to the marble fireplace and turned his back on it and rested his arms along the length of the mantelpiece.

'One side or another is going to win in Russia,' he said. 'It might be Denikin's White Army. He wants to restore what he calls One Russia, Great and Undivided. That means the Empire of the late Nicholas II – including all the bits and bobs

135

around the edges that are now free and independent, from Finland and Poland in the north to the Caucasus in the south.'

'Correct me if I'm wrong,' Fitzroy said cautiously, 'but hasn't Denikin said he does not wish to be a new Tsar? Isn't his aim to give Russia back to the Russians?'

'So he says. But he doesn't behave like a democrat. He's hanged quite a few Russians who disagreed with him. However, that's not our concern. Our concern is that if he gets his One Russia, Great and Undivided, he'll want India too. Why? Because Russia has always wanted India. On the other hand, Lenin and Trotsky might win. If they do, there's every sign that they, too, will want the whole of Russia with all the trimmings. Imagine a Bolshevik Poland, gentlemen. A Bolshevik Lithuania, Latvia, Estonia. How long before the Bolsheviks get Germany, Czechoslovakia, Austria? Was it for that sort of Europe we fought and won the Great War?'

There was a gloomy silence.

'Alright,' Charles Delahaye said, 'That's all conjecture. But even supposing it's true, what can we do to stop it?'

'I know what you can do,' General Stattaford said confidently. 'Denikin's troops are tired. Trotsky's rabble is a shambles. Give me two divisions – no, damn it, two brigades – of frontline British regiments, and I'll guarantee to take Moscow before the first snow falls.'

That surprised everyone. 'So ... our recommendation to the P.M. is what?' Fitzroy asked. 'Seize Moscow?'

136

'They won't go,' James Weatherby muttered.

'We can't invade Russia when we haven't declared war,' Sir Franklyn said.

'They'll mutiny,' Weatherby said.

'Shipping? Food? Equipment?' Charles Delahaye asked. 'The cost is prohibitive.'

'The troops simply won't go!' Weatherby said. 'You can't force them.'

'They'll do as they're bloody well ordered,' Stattaford declared. 'This is the British Army and–'

'And they won't kill Russians. The troops' war is over. Look: British troops don't want to go to Ireland and shoot Irishmen who were fighting alongside them last year, so they certainly won't obey orders to go to Russia and kill Russians who were our allies against Germany.' Weatherby flourished a copy of the *Daily Mail*. 'Just to put together a small Relief Force for Murmansk and Archangel you have to appeal for volunteers. Ex-soldiers.'

Stattaford took the paper from him.

'Money wouldn't *necessarily* be a problem,' Fitzroy said.

'Yes it would,' Delahaye said. 'Put up income tax again to pay for your Russian adventure and see what the public thinks.'

'Listen to this,' Stattaford said. *'The fighting spirit of the old army is aflame... Recruits are still pouring in with medal ribbons on their waistcoats... The officers too are excellent...'* He looked up. 'How d'you explain that keenness? What?'

'Half of them can't get a job in civvy street,' Weatherby said.

'The other half are on the run from Scotland Yard,' Delahaye said.

'Gentlemen, gentlemen... Please, please,' Fitzroy said. 'We're straying ever further from the point. How can we best help the Prime Minister retain the confidence of the nation?'

'The British people want two things,' Weatherby said. 'First, no more war. Ever. Second, make the Germans pay. My department gets reports from throughout the kingdom, and especially from the four million who did the fighting, and they all say: "Make the Huns pay every penny for the damage they did, even if it takes a thousand years." That's what matters.'

'Gratifying,' Charles Delahaye said. 'But self-defeating. It's the economics of the madhouse.'

'They don't know economics. They *do* know atrocities. We've been feeding them Hun atrocities for four years. Now their answer is: Squeeze the swine till the pips squeak.'

'And Russia?' Fitzroy asked. He was beginning to sound defeated.

'Oh, let them stew in their own juice,' Weatherby said. 'That's not my opinion. It's their opinion.'

A long, thoughtful pause.

'I've been scribbling down a few words,' Sir Franklyn said. 'What d'you think of *A decent life for all Russians?*'

They thought of it, and nodded agreement. 'And hang the Kaiser,' Weatherby said. 'That would be the cherry on the bun.'

9

The Nines and the Camels landed at Beketofka.

138

Immediately, Griffin ordered Jessop and Maynard to refuel and rearm and go and look for the missing bomber. 'Take a bottle of whisky,' he said. 'Pedlow and Duncan might be a bit shaken up. Look for them halfway between here and Urbàkb. Maybe a bit further. Scout around.'

Count Borodin had been on the aerodrome, counting the machines as they landed. 'Three missing in all,' he said. 'Two Russian and one English.'

'Your two crashed and burned,' Griffin said. He shouted at Hackett and Oliphant and beckoned to them. 'Lucky it wasn't more. Your White bomber boys were all over the sky. They never kept formation. I've seen more discipline in a herd of cows. Their defensive fire was worse than useless.' Oliphant and Hackett arrived. 'Our Nines kept formation, they used crossfire, kept the Reds at a distance,' Griffin said. 'Your lot...' He gave up.

'All chiefs and no Indians,' Hackett said.

Borodin gave a sad smile. 'They fight when they want to and they fly as they like. Their commander is a good man but he cannot control them. They all flew for the Tsar, in the Imperial Air Service, and now they hate the Bolsheviks, but they don't respect Wrangel. And some are lazy and drink too much.'

'Sack them,' Griffin said.

'No replacements.'

'What have they got against General Wrangel?' Oliphant asked. 'He's a baron, isn't he? Isn't that imperial enough for them?'

'Alas, no. We have many barons. Wrangel is from the Baltic, which is Russian but not old

139

Russia. These pilots are from true Russian nobility. They look down on Baltic barons. A question of breeding, you see.'

'Extraordinary,' Oliphant said.

'Yes. I think you have something similar with Ireland. I shared rooms at Cambridge with the son of an Irish peer. Not a happy man. The British police kept reading his letters, he said. He grew quite bitter and went to America. Texas.'

'Big mistake, that,' Hackett said. 'In France the Yankee infantry attacked wearing cowboy hats. Texas is cowboy country. I expect they shot your Irish friend.'

'Yes, they shot him.' The count's brief, bleak words silenced them. 'An argument in a bar.'

'Bad luck,' Griffin said. 'Back to business. Today's raid. Pity the Red fighters were yellow but we strafed the machines on the ground and then we saw off that crowd that bothered the bombers. Good. Any observations?'

'They know we're here,' Oliphant said. 'Maybe they'll come and strafe us.'

'We'll go back there tomorrow,' Griffin said. 'Last thing they'll expect. Catch 'em with their pants down.'

'They're not stupid. They tricked us today,' Hackett said. 'If we'd stayed with the bombers–'

'We wouldn't have strafed the aerodrome.'

'Those Red fighters weren't interested in us. They wanted the Nines and they caught them. Same fighters?'

'No. Different crowd.'

'I thought I recognized a few,' Oliphant said.

'Not important,' Griffin insisted. 'Anything else?'

140

'They fooled us,' Hackett said. 'Our job–'

'Your job is to do what you're told.' Griffin turned to Borodin. 'And someone should kick your boys' backsides until they learn to fight. Don't look at me, I'm not going to volunteer. Not my job.'

'They probably wouldn't listen to us anyway,' Oliphant said. 'We haven't got the breeding. Some of us are scarcely bred at all. I mean, Bellamy's Canadian.'

'Bellamy's dead,' Borodin said. 'Your medical sergeant told me an hour ago. It wasn't malaria, it was typhus. I advise a speedy burial.'

'Sweet Jesus suffering Christ AllbloodyMighty,' Griffin said.

'And General Wrangel invites you to a banquet to celebrate Tsaritsyn's capture. Seven tonight. Carriages will call.'

10

The village was only a mile from the crash, but it was hidden in a long fold in the ground. It had about a hundred houses, all small and mud-coloured. Pedlow and Duncan were taken to a slightly larger house, built of brick, and invited to enter. They were given stools to sit on. The room was gloomy. The windows were tawny with dirt. In one corner, a small and flickering lamp cast a weak light on a pair of icons, drab with age.

Cobwebs hung thickly from the roof. The warm air smelled of dried dung. Duncan suddenly sneezed, twice, and a long, thin cobweb detached itself from a rafter. 'Now look what you've done,' Pedlow said. They watched it drift down, slower than time, and reach its end. 'Too thrilling,' Duncan said. 'It's more than a chap can take in.'

Outside, a crowd was gathering. The man who had found them climbed onto his cart and made a speech, with much gesturing at the sky. His words aroused his listeners. One by one they entered the room. A brief prayer to the icons, and then the wings on Pedlow's tunic got their full attention. The men touched them, the women kissed his boots, everyone stood around and put their hands together and prayed, loud and strong.

'I seem to be doing rather well,' Pedlow murmured. 'Don't you wish you were a pilot?'

'That woman on your right is fascinated by your groin,' Duncan said. 'She can't get enough of it.'

Pedlow looked. 'Perhaps her head is bowed in deference.'

'No. They all took a good squint at your crotch. Is your fly unbuttoned? Wedding tackle on display?'

Discreetly, Pedlow felt his fly. This small action startled the crowd. Some gasped, some moved to get a better view, faces brightened. 'All correct.' he said softly, and folded his arms. The onlookers slowly relaxed. There was a sense of anticlimax.

'Maybe they plan to eat us,' Duncan said. 'I'm told the family jewels are considered a great delicacy.'

'I wish they'd stop staring. They expect something. Maybe I should make a speech.'

'I'll do it.' Duncan stood. All eyes swivelled to him. 'On the breast of a barmaid from Sale,' he

142

announced, 'was tattooed the price of brown ale. And on her behind, for the sake of the blind, was the same information in Braille.' Their eyes were wide. They said nothing. He sat down. They turned and shuffled out of the room. 'They've gone to tell it to their friends,' he said.

After a while, men brought milk, black bread and boiled eggs. Also armfuls of sheepskins. Pedlow and Duncan ate and drank and stretched out on the sheepskins. When in Rome, take a siesta. That's what everyone else was doing.

The search party landed and reported no success. 'We flew up and down and round and round,' Jessop said. 'Nothing but steppe, I'm afraid.'

'Very empty,' Maynard said. 'Jolly hard on the eyeballs, looking at nothing.'

'Not good enough,' Griffin told them. 'Get yourselves a sandwich and go back and look again. That Nine's got to be somewhere.' He watched them trudge away. 'The squadron never gives up!' he shouted. 'It could be you lying out there. Or me.'

'Then why don't you bloody well come and help?' Jessop said, very quietly. As the day had grown hotter, the air had got bumpier. The Camel was not built for comfort. After two long flights his backside ached. Now they were going back again. This wasn't why he came to Russia.

11

Captain Brazier was bored because he had

nothing to do. In France, when he was adjutant of an R.F.C. squadron, he had had power: he was the man to whom new arrivals reported, he told them the drill, allocated their billets, chose their servants. He organized funerals, trained the pall-bearers, made sure the firing party discharged in unison, and God help anyone who cracked a smile. He met visiting generals, inspected latrines, forwarded recommendations for decorations, blasted mechanics who needed a haircut. In France, he mattered.

Now he was what the Army called a 'useless mouth', a commander with nothing to command, as bad as a pay clerk or a bandsman, fit only to be evacuated when the battle approached. He lived in a railway train among a waste of prairie, sur-rounded by natives who never washed, never shaved, and talked gobbledegook. It was a pity the Kaiser's war had to end. It wasn't perfect, but at least it was fought in the King's English. In France, if you told a chap the Boche had put the kibosh on the frogs, the other chap understood you. God knows what it'd sound like in Russian.

He sat in his Orderly Room and rolled a bit of blotting paper into a pellet. Only half the Pullman car was his, the other half was Lacey's office and radio room. He flicked the pellet at Lacey but it fell short. Lacey, listening on headphones, noticed nothing. Brazier made another pellet and fired again, but too hard: it flew over Lacey's head. 'Alright,' he growled. 'One under, one over. Now watch out.' He fired again, just as Lacey reached down to open a desk drawer, and the pellet flew through the space where his head had been.

144

'Hell's teeth!' Brazier roared. 'Play the white man, can't you? I blew your head off, dammit.'

'I'll call you in fifteen minutes,' Lacey told someone.

He unplugged the headphones and let them slip to his neck. Brazier aimed carefully and nearly hit a hat stand. 'Back in the schoolroom, are we?' Lacey said.

'Very dull war. No enemy. Bloody boring.'

They made a curious contrast. Brazier wore a double row of medal ribbons, which looked like miniatures on his khaki tunic. Lacey's sole decoration was his neatly groomed moustache, and in silk-lined RAF blue barathea he seemed almost dapper. Brazier sat hunched over his desk, his fingers still destroying the blotting paper, cheated of an enemy to duff up. Lacey stood and strolled to the window where he could enjoy the late afternoon sun. He spun the end of his headphone cord. He needed the exercise.

'I don't find it boring,' he said. 'I've just sold five thousand steel helmets, for cash. The thrill of the marketplace, the pulse of profit.'

'British Army issue. That's government property. You can't sell them.'

'Well, nobody wanted them. Russian troops won't wear them, they prefer to get their heads blown off in fur hats. Perhaps astrakhan, for the more stylish.'

'Still not yours to sell.'

'My dear captain, they were going nowhere on the docks at Novorossisk, while Russian housewives everywhere are crying out for good, sturdy cooking pots. An unusually honest Russian

145

dealer bought the lot from our man in Ekat.'

'Give me his name. I'll have the blighter court-martialled.'

'Henry. You can't touch him, he's an American civilian. You should be grateful to him. He sold forty thousand British Army horseshoes last week. Best Sheffield steel. Or do I mean iron?'

'He stole them.'

'No. If anyone did it was our man in Novo. Lieutenant Waxman, delightful chap, you'd like him.'

'Waxman. Good. I'll have *him* court-martialled.'

'That might be difficult. Once the cargo is unloaded, it's no longer British, it's Russian. Denikin's property. He won't court-martial a British officer. He needs our guns and things. But not our horseshoes. Guess why?'

Brazier tore the blotting paper into halves and then quarters. 'Astonish me.' He threw the pieces over his shoulder.

'Russian horses are smaller than British Army horses. They have far smaller feet. Evidently London didn't know that.'

'*But.*' Brazier raised a finger. 'Russian women pull the plough. And they *do* have big feet.'

Lacey looked around in surprise. 'A jest. How droll. I feared that life amongst the crude, licentious infantry might have coarsened you. No, our buyer is in armaments. He melts down the steel to make rifles.'

Brazier stood up and put on his cap. Lacey knew what that meant: now the adjutant was on parade, and King's Regulations applied to everything. 'Look here, Lacey. You're not in France any more, swapping disinfectant for Canadian

146

bacon. We're guests of the Russian people. Stealing's got to stop.'

'The Russians steal from each other all the time. And it wasn't disinfectant in France, it was linoleum. I seem to remember you enjoyed the bacon.'

'There's a difference. What you're doing now is black-market trading. That's fraud. Penal servitude.'

'And without it, the squadron would have no petrol. I buy our petrol with the profits of my trading.'

'Rubbish. Denikin's people supply our petrol. Our military mission in Ekat said so.'

Somewhere, a gramophone began playing dance music. Lacey put his hands in his pockets and began a slow fox-trot across the compartment. 'Denikin's man cheats,' he said. 'He sells half of our petrol to his friends. The railway people sell a lot of the rest *en route*. We're lucky to get the dregs.' He reached the door and swivelled on his toes and started back.

Brazier snorted. 'Everyone's a crook, are they? I don't believe it.'

'Henry isn't a crook. He buys our petrol back from the men who stole it. Result – everyone's happy. And Merlin Squadron flies again.'

Brazier went out and slammed the door.

'A poor critic,' Lacey said, 'but a steady performer.'

12

Griffin told Wragge and Hackett to find a good

spot to bury Bellamy. They asked the adjutant's advice. In France or England there had always been a handy church with a graveyard, but here... Brazier told them to look for low ground, no rocks, easy digging, away from running water. 'Typhus,' he said. 'Nasty stuff. Go down six feet minimum.'

They found a sharp stick and set off.

'Tough luck on old Bellamy,' Wragge said.

Hackett grunted.

'Best Mess president we ever had,' Wragge said. 'Those dinners at Butler's Farm were stunning.'

'Too much fish. The British are in love with haddock. Ever seen a whole haddock? Very ugly. No haddock in Australia. We passed a law, it's banned. And anchovies. Bellamy was always giving us anchovies, for God's sake. Why?'

'I don't think anchovies are actually fish.' Wragge tried to remember what an anchovy looked like. 'Anyway, you never had any problems with the roast beef. You tucked in like billy-ho to the roast beef. Second helpings?'

'Because the first was feeble.' Hackett stopped. 'Where are we going?'

'Beats me.' They looked around: steppe everywhere: a flat nothing-much stretching to the horizon beneath an overcast sky totally empty. 'Fancy coming all this way, just to cop it,' Wragge said. 'Not even a Bolo bullet. Just some filthy plague.'

'Here is as good as anywhere.' Hackett pointed, and spat. 'There. Put him there.'

They screwed the sharp stick into the ground, and turned back. 'I bet Griffin makes us take the burial service,' Wragge said.

'I can do it. I've seen plenty. A bit of God-stuff, plant the body, more God-stuff, throw in some earth, fire the rifles, God-stuff, march off, sherry in the Mess, hello replacement, what's for dinner?'

'I knew a boy at Harrow got killed by a cricket ball,'Wragge said. 'Fast delivery smacked him on the heart, stone dead. Big funeral... Hullo, they're back.' A pair of Camels was descending. Before they landed, a mechanic had reached Hackett and Wragge with a message. The squadron was bombing up for another raid.

'Bellamy will have to wait,' Hackett said. 'He'll get used to it. He's got all eternity.'

Jessop and Maynard reported still no sign of Pedlow and Duncan or their presumably crashed Nine, but they had found a large black scorch-mark on the steppe, and it wasn't made by the missing White Russian bombers, because their wrecks were miles away.

'Scorch-mark,' Griffin said. 'No bits lying around? No engine? Should be a damn great Puma lying somewhere.You can't burn an engine.'

'We flew very low,' Maynard said. 'If there was an engine, we'd have seen it. We'd have seen a cylinder. Nothing.'

'Well, we haven't got time for that. Get fuelled up. The squadron's been given a nice juicy target.'

They walked away. 'My bottom feels as if it's been beaten with a hockey stick,' Maynard said.

Jessop was too hungry to sympathize. 'What school did you go to?'

'Sherborne.'

'Lucky you. If you'd gone to Tonbridge, your delicate bottom would be used to that sort of treatment.'

The target was a group of Red gunboats, said to be coming down the Volga towards Tsaritsyn. Nobody was sure how many or how big or how well armed, but Griffin had promised Wrangel to send them packing. The squadron – five Camels, five Nines – got airborne about 4.00 p.m. Just before take-off, Jessop's ground crew gave him a bar of chocolate; Maynard got half. They ate chunks as they flew. Their taste buds salivated with gratitude. Colours brightened, sounds sharpened, suddenly the afternoon improved enormously.

The squadron cruised up the Volga at a thousand feet for ten, twenty miles, until Oliphant started wondering if the gunboats existed. Maybe this was a trap. The river was vast, magnificent, it made the Thames look like a stream, but the banks were broken and scarred, you wouldn't want to make a forced landing down there. Then he saw smoke ahead, and soon the funnels of four, no, five gunboats, pumping it out. They looked to be too small to be dangerous, but that was because the river was so wide.

The Camels curled away to the left. Oliphant led the Nines away to the right. The gunboats began firing.

Griffin's tactics were simple. The Camels came in, weaving and jinking, twenty or thirty feet above the Volga, and threatened the largest gunboat, firing a short burst and then sheering off and threatening it from another angle, anything to distract its gunners while the Nines made their bombing run from the other flank. He didn't expect it to work. This was war; nothing works quite as planned. But the bombers found gaps in the shell bursts and by determination and a fat slice of luck somebody's bomb went down the gunboat's funnel. Or so the pilot claimed. The truth didn't matter, because the bomb exploded somewhere crucial, maybe in the magazine, and the gunboat got blown up by its own shells.

The detonation was spectacular. The boat erupted, flung apart by the intensity of flame and fury. *Volcanic* was the word that Maynard thought of. Wragge said later that a white-hot lump of metal flew past him, as big as a barn door, he heard it go *whizz*. When the Flights got over their surprise and found some sort of formation, the gunboat had gone. And the other gunboats had turned and were making all speed upstream. The squadron harassed them and a few near-misses blew spray over them, but none was sunk. Still, the squadron had sent them packing, just as Griffin promised. Typical Bolo behaviour. Wave your arms and they all run away.

13

It was late afternoon when a man ducked his head and came into the brick hut. He was head and shoulders taller than the rest of the village, red-bearded and better dressed. He gave a passing nod to the icons and began to speak. His voice was rich and deep and his gestures were confident. He had quite a lot to say.

'He's the headman,' Pedlow said. 'They always pick the tallest chap.'

'Ask him if he can do something about the bedbugs,' Duncan said.

'I only know one Russian word, and that's the one Lacey taught us.'

Pedlow clicked his fingers. 'Damn. I've forgotten it.'

'It's *nichevo*,' Duncan said. 'Try *nichevo* bedbugs.'

The word abruptly silenced the headman. He stood with his mouth half-open and his arms frozen in mid-gesture. *'Nichevo,'* he whispered.

'That's it. *Nichevo*,' Pedlow said firmly. The headman dropped his arms, bowed, turned and left. They followed him. 'I've forgotten what it means,' Pedlow said.

'According to Lacey it means don't worry, *san fairy ann* as the French say. Sort of vaguely encouraging.'

'Didn't work, did it? We seem to have scared him off.' The headman was half-running away. Soon he vanished between huts. They stood, blinking in the mild sunlight. 'I suppose we could walk to Beketofka.'

'In the dark? It's forty miles at least. Meanwhile ... my bladder's about to burst. Can you see anything that looks like a lavatory?'

'This whole village smells like a lavatory, old chap,' Pedlow said.

'Perhaps there's a bog at the back. Traditional place.'

They went and looked. No bog.

'Since the locals seem to believe I've descended

from heaven, and as this is Tuesday,' Pedlow said, 'I shall make water, and I command you to do likewise.' They unbuttoned and were making water, lots of water, when they saw two small boys watching. 'Hullo!' Pedlow called. 'This will be the Garden of Eden one day. You'll thank me for it then.' They bolted.

Nothing much happened for the next hour; the villagers seemed to be avoiding them. They went indoors. It was dusk when the headman returned, escorted by the villagers. He wore a white stove-pipe hat with no brim, a dark red robe that reached his ankles, and rope sandals. His escort wore long green robes. He said a few words and his gestures clearly invited them to go with him. 'Might as well,' Duncan said. 'Could be supper.'

They heard singing, and it was impressive, as skilled as any cathedral choir, but much larger, hundreds of men and women passing the melody back and forth like questions and answers. Then they saw the assembly. The whole village had gathered in a wide circle. The strength of the voices was not just their power but also their conviction. Joe Duncan had read ghost stories that told of men whose hair stood on end and he hadn't believed them. Now he felt a bristling at the back of his neck.

The headman led them through a gap in the circle and instantly the singing ceased. That was the first surprise. The second was the remains of their Nine. They were carefully stacked in the middle of the circle.

They walked over to it. Most of the machine had gone up in flames, but somebody had searched hard. Around the engine were bits of wing and tail unit, a wheel, the Lewis gun, an empty ammunition drum, chunks of broken propeller. 'Don't touch anything,' Pedlow muttered.

'Why not?'

'I don't know. Just don't.'

There were two chairs, so they sat in them, and the evening began.

The headman was clearly a priest or prophet. He held what looked like a Bible and he read from it. His followers liked that: every reading brought a thunderous response. Then they sang. By now it was night; a fire was lit. The priest walked around the broken bomber, delivered what sounded like a sermon, made much of the airmen's presence. They sat and watched and didn't understand a damn word. 'I could do with a beer,' Duncan said. The villagers sang again, but now it had a faster tempo, a thumping melody, and some of them were dancing. Furiously.

They formed two rings, one inside the other: women on the inside danced one way, men on the outside danced the other. Pedlow and Duncan found it hypnotic but exhausting. This was only the beginning, the warm-up. The dancers started spinning, competing in a tireless contest to dance harder, spin faster. 'They're crazy,' Pedlow said. A few dancers collapsed. Their mouths were foaming and their shouts blew foam. Clothing was thrown off. Many of the remaining dancers, men and women, were naked. 'What now?' Duncan asked.

'I hate to think,' Pedlow said.

But within minutes the dance was over, the

154

singing had stopped, the dancers were sprawling. That was when the priest approached the airmen with a young man on one side and a young woman on the other. Both were naked. He held a knife in each hand.

'Ritual sacrifice,' Duncan said.

'I think it's worse than that,' Pedlow said.

The young man took a knife and began slicing off his left testicle. The young woman took a knife and began carving away her right breast. Duncan groaned and fainted. Pedlow grabbed him and carried him away. When he looked back the amputations were done and blood painted the figures red.

JOLLY BOATING WEATHER

1

Wrangel sent two open carriages, horse-drawn, each with room for four guests. Griffin took with him the adjutant, Count Borodin and Hackett. In the other carriage went Oliphant, Wragge and a couple of bomber pilots, Tommy Hopton and Douglas Gunning. Their *plennys* had worked hard. Buttons were bright, creases were sharp.

The carriages crossed the aerodrome and turned south. The weather had cleared and the evening skies were an immense eggshell blue fading to yellow. Squadrons of little birds took off and circled and settled. Griffin stretched his legs. 'This is the way to travel, adjutant. We never had this in France.'

Brazier nodded. He was looking to the left. 'What's going on over there, count?'

Two hundred yards away, a crowd of men were digging a hole. It was long and deep; already they had created a heap of earth along one side. The setting sun caught the steady action of shovels being swung. Nobody paused, nobody looked at the carriages. At least two hundred men were at work. Probably more.

'A place to bury the typhus victims,' Borodin said. 'The disease is raging in Tsaritsyn, I'm afraid.' End of conversation.

Two miles on, the carriages reached the drive of a handsome country house, busy with arrivals. It was not yet dark but the windows were blazing with lights. At the portico, the airmen were greeted by someone who was so magnificently dressed that he could have been the butler or the Brazilian ambassador. Borodin made the introductions. The man turned out to be Denikin's brother-in-law. 'The owner is in Switzerland. It's a long story,' Borodin said. 'Please follow me.'

The house throbbed with male talk. This was not an evening for the ladies, although the fragrance of eau-de-cologne was everywhere. The uniforms of the Russian guests were never less than brilliant, the tunics rich with decorations, the epaulettes heavy with gold braid, the calf-length boots as glossy as glass. Every man wore a sword and every sword hilt glittered with jewels. 'How many generals are here?' Hackett asked.

'About seventy or eighty,' Borodin said. 'And a few colonels and one or two admirals. The Bishop of Tsaritsyn is somewhere.'

'They stare at me as if I'm in my underwear.'

'Pay no attention. This is just the throng. We shall join the favoured few.'

He led them to an anteroom. The chandeliers were dazzling and the uniforms were even more heavily hung with awards, gold-tasselled lanyards, silk sashes. General Wrangel left a group of a dozen and shook hands with Griffin. *'Dobry vecher,'* he said.

'We are honoured by your invitation to such a distinguished gathering, sir,' Griffin said.

Wrangel looked at the count, who translated:

157

'Congratulations on your brilliant victory over the fiendish enemy.'

'They don't speak our language, do they?' Wrangel said to him. 'Well, tell them that half the guns they've sent are useless and their boots are too big for my soldiers, but we are glad to get their money and please send more.'

'The general admires your famous British courage,' Borodin told the airmen, 'and he applauds the way your skilful flying terrifies the enemy.'

Wrangel gave them a nod and went away.

They turned to the delights on display. A cut-glass bowl as big as a baby's bath was full of vodka. A swan carved from ice appeared to float in the middle. Lying on the bottom were what seemed to be gemstones, and probably were. The goblets were of crystal and the ladle was solid silver. They helped themselves.

Pancakes were being served, in abundance. 'These are *blinochki*,' Borodin said. 'Famous in Russia as an appetizer. The stuffings are too many to mention. Next will be *blinochki's syrom*, a Ukrainian speciality, filled with numerous cheeses. Then there are *bliny*, served with melted butter and caviare.' For the airmen, lunch was a distant memory. They sampled everything, washed down with vodka. 'I should warn you,' Borodin said, 'these are merely *hors d'oeuvres*. The true banquet is yet to come.'

'The Russian Army does things in style, doesn't it?' Wragge said. 'What a pity Bellamy isn't here to enjoy it.'

'Here's to Bellamy!' Hackett said. They all drank to that. The vodka was beginning to work. 'He

158

owed me a quid, so I've bagged his flying boots.'

'That's in very poor taste,' Wragge said.

'I agree,' Oliphant said. 'Show some respect for the dead.'

'Why?' Hackett said. 'He didn't die for me, or for you. He ran out of luck, that's all. He's gone and I'm still alive. What else matters?'

'There's no point in arguing with him,' Wragge told Oliphant. 'He went to the wrong school. Not his fault.'

'Boolabong Academy,' Hackett said. 'Very exclusive. Highest standards. If you couldn't spell "illicit intercourse" properly, they beat the living shit out of you.' But Wragge and Oliphant had moved on.

James Hackett's former C.O. was right: he was a tenacious bugger. At the age of twelve he knew what he wanted: to be the best swimmer in Sydney, in New South Wales, in all of Australia. He swam every day until he could easily swim twenty-five yards underwater. When he was fourteen his chest was two sizes larger than normal and his shirts wouldn't fasten at the collar. Then his father, who was a printer, got a savage pain in his side and a burst appendix killed him. Peritonitis, the doctors said. Dead, whatever you called it.

The unfairness of his loss left James stunned, and then angry. He abandoned swimming and decided to become a surgeon.

After that, in every spare minute, he read second-hand medical books. His friends said he was off his trolley, his mother said it was unhealthy, all this reading, it wouldn't bring his dad back, why didn't he get a job at the printer's, bring in some money, God knows they needed it. Within a year she had remarried. Soon there was an infant brother and she had no time left for James. He decided to go to Victoria College. 'Not on my money, you're not,' his stepfather said. 'You'll work in my butcher's shop. Get some real blood on your hands.' By then James was out the door, out the house. Soon, out of Sydney, out of Australia. He lied about his age and joined the Royal Australian Navy.

He shovelled coal in a cruiser for a year. Off-duty he learned semaphore and got promoted to Signals, had a spell in Guns, finally won a place on the bridge as captain's messenger. It was from the bridge that he saw his first aeroplane, a seaplane, and knew at once that he had to learn to fly. They were at war; the cruiser was in England, in Portsmouth harbour; he couldn't escape a grinding tour of Atlantic patrols. This almost certainly saved his life. Only in 1917 did the Australian Navy grudgingly agree to his transfer to the Australian Army. The army was happy to give him a commission and send him to the Royal Flying Corps, which was eager for any volunteer to replace the wastage in France.

He handled engine controls as clumsily as most trainee pilots, but once in the air he managed the lurching, wandering, underpowered craft with the skills he had learned from keeping his balance in a cruiser that was battling the Atlantic gales. For Second Lieutenant Hackett, aeroplanes were an extension of boats: you sailed on the air and you paid close attention to the wind and the weather. Forward momentum made it possible to steer. Watch the birds and learn.

And get your hands dirty. At the end of a day's training, most pupils headed for the Mess and aimed to get blotto. Hackett went to the hangars and talked to the mechanics. When he got posted to France, he knew almost as much as the ground crew about the Sopwith Camel and its Rhône rotary engine.

2

The mechanics knocked some planks from a packing case and they made a coffin. The *plennys* dug a grave in the steppe, two feet wide, six and a half feet long, six feet deep. They struck clay, and it was dusk by the time they finished.

Lacey was acting C.O. during the period of the banquet. The sergeant medic told him that Mr Bellamy had to be taken care of now, they couldn't wait until morning. The smell was bad and getting worse. Lacey told Maynard to select five other officers who would form a firing party. A sergeant gave them rifles and showed them how to load and fire. Some wanted to practise. Lacey foresaw trouble and said there was no time for that. A fresh squad of *plennys* – the first lot were wet with sweat and stained with clay – lifted the coffin from the train. Lacey and the sergeant carried hurricane lamps and the whole party set off.

The moon had not yet risen and the night was black. After two minutes, Lacey said: 'Stop. This is too far. You've missed it, Sergeant.'

'I thought you were leading, sir.'

'Don't you know where it is?'

'Never seen it. I wasn't here when the *plennys* dug it.'

Lacey sent Maynard back to fetch one of the diggers.

The *plennys* put down the coffin, and moved well away from it.

One of the hurricane lamps began to flicker. 'I hope someone remembered to fill these things,' Lacey said sharply. The sergeant took a firm grip of the lamp and shook it. Liquid sloshed. 'Well, it's not empty, anyway,' he said. Lacey took a deep breath. 'If it were empty, sergeant, I think we should have known by now.'

The flickering flame cast an erratic, dancing light on the scene. The *plennys* huddled together and whispered. An officer sat down and immediately got up. 'Grass is soaking wet,' he complained.

'That'll be the dew, sir,' the sergeant said.

'Christ... My rear end is drenched. Totally drenched.'

He got no sympathy from the rest of the firing party. 'Oh dear,' one said. 'Mickey's gone and wet himself again.'

'Oh, I say, Mickey. Play the game. You're letting the side down.'

'Poor old Mickey. He could never hold his drink.'

'Look at who's talking,' Mickey said. 'A glass of port and you're legless.'

'That's enough!' Lacey said.

'More than enough,' Mickey muttered. 'Half a glass.'

'You're *on parade*,' Lacey said. 'Kindly remem-

162

ber that.'

'The fact is, we're bloody lost,' someone said.

'I don't see why this couldn't wait until morning,' another said. 'Leave the box here. Perfectly safe.'

'Unthinkable,' Lacey said. But the idea provoked discussion.

'Nothing's safe out here,' Mickey said. 'Some thieving Russki might steal him in the night, open the box, heart attack.'

'Now there's *two* bodies. Doesn't look good.'

'Got the makings of an international incident.'

'Diplomatic uproar. High-level complaints. All because of you, Lacey.'

'Only one complaint matters,' Lacey said, 'and that's Jeremy Bellamy's. We are here to send it to the lowest level. If you want a second opinion, smell the coffin.' Nobody moved. 'Very wise.'

A *plenny* came out of the night. Maynard was behind him, waving his rifle. 'About time,' Lacey said.

'I had the devil of a job persuading him to leave the train,' Maynard said. 'He thought I was going to shoot him. I couldn't explain because I couldn't.'

The *plenny* hurried to his comrades. There was much gesturing and excited talk and finally suppressed laughter. The *plenny* went back to Maynard and saluted, and pointed into the night. The funeral party set off. 'We nearly didn't find you,' Maynard said. 'One of your lamps is on its last legs.'

'I know,' Lacey said. 'It's one of the few things I do know.'

'Perhaps it's low on fuel.'

'Perhaps. We're all rather low on fuel, Maynard. All except for poor Bellamy, who's empty, so let's put him to rest, shall we?'

Maynard knew that tone of voice. He had often heard it from parents and schoolmasters and, more recently, adjutants. It meant: *If that's the best you can say, then shut up.*

Ten minutes of wandering finally paid off, and they found the place.

The *plennys* laid Bellamy on the grass at one end of the grave and the sergeant gave them two long straps of khaki webbing. They slid the straps under the coffin. Two *plennys* stood on each side and wrapped the webbing around their fists.

Lacey opened Brazier's copy of the *British Army Pocket Book, 1917,* and knew at once that the Burial Service was too long. He cut to the middle and read: 'Man that is born of woman hath but a short time to live, and is full of misery.' (Total tosh, he thought. No R.A.F. squadron is full of misery. Not even half-full.) 'He cometh up, and is cut down, like a flower; he fleeth as it were a shadow, and never continueth in one stay.' (Some truth in that.) He looked up and made a vaguely priestly gesture towards the grave.

The *plennys* tightened their grip, lifted the coffin, and began to shuffle sideways. All the earth had been thrown out on one side, and the pile left little space to walk. The light was poor; the unhappy lamp was flickering more violently and making smoke. The *plennys* got there in the end. The coffin was poised over the hole. They looked at Lacey. He pointed downwards and they began to pay out

164

the webbing. 'For as much as it hath pleased Almighty God of his great mercy...' (He didn't show Bellamy much mercy, did He?) '...to take unto himself the soul of our brother here departed...'

A *plenny* cried out. Lacey looked up. The coffin was out of sight. The *plenny* was standing on the narrow edge and the earth was crumbling under his feet. As he struggled, his hands lost their grip. The strap raced away in a flourish of release. One end of the coffin hit the bottom of the grave with a sombre thud, and he tumbled after it. The other *plennys* let go, and the coffin made a much louder thud. The fallen *plenny* scrambled out. 'Earth to earth,' Lacey said, 'ashes to ashes, dust to dust. Sergeant! Carry on.'

'Firing party!' the sergeant roared. 'Prepare to fire! Charge your rifles! Aim your rifles! Fire!'

It would have been too much to expect a concerted, impressive volley. Merlin Squadron was not the Grenadier Guards. The night was cold, trigger-fingers were chilled, the weapons were unfamiliar. The volley went off like a firecracker, a shapeless ragbag of shots. Given the rest of the accidents, it was a suitable farewell to Bellamy.

3

Each of the British guests was seated next to a Russian officer. The first course might have been stuffed trout. Hard to tell, when it was covered in white sauce and stuffed with caviare. Whatever it was, they all enjoyed it, with plenty of vodka, essential because toasts kept being proposed and then everyone stood and drank. Warm patriotic greetings came from all parts of the table and they too had to be acknowledged. In vodka.

'It's an acquired taste,' Wragge told Brazier. 'I think I'm acquiring it, Uncle.'

'Don't spill it on your skin, lad. You'll carry the scar to the grave.'

Hare stuffed with chestnuts came next. Roast parsnips and hot buttered mushrooms accompanied it. There was a very dry white wine, which was not a substitute for vodka. The toasts continued.

'Are there a lot of hares in Russia?' Oliphant asked Count Borodin.

'Not as many as there were last week.'

Baked mutton was sliced by the chefs alongside the table. It was as tender as butter, and went well with sweet cabbage. The wine was red and peppery.

'Not to your taste?' Hackett said to Griffin. 'Off your feed?'

'Reached my limit. Got to watch my weight.'

Next was roast duck with a different kind of caviare and small new potatoes. Followed by quail stuffed with apricots. Followed by fluffy pancakes enriched with flaked ham. Followed by... Griffin didn't care. He waved it away and sipped his vodka while he smiled at everyone. His face ached from smiling. Russia was nothing to smile at.

4

Pedlow found a tobacco pouch in an inside

pocket, together with a pipe, and he thought he might as well smoke it. 'My good luck token,' he said.

'Not much help so far, is it?'

They were standing in the doorway of their brick hut. After Duncan recovered from his faint, a villager had given him half a bottle of vodka. He sipped it and was sick, but not so sick as to let go of the bottle. It was the only bright spot in an otherwise grisly evening.

'I bought this pipe when I was sixteen,' Pedlow said. 'A girl called Monica said it would go well with my curly black hair, so I got one, and next time I kissed her she seemed to enjoy it, so I put my hand on her breast and she hit my face so hard I saw stars. I didn't know girls could punch like that.'

'Bloody women.'

'I let fly. Hit her. Instinctive reaction. Made her nose bleed. Never saw Monica again. Always kept the pipe, though.'

'What are you smoking? Apart from kippers.'

'Rough shag. It cuts down the local stench.'

Duncan sniffed. 'Not noticeably.' No sound came from the village except for the howling of a distant dog. It howled sadly, as if it had forgotten why it began. 'We can't stay here, Gerard.'

The sky was loaded with stars. Pedlow looked at them too long and too hard, until he could feel the heavens wheeling. He said, 'Some people navigate by the stars.'

'I can't.'

'Nor me. Anyway, the trip would take forever and hurt abominably. I don't fancy hiking in these

167

flying boots. Not made for hiking.'

'Well, we can't stay here. You saw those knives. Like razors. These brutes are cannibals. Worse than cannibals.'

'Trouble is,' Pedlow said, 'they've got it into their tiny minds that I'm an angel, and they're very pleased they've got their hands on me.'

'And your bollocks,' Duncan said. 'They'll have those too.'

5

After the ninth or tenth course, Griffin told Count Borodin that it was getting stuffy and he needed fresh air. 'Explain to General Wrangel, would you? I'll be back before the goings-on end.'

'No explanation needed. Chaps are free to answer when nature calls. I'll come with you.'

The adjutant saw them go, and followed. Oliphant and Hackett made their excuses and went too, weaving slightly. They gathered on a balcony. 'Thank God for some cool night air,' the C.O. said. 'I need oxygen. This bun fight isn't what I expected, Count.'

'Such banquets are traditional in Russia. Especially after a victory.'

'Let's hope the Bolos don't attack tomorrow,' Oliphant said. 'Half your top generals are pretty squiffy.'

Borodin laughed. 'Squiffy. Yes, that's the word. They were mostly in the Tsarist Imperial Army. Not what you'd call fighting generals.'

'This is a war zone,' Brazier said. 'What are they

doing here, if not fighting?'

'Denikin's orders. He sent an express train full of food and chefs and superfluous generals. They decorate the banquet.'

'Look here, Count,' Griffin said. 'When can we decently say our thank-yous and leave?'

'First there will be speeches and toasts. You, as commanding officer, must make a speech. Later there will be patriotic songs. Including British songs, of course.'

'Oh ... sweet Christ on crutches. We'll be here till dawn.'

'Yes, that is normal. Russian hospitality is considered to have failed if the guests can walk, unaided, to their carriages.' He stopped: a faint spattering of rifle fire rattled, far away. Quite a lot of rifles. They all looked at him. 'The mass grave is complete,' he told them. 'The shots are a tribute to the dead.'

'I've got to make a speech,' Griffin said to Brazier. 'Bloody hell.'

'No politics. Nothing about the Tsar or Lloyd George. No jokes. No promises. Flattery, flattery, flattery.'

As they drifted back inside, more rifle fire could be heard. 'Another tribute?' Brazier said. The count nodded sombrely.

Once the immensely long mahogany table had been cleared, speeches were made from all parts. They were passionate, they were dramatic, they were loud, they were totally meaningless to the R.A.F. guests except for the final toasts, which usually ended with *'Na Moskvu! Na Moskvu!'* and

169

always the empty glasses were hurled at the walls. Servants hurried forward, their boots crunching the shards, bringing fresh glasses and more vodka. Then it was Griffin's turn.

Amongst all these peacocks he was a sparrow. Many couldn't see him, and everywhere arms gestured *up! up!* He climbed onto the table. Somebody handed him a glass of vodka, and in taking it he dropped his notes, ideas scribbled on scraps of paper, and everyone roared with laughter. Well, that was a good start.

He announced how proud and privileged he felt to be serving alongside such staunch and ... and doughty (What did that mean? Oh well. Press on) yes, doughty warriors, men whose valour, and gallantry, and ... um... (Think of a third!) ... um ... dash, yes, sheer dash, quite rightly ring around the world.

He took a swig, while Borodin translated. They liked it, and thumped the table. He took a deep breath and everything went wrong. He tried to say Cossacks and it came out *cassocks*. He tried to explain what *cassocks* were and, too late, knew he was talking about *hassocks*, so he abandoned that explanation and finally mastered *Cossacks*. 'Jolly fine bunch of men!' he shouted. Borodin translated. Prolonged applause. Another swig.

'I want to thank you,' he said, 'for your hostile artillery. No, I don't mean... Well, yes I do, you have lovely guns, biff the Bolos, hit 'em for six... But what I wanted to say was ... this amazing feast...' He was lost for words. Took another swig. Tried again. 'Your hospitallyho,' he said, and hiccuped. 'Damn. I've got the Cossacks!'

170

Borodin translated, and at last Griffin dimly understood that it didn't matter what he said, because the count always made it wonderful. So he blundered on, and had the wit to end by shouting 'Na Moskvu!' They all stood up and cheered. They drank to the R.A.F. More glasses smashed.

Songs were sung, melancholy ballads of Russian tragedy that had the listeners in tears. Count Borodin got the pilots together and told them that they must sing a song. It was essential. National honour depended on it.

'I can do "The Ball of Kirriemuir",' Hackett said. 'Four-and-twenty virgins went out from Inverness, and when the ball was over there were four-and-twenty less. All join in the chorus. Twenty-six verses. Some are a bit saucy.'

Oliphant shuddered. 'Look here, Tommy. You were at Eton. Isn't there a nice tune you can sing?'

'I know the Eton Boating Song, if you like. In fact there's a stunt we used to do at Old Etonian dinners. We need a couch on wheels. Big wheels. A long, flat couch, with no back. Long enough for four chaps to sit astride.'

Borodin sent servants to fetch a couch on wheels. Tommy Hopton explained the stunt.

'Sorry if I'm a bit dense,' Oliphant said. 'Must be all this cigar smoke. You say we pretend to row, and the couch ... that is, the boat ... it really goes.'

'Kick the floor with your heels. All kick together. Kick hard and she'll skim along.'

Servants placed the couch lengthwise on the table. It was upholstered and its wheels were as big as saucers. The pilots climbed up and sat

171

astride it. The count made a short announcement and the room fell silent. 'This had better bloody work,' Wragge whispered.

'Too late now,' Hopton said.

He stood at one end, with the four pilots facing him. 'Come forward!' he ordered, and four pairs of arms stretched out, holding imaginary oars. 'Follow my stroke, chaps. *In* when I'm in, *out* when I'm out. And remember to kick.' He took a lungful of smoky air, and began to sing.

Jolly boating *weather,*
And a *hay* harvest *breeze.*
Blade on the *feather,*
Shade off the *trees...*

They got the idea. Lean *forward* at the start of each line, lean *back* at the end. Four pairs of heels kicked hard and the couch raced away. Hopton followed. His voice had the clarity and purity of youth.

Swing, swing *together,*
With your *bodies* between your *knees.*
Swing, swing, *together,*
With your *bodies* between your *knees.*

They squeaked to a halt ten feet from General Wrangel. Tommy Hopton led them in three huzzahs for Wrangel's army. The performance was a huge success. One word was roared, again and again.

'*Encore,*' Borodin said. 'They want more.'

The crew reversed their positions while Hopton

rehearsed the Russians. 'Swing, swing together,' he sang to them, and they shouted it back to him. He took his place, and the crew, expert now, made the couch whizz to the rhythms of the next verse:

Rugby may be more *clever*,
Harrow may make more *row*,
But *we'll* row for *ever*...

'I'm not a sentimental man,' the C.O. said to the adjutant, 'but you must admit, Uncle, this warms the heart.'

'Those wheels are playing merry hell with that table.'

'Oh, bugger the table. These boys fought for England. Now for Russia. True patriotism.' He had a little trouble with the word, so he took another stab at it. 'Patriotism.' Better.

Hopton finished the verse and the Russians took their cue. 'Sving, sving togezzer,' they sang, a hundred and fifty of them, all swaying from side to side. Hopton responded: 'With your *bodies* between your *knees*...'

'King and country,' Brazier said. 'They swallow that claptrap when they enlist. It gets blown away in battle. Battle's the only test.'

'Nonsense. Loyalty's what matters.'

'Loyalty to your pals. Nobody else.'

The couch rolled to a halt. The crew had done two lengths; panting and sweating, they thought they had finished. Relentless, thunderous slow handclapping told them otherwise. Again, they reversed their positions. Hopton began verse three, and they sprinted away.

Others will fill our *places,*
Dressed in the old light *blue,*
We'll recollect our *races,*
We'll to the flag be *true...*

Griffin pointed. 'Hear that? We'll to the flag be true! We're here to save this world from bloody Bolsheviks.'

'Bully for you. I've fought all sorts of ruffians. Boers. Fuzzy-wuzzies. Huns. Not to save the world. Save the regiment. Sometimes the platoon.'

'Airmen are different, Uncle.'

Brazier grunted. 'You live and die for your friends.'

Sving, sving, togezzer, the Russians chanted, and then the stunt began to go wrong. Tired legs gave an unequal shove and the couch veered to the left. Hopton shouted a warning. They thought he was urging them on and their feet kicked harder until the whole gesticulating contraption shot over the edge and fell into the laps of half a dozen generals too fat and old and squiffy to avoid it. Everyone else cheered. The Royal Air Force could do no wrong.

Dawn was nudging the eastern horizon when the carriages left for Beketofka, moving at a gentle trot to avoid awakening the pilots. The drivers knew how best to earn a fat tip.

Only Brazier and Count Borodin were awake, and after the din of the banquet they enjoyed the silence of the countryside. Mist as soft as smoke filled the hollows. Sometimes a pair of ducks

174

emerged, flying fast and noiseless, and vanished. A rim of sun showed itself. It picked out the mist tops and soon it was making long, elastic shadows of the carriages. It washed the sky clean of stars. Another fine day on the way.

As it rose, Brazier turned his face towards it and welcomed the warmth. The dazzle made his eyelids almost close. Almost. He made out a shape, a low silhouette. He shielded his eyes.

'Borodin,' he said quietly. 'Isn't that your mass grave?'

'Yes, I expect so.'

'I'd like to see it.'

The count looked at him. If he said, *No, that's not possible,* or *Why? It's just plague victims,* if he said anything at all, the adjutant would not argue, he would simply get out and go. 'If you must,' he said. He told the driver to stop and wait.

They walked across boggy heathland and stood on the edge of the hole. It was at least thirty yards long. It was half-full.

'All male, I see,' Brazier said. 'A very selective plague.' He walked along the side. 'But no boots. Perhaps they caught the disease through their feet.' He walked on. 'And some without breeches. They don't look very sick, do they? Dead, yes. Sick, no.'

'Bolshevik commissars, officers and N.C.O.s,' Borodin said. 'When we take prisoners, we recruit the ordinary soldiers into our army. We shoot the rest. Boots and breeches are scarce in our army.'

'How many?'

'About three hundred. And you have my word that when the enemy take prisoners, they do not kill them as humanely as we do.'

They walked back to the carriage.

'You take it all very calmly,' Brazier said.

'How would it help if I were otherwise?'

'Ah. A good point.'

6

Jonathan Fitzroy's ad hoc committee met in a filthy temper.

It was Monday, it was bucketing down with rain, it had been raining everywhere all weekend, the entire county cricket programme had been washed out. The prospects for Wimbledon were grim. All the best salmon and trout rivers were in flood, the water looked like cocoa, two Welshmen had been drowned while trying to fish the Usk, probably poachers using worm as bait, so nobody grieved too much. Today's papers didn't help. They gave the government a good kicking for the unemployment figures (up again). They gloomed about farmers' warnings that the harvest would be ruined. And the Metropolitan Police had found a member of the House of Lords behind a bush in Hyde Park with a trooper from the Coldstream Guards, both stark naked, at three in the morning.

James Weatherby was reading the report in the *Mail* when General Stattaford sat beside him. 'Look on the bright side,' the general said. 'His Lordship is sixty-eight. The night was black as sin, the rain fell in torrents, and he was stripped to the skin. Makes you proud to be British, doesn't it?'

Weatherby grunted. 'You can replace a trooper,'

176

he said, 'but we've lost a vote in the Lords. And that's serious.'

'Gentlemen,' Jonathan Fitzroy said. 'May we start? Our last recommendation was, I'm afraid, rather kicked into touch by the P.M. "A decent life for all Russians" is good as far as it goes, but it doesn't go anywhere. His words. Rather like being kind to one another. Even the Cabinet agrees it's desirable, but *how?*'

'Do they want us to make policy?' Sir Franklyn Fletcher said. 'Because that wasn't in the original prospectus.'

Fitzroy was built like a bruiser but his footwork was nimble. 'I think it revolves around what we feel the British people believe to be right and apt,' he said, 'which in itself is a product of what they feel *can* be done. Thus what *should* happen and what *can* happen are so closely linked as to be virtually identical? He beamed at each man in turn.

'Smooth,' Sir Franklyn murmured. 'And slippery.'

'The people have had a bellyful of war,' Weatherby said. 'I keep saying it because it keeps being true. No more war. I can think of only one thing that might conceivably change that. If the Bolsheviks start exploding bombs in Whitehall and St Paul's and Arsenal football ground, people might get angry enough to want to drop a few shells on Lenin and his friends.'

Sir Franklyn stretched his long legs and slid deeper into his armchair. His hands steepled until they touched his chin. 'You make it sound like stamping out piracy in international waters, James,' he said.

'So it is. They're brigands, savages. What they've done in Russia...' Weatherby shook his head. 'We don't want that here.'

'Foul baboonery,' Fitzroy added helpfully. 'That's what Churchill called them in the Commons.'

'They boast about world domination,' Stattaford said. 'Did their worst in Austria and Germany. Why wait? Retaliate first. Avoids a lot of bloodshed.'

'Alone?' Charles Delahaye said. It was the first word he had spoken since he arrived and it hung in the air. Nobody wanted to be the first to answer.

'Oh, bother,' Fitzroy said. 'And we were going along so well. I suppose the question must be faced. Foreigners, I believe, are the province of the Foreign Office.'

Sir Franklyn sat up straight. 'If you are hoping for allies to assist in a punitive expedition, then the list is short. Not Italy. Italy's manpower died on the battlefield. Not Japan. It has two divisions in Vladivostock, which is about as far from Moscow as we are from Canada, the journey takes a month, and Japan doesn't give a toss what Moscow does anyway. Not America. They've picked our chestnuts out of the fire once already, and they've got elections coming up. Not the Empire. We played the Mother Country card in the war, and we can't play it twice. That leaves France. After the Armistice they sent two divisions into the Ukraine and kicked out the German occupying army, the only real force for law and order, treated the place like a French colony and made

178

themselves despicable. French troops never wanted to be there, they mutinied, they departed faster than they arrived. Forget France. Yes, it's a very short list.'

Nobody spoke. Stattaford got up and walked to a window, exercising his left leg as he went. Rain turned the glass to a wandering blur. 'Bit of Hun ironmongery,' he said, still flexing. 'Doesn't like this weather.'

A tap on the door, and a maid came in, wheeling a trolley. The ceremony of tea helped dispel the feebleness of Allies. Well, former Allies. Platitudes about the weather were exchanged. They all agreed it was beyond a joke. 'I've got a beat on the Test,' Sir Franklyn said sadly. 'Can't cast a fly in this deluge. Hampshire's just a lake.' He bit into a custard cream.

'If it keeps up, the whole country will be washed away,' Jonathan Fitzroy said. 'End up floating into the Atlantic, I expect.'

'The Navy will save us,' Weatherby said. 'Always does.'

'The Navy's in the Baltic,' Charles Delahaye said. 'How do I know? Because the Treasury pays its bills. Hefty bills, too.'

'Not the whole Navy, surely?' Fitzroy said.

'A significant fleet. Not cheap.'

That took their minds off the rain.

'Doing what?' Weatherby said. He looked at General Stattaford.

'I'm a soldier, old chap. Ask an admiral.'

'Doing its duty,' Sir Franklyn said. 'We are mounting a vigorous diplomatic campaign to protect the Baltic States against Bolshevik attempts to seize them. The Navy provides a presence.'

'A presence,' Weatherby said. 'Does it go bang-bang, by any chance?'

'When requested, the Navy assists by discouraging enemy troop movements. We also discourage interference by the Soviet Navy. It has a large base at Kronstadt, at the head of the Baltic. Guarding Petrograd.'

'Discourage. Is that a diplomatic word for "sink on sight"?'

Sir Franklyn had said enough. He found a handkerchief and blew his nose and re-folded the handkerchief and took his time over it.

'In brief,' Fitzroy said, 'we keep this fleet in the Baltic to bombard Bolsheviks ashore and afloat. Since this is not common knowledge, nor likely to be, I don't quite see how it helps us to reassure the British people about why we are in Russia.'

'I do,' Stattaford said. 'The railway runs from Petrograd straight to Moscow. Five hundred miles. Give the Navy a free hand. Sink the Russian fleet. Land two brigades of Guards, and I guarantee we'll be in Moscow in a week. The Reds will be dead. Problem solved.'

'Splendid,' Delahaye said. 'Just as long as we don't interfere in Russia's internal affairs.'

Weatherby chuckled. Fitzroy sighed. Sir Franklyn stared at the ceiling and stroked his jaw. Stattaford glared. 'Is that a joke?' he demanded.

'Only if the Prime Minister was joking,' Delahaye said. 'It's what he told the House of Commons. I was there, I heard. He said you should never interfere in the internal affairs of another

180

country, however badly governed.'

'The *Daily Express* agrees,' Weatherby said. 'They say – and I quote – the frozen plains of Eastern Europe are not worth the bones of a single British grenadier. Big circulation, the *Express*.'

'Beaverbrook's grubby rag. The man's a damned Canadian. Got no loyalty to this country.'

Fitzroy clapped his hands. 'Gentlemen, gentlemen. Aren't we barking up the wrong tree? Surely it's not intervention when we are simply assisting the Russians to cleanse their own house? Help them achieve what all honest, decent, patriotic Russians are fighting for?'

'The damn plains aren't frozen,' Stattaford growled at Weatherby. 'It's summer, for God's sake. Have some common sense.' He sat in silence for the rest of the discussion. Eventually Sir Franklyn suggested something along the lines of *Answering the call of freedom and justice*. Nobody cheered, but nobody could improve on it.

7

There was nothing seriously wrong with the Chevrolet ambulance. Russian drivers, both Red and White, had failed to service it and after much bullying its engine had quit. A couple of springs were broken. The steering had hit so many pot-holes that it was cross-eyed. But all this was nothing that an R.A.F. squadron of fitters and metal-bashers couldn't repair overnight. They gave it back to Lacey after breakfast. 'Thanks awfully,' he said. 'I shall have you all Mentioned in Despatches.' He gave them a case of Guinness.

Count Borodin turned up at ten, freshly shaven and alert.

'All our party-goers are sleeping like the dead,' Lacey said. 'How do you do it?'

'I'm accustomed. Banquets like that are routine in Russia. One learns to pace oneself... Is the ambulance tickety-boo? We should drive somewhere.'

Lacey looked around. 'Is there somewhere? It's all anywhere. Steppe is steppe.'

'I've been thinking about your missing Nine. If Pedlow and Duncan are dead, they deserve a decent burial. And if they're not...'

'Two British airmen can't just vanish. Even in Russia.'

'Well, you're still the C.O. Take command of the situation.'

Lacey saw Maynard admiring the Chevrolet, and went to him. 'Good news, Maynard. I'm delegating my authority,' Lacey said. 'You're temporary acting C.O. in my absence.'

'I say, Lacey. That's a bit thick. Where are you going?' Lacey told him. 'I shan't know what to do,' Maynard said.

'You were captain of cricket at school, weren't you? Well, play a straight bat,' Lacey said. 'That always worked for me.'

Hard-boiled eggs and black bread for breakfast.

Joe Duncan had been working on plans of escape. Set fire to the village and do a bunk in all the smoke and the panic. Or get some paint and write BEKETOFKA on a wall... No. They've probably never heard of it, and most of them can't read. Or, tell the tall chump, the priest or whatever he was, that they were leading a crusade. 'You're a bloody angel, Gerry,' Duncan said. 'Get on a donkey and lead the buggers out of here.'

'There's some precedent for that,' Pedlow said. 'Tell you what. You explain it to them and I'll do the rest.' He scratched his ribs and his crotch. Something was biting. Suppose they became lousy; what could they do about it? A wash and a shave would be wonderful. Nobody in the village seemed to have time for either. He was thirsty. He remembered stories of how a chap got dysentery. Better to be thirsty.

Later a choir in green robes turned up and sang. Then the red-bearded headman led a small delegation into the hut. Pedlow stood on his stool and announced: 'I'm a sodding angel. Don't you bastards forget it. I'll bring down the wrath of God on you, so I will.' He gave them a casual papal blessing.

'The redhead has a knife in his belt,' Duncan whispered.

The visitors performed a chant, with the redhead booming out the declarations and the others giving the response, ending with a climactic shout. They all stared at Pedlow. They'd done their bit. A reply would be nice.

He held his arms as wide as possible and spread his fingers. 'The train now standing at platform three,' he cried exultantly, 'is the nonstop express to Glasgow! The dining car is open, and I recommend the pork chops!'

The crowd looked at each other and muttered.

They shuffled out, leaving their leader. He folded his arms and cocked his head and stared, frowning. Pedlow folded his arms and frowned back. 'Play suspended,' he said. 'No refunds.' The man didn't like that. He walked to the door, stopped and stared again, and left.

'He's gone broody,' Duncan said. 'You've let him down.'

'Too bad. I can't help them when I don't know what they want.'

'I know what they want. They want mine too. On a plate. With lots of Worcester sauce.'

Cabbage soup for lunch. No bread.

The midday heat baked the village until even the flies gave up. The airmen sat inside the hut with their backs to the wall and dozed. Faraway gunshots made them blink but it was too hot to move any larger muscle. Then a car engine rapidly expanded its roar and charged past the open door, and by the time they got outside it was a cloud of dust, disappearing around a bend.

'Could be Bolsheviks,' Duncan said. 'Come to grab us.'

'Could be a London bus,' Pedlow said. 'Number eleven goes past here.'

'Number eleven goes down Piccadilly, old chap.'

'Does it? No damn good, then. Miles out of our way. Might as well walk.'

They joined the stream of people, all hurrying to find the cause of yet another visitation, the second in two days. They found the answer on the village green, a Chevrolet, as miraculous as a meteorite. Lacey and Borodin were examining the scorched wreckage of the bomber. Lacey had

184

a shooting stick, and he was prodding the engine.

'If you break it, you pay for it,' Pedlow said.

They straightened up. 'Did you crash in the middle of this built-up area?' Lacey asked. 'Or have they built the slums since you crashed?'

'It's a sacred spot,' Duncan said. 'They're all a bit dotty about Gerard. Think he's an angel.'

'Awfully glad you're not dead,' Borodin said. 'Two bodies in the car. This heat. Wasn't looking forward to it.'

'Not dead,' Pedlow said. 'Slightly immortal, however.'

'And very soiled,' Lacey said. 'Squalid, even. What happened to you? Have you gone native?'

'I don't think we should stand around and chat,' Duncan said. 'You see the heavyweight with the red beard? We're his property.'

'Leave him to me,' Borodin said. As he walked towards the headman, the crowd of villagers parted like a bow wave.

'How did you find us?' Pedlow asked. 'I came down miles away.'

'The count asked a passing shepherd,' Lacey said. 'You're big news in these parts. Everyone knows.'

'We heard shooting. Did you have to fight your way into town?'

'Backfires. If you jiggle the controls you can make the car backfire. Borodin showed me. He says he learnt the trick at Cambridge.' There was a pause. The silence of the crowd, and its permanent stare, was disturbing. 'Have they been feeding you well?' he asked.

'Boiled eggs,' Duncan said. 'Radishes.'

185

'As many as you like. Awfully healthy,' Pedlow said. 'I think I'll stay for supper.'

'Beef Wellington for dinner in the Mess to-night,' Lacey said. 'Roast potatoes. Brandied peaches. A sharp Cheddar.'

'Yes? I quite fancy a sliver of Cheddar. Maybe I'll give the radishes a miss.'

Borodin came back. 'I thanked him for his efforts and said his reward would be in the Here-after, where God would keep a warm seat for him in the ranks of angels, not too near the harp section, and he seemed satisfied. So now we can go.'

As Pedlow and Duncan got into the car there were signs of distress on the faces of the villagers. 'You're abandoning them, Gerry,' Duncan said. 'You're a rotten angel.'

'Am I? Well, tell them I'm going to ascend to heaven, and thank you and goodbye.'

Borodin let in the gear and sounded the horn and drove off, backfiring hard. 'Not a fanfare,' Pedlow said. 'But better than nothing. Jolly comfy car.' He felt weary and drowsy. Soon he was asleep.

He spent what seemed a lifetime not crashing the DH9. He sat in the cockpit, stick pulled back into his stomach, watching the ground magnify until its size stretched his eyeballs. It rushed at him with a speed that was uncontrollably fast and at the same time cruelly slow. The horror never lessened and it never ended until he shouted at it, and it vanished. Good. Now he was dead. All over. You couldn't die twice. Then it began again. And again. What was worse, that bloody fool Duncan was shaking his arm, trying to make him let go of the stick. He shouted, 'Sod off, you maniac!'

'You've got snot on your chin and blood on your lip, and it's teatime,' Duncan said, and went away.

Pedlow relaxed his body. All his muscles ached. His head was wet with sweat. He licked his lips and tasted the salt of blood. His pulse was galloping. Breathe in slowly, breathe out slowly. His pulse came down to a canter. He felt strong enough to look out of the window. The car had stopped. Lots of steppe. Somewhere in his brain the DH9 was still crashing, but the image was faint, like a weak sepia photograph left in the sun, and it faded to nothing. He got out of the car.

'Is Earl Grey alright?' Lacey asked. A kettle was steaming on a Primus stove. 'We brought a hamper. I think you've bitten your lip.' He gave Pedlow a bottle of water and a hand towel. 'I'm afraid we forgot the soap.'

They were in the middle of a flat sea of grass. The sun was benign. A breeze wandered by, bending some of the grasses. Nothing violent. Just fun.

They sat on a travel rug and ate cucumber sandwiches and Dundee cake. Pedlow rested his battered brain, and let the others make conversation. Borodin identified the various butterflies that came in sight. He knew a lot about butterflies, having studied them at Cambridge. 'The brain is smaller than a pinhead,' he said, 'yet in the face of a strong wind, a butterfly knows how to crab sideways and make remarkable progress. Clever little beasts.'

'They can fly jolly high too,' Duncan said. 'I've seen them at a thousand feet.'

'Up there with the skylarks,' Lacey said.

'They wanted to cut my goolies off,' Pedlow said.

That got their attention. His lip was bleeding again, and a fat drop fell onto his cucumber sandwich; but he said no more. Duncan told them the rest of the story. 'Horrible business,' he said. 'They seemed quite proud of it.'

'It's a mark of purity,' Borodin said. 'You had the bad luck to fall in with one of our religious sects. We have a lot of them, some very odd indeed. This particular crowd believes that the road to salvation is purification by self-mutilation, which subdues the flesh. They believe the flesh is the product of evil.'

'So they cut it off,' Duncan said.

'Self-castration for the men. Amputating the breasts for the women. The sect is called *Skoptsi*. Roughly translated: eunuchs.'

'Bloody hell. And I thought the Plymouth Brethren were peculiar.'

'The *Skoptsi* get it from the Bible. Matthew nineteen, verse twelve. The formula for perfection.'

'All this purification,' Lacey said. 'Isn't it self-defeating? If the men carry on mutilating themselves, the cult won't have the wherewithal to reproduce, and they'll vanish. Yet they looked quite vigorous.'

'I put it down to radishes,' Pedlow said. 'Radishes can work miracles. Believe me. I got it straight from God.'

UNQUENCHABLE GALLANTRY

1

The C.O. woke at eleven o'clock with a hangover that felt like a kick in the head and a tongue that tasted of old socks. He drank a mug of black coffee and told Brazier to assemble both Flights on the grass.

He came out and led them in twenty minutes of brisk non-stop P.T., with ten press-ups for any slackers. Then he split them into teams of five, lined them up, and sent them on a leapfrogging race the length of the train. Wragge leapfrogged three of his team and collided with the last, who was Maynard. Both fell heavily. 'Don't bloody lie there!' Griffin shouted. 'Idle on parade! Asleep in the sky! Bolos will biff you!' They scrambled to their feet. When the last team reached the finish, everyone was gasping and some were being sick. 'Flabby!' Griffin roared. 'Pathetic! Unfit for duty! Fall in and do it again.' They leapfrogged back down the length of the train to the locomotive, working hard and failing often. The *plennys* watched, amazed and amused.

'Take-off in thirty minutes,' Griffin announced. 'We'll fly up the Volga and sink a few gunboats.' He felt a little better. Every squadron needed to be licked into shape now and then. Exercising power made him hungry. He strode to the dining

189

car and ordered a bacon sandwich, lickety-split. No time to waste. There were Bolos out there to be bashed.

The squadron sat on the grass and rested its aching joints.

'What brought on that lunacy?' Oliphant asked.

'He's got a sour apple up his ass,' Douglas Gunning said. 'Old English saying.'

'We had a games master like that,' Maynard said. 'He had the rugger team out doing tackling practice every morning before breakfast. We all had big bruises. Did no good, we lost anyway. Silly bastard.'

'Leapfrog isn't going to beat the Bolsheviks,' Wragge said. 'And I didn't come to Russia to play the fool.'

'He shot himself,' Maynard said. 'Not because we lost the rugger. The police wanted him. Fraud.'

Oliphant got to his feet. 'We shouldn't complain, I suppose. He's the C.O., naturally he wants a top-notch squadron.'

'He killed Bellamy,' Hackett said. 'Bellamy was sick. Should never have been flying.' That left a long silence. Nobody wanted to argue, not with Hackett. They got up and went to put their flying kit on.

Half an hour was not enough.

The bombs had to be carted from their dump in a distant corner of the aerodrome, and then fused and hung on the Nines. Some bombs turned out to be old and corroded – no surprise – and they had to be replaced. One bomb was too big and broke its hanger; more work. One was

190

successfully hung before an armourer saw that it was a practice bomb: a dud. More delay. Griffin growled at them to get a move on. 'You can have it fast, sir,' said a flight sergeant. 'Or you can have it good. Which d'you want?' Half an hour was not nearly enough.

The crews, and those not flying who had come to watch, were glad of the rest. They sprawled on the grass and speculated what Russian women might be like. Not the peasants. They all seemed to be short and thick. Probably a bit aromatic too. Noblewomen must surely be different. Also Russian ballet dancers. They had legs, long lovely legs. Where were all the ballet dancers? Maybe in Moscow. *'Na Moskvu!'* Jessop said, and nobody laughed. Moscow was a thousand miles away and Jessop was all mouth and no brains.

The adjutant didn't attend. He was in his Pullman car when his *plenny* came in, highly excited about something, which turned out to be a train, pulling into an adjacent siding.

It was the personal express of Colonel Guy Kenny, V.C. and much more. The V.C. alone was enough to make Brazier suck in his gut and put extra snap into his salute. He knew about Kenny. Kenny was a legend in the British Army. Six feet three inches tall, the build of a rowing Blue, an eye-patch and a cheery smile. A couple of bullets had rearranged his left ankle, so he used a cane to help him walk. He wore a khaki kilt and a Glengarry bonnet and the purple ribbon of the Victoria Cross, the only British decoration whose ribbon carried a miniature replica of the medal, dull bronze, as tiny as a sequin. Brazier himself had a few medal ribbons, but that miniature turned every other award into a trinket.

'I'm afraid there's nobody here, sir,' he said. 'They're all at the aerodrome. Preparing for an attack.'

'Perfect. We'll go and watch.'

Three years earlier, Guy Kenny had been a captain in the London Scottish Regiment. He was thirty. The regiment had been given a section of the German line to capture. That was on 1st July 1916, when one hundred thousand troops climbed out of their trenches and walked – as advised; there was no need to run; seven days of shelling had battered the enemy into silence – across the dry plain of the Somme, so much better than the clogging clay of Flanders. Quite quickly, they found that the artillery barrage had failed to silence the enemy. By nightfall – probably by midday – twenty thousand of that army were dead and forty thousand more were wounded. So began the Battle of the Somme. It was to last another eighteen weeks, but Guy Kenny's contribution was all over on the first day.

The London Scottish took their objective. Most attacks failed, but London Scottish was one of a few regiments to get through the German wire and kill the machine-gunners and capture the trenches. At a terrible price. Half the soldiers fell, either dead or wounded. In Kenny's section, all the other company commanders were killed; he was the only surviving officer. Now his men were fighting to hold trenches that had been knocked shapeless by the British bombardment and were cut off by a German barrage that turned no-man's-land into exactly that. They were running out of ammunition. A relief party of fifty-nine men left the British trenches with fresh supplies. Three got through. Yet the remnants of the London Scottish fought off German counter-attacks all day, and Guy Kenny won his Victoria Cross.

He should have been shot. Statistically, and by any military measurement of risk, his leadership in moving from trench to trench across open ground, often standing upright and directing fire where it was most needed, was sacrificial. It should have been swiftly ended by the enemy. They certainly tried. Shot in the ankle, he hopped and hobbled, and kept command. As the day wore on, and ammunition ran out, he had his men firing captured enemy rifles. When night fell, he counted the survivors, made the only sensible decision, and took them back to their own lines. One eye was closed by a sliver of shrapnel. He didn't need it. The night was too black to see much.

Griffin was squatting beneath the wing of a Nine, trying to see why an armourer was having so much trouble with the bomb-release mechanism, when he became aware that a couple of mechanics were suddenly standing at attention, and he straightened up too quickly and banged his head and lost his cap.

'Colonel Kenny, sir,' the adjutant said. Griffin grabbed the cap; an R.A.F. officer couldn't salute bareheaded; besides, he was the C.O., for Christ's sake. The man he saluted was a giant. Griffin was looking at the ribbon of Britain's supreme award for valour. This was worse than being in the presence of royalty.

'We should have been flying twenty minutes ago, sir,' he said. That sounded apologetic. It pained him more than the bang on the head. 'Problems with bombs. Too many duds.'

'I know how you feel. We had the same trouble with grenades on the Somme. Infuriating, isn't it?' Kenny's massive hand squeezed his shoulder. 'Never mind, old chap. Soldier on.' It was meant to sound comforting. Griffin didn't want to be bloody comforted. He wanted to get on with his blasted job. He had to say something. He grunted.

'I'm doing a tour of the battlefields,' Kenny said. 'Mission H.Q. sent me. While I'm here I give a little talk, tell your chaps how this show fits into the Grand Strategy. These are bombers, are they?'

'Yes, colonel. These are bombers. Those are fighters. And that rabble over there are pilots and observers.' Sarcasm leaked into Griffin's voice. Nothing was going right. Hangover. Unfit pilots. Unready bombers. Now this interfering hulk of a hero.

Kenny laughed. He seemed easily amused. 'D'you know, I've never been up in a machine. Could I fit in a, what d'you call it, a cockpit?' He stepped onto the wing root of the Nine. 'Ah, the faithful Lewis gun. Jolly reliable weapon, the Lewis...' He paused, and cocked his head to listen. 'Are those more of your chaps returning?'

'You're too big, sir. You won't fit' Resentment simmered inside Griffin. His R.A.F. competence was being challenged by a colonel in a kilt.

194

'Please get off that aeroplane and let these men work on it.'

'Somebody's definitely coming.' Kenny searched the sky, trying to locate the sound. 'Hear them?'

Griffin heard. 'Not ours. Not Pumas, not Le Rhônes...' He suddenly realized the stupidity of his words, and turned and ran towards the air crews. Some had heard, and were standing. 'Take off, take off!' he shouted. 'Reds! Reds! Start up all machines! Get in the air!' Everyone ran. Ground crew sprinted. Pilots, heavy in flying kit, lumbered. Kenny got down from the Nine and joined Brazier. 'By Harry, this is a stroke of luck,' he said. 'Never expected to be in the thick of the action so soon.'

'There's a dugout nearby, sir.'

'No fear. Front-row seat for me.'

The noise became a roar and ten Red fighters in a ragged line abreast flew over the hangars, fifty feet up, low enough for Kenny to see a pilot's face when he looked down. They passed over-head before they had time to attack. A few were two-seaters. As they went out of range, their gun-ners squirted brief bursts. The bullets made clods of grass jump like frogs. The line kept going.

'Not interested in us,' Brazier said. 'They're after the White squadron over there.'

'Golly,' Kenny said. 'Sitting ducks.'

All around, mechanics were trying to start en-gines. The procedure could not be hurried. Rush it and the engine would choke on fuel. Griffin and Hackett had ground crews who rushed nothing. They got it right and the Camels taxied fast and the tails came up and they were flying. Wragge's

195

machine was moving, but slowly. Dextry followed. Jessop and Maynard made clouds of black exhaust and went nowhere. One bomber began to taxi. The other three coughed as their propellers kicked and stopped, and ground crews cursed and pilots sat and waited.

'I suppose those are Reds, too,' Kenny said. A thousand feet up, a neat arrowhead of three twin-engined aircraft had appeared.

'Big brutes, aren't they?' Brazier said. 'Probably got big bombs, too.'

Griffin's Camel was still cranking up its airspeed – seventy, eighty miles an hour. It wasn't a fighting speed. He turned away from the enemy and climbed. Height gave advantage.

Hackett was behind him and below. He counted the Red fighters. Two Spads, two Nieuports, maybe a Fokker, and the rest were strangers. As he watched, the Reds dropped to twenty feet and stretched their line and hit the White squadron with a blaze of fire that was speckled with tracer. It was perfectly timed, lasted three seconds and then up and away. Hot stuff, Hackett thought. Some of the White DH9s had collapsed, others were burning. He looked down. Now Wragge and Dextry were in the air, and the other two Camels were finally moving. Give them a couple of minutes; the odds would be ten to six. Bloody sight better than ten to two. When he looked, the C.O. had gone.

Hackett wasn't altogether surprised. Once you reached five or six hundred feet, the immense sky could quickly swallow a little fighter like a fly in a ballroom. He searched above him until he was defeated by the glare of the sun. He searched to right and left and saw nothing among the pink images turning green. He tipped the Camel on its side and scanned below. Nothing.

By then Griffin was far behind him, and heading flat-out for the Red fighters.

They were at five hundred feet, cruising lazily while the three Red bombers made their runs over the smoking wrecks of the White squadron. Griffin saw the bombs tumble out, just specks, too small to do much damage but their explosions sent a blast wave that made his Camel shudder. 'Damned cheek!' he said. 'You think you can just wander in here and...' Then he was amongst the enemy fighters, working rudder bar and stick as he hunted for a target.

Even in loose formation, the ten Reds made a swirling cloud. An all-brown Spad loomed up and soared away just as he thumbed the gun-triggers. Other guns were firing: bullet holes made a slick row of tatters in his lower left wing and he chucked everything into a right-hand bank, the Camel's best escape, made a vertical turn on a sixpence, and he was rewarded when a chequerboard two-seater wandered into his sights and all he had to do was fire and his twin Vickers battered the cockpit. The pilot threw up his arms. 'No surrender!' Griffin shouted. That was his last word on the subject. Crossfire from a second two-seater smashed his propeller. Now he was easy meat. A Spad's guns shot him in the back. A burst from a Nieuport tore into his petrol tank. The Camel ignited, blew apart, trailed long sheets of flame on its brief journey to the ground.

Kenny was watching through binoculars. 'Damn,' he said. 'That doesn't look good.'

'It never does, sir,' Brazier said.

By now the rest of the Camels, and all but one of the Nines, were in the air. The crew of the broken Nine got out and walked away. Mechanics had removed the cowling and were looking at the engine.

'What next?' Kenny asked.

'It's what's called a tactical withdrawal, sir.' The Nines and the Camels had grouped and were droning to the west, away from the enemy. 'We're outnumbered. If we do battle, we might lose all our bombers. Let's hope the enemy don't give chase. Low on fuel, perhaps.'

'Perhaps. But they're coming this way.' It was true: the line of Red fighters was recrossing the aerodrome, dropping low as it came. Now they were in line astern.

'Dugout!' Brazier snapped, and ran.

Kenny frowned, and made a decision. 'It is time to stand and fight,' he said. He walked to the Nine and heaved the Lewis gun from the observer's cockpit. A mechanic was running past when he saw Kenny and paused in surprise. 'You,' Kenny said. 'Bring spare drums.' He moved away, into an open space where he had freedom of fire.

The fighters strafed the Nine. As they passed overhead, Kenny braced himself and fired brief bursts, swinging his body again and again, until the line had passed and the Lewis was empty.

'New drum, please,' Kenny said. 'You have to lead the target,' he explained to the mechanic. 'Like shooting grouse.'

198

'Yes, sir.'

'Good man. Look and learn, look and learn. You're doing a fine job, laddy.'

'They're coming back, sir.'

Only a very strong man could handle a Lewis gun as if it were a rifle, and even Kenny's arms were getting tired. The Red fighters circled, and attacked again, and this time they strafed Kenny and bowled him over while he still had a full drum. They strafed his mechanic, too.

2

'Courage above and beyond the call of duty,' the adjutant said. 'Complete indifference to his personal safety. Resolution in the face of overwhelming odds. Look, I've written it down. Ah, thank you, Chef.' He took a black coffee and poured a slug of rum into it.

Hackett and Oliphant read the adjutant's notes. The three men were alone in the dining car. 'I suppose it's one point of view,' Oliphant said. 'The other is he was a bloody idiot.'

'That's unacceptable.'

'If you ask me, he was doolally,' Hackett said. 'I've seen it coming. Several screws loose.'

'Not Griffin, you fools. Nobody in London will lose any sleep over Griffin. Casualty of war. Might have been knocked down by a tramcar. But Colonel Kenny V.C., killed *here*, on the premises, *that's* what we have to sort out.' He rapped the table. '*Think*, for God's sake. He'll probably have a memorial service in Westminster Abbey. You must get it right.'

'I never saw it. I was miles away,' Hackett said.

'Beside the point. You still have to sign the report. You command the squadron now.'

Oliphant groaned, and put his head in his hands. 'This is all a bad dream,' he muttered. 'Too much vodka.'

'Why me?' Hackett said. 'I've done nothing wrong.'

'You're senior officer,' Brazier said. 'Acting squadron leader, with effect from now. It's all in *King's Regulations*.' He waved the book. 'Write a draft report. Lacey will polish it.'

'Hackett can't write,' Oliphant said. 'He can barely speak. He counts on his fingers. He's a Colonial, for God's sake.'

'Squadron leader, you say,' Hackett said to the adjutant.

'Paid.' Brazier finished his coffee, and stood. 'Must go. Bodies to organize.'

They watched him leave. 'I wouldn't have come to Russia if I'd known you were going to be in charge.' Oliphant said. 'All of a sudden the squadron's gone to pot.'

'Look on the bright side, Olly. When I get killed, you get command. Now shut up or I'll clap you in irons. We Australians are good at doing that. The bloody English showed us how.' Hackett sat back, feeling oddly satisfied. He looked out, at the endless, changeless steppe. He was master of all he surveyed. It wasn't worth a damn, but it was all his. 'Olly,' he said. 'Get hold of Lacey.'

'Can't,' Oliphant said. 'He's not here. And you're corrupted by power already. I suppose you learnt that from the English too.'

There was little the adjutant could do about the bodies.

Colonel Davenport's men had reached Griffin's wreck first and thrown buckets of water at it, but they were far too late: nothing could reverse the impact of the crash and the fierceness of the fire. They shovelled up what looked as if it had been human, piled it on a stretcher, covered it with an old gas cape and carried it to a hangar. Davenport sent a Union Jack to go over the cape. Dammit, the C.O. deserved some recognition.

The bigger problem was Colonel Kenny. He too lay on a stretcher in the same hangar. Twin machine guns of several Red fighters had raked the body and killed it ten times over. Brazier was not affected by the sight of multiple wounds; he had seen a lot worse; but these legs were knock-kneed and the feet were pigeon-toed, and that looked silly on such a big man. He tried to straighten them but they flopped back to their unsoldierly position. Someone had thoughtfully covered the face with Kenny's Glengarry, and Brazier did not move it.

The dead mechanic was in a similar state, but he was no problem: he would soon go underground. Kenny was different. Brazier sent for the medical sergeant and waited in the fresh air.

'Here's the thing,' he told the medic. 'The big lad in the kilt had a V.C., and he's got to go to London. In a coffin. Smelling of roses.'

'Contrary to nature, sir.'

'Suppose we got him to Salonika. Fast express

to Calais, ferry to Dover...'

The medic was shaking his head. 'That's a week at least. He'd stink bad enough to stun an elephant. This heat, two elephants.' He saw what the adjutant was thinking. 'Embalming, sir. I don't do it. Wouldn't know where to start.'

'No more would I, sergeant. When Nelson died at Trafalgar, they pickled him in salt and brought him home in a barrel.'

The medic took another look at Kenny. 'Bloody big barrel, sir.'

The adjutant nodded sadly, and walked away. Bloody V.C.s, he thought. Raving lunatics when they're alive and a thundering nuisance when they're dead.

3

Most of the squadron was sitting in the shade of the train when the Chevrolet came in sight. Borodin made the car backfire twice, just to let everyone know, and he stopped where everyone could see it. The dust made by the wheels drifted away. Nobody got up.

'Less than delirious,' Lacey said.

'I must say I expected mild applause,' Borodin said. 'Perhaps even a glad huzzah or two.'

'Maybe they've been worried sick about us,' Duncan said. 'Too full to speak.'

They all got out of the car. Oliphant stood up and walked towards them. 'I'd written you off,' he said. 'We couldn't find any wreckage.'

'It's a long story,' Pedlow said.

'I started doing the paperwork. Next-of-kin, and so on.'

'Tell you what,' Duncan said. 'We'll go back and die, and then you can get on with your paperwork.'

'Don't joke about it. We've got enough funerals without yours too.'

'Who's dead?' Lacey asked. 'Besides Bellamy.'

'Bellamy's gone?' Pedlow said. 'You might have told us.'

'You had rather a lot on your mind,' Lacey said. 'And you fell asleep. Then we had tea, and that didn't seem the right moment.'

A few other pilots had joined them. 'You had tea?' Tommy Hopton said. 'Is that where you've been all this time? Drinking tea?'

'Stroke of luck,' Pedlow said. 'Found this Russian tea shop. Damn good cream buns. Recommended.'

'I could do with a drink,' Duncan said.

'Well, you can't go into the bar looking like that,' Oliphant said. 'How did you get so filthy? Where did you spend the night? And what's that curious smell?'

'Another long story,' Pedlow said. 'Russian village. Simple folk. Bit short on plumbing.'

'They wanted to chop his bollocks off,' Duncan said.

That caused some laughter. 'Was this in the tea shop?' Hopton asked. 'I hope they let you finish your cream bun.'

'On a point of fact,' Borodin said. 'Gerard himself was meant to perform the act, not the villagers. They would provide the knife.'

'So what's all the fuss about?' Jessop said.

'Worse things happened to me at Tonbridge.'

Hackett had arrived. 'Tonbridge what?'

'Tonbridge School. Believe me, after Tonbridge, the war was a blessed relief.'

'Sorry about the smell,' Pedlow said to Hackett. 'And I'm afraid we rather broke the aeroplane. Good God.' He noticed the extra stripe on Hackett's sleeve. 'You're a squadron leader.'

'Griffin went west. I'm the C.O. Are you fit to fly?'

'Now I really need a drink,' Duncan said. 'A big drink.'

'You've turned into a raving dipsomaniac,' Hopton said.

'It's the tea in the tea shop,' Pedlow said. 'Twelve per cent proof. They make it in a bathtub while you wait.'

4

Hackett inherited the C.O.'s Pullman compartment. He gave Lacey the chair, sat on the bed and explained what had happened in his absence. Ten Bolo fighters and three bombers blew the White squadron to buggery on the ground and the C.O. went off his head, attacked the Reds on his own, ten seconds later he was a flamer. At the other end of the field a visiting colonel with a V.C. did exactly the same bloody stupid thing except that he stood and fired a Lewis gun but he got the same treatment. Without the flames. Maybe he wanted to win another V.C. Christ knows. Anyway, Mission H.Q. in Ekat would have to be told.

Hackett gave Lacey the adjutant's notes. 'Draft a signal,' he said. 'You've got half an hour. There's two g's in buggery.'

'I'll do it now,' Lacey said.

Ten minutes later he finished the draft. Hackett read:

In single-handed combat against overwhelming odds, Wing Commander Griffin lived and died in the finest traditions of the Royal Air Force. His skill, audacity and resolution were more than a match for the Bolshevik pilots, who got the better of him only when his ammunition was exhausted. His spirit and his gallantry remained unquenchable.

'Um,' Hackett said. 'Dunno. Bit brief, isn't it?'

'The more we say, the more there is for H.Q. to pick holes in.'

Hackett read it again. The paper crinkled between his restless fingers. 'We don't know his ammunition was exhausted.'

'We don't know it wasn't.'

Hackett thought about that, and soon gave up. 'This last bit...' His spirit and his gallantry remained unquenchable? What's that supposed to mean? The stupid bastard picked a fight with ten Red machines and got himself killed. That must have quenched his spirit.'

'It means...' Lacey made his eyes big, and searched the room. 'Whatever you want it to mean.'

Hackett massaged his face while he reviewed that, and got nowhere. 'Where's the other fellow?'

'Turn over.'

Hackett looked at the other side.

The unflinching courage that earned Colonel Guy Kenny his Victoria Cross in France came to the fore when he unexpectedly found himself alone in the face of low-flying Bolshevik aircraft. With no thought of personal safety, he displayed gallantry above and beyond the call of duty, exposing himself to danger time and again in order to protect others. He made the supreme sacrifice for the country he loved and the cause he held dear.

'What cause is that?' Hackett asked. 'Don't tell me. It's any cause I want it to be.'

'The trick of writing these things is telling people what they want to hear,' Lacey said. 'Without actually lying.' He watched Hackett sign the paper. 'We should go and search the colonel's train,' he said.

Hackett added *Squadron Leader, Officer Commanding, Merlin Squadron,* before he asked: 'Why?'

'It's your train now. And our man in Ekat has sent me a hundred thousand roubles to pay the squadron. I bet it's under the colonel's bed.'

'We'd better take the adjutant.'

'Good idea. He's bored. He hasn't shot a British soldier since last year.'

The colonel's train was compact: just a couple of Pullman cars and a goods truck, hauled by a locomotive. A Vickers machine gun was bolted to the roof of a Pullman. A Royal Marine sentry guarded the doorway of the main coach and refused to admit anyone without Colonel Kenny's permission.

'The colonel's dead,' Hackett said. The sentry blinked, and did not move.

'Death revokes all contracts,' Lacey suggested. The Marine pursed his lips. If he thought about it, he didn't think much.

Hackett turned and looked at the setting sun. It had been a bad day. He was fairly sure he could rush this man and knock him down, but what if there were more Royal Marines waiting inside? A bad day would get worse. Then the adjutant cleared his throat.

'I congratulate you,' he said. 'You have done your duty as a Royal Marine should. You are clearly a loyal and intelligent man. You can see that we all face a problem. This officer is Group Captain Hackett. He commands all British forces in this battle zone. As such, he outranked Colonel Kenny. Before he was killed, Colonel Kenny handed control of this train to Group Captain Hackett, to operate as part of his strategic war plan. If you continue to rely on orders that have in fact expired, you tamper with Group Captain Hackett's strategic war plan. However...'

Brazier paused to let all that sink in.

'However, a lucky solution is at hand, a solution to your problem and ours. This is Lieutenant Lacey. The Honourable Lieutenant Lacey. He is a cousin of the Prince of Wales, who is the son and heir of George V, our monarch – yours and mine – who commissioned both the colonel and the group captain in his service. The Honourable Lieutenant Lacey is twenty-sixth in line to the throne. He will remain here with you as a guarantor of correct behaviour. His presence allows you to give access to this train to Group Captain Hackett, as Colonel Kenny ordered.'

The marine had stopped looking at Brazier. His eyes had swivelled to Lacey, and they were large with awe. Lacey stood like a full-page portrait from *Tatler,* right leg slightly flexed with the foot pointing at two o'clock, chin up and the peak of his cap shielding eyes that gazed at nothing except perhaps the responsibility or being twenty-sixth in line to rule the greatest empire in the world.

The sentry stepped aside. Hackett and Brazier climbed onto the train. 'Look here,' Lacey said, and found a drawl he did not know he owned. 'Stand easy, if you like. Unless you'd rather not?' The Marine stood easy.

Colonel Kenny's quarters were spacious. Hackett and Brazier went through a kitchen and a bathroom and into a sitting room that was the full width of the train and twenty feet long. A corporal of Marines was playing cribbage with a young woman in nurse's uniform. 'That will be all, corporal,' Brazier said, and the man left at speed.

The woman did not move. 'If you two are officers, you should take your hats off,' she said; and they did. She had a measured, casual, confident voice. Once, in London, Hackett had gatecrashed a ball and asked a debutante for a dance. She had told him his fly was unbuttoned, and she had used the same cool tone of voice.

Brazier introduced them. 'May I ask...' He wasn't sure what to ask. 'Are you a friend of Colonel Kenny?'

'You mean, am I his mistress? No. I am his

nurse. Susan Perry. He is asthmatic.'

'Was, I'm afraid,' Hackett said. 'Killed in action a few hours ago. That's why we're here.'

He expected the news to jolt her, but all she did was frown a little, and that only briefly. She stood up, and Hackett was surprised to see how small she was, *petite* as the French would say, yet strong in the face and wonderfully well shaped. It was many weeks since he had met anyone like this. He knew his fly was completely buttoned, yet he felt a stupid need to check it. He locked his hands behind his back.

'You trained as a nurse in ... um ... England?' Brazier said. 'I only ask because there are many so-called nurses in Ekaterinoslav. Every other woman wears a British nursing uniform.'

'Yes. Stolen. Denikin's officers give them to their wives, mistresses, daughters. Not because they want to be nurses. They would run a mile rather than touch a wounded soldier.' There was no scorn in her voice; it was a matter of fact.

'With your permission,' Hackett said, with a delicacy that surprised him, 'we'd like to sort of, you know, look around.'

'I expect you want the money,' she said. 'It's under the bed.'

She led them into the bedroom, and there it was: two big leather suitcases. Brazier dragged them out, undid the straps, clicked open the locks. Bundles of fresh roubles lay like bricks. 'Pay for the troops,' Hackett told her.

'And you might as well have this.' She pointed to a despatch case. 'It's no use to me.'

Brazier carried the suitcases into the other

209

room. Hackett picked up the despatch case and gestured that she should go next. He followed her. She had black hair that curled around her ears and left her neck bare. He felt a great wish to touch the neck, to stroke it with his knuckles. He fished out a handkerchief, wiped his lips, took his time putting it away. Anything to busy his hands.

'Thank you for your help,' he said. 'Is there something ... anything ... we can do for you?'

'Perhaps.' For the first time, she had the makings of a smile. 'I'm now an unemployed nurse. Do you have a medical emergency in your unit? Sprained ankle? Black eye? Broken leg?'

'Can you embalm a corpse?' Brazier asked. 'I've got to get Colonel Kenny back to London in A1 condition. That is to say ... not exactly A1 but–'

'Before decay sets in. I know the principles, I've seen embalming done in France. Usually some young officer who had to be shipped home to the family burial plot. I'll need embalming fluid. Three gallons.'

'Good grief. I thought a couple of pints...'

'Three gallons, minimum.'

'Count Borodin,' Hackett said fast. 'If anyone can get you three gallons of the stuff, it's Borodin. Leave it to us.'

5

Borodin took the car and tracked down the Bishop of Tsaritsyn, who was living in the cellars of his ruined palace, and gave him a bottle of whisky as a gesture of appreciation from R.A.F. Merlin Squadron. The bishop, black-bearded to the waist, raised a jewelled hand and blessed the bottle, blessed the squadron, and blessed the embalming of the martyred colonel. He sent for a priest who knew a man who knew another man who took Borodin to, allegedly, the best undertaker in Tsaritsyn. Business, the undertaker said, was like his premises: in ruins. Look around: nobody has any respect for the dead, who lie everywhere, broken and useless, not worth spending a kopek on, not that anyone has a kopek. He gave Borodin three gallons of embalming fluid in exchange for a bottle of rum and seemed pleased with the deal.

The adjutant heard the car return. He thanked him for the embalming fluid and sent for the medical sergeant. They took nurse Perry and two boxes of her equipment and drove to the hangar. It was sunset. A dozen hurricane lamps gave the place a warm glow. Colonel Kenny lay on his back. His uniform was soaked with blood that had dried brown-black.

'He wasn't shot,' she said. 'He was destroyed. This is going to take a few hours.'

'I've arranged for coffee and sandwiches to be sent over,' Brazier said. 'I'll stay and watch, if that's alright.'

'As you wish. I may need your muscle-power later.'

The first task was to get the uniform off. The body was stiff and awkward, and the sergeant had to scissor much of the clothing into strips. The Glengarry came away to reveal a face that was unrecognisable under a mask of blood. 'Hell's bells,' Brazier said softly. 'The family aren't going to like that.'

'Could be worse.' She splashed some water on the face and touched it with her fingertips. 'The features seem intact. All this gore came from a head wound. Maybe two. It will wash off.'

She poured a quart of disinfectant into a bucket of soapy water and cleaned the body. When she finished the right arm and leg, she told Brazier: 'Rigor has set in. I need you to flex those joints. Keep bending. Give the muscles some massage. Make him supple.' She washed the other limbs, and they turned the body over and she washed the back. Brazier had his tunic and tie off and his sleeves rolled up. There was a lot of Kenny to work on.

They put him face-up again. Without the blood, the wounds made by the bullet-strikes were very obvious. Brazier began silently counting the sites of torn flesh, and gave up. What would it prove, anyway?

'Glue,' she said. 'We need glue. Or some sort of adhesive.'

Brazier went away and talked to ground crew and came back with a small tin of aircraft dope. 'For aeroplanes,' he said. 'They use it to stick patches onto the fabric.'

She sniffed it. 'Exciting smell. We'll try it.' She threaded a needle and made a single stitch that closed Kenny's right eyelid, and brushed dope along the lids where they met. 'Rather glossy,' she said. 'But it seems to work.' She closed the left eye, and then did the same operation with his mouth. 'Nobody likes to see a corpse with his

212

mouth open,' she said. She stroked Kenny's chin. 'He needs to be shaved. Is your hand steady enough?' The sergeant said he thought so. 'You shave. And wash his hair. I'll start on the serious business. Emptying the arteries and so on,' she explained to Brazier.

'I'm surprised he has any blood left in him.'

'Be ready to be surprised.'

The sergeant had brought a large syringe that he thought belonged to the Veterinary Corps. She filled it with embalming fluid, opened the right carotid artery in Kenny's neck and the right femoral vein behind his knee, inserted the syringe in the carotid and began pumping. Old blood and other fluids spurted from the femoral, and from a few other gashes in the torso. She refilled many times and pumped many times, before she was satisfied that only embalming fluid was emerging. She stitched him up, and washed her hands in the bucket. 'I'm starving,' she said. 'I hope they remembered the mustard.'

They sat on ammunition boxes and ate roast beef sandwiches.

'If I may say so,' the adjutant said, 'for a nurse you make a very competent surgeon.'

She chewed, and looked out at the night, and drank some coffee. Brazier was beginning to regret his remark when she said: 'Great-aunt Phoebe died and left me enough money to go to Cambridge. They allowed me to attend medical lectures but they wouldn't let a woman take a degree. So, no Doctor Perry. Went to London, to Guy's Hospital. Surgical nurse. Got my hands wet, learned a lot. I became the third hand when

213

the surgeon got sweat in his eyes. Sometimes I was the fourth hand. After that, France. Plenty of work there, too much sometimes. Nobody cared about gender when his leg had been blown off. Isn't that right, sergeant?'

'Ah, the war. Those were the good old days,' the sergeant said.

'Then they asked for volunteers for Russia. I told the Military Mission in Ekat I had as much experience as any doctor but they laughed. Actually laughed, ha-ha. So I joined the colonel's train. And here we are.'

'Interesting,' Brazier said. 'The squadron needs a doctor. And if anyone laughs ha-ha, I'll knock his block off.'

'And he'll come running to me.' Which made them chuckle. Nobody was laughing, not with the smell of formaldehyde heavy in the air.

She finished her sandwich, washed her hands, and got down to the heavy work. 'This is what's known as the body cavities,' she said as she punctured the abdomen just north of the navel. 'Here's where we find out what he had for breakfast. Also supper and maybe lunch. I shall need more buckets.'

The rush of escaping gases made the adjutant retreat a few paces.

'You'll need another uniform, won't you?' he said. 'I'll fetch it.'

'Don't hurry,' she said. 'The stench tends to linger.'

Both flights assembled for dinner in the dining car. Conversation was sparse. Wragge and

Oliphant, the flight leaders, discussed shows on the London stage. Oliphant spoke admiringly of 'Chu Chin Chow' Wragge recommended a revue at the Trocadero. They talked just loudly enough to avoid the discomfort of a total silence.

Then the new C.O. came in and they stopped. Everyone stood. Hackett reached his place at the top table but he did not sit. He said: 'Pilot Officer Lacey will read a message I have sent to the Military Mission H.Q.'

'In single-handed combat against overwhelming odds,' Lacey began. His voice had the clarity of an actor with the gravity of an air marshal. Finest traditions ... skill, audacity and resolution ... ammunition was exhausted ... gallantry remained unquenchable: phrases that made the younger pilots breathe deeply and stand tall.

'Wing Commander Griffin's funeral will be at ten tomorrow,' Hackett said. 'Together with that of Air Mechanic Henderson.' He waited five seconds: a decent interval. 'Now let dinner be served.'

Chef had added a dash of sherry to the mushroom soup. Pedlow and Duncan each finished two bowls. Their concentration was impressive, and nobody interrupted them with conversation. Talk elsewhere was tentative and brief. 'Merlin Squadron,' Maynard said. 'Wasn't there a wizard called Merlin?' Nobody cared to comment. Maynard gave up.

The Beef Wellington was a big success, and there was a local red wine which wasn't claret but by God it punched above its weight. Everyone relaxed. Maynard forgot his Merlin failure and said: 'Good Lord. Just realized. Today's my birthday. I'm twenty.'

'Damn bad luck,' Wragge said. 'The best is behind you, Maynard. Nothing left to look forward to but impending doom.'

'Marriage,' Jessop said bleakly. 'Fatherhood. Children.'

'Deepest sympathy,' Dextry said. 'Here's to Daddy Maynard.' Everyone drank to that. Maynard squirmed, and felt his cheeks turn pink. 'Daddy Maynard,' he muttered, trying to sound dismissive. Secretly he was pleased. He had a nickname. He was accepted.

Dominic Dextry saw Pedlow align his cutlery and lean back. His plate was empty. He looked content.

'I pinched your fly-rod, Pedders,' Dextry said. 'And the reel.'

'You're a beast.'

'I put them back.'

'A cowardly beast.'

'Well, the general opinion was that you were dead. Tommy Hopton had his greedy eye on the rod but I got in first.'

'I took your fountain pen instead,' Hopton said. 'I suppose you want it back now. Doesn't work, anyway. No ink. Where d'you hide your ink?'

Pedlow gave him a twisted smile. 'Nowhere. It's invisible ink. You'll never find it. I hope that makes you feel really stupid.'

'Oh ... shattered. Quite flattened.' Hopton closed one eye and squinted at him through the other. 'Why would you wish to use invisible ink?'

'Damn the ink,' Dextry said. 'Tell us about the crash.'

'Didn't crash,' Pedlow said. 'Not as such. What happened was, Russia was five feet higher than indicated on my altimeter. If Russia had been in the right place, fine, no problem, three-point landing. As it was, I wiped out the undercarriage.'

'Blame the instruments,' Duncan said.

'After that we lost the prop, most of the wings, the fuselage and the tail. But not the engine. We could have rebuilt the aeroplane. Joe had a hammer and a ball of string.'

'Then it caught fire,' Duncan said. 'Not our fault. We were nowhere near. Hairy villager jumped on it and it burst into flames.'

'Hairy villager,' Hopton said. 'Was he the one who wanted your private parts on a plate?'

'Oh, you know about that?' Pedlow said.

'The whole squadron knows.'

'They weren't very private,' Duncan said. 'Not in that village. They were on display at the drop of a hat.'

'They dropped their *hats* to expose themselves,' Dextry said. 'What peculiar people. In Ireland they'd say you were away with the fairies.'

'Well, they *were* peculiar,' Duncan said doggedly. 'They thought Gerry was an angel. Because of his wings.' That produced a roar of laughter. Duncan didn't join in. He aimed a finger at Dextry. 'It's no dafter than half the stuff you Irish Catholics believe about seeing the Virgin Mary up a tree and so on.'

'Not guilty. Since Passchendaele, I'm an atheist.'

'That's nothing. I'm a Protestant,' Pedlow said. 'All my family are Ulster Protestants. The worst kind. Ulster Prods are never happy unless everyone's miserable.'

Hackett murmured something to Oliphant. 'No religion in the Mess,' Oliphant told them. 'No religion, no politics, no women.'

'Not much left,' Dextry said. 'Oh, well.' Brandied peaches had arrived. Then there was the unusually sharp Cheddar. They felt well fed and unworried now that Pedlow's crash had become a big joke. They settled down to inventing nicknames. In the R.F.C., every good squadron had lots of nicknames. Drunken Duncan was a start. Jessop talked balls so he was Junk Jessop. Oliphant sounded like an elephant: Tusker Oliphant. Dextry had crashed so often he was called Wrecks. Or even Rex. Tiger Wragge was obvious. The adj was always Uncle.

Hackett wasn't there to comment. He had left with Lacey. Nobody suggested giving Lacey a nickname. He was on the squadron but he wasn't in the club.

6

'Uncle wants the colonel's nurse to stay on as squadron doctor,' Hackett said. 'You've got to be a captain to be an army doctor, haven't you?'

'Commission her,' Lacey said. 'Make her a flight lieutenant.'

'Can I do that? Yes, of course. Promoted in the field. Flight Lieutenant Perry. Good. I've done it.'

They were in Lacey's radio room, drinking port

while Lacey tried to open the despatch case, using a bunch of keys found in Kenny's bedroom. 'Nothing works,' he said.

'That bag's damned heavy,' Hackett said. 'He didn't come here just to see we got paid.'

The adjutant came in, carrying his tunic, his sleeves rolled up. 'Well, he's cleaned and gutted and sewn up and preserved and dressed in his best and boxed up for London,' he said. 'And I hope they say thank-you but I don't suppose they will. Is that port?'

Lacey poured him a glass. 'We're stymied here. Maybe the colonel kept the key on his person.'

'We would have found it. She emptied him of everything that mattered. Also a lot that you don't want to hear about. Nurse Perry is a godsend.'

'She's Flight Lieutenant Perry,' Hackett said. 'You've got your doctor. Now we need a locksmith. Is there a safe-cracker on the squadron?' Brazier shrugged.

'In the cinema,' Lacey said, 'they just shoot the lock out.'

'It's quarter-inch steel,' Brazier said. 'A bullet would jam the mechanism.' His meaty fingers prodded the case. 'Ox hide.' He opened a desk drawer and took out a trench knife. He hacked and slashed until the case fell open and despatches spilled onto the floor. 'What you might call a short cut,' he said.

Much of the mail was routine, but Hackett picked out a heavy buff envelope, sealed with red wax, addressed to Griffin. Inside it was a smaller envelope marked SECRET. Inside that were orders for the squadron to proceed to Ekaterinoslav with all speed. 'Good,' he said. 'We're leaving. Off to join Denikin's mob. I'm getting tired of this place.'

'And you've got the D.S.O.' Lacey waved a letter. 'Apologies from the War Office. Regrettable delay. They got you mixed up with another Hackett in the Pay Corps.' He shook the envelope. 'No sign of the medal. Or the ribbon.'

'Here, take this,' Brazier said. 'Belonged to Kenny. His tunic was in tatters but I saved the ribbons.'

Hackett smoothed out the little dark-green-and-blue strip. 'Well, hell,' he said. 'I must have done something to deserve it, but I'm buggered if I can remember what.' He heard the flat voice and asked himself if that was how a commanding officer should sound. Would Griffin have talked like that? Griffin talked big and aimed high. And was dead. Hackett cleared his throat and squared his shoulders. 'First things first. Tomorrow's funerals. Lacey: you'll read the service. Uncle: get the graves dug; drill the pallbearers and the rifle-volley men. No cock-ups. I suppose I should say a few words.'

'Lacey's good at that,' Brazier said. 'He'll knock something together for you.'

They sipped their port. Faintly came the sound of singing from the dining car. Lacey took a pencil and poked the ruined despatch case. 'Damaged in action' he said. 'Strafed by Bolo fighters.'

'Bastards,' Hackett said. 'Ruthless bastards.'

The squadron walked through the morning mist to the graves. Marching in formation was not possible on this springy turf with its patches of wet heather. The air crews and the ground crews formed a hollow square and waited. Nobody spoke, nobody moved. Everything was grey and damp and motionless. Jessop muttered: 'What's keeping them?'

'Patience,' Dextry whispered. 'Give the poor men their due. They'll only die the once.'

When the burial party came out of the mist, there was no precedence: the air mechanic was carried alongside the wing commander. The pall-bearers trod carefully, looking at the ground: nobody wanted to stumble. The C.O. walked behind, with the adjutant and Lacey. Then came six sergeants with rifles. Brazier had heard all about officers and their nervous trigger-fingers. He wanted trained and reliable men.

'Hats off,' Oliphant said.

Brazier lengthened his stride and got to the graves first. Planks had been placed across them. He watched carefully as the coffins were lowered onto the planks and the pall-bearers took a pace back. There was ample room; Brazier had been up at dawn, showing the *plennys* exactly where to throw the earth. He nodded to the C.O. Hackett did not respond. He was looking at the eastern sky, at a yellowish hazy blur where the sun was failing to burn through the mist. Brazier turned to Lacey and raised his eyebrows.

'We are gathered here to bury our two comrades,' Lacey said. It sounded fatuous, as he knew it would: everyone knew why they were there. Still, the padre always said it, so maybe it was a legal requirement. 'I am the resurrection

221

and the life, saith the Lord,' Lacey announced confidently. 'He that believeth in me, though he were dead, yet shall he live, and whosoever liveth and believeth in me shall never die.'

That was a very sound opener. Lacey had given some thought as to how he should handle this burial service, and he knew that he couldn't beat a solid, simple yet familiar reassurance that things aren't as bad as they look. The Church knew how to buck up a glum congregation. *Never die*. Promises. Rich promises. After that, warm their hearts with loud hurrahs. He had some ideas for that too. But first there was Psalm 130.

Apologetic. That was the tenor of 130. It was full of suffering and inadequacy and pleading for help. God knows why the adjutant's *British Army Pocket Book, 1917* put Psalm 130 in Appendix III, Burial Service, but Lacey wasn't going to waste the squadron's time by telling them, for instance, that the Lord shall redeem Israel from all his sins. He was prepared to make a gesture towards the Almighty, and so he read verses one and six:

'Out of the deep have I called unto thee, O Lord; Lord, hear my voice... My soul fleeth unto the Lord: before the morning watch, I say, before the morning watch.'

Enough of that. The morning had already begun; this was it. He closed the Pocket Book. Now for the heartwarming fanfare. He filled his lungs and orated:

Now God be thanked
From this day to the ending of the world!
Blow, bugle, blow! Was there a man dismayed?

Who rushed to glory, or the last parade?
Land of our birth, we pledge to thee:
Dulce et decorum est pro patria mori!

He glanced at the adjutant. Brazier had a small, sardonic smile. He was shaking his head, almost in wonder. Lacey charged on:

Armed with thunder, clad with wings,
Men like eagles hunt their foes.
At home in the heavens, and heaven's their home.
See! In the sunrise their epitaph glows.

Hackett heard none of it. He was thinking of the other funerals he had attended, a few in England, where pilot training was famously deadly, the rest in France. Too many to remember. Long ago he had learned the trick of coping with funerals: you told yourself that the coffin was empty, the chap had been posted, so forget him. Often it really was half-empty, with sandbags to make up the weight. But this show was somehow different. He hadn't come to Russia for this. He'd come to fly, to put on a show for the Russkis, to bag a few Bolos. Not to put men he knew in holes at ten on a foggy morning.

There was a long silence. Everyone was waiting.

He stepped forward and spoke the few words that Lacey had written for him, sturdy stuff about the supreme sacrifice and the fighting spirit that beat the Hun and about memories that would never fade. He ended with a scrap of verse which Lacey said was written by a British soldier who

223

now lay dead, far from home. 'If I should die,' Hackett said, 'think only this of me: that there's some corner of a foreign field that is forever England.'

The pall-bearers stepped forward and grasped the straps. The planks slid away. Lacey said his bit about man that is born of a woman hath but a short time to live, and so on. Wing Commander Griffin and Air Mechanic Henderson vanished smoothly from sight. Brazier gave the order and the six sergeants fired a perfect volley, reloaded, fired again. Those who wished, came forward and scattered earth on the coffins. That was that. Two more chaps had been posted.

HANG THE KAISER

1

A night of rain had cleared the sky over London and washed the smoke away. The lapse was temporary: the smoke would be back; but for one morning at least, London got the full benefit of a summer sun in a cloudless sky, and the warmth put the city in a good temper. In the parks the grass was greener. At street corners the flower stalls were brighter. And on the steps of the Home Office, Jonathan Fitzroy felt too cheerful to stand still, and he clicked his fingers in a bad imitation of a gypsy rhythm. He stopped when an army officer got out of a taxi and limped towards him. 'Colonel Johnson?' he said. 'I'm Fitzroy.'

'Lieutenant-colonel, actually.' He was grey-haired and his face was as windbeaten as a ploughman's but a lot thinner.

'My apologies. I'm afraid I'm not very clever with ranks.'

'Neither am I. Admiral Kolchak offered to make me a general in one of his armies, but I had to decline.'

'Yes.' They went inside. 'How long have you been back?'

'Landed two days ago. Barely had time to get my uniform cleaned.'

Fitzroy glanced at the faded khaki. 'It's been in

the wars, hasn't it?'

'The wars? That's about the only thing it hasn't been in.'

'Well, you must tell us all about it. We're a small committee on Russian affairs, to advise the P.M's office. First-hand news is exactly what we need.'

They went into a conference room and Fitzroy introduced him to the team. 'Lieutenant-colonel Johnson commanded a battalion of the Hampshire Regiment in Siberia,' he said. 'As soon as I knew he was in London I got in touch. We're very fortunate to meet a man who knew Admiral Kolchak personally.'

They took their seats.

'Hampshires,' General Stattaford said. 'Regular or Territorials?'

'Territorials,' Johnson said. 'First-class men. It was an honour to lead them. We were all set to fight in France but we got sent to India instead.'

'See any fighting there?'

'A little. Some police action.'

'Oh. No real campaigns, then.'

Johnson sat very still, with his arms resting on the arms of the chair. He kept his head slightly tilted, as if his neck muscles were tired. His eyes had the weary look of someone who has gazed too long at distances too great. 'We served where our country sent us,' he said.

'India to Siberia,' Stattaford said. 'Somewhat different climates.'

Johnson had nothing to add to that.

'What were your orders?' James Weatherby asked. 'When you left India, that is.'

'To take my battalion to Omsk and to assist the

White Russian Army to establish a new eastern front against the Germans. Omsk is about a thousand miles east of Moscow, and so not in any danger from the Germans. But that didn't matter because it took us two months to get to Omsk, and by then Germany had surrendered.'

'Two months,' Stattaford said. 'Less than speedy.'

'Shipping was scarce. We sailed to Ceylon, then to Hong Kong, and to Singapore, and finally to Vladivostok, on the Russian Pacific coast. From there we took the Trans-Siberian Railway. It's a long way to Omsk, at least two thousand miles, and the train goes slowly. Sometimes not at all.'

'And when you arrived?' Weatherby said. 'How did that go?'

'I believe we did our duty,' Johnson said slowly. 'I believe we performed as well as any men could.'

'Splendid, splendid,' Fitzroy said. It wasn't splendid at all; it was rather dull. 'How did you get along with Admiral Kolchak? What were your impressions of him?'

'Kolchak.' Johnson gave that question some thought. 'A brave man. Energetic. Knew what he wanted. He was the only totally honest man I met in Russia.'

That amused Charles Delahaye, from the Treasury. 'Honesty is a rare commodity, is it?'

Johnson took a deep breath, held it for a second, and released it. 'Gentlemen,' he said, 'I am very proud of my Hampshires. But if anything I say here were to appear in the Press, the name and reputation of the regiment might suffer in the eyes of some people. That would be grossly unfair.'

'Nothing said here leaves this room,' Fitzroy told him. Everyone nodded agreement.

'Well then. You ask about honesty. All of the White Russian generals whom I met, and my officers met, were corrupt or incompetent, and most were both. The same went for the regimental officers. They treated their rank as an opportunity to make money at the expense of the ordinary Russian soldier, who is half-starved, abominably clothed, badly armed, and ill-led. Officers regard their men with contempt and steal the money which is meant to feed and clothe them. There is no common purpose, no *esprit de corps*. The generals conspire against each other. All of them drink too much and some are permanently drunk.'

'Goodness,' Fitzroy said. 'Rather a bombshell.'

'But surely,' Stattaford said, 'you could train the soldiers. You could take a rabble and turn it into something like the British Army. We did, in the war. Made good troops out of useless civilians.'

'Mmm. A nice idea. But the comparison is not apt, general. We moved the whole battalion five hundred miles from Omsk, by rail, to Ekaterinburg. Not to be confused with Ekaterinodar or Ekaterinoslav, near the Black Sea. Ekaterinburg is in Siberia. We took charge of eight thousand Russian recruits. They were – it gives me no pleasure to tell you this – all filthy, all lousy, thoroughly infested with vermin. Our first task was to strip them and wash them, they could not be relied on to wash themselves. Their rags of clothing were burned and the recruits were disinfected, head to foot. Only then could we equip them with British

228

Army uniform.'

Sir Franklyn Fletcher stirred himself. 'How many of your officers spoke Russian?'

'A few had a smattering. Not a problem, because many recruits spoke no Russian either. They came from Mongolia. Moslems, most of them.'

'Ah,' Stattaford said. 'French Army had a spot of bother like that. Colonial troops, Moroccans, very keen on prayer.'

'One learned to adjust,' Johnson said. 'If half the squad disappears during bayonet practice, so be it.'

'The key question is,' Delahaye said, 'did your training pay off? I mean, did you end up with an *élite* group, keen as mustard to fight the Bolsheviks?'

'It wasn't as simple as that.' Johnson stood up. 'Excuse me, gentlemen.' He limped to and fro. 'My legs have taken a bit of a hammering lately. Knees get stiff.' He returned, and stood behind his chair, gripping the top. 'What I should explain is that Siberia is a shambles, a state of anarchy. Admiral Kolchak's men control the railway – well, some of it, some of the time – but there are tens of thousands of square miles on either side that are full of warlords, guerrilla groups, private armies, bandits, leftover German and Austrian prisoners of war, all sorts of odds and sods. They don't support Kolchak, and they certainly won't fight for him, because they believe he wants to be the next Tsar of all the Russias.'

Sir Franklyn asked: 'And does he?'

'He claims to be the Supreme Power.'

'And you think that is a fiction?'

229

'His grip is tenuous. Conspiracies against him abound. A plot by his generals to overthrow him would have succeeded if the Hampshires hadn't been there to quash it.'

'Yet he's running the show in Siberia,' Weatherby said. 'How did that happen?'

'Oh ... I can think of three reasons. Firstly, he has more money than anyone else. He has the Imperial Gold Reserve, acquired I don't know how, and worth a hundred million pounds. Secondly, he has the Czech Brigade. Sixty thousand men, very disciplined, very tough. Thirdly, all the other White Russian leaders are quite hopeless.'

It made them laugh. Johnson shrugged, and did not laugh.

'Well, that certainly clears the air,' Fitzroy said.

'It's not as simple as it sounds,' Johnson said. 'The gold is an enormous hazard. Everyone wants to steal it. The Czechs are tired of fighting. They want to go home, now. And the other White leaders are too stupid to realize how stupid they are. They will overthrow Kolchak even if it kills them. Which the Bolsheviks will gladly do.'

There was a knock on the door. 'Coffee,' Weatherby said. 'Praise be. We need some stimulus.'

The coffee circulated. Everyone left their seats and enjoyed a little exercise. James Weatherby and Sir Francis strolled around the room, looking at portraits of long-dead statesmen.

'Delicious coffee,' Sir Francis said. 'What's wrong with the Royal College of Embroidery?'

'Out of bounds. Influenza struck down the staff. You probably recognise this chap. Lord Palmerston. Diplomacy was a lot easier in his day. Any problem, send a gunboat.'

'Not a formula that would apply to Siberia. It's rather a long way up the Volga.'

They moved on. 'What do you make of our guest?' Weatherby asked quietly.

'Well, I happen to know he was President of the Union when he was at Oxford. He's nobody's fool.'

'Too clever for the Army?'

'Perhaps. I say: who was this handsome fellow?'

'Um ... Spencer Perceval. The only Prime Minister to be assassinated. His murderer ran up a lot of debts in Russia, blamed them on the government, and when it refused to pay, he shot poor Perceval.'

'Dear me.'

'Gunned down in the lobby of the House of Commons. 1812.'

'A very Russian solution. We have elections, they have assassinations.'

'Doesn't make them any happier, does it?'

Sir Francis shrugged. 'I don't think Russians expect to be happy. But they do like to register their disapproval.'

General Stattaford was talking to Delahaye. 'Did I see a little glint in your eye at the mention of a hundred million in gold, Charles?'

'It would make a dent in their debt, certainly.'

'Russia's flat broke. They'll never pay.'

'No, probably not. Our friend makes Kolchak's crowd sound like a grisly lot. And why must they keep slaughtering the Jews?'

'Force of habit, old chap.'

'It doesn't help either side win the war, that's

what puzzles me. Jews are the only Russians with brains, and everyone kills them. Makes life difficult for Lloyd George, I can tell you. Whatever he does, he ends up backing a mob of butchers.'

'War is war, Charles. Omelettes and eggs, you know.'

'Try telling that to the Jews.'

Fitzroy was chatting to Johnson about cricket. 'Stroke of luck,' Johnson said. 'Hampshire are playing Middlesex at Lord's today. Sort of thing I dreamt about in Siberia. Sunny day, Hampshire in fine form, that's my idea of heaven.'

'Then we'd better finish up here and let you go on your way.' Fitzroy tapped a teaspoon against a coffee cup. 'Gentlemen ... Lieutenant-colonel Johnson has kindly agreed to answer your questions.'

They settled into their chairs.

'Haven't you been a little unfair on Admiral Kolchak?' Sir Franklyn said. 'He has had some success, hasn't he?'

'Indeed. His armies advanced hundreds of miles early this year. Bolshevik opposition was weak. His staff even spoke of taking Moscow. Then some strong Red armies appeared and Kolchak's men have been retreating ever since. His advance looked good on the map, but he didn't administer his gains, he didn't win over the population, because...'

'Because he's a sailor,' Stattaford said cheerfully.

'It's not like the Western Front. Battles may be hundreds of miles apart. Capturing a great slice of Siberia is meaningless unless the people support you. And–'

'They don't like Kolchak,' Stattaford said.

'Will the Siberian people prefer the Bolsheviks?' Weatherby asked.

'The peasants prefer the Revolution to the Romanovs,' Johnson said. 'Nine out of ten Russians are peasants.'

'You make it sound as if we've backed the wrong horse.'

'It's their country. They must decide.'

'Meanwhile, your Hampshires are still there,' Stattaford said. 'Why did you leave them?'

'Orders. I was recalled. I'm doing my utmost to get them out of there.'

'I hear you had an exciting trip,' Fitzroy said hopefully.

Johnson thought about that. 'Challenging,' he said.

'The Trans-Siberian again?' James Weatherby asked.

'If I'd gone to Vladivostok I'd still be on the train now. I took the short route. Overland to Archangel, and then by ship.'

'How far was this short route?'

'From Ekaterinburg to Archangel? About a thousand miles.' Johnson unfolded a foolscap sheet of paper and spread it on the table. 'Local maps aren't very reliable, so I've drawn my own. The battalion had a dozen married men, all released on compassionate grounds, and they came with me. Archangel's north-west of Ekaterinburg. Went by train from Ekaterinburg to Perm, two hundred miles. Steamboat up the River Kama, then we took this tributary of the Kama.' His fingers traced the route. 'Too shallow for the

233

steamboat. We transferred to rowboats.'

'Upstream?' Fitzroy said. 'Against the current?'

Johnson nodded. 'Rowed as far as we could. Then we walked to another river, the Pechora. Only eighty miles, but it meant hiking through forest, thick forest, and that presents its own problems. Reached the Pechora, very shallow, more rowboats. Eventually we found another river steamer. It took us four hundred miles, almost to the Barents Sea. Unfortunately ice blocked the river mouth. We had to tramp two hundred miles through yet more thick forest.' He glanced up. 'There is no such thing as thin forest in Russia.' They smiled. The old stick had a sense of humour after all. 'Another river. Rowboats again. Rowed to the sea, and a Royal Navy destroyer found us.'

'Well done!' Fitzroy said. He pounded the table with his fist, and the rest joined in, except General Stattaford.

'Strenuous,' he said. 'But I wonder if there wasn't a better way. More direct, less exhausting. You left the train at Perm. Perm is not the end of the line.' He took a pencil and traced a more westerly route. 'The railway continues for six or seven hundred miles to this town, called Kotlas.' He drew a circle around it. 'From Kotlas it's riverboat all the way down the River Dvina to Archangel.' His pencil raced down the river and underscored Archangel. 'Hop on a boat. That's the sensible way to travel.'

Johnson was starting to feel weary. 'The Bolsheviks hold Kotlas, general. Admiral Kolchak sent an army to capture it and link up with Archangel but the Red Army destroyed it. Beyond

Perm, the Red Army owns everything. That's why I took a different route.'

Stattaford was blithely untroubled. 'Just testing your strategy,' he said. 'Seems sound.'

Everyone shook Johnson's hand, and Jonathan Fitzroy escorted him out of the building. 'Quite fascinating,' he said. 'We're enormously grateful to you.'

'If you have the P.M.'s ear,' Johnson said, 'please get my Hampshires out of that dreadful country.'

Fitzroy went back and met the rest of the party coming downstairs. 'Tell Lloyd George to wash his hands of the whole scurvy crew,' Charles Delahaye said, without stopping.

'The odd thing is,' Sir Franklyn said, 'they write such damned fine symphonies.' Then he too was gone.

2

The Camels and the Nines had been dismantled and loaded on to flat cars. The ponies and the Chevrolet went into boxcars; so did all the ground crews' stores and toolkits, the fuel, bombs and ammunition, and the canvas hangars. Wrangel had released Count Borodin from his army duties; he joined the squadron and took Colonel Kenny's coach. The colonel's coffin travelled in the Marines' quarters. Flight Lieutenant Susan Perry moved into Hackett's old Pullman compartment. Hackett, of course, had the C.O.'s place.

After many warning blasts on all three locomotive whistles to get everybody aboard, Merlin

235

Squadron trundled out of Beketofka. For the first mile it moved at a slow walking pace, while the ground crews made sure that none of the loads fell off. Then, with final blasts, the trains gradually worked up to fifteen miles an hour and stuck to it.

The C.O. called a meeting with his senior officers.

'I can run backwards faster than this,' Hackett said. 'Can't we speed it up?'

'The drivers say this is the most economical speed,' Borodin said. 'The locomotives are low on fuel.'

'What's wrong with the railways? Haven't they got fuel dumps?' Tusker Oliphant asked.

'Not for a hundred miles.'

'If we went faster, we'd reach the dumps sooner,' Hackett said.

'I don't think it works like that,' Tiger Wragge said. 'The faster, the slower. In the long run.'

Hackett gave him a hard stare. 'Bollocks,' he said.

'Well, I can't compete with your intellectual firepower,' Wragge said. 'And I hope you're not turning into another galloping warhorse like our late lamented wing commander?'

'Oh, I say ... that's a bit below the belt,' Oliphant said. 'Sniping at a chap who's not here to defend himself.'

'Why isn't he? Because he couldn't wait. Dashed off on his own. Outnumbered. Dead. Good way to lead the squadron? Or have I overlooked something?' Wragge stared at Hackett, but Hackett just stared back.

The adjutant cleared his throat, with a sound like gravel being shovelled. 'I'm not an airman,' he said. 'I'm just a simple soldier, me. But could Griffin have been trying to divert the enemy? All our machines were not yet in the air. Might he have attacked to distract the Bolsheviks?' He raised his eyebrows, and then his hands. 'Just a suggestion. A possibility.'

Hackett said: 'If he'd waited two minutes, we could all have distracted them.'

'Two minutes can be a long time in a battle,' Brazier murmured.

'Not in that battle.'

'Captain Ball,' Oliphant said. '56 Squadron. I met a chap from 56 who told me Ball liked to dive into the middle of a Hun circus because they didn't dare fire at him for fear of hitting one of their own. He got three D.S.O.s, a V.C., God knows what else. So it worked for Ball.'

'Until one day it didn't,' Wragge said. 'Ball played his joker too often. Griffin played it once, and that was once too many.'

'I don't suppose...' Count Borodin began, and waved the thought away as if it were smoke from a cigar. 'No. Silly idea.'

'Most of war's a bloody silly idea,' Hackett said. 'Spit it out.'

'Well ... I saw some heroic acts when we were fighting the Germans. Truly heroic. The survivors became heroes, and sometimes the Tsar, in person, presented them with the Order of St George, first class, and they were speechless, they felt they had been touched by the hand of God. It begs the question: why had they risked death

237

so recklessly? It wasn't to win the battle. Usually the battle was lost already. So why...' He gave up.

'Griffin had just met Colonel Kenny, hadn't he?' Wragge said. 'Kenny V.C. The hero of the Somme.'

'He took on all those Bolos just to win the Victoria Cross?' Oliphant said. 'That's crazy.'

'Men on the battlefield are not completely sane,' Brazier said. 'I've seen soldiers crawl into no-man's-land in broad daylight just to dig some potatoes. Risk of getting snipered, maybe twenty to one. They weren't crazy. They just wanted a few new spuds.'

'Maybe it wasn't a spur of-the-moment thing,' Wragge said. 'Maybe Griffin came to Russia to win the V.C.'

'He might get one,' Hackett said. 'I bet the Mission in Ekat is tickled pink with him.'

Further down the train, Lacey was playing backgammon with Stevens, the medical sergeant.

'Your pay parade was a big success,' Stevens said. 'We all got five times what we expected.'

Lacey threw his dice and made his move.

'I asked the adj how it was done,' Stevens said. He threw his dice and studied the board. 'He seemed a bit awkward. Almost shifty. Said it was all up to you.' He made his move and hit a piece left by Lacey and removed it. 'Was it all up to you, Mr Lacey?'

Lacey took his time over his throw and got a two and a five, exactly what he didn't want. 'Come on, God,' he said. 'Play the game.' He tried a possible move, didn't like it and took it back.

'You nearly fell in a yawning cesspit there, sir.'

Lacey massaged his eyes. 'Before now, you were paid at the official exchange rate, twenty roubles to the pound. That was very stupid, it bought almost nothing. The unofficial rate – on the street, any street – is at least eighty roubles. The Paymaster at the Military Mission gives our man in Ekat our pay in pounds, he gets the street rate, or better, and sends the roubles to me. Simple.'

'Doesn't sound legal, sir.'

'Of course it's not legal. This war isn't legal. The difference is what I do doesn't hurt anybody. Your move.'

'No, it's still yours. Any move you make is a disaster. You can concede now, if you like. If not, I'll clobber you.'

'Where did you learn to play?'

'Salonika. Greeks taught me. Best in the world.'

Lacey decided to play on. He quickly threw a string of double-sixes and played a long, dour defensive game and won by a whisker. 'Another?' he said.

'Bloody officers,' Stevens said.

The bar-dining-room had been renamed; it was now known as The Dregs. Several crews from the bomber flight were there, attracted by the poker game. Everyone was flush with Lacey's roubles. A hazy setting sun warmed the air. The train rumbled along, unhurriedly. There was a feeling of contentment, of a well-deserved holiday after hard work. Memories of non-stop P.T. and leap-frog races on top of a hot breakfast had been rapidly forgotten. Nobody mentioned Griffin.

Daddy Maynard was reading some old copies

239

of the *Daily Mail* that Lacey had found in Colonel Kenny's train. 'Hullo,' he said. 'They're going to hang the Kaiser.'

'About time,' Junk Jessop said. 'That bloody awful moustache. Looks like seaweed. Definite hanging offence.'

'Who's going to hang him?' Hopton asked.

'Not like seaweed,' Drunken Duncan said. 'Seaweed's green.'

'The French seem first in line,' Daddy Maynard said.

'German seaweed isn't green,' Jessop said. 'German stuff's all grey and slimy. Ask any sailor.'

'I bet the French won't hang him,' Gerry Pedlow said. 'I bet they guillotine him.'

'Yes. On the Champs Élysées,' Hopton said. 'And their top man, Clemenceau, will sell tickets. Make a fortune. Typical frog thing.'

'I suppose you learnt that at your rotten school,' Rex Dextry said to Jessop. 'Got beaten senseless all afternoon and then wrote essays on German seaweed.'

'You can't write on seaweed,' Jessop said. 'The ink keeps running.' Nobody laughed.

'They wouldn't do it on the Champs Élysées,' Pedlow said. 'It's just a road. If they sold tickets, people would get a lousy view. The frogs would riot.'

'They might guillotine Clemenceau too,' Hopton suggested. 'Two for the price of one.'

'That was a good joke, writing essays on seaweed,' Jessop said. 'Wasted on you peasants.'

'The Bois de Boulogne is the place to hang him,' Pedlow said. 'Tons of room. Or maybe the

Eiffel Tower.'

Maynard had moved on to a later copy of the *Daily Mail*. 'They can't hang the Kaiser,' he said. 'He's done a bunk to Holland, and Holland's neutral.'

'You're a large fart, Daddy,' Gerry Pedlow said.

'Anyway, Tonbridge wasn't as rotten as Rugby,' Jessop said to Dextry. 'At least we didn't invent that stupid game where you hack each other on the shins all afternoon.'

'What was the seaweed joke?' Maynard asked Jessop. 'I didn't hear it.'

'I've forgotten,' Jessop said. 'And it was too clever for you, anyway.'

3

All three trains came to a gradual halt just as the Camel pilots were sitting down to dinner. 'Where are we?' Hackett said.

Daddy Maynard got up and looked out. Dying sunlight made a soft yellow backdrop to the steppe. 'Nowhere,' he reported. 'We're in a siding in the middle of nowhere. The other trains have stopped too.'

'Locomotive crews must eat,' Count Borodin said. 'And rest. We'll move again at dawn.'

Fair enough. Mushroom soup laced with cream and brandy was served. 'Signal Mission H.Q. at Ekat,' Tiger Wragge told Lacey. 'Tell them to keep the war hot until we get there.'

They were well into the beef stroganoff when the far-off crack of rifle fire stopped all con-

241

versation. They looked at Borodin. 'Not hunters,' he said. 'Nobody hunts in the dark. Nothing to hunt, anyway.'

'I posted a guard,' the adjutant said. 'Maybe they saw something.'

He left the Pullman coach and walked along the track to a boxcar with a fixed ladder. He climbed to the roof. Starlight showed the black shapes of two men and a Lewis gun on a tripod, 'See anything, sergeant?'

'Bugger-all, sir. Harris thinks he heard something. Black as sin out there.'

Brazier looked. It was impossible to tell where steppe ended and night sky began. There was nothing to focus on.

'Might be some fuckin' peasant,' the sergeant said softly. 'Fucked his brain with fuckin' vodka, got kicked out by his fuckin' wife, went and shot his fuckin' self.'

'Probably fuckin' missed,' Harris said.

Brazier walked slowly up and down the boxcar roof. His stroganoff was getting cold, all because a drunken nobody couldn't shoot straight. Then a rifle cracked the night on the other side of the train, the bullet ricocheted off iron and sang as it soared and died in the night. Then another shot. This time Brazier saw the tiny splash of flame. As Harris swung the Lewis, Brazier said: 'Watch for the next muzzle-flash and give it a short burst. Four rounds maximum. This could be a long fight.'

He swung down the ladder. Lit windows in all three trains were turning black. He hurried back to The Dregs and met Hackett at the door. 'Tell everyone to lie flat,' he said.

Hackett disappeared, shouted orders, came back, 'What's up?' he asked.

'God knows. No moon yet. You could hide two or three battalions out there.' Lewis guns made short statements. 'I bet the bastards didn't expect *that*,' Brazier said.

'This is your kind of show, Uncle. You're in command.'

A bullet sighed overhead. High overhead. 'Sloppy,' Brazier said. 'No discipline. But a random shot can still kill you. I'll get some rifles sent here.'

'Thanks. We officers can shoot at random too. Might even hit it.'

The adjutant chuckled, a rare sound.

He made his rounds of the trains, talking to the flight sergeants, making sure that all the ground crews were armed. He added four more Lewis guns on top of boxcars. Sporadic shots continued. A couple punctured windows, but there seemed no obvious plan to the firing. Brazier walked to Kenny's train and found, as he expected, that he could teach its Royal Marines nothing. They welcomed the change in routine. They could fire, reload and fire again so fast that a rifle sounded almost like a light machine gun. All they needed was a target.

In The Dregs everyone was on the floor, including Hackett. He felt restless: annoyed that the evening had been spoiled by a few bad marksmen, God knew how many, a dozen, a thousand? Merlin Squadron could strafe the scruffy bastards to bits in five minutes. If it was daytime. If the

Camels could be assembled. If the scruffy bastards would stand and fight, which they probably wouldn't... That was when he remembered the squadron doctor.

Susan Perry was in her Pullman cabin, sitting on the floor, finishing her supper by candlelight and reading a tattered copy of *Horse and Hound.*

'Just wanted to check that you're O.K.,' he said. 'Nothing to worry about. Just a few trouble-makers. Soon send them packing.'

She ate the last bit and gave him the plate. 'In France I worked with surgeons in a Forward Dressing Station,' she said. 'Blood up to the elbows and Hun shells dropping like autumn leaves. So this doesn't worry me.'

'All the same, I think you should be with the pilots.'

'Is there pudding?'

'Um... Treacle tart. Cream.'

'I'm not going to miss out on that.' She got to her feet and picked up a Colt revolver. 'Belonged to Colonel Kenny. Don't worry, it's loaded.'

'I hope we won't let any blighter get that close.'

'I'm sure you won't. This is to fight off randy pilots in the dark.'

'You can trust my chaps.'

'When a man tells a girl she can trust him,' she said, 'she knows she can't trust him.'

They went to The Dregs. 'Listen here,' he announced. 'There's a lady present. Mind your manners.'

'God, I hope not,' she said. 'I can take war or good manners but I can't take them both to-gether.'

The night passed slowly. Some of the pilots fell asleep. Hackett organized a system of watches so that two were always awake and alert. The firing lessened but never completely stopped. Brazier would have liked to lead a few volunteers from the ground crews, stealthily patrolling the steppe with blackened faces and sharpened knives, but he knew that such tactics ended with the last war, the one with trenches and no-man's-land and abundant Huns to be poached. Instead, he made sure that hot cocoa and bully-beef sandwiches were available. The hours drifted by, and just as a tinge of grey began to soften the darkness, the enemy attacked Kenny's train.

The Marine who was manning the Lewis gun on the roof swung it in a steady, scything action, changed the drum, did it again. Marines at the windows picked off the ghostly shapes that got past the Lewis gun. Brazier, watching from the roof of 'B' Flight's train, said: 'They'll come at us from both sides. Spray the ground on the left. Four-second bursts. Don't stint the bullets. Where are the grenades?'

He took four grenades, climbed down and walked to the front of the locomotive. There was much shouting and blowing of whistles, and he threw two grenades to left and to right, aiming for the centres of the noise. Brazier had a strong arm. The grenades flew like clay pigeons and exploded like the crack of doom.

When the smoke cleared, the pre-dawn twilight showed attackers running away on both sides of Kenny's train. The Lewis guns chased them. Some fell.

Brazier walked back to The Dregs. 'I think you can safely tell Chef to prepare breakfast,' he told Hackett.

'They weren't Bolos, were they? Too far south. What did they want?'

'They were rabble,' Brazier said comfortably. 'And they wanted what every Russian wants, anything that isn't nailed down. Given enough time, they'll steal the nails too.' He patted Hackett's arm. 'This isn't the Varsity rugger match, squadron leader.' They went into the bar car. Brazier hadn't felt so satisfied since he watched the lid of Kenny's coffin being screwed down.

'The bandits have been sent packing,' Hackett told the pilots. 'Back to normal again.'

'Congratulations to the adjutant and his men,' Count Borodin said. 'As to normal ... I wonder if that might be premature?'

'What's the problem?' Hackett asked. 'Fuel dump's not far. We steam on, grab some coal. Easy.'

Borodin went to a window and tapped his knuckles on the glass. 'Double tracks out there. But no train has passed us, going either way, since we left Beketofka. Isn't that unusual?'

'I smell coffee,' the adjutant said. 'Let us examine the situation over the black stimulant. And perhaps also an egg.'

Over coffee, they listened to Borodin. The train drivers, he said, told him that the fuel dump and water tower were in a small town about twenty miles away. He told them its name, and wrote it on a piece of paper.

'You've left out the vowels,' Brazier said. He

246

clutched the paper and took a stab at the name, and failed. 'Let's call it Walsall. Near Birmingham. Sounds a bit like Warsaw.'

'That's in Poland,' Hackett objected.

'Warsaw will do nicely,' Borodin said. 'I rather think this Warsaw may be in unfriendly hands.' That might explain the absence of trains. Could the Reds have captured Warsaw? Unlikely. But there were other rogue forces roaming the land. Bands of guerrillas. Hordes of deserters. Warlords' armies. Why Warsaw? Because trains worth looting would stop there. And maybe a handful of bandits had chanced on Merlin Squadron in the dark, and didn't know the trains were full of fighting men.

Well, it was possible. Anyway, what next?

No point in steaming into Warsaw if it was stuffed with bad hats. No point in sitting here if it wasn't.

Borodin offered to go on ahead, by pony, and find out more. Talk to a few peasants. 'They'll tell me,' he said. 'They won't tell you.'

Nobody could think of a better idea. 'We'll look at the battlefield first,' Brazier said. 'Might find some clues.'

The Marines were counting the bodies and dragging them into lines. A few of the dead wore odd bits of uniform; most did not; many were barefoot. 'Funny thing, sir,' a Marine corporal said. 'No wounded. Not many rifles, either.'

'The survivors took all the rifles,' Borodin said. 'And the boots. Both are scarce. And the wounded expected to be shot. Or worse. The lucky ones would have been carried away by their friends. The rest...' He waved a hand at the sweep of the

247

steppe. 'Crawled off to die in the grass.'

'Bloody hell,' the corporal said. 'Sir.'

'Don't go looking for them, corporal,' Brazier said. 'They won't thank you for it.'

Borodin walked along the line of bodies. He stooped and picked up a black flag. 'Nestor Makhno's badge,' he said. 'He leads an Anarchist guerrilla force. They fight anyone and everyone. Makhno calls them his Green Guards.'

'Green Guards,' Hackett said. 'With a black flag.'

Borodin shrugged. 'They're Anarchists. They do what they like. They like attacking trains.'

'They didn't like our Lewis guns, sir,' the corporal said. 'Made a big mistake there, they did.'

Count Borodin took some old and soiled pieces of clothing from the bodies: a sheepskin coat, canvas trousers, a felt cap. 'Camouflage,' he said.

4

The squadron caught up on its sleep. The adjutant kept a few guards on top of the boxcars. Fifty yards from Kenny's train, *plennys* dug a mass grave. They worked steadily, but they were silent and sombre They were Russians burying fellow-Russians killed by foreigners. The bloodshed had been unavoidable. If the attackers had got into the trains, they might have slaughtered everyone. All the same, the *plennys* didn't like it. Some of the drops that fell in the grave were sweat. A few were tears.

Hackett woke at midday, dressed and walked

alongside the trains, looking for damage. He found some bullet holes and Flight Lieutenant Susan Perry. She was changing the dressings on a couple of ground crew, cut by fragments of glass from broken windows. She tied the knot on the final bandage. 'Does that hurt?' she asked.

'Agony, ma'am.'

'That's odd, I didn't feel a thing.' He laughed, and she dismissed him with a nod and a smile. 'I need some exercise,' she told Hackett. 'Will you come with me? I don't want to get massacred by some smelly bandit.'

'Of course. I'll get my gun.'

'No need. I have the colonel's revolver in my bag. You hold the rotter and I'll shoot him in the head.'

They strolled towards the steppe. 'You seem very ... um ... refreshed,' he said. What he meant was *delightful,* but he was the C.O. and duty came first.

'It goes with the job. A nurse can be dead on her feet, but if she yawns, matron will kill her. Lesson one.'

'I see, I see.' Hearing her voice – after weeks of male gruffness – gave him amazing pleasure. It had a light and easy lilt that was a reward in itself. Never mind the words. Just enjoy the voice. 'Yes, I do see.'

'We're walking in step,' she said. 'D'you mind awfully if we don't? Your legs are longer than mine.'

'Yes, of course, of course.' Why must he say everything twice? It made him sound stupid. He broke step, and to make sure that they stayed out of step he watched her feet. She had legs like a

249

dancer's. What he could see of them. But she was so slim that he could easily imagine

He sniffed hard and filled his lungs. A rabbit hole gave him an excuse to sidestep away from her. They walked at a safe distance. 'Uncle tells me you embalmed Colonel Kenny superbly well,' he said.

'Does he? I'm pleased he's pleased.'

A touch of tartness in the words surprised him. 'Well, it got us out of a serious hole.'

She stopped and picked a small yellow flower and tucked it into a buttonhole in his tunic. 'Kenny looked quite satisfied with the results.'

'Thank you,' he said, for the flower; and then: 'I don't know what you mean.'

'There's nothing noble about a dead man's face. Quite the reverse. I gave his features a human look. Not a smile. Just the kind of expression that a colonel with a V.C. should have. Oh dear. Now I've shocked you.'

'Not a bit.' They walked on. Not entirely true: what had shocked him was the sight of the wedding ring on her finger as she fixed the flower. Why hadn't he noticed it before? He felt cheated, and hated the feeling, it was a sign of weakness, unworthy of a C.O. 'After France, nothing shocks me,' he said. 'All that blood and guts.'

'It may be blood and guts to you, but it's bread and butter to me,' she said. 'Old medical joke. Very old.'

He laughed, and enjoyed a great relief of tension, so he took another risk and said: 'How does your husband feel about all this?' He waved at the steppe. 'An Englishwoman in the wilds of Russia.'

'Nothing. He...' She stopped, and faced him. 'Look: if you must walk such a long way away, we shall have to communicate by postcard.' He took a cautious pace towards her. She shook her head. 'Dear Sir,' she said. 'Ref yours of the tenth inst...' He took a larger step. 'Better,' she said. 'Short story. We met at Cambridge. His name was Tristram. Not his fault, blame his dotty parents. Fell in love. Not our fault, blame the biology. Tristram was very dashing. As soon as he could, he dashed off fast to join the war before it stopped. Queen Victoria's Rifles, second lieutenant. Dashed over to France, dashed over the top at Festubert in 1915. Pointless battle that nobody remembers. End of story. Not his fault, blame ... I don't know who. But I hope you're not all dash.'

'I ran away from home when I was fifteen,' he said. 'Does that count?'

They turned to walk back to the trains, and she took his arm. 'Hullo!' he said. He glanced ahead and saw distant figures watching them. 'What will the neighbours think?'

'They'll think what we both thought as soon as we saw each other on Kenny's train,' she said. 'Yum-yum, we thought. That's for me.'

'Oh,' Hackett said. 'Yes. I suppose that's true.'

She squeezed his arm. 'Men can be so slow,' she said. 'It's a wonder the race has survived.'

Prod Pedlow had borrowed a Bible. He sat in the shade of the train with Drunken Duncan, and tried to look up the part that Borodin had mentioned during tea on the way back from the village of the Skoptsi. 'Whose gospel was it?' he

251

asked. 'I've forgotten.'

'Matthew. I remember because I've got a cousin called Matthew. Brilliant opening bat. He hit the ball so hard it made holes in the boundary fence. Bound to play for England one day, everyone said so. But...' Duncan shrugged.

'But what?'

'Fell in love. French ambassador found him in bed with his wife, said the embassy was French territory and under French law he could kill him, it was justifiable homicide. Very nasty. Last I heard, Matthew was an assistant bank manager in Cape Town. Tragic.'

'Serve him right.' Pedlow was searching the pages for St Matthew. 'Anyway, it's only cricket.'

'You're an Ulster Prod,' Duncan said. 'You wouldn't know a cover drive from a dustbin lid.'

'Ah, here he is. Matthew.'

'You need chapter and verse. I can't remember what Borodin said.'

'I can. He said 1912 – chapter 19, verse 12. Big year, 1912. I was a chorister, the choir was processing around the church, and I was singing like a bird when my voice broke. Cracked. It fell two octaves in one breath. 1912. Turning-point for the nation. Here we are...' He read the verse. 'Bloody hell' he said bleakly, and handed the Bible to Duncan. 'Verse 12.'

Duncan read it in silence. *For there are some eunuchs, which were so born from their mother's womb: and there are some eunuchs, which were made eunuchs of men: and there be eunuchs, which have made themselves eunuchs for the kingdom of heaven's sake. He that is able to receive it, let him receive it.*

'That's only someone's opinion,' Duncan said. 'Who was it, anyway?'

'Jesus Christ,' Pedlow said. 'Preaching to the disciples. I suppose those chaps in the village thought that, if it got them into the kingdom of heaven, it was worth a swift chop.'

'We could show this to the squadron,' Duncan said. 'No. They still wouldn't believe us.'

'I wonder what a swift chop does to a chap's vocal cords? It might boost him up a couple of octaves.' Pedlow sprawled in the grass, propping himself on his elbows, and looked at the vastness of the sky and the spotless purity of its blue. 'Enough to get you into the heavenly choir. Not that it exists. That kind of mumbo-jumbo is all codswallop. But if you were an ignorant villager standing stark naked with a sharp knife in your hand, it might be enough to get you to de-bollock yourself. If you'd started having second thoughts, I mean.'

'Oh ... Christ on crutches.' Duncan had not been listening; he had been scanning the page opposite Matthew 19, 12. 'It gets worse,' he said. 'Listen. *And if thy hand or foot offend thee, cut them off, and cast them from thee: it is better for thee to enter into life halt or maimed, rather than having two hands or two feet to be cast into everlasting fire.'* He looked up. 'More friendly advice from the Son of God.'

'They wouldn't dare cut off my feet,' Pedlow said. 'I wouldn't stand for it.' Duncan yawned. 'Anyway, I outranked them,' Pedlow said. 'I was a Top Angel. Air Commodore, at least. Maybe Air Vice-Marshal.'

'Didn't stop your feet stinking. Another night

in that lousy hut and I'd have cut them off.'

'You can be very selfish sometimes, Dudders.'

'It's for your own good, Gerry. To keep you out of the everlasting fire. And I haven't finished.' Duncan's forefinger pressed the page. *'And if thine eye offend thee, pluck it out, and cast it from thee...* You can guess the rest. Keep a duff eye and you go straight to hell.'

Pedlow stood up and brushed bits of grass from his sleeves. 'They really believed it. I mean, we saw the knives and the blood and...' He squeezed his eyes shut as the memories returned. 'And the mutilations. Thank God Borodin and Lacey turned up. Those fanatics were capable of anything.' Duncan grunted. For a moment they were both silent, trying to forget the unforgettable. 'Bloody Russians,' Pedlow said. 'D'you fancy a beer?'

'Nothing against it in St Matthew,' Duncan said. They headed for The Dregs.

Hackett was restless. He wanted to send a signal to Mission H.Q. in Ekat, reporting his situation. Lacey's radio batteries were flat. Being recharged. Ready tomorrow. Well, send a cable. Telegraph lines ran alongside the track, so tap into them. No good, they'd been cut. Maybe by Nestor Makhno's men, in Warsaw.

There was nothing to be done. No train passed, in either direction. Hackett sat on the bottom step of his Pullman car and began to dislike this corner of Russia. Didn't hate it, there was nothing to hate, how could you hate *grass?* But he resented being dumped in the middle of this emptiness. From time to time a fly came wandering by, curious to taste his unusual sweat, and he let it take a look before he made a grab. It always got away. It was just a stupid fly, all buzz and no brains, and it won every time. He looked around and saw his squadron lying in the sun, shirts off, waiting for him to tell them what to do. He sent for the flight leaders, the adjutant and Lacey.

They met in his Pullman.

'It's forty miles round trip to Warsaw,' he said. 'Borodin won't be back tonight. I'm not waiting here to be shot at from dusk to dawn. We're leaving. We'll head back east, find somewhere to lie up, return here tomorrow.'

The adjutant didn't like the risk. Borodin might return earlier than expected, might have urgent intelligence, might need protection. He volunteered to remain. Not alone, obviously. Wragge suggested leaving Uncle and ten picked men. Oliphant said twenty would be better, with four Lewis guns. Then there was food. A squad that size had to eat. Alright, add a cook. And the medical sergeant, just in case. Perhaps a couple of *plennys*. Hackett cut short the discussion. 'You can keep the Marines and Kenny's train, Uncle:' he said. 'I'll take everybody else.'

'Excellent decision,' Brazier said.

'You're in your element, aren't you?' Wragge said. 'You'll command a little local war. Enormous fun.'

'Look at it this way. We'll be shooting them before they can start shooting you.'

'Russians can't shoot straight,' Lacey said.

They looked at him with surprise. 'I thought you were here to take the minutes,' Oliphant said.

'Count Borodin told me. He said that Russians have never had much faith in rifles. They believe in fighting with the sword, the lance and the dagger.'

'How quaint,' Wragge said. 'But it won't win this war.'

'Somebody must win,' Oliphant said.

'Not necessarily. Maybe they'll both lose. All die from exhaustion.'

'That's all.' Hackett stood up. 'We'll move in an hour.'

As they left the Pullman, they heard the *plennys* singing. They were standing around the mound of the mass grave, and their hymn had a depth and strength not found in Western choirs. The boom and rumble of the singing contained a sadness that went far beyond these victims of war. Here was the voice of Russians who grieved for their whole country. While they sang, nobody in the squadron moved. Then the hymn ended.

'That's one thing these jokers are good at,' Oliphant said. 'They can sing in tune. After that, they couldn't pour piss out of a boot if the instructions were printed on the sole.'

The trains moved out, and Brazier spent the night with the Marines, waiting for trouble that never came. He was not unhappy. He had been soldiering long enough to know that there was always more trouble on the way. The supply was inexhaustible. In times of uncertainty, while other men worried about the future, Brazier was certain that it would always bring problems that could be tackled only by high explosive and cold steel. Someone, somewhere, would always need his skills. That was a comforting thought.

5

Count Borodin took a pony without a saddle. He told himself that no peasant could afford a saddle, and he was a peasant. Big mistake.

After five miles, the base of his spine ached from bouncing on the pony's backbone. He tried sitting on his hat, but it was no better. He pressed his thighs against the pony and raised himself and took the pressure off his spine. The relief was good, but the constant effort soon made his thighs ache. He tried sitting sidesaddle, and liked it, but the pony didn't. It swung its head and tried to nip his legs. He cursed it, not as a peasant would but in the elegant language of the Imperial Court, which meant nothing to the animal, so it stopped and listened. 'You're useless,' Borodin said in English. 'You're cutting me in half and you're as slow as cold treacle.' He got off and massaged his thighs, and began walking. The pony munched grass and watched him go.

Soon it would be dusk. He had no need to think about his route; he followed the railway track. He thought about what he was doing. What he was trying to do.

Seeking out intelligence was new to him. He had served with his regiment until it was virtually destroyed by death or desertion. He had a spell in the Imperial Air Service until it ran out of aero-

257

planes, and then he got a position on the staff at supreme army headquarters. He witnessed a different scale of carnage there.

The death-blow was struck when Tsar Nicholas II, appointed by God to be Supreme Ruler of the Holy Russian Empire and therefore Head of the Armed Forces, sacked the C-in-C of the Army and took over operational command. The saying goes: *A fish rots from its head*. Borodin saw the Russian Army rot from the Tsar down, until the soldiers gave up and walked home and abandoned their war.

When he was a boy, Borodin had often lived on the fringe of the Imperial family: such was the accident of his birth and the fact that Nicholas was in love with Russian music – Rimsky-Korsakov; Balakirev; the boy's father, Aleksandr Borodin; Tchaikovsky: a golden age. The Tsar's idea of heaven was watching *Sleeping Beauty* from his box at the Imperial Conservatory.

Borodin knew him as a mild young man who liked playing with dogs and gathering mushrooms. When he was twenty-five he still enjoyed a game of hide-and-seek. He had no curiosity about the outside world and absolutely no ambition to be Tsar. 'What am I going to do?' he asked when his father died, and he never found a happy answer. He adored his wife more than his people, let her dominate him, scold him and urge him to be a second Peter the Great. Perhaps he put himself in charge of winning the war in order to please her. In so doing, he condemned them both, and their children, to death; but not before he had killed another million or more Russian troops.

So: no room for Intelligence in Borodin's time on the Staff. Now he wondered just what he would do in this little town renamed Warsaw, how he would discover whether or not it was in Nestor Makhno's hands and how he could escape without getting shot. Even in these rags, he didn't look like a peasant. Too tall, too erect. He rubbed dirt on his face and neck, and walked like a ploughman, feet well apart, knees bent, a bit of a stoop, elbows out. Night fell. Walking like that, in the dark, grew more difficult. He often stumbled, partly because he was tired. And every step he took was a step he would have to take again when he came back. Perhaps this adventure was not such a good idea.

The moon came up, which helped, and at last he saw a light, which was very welcome. It was a farmhouse, and the light was a fire. A woman, not young, was bagging potatoes by the light of a fire, and she was not glad to see him. He stopped a good distance away, told her he was alone, and asked how far it was to town.

'Walking?' She had a knife, and made sure he saw it. 'An hour. Maybe less.'

An hour was three miles. Maybe only two. At once he felt better. 'You grow potatoes? Sell me a sack of potatoes.' A peasant bringing potatoes into town: nobody would look twice at him. Then he remembered: it was two miles. Maybe three. 'Make it half a sack,' he said.

They argued over the price and he paid more than they were worth. 'You'll get double that in town,' she said. 'If you're lucky.' And laughed. Or cackled.

About an hour later, maybe more, maybe less,

Borodin slouched along the railway tracks into Warsaw. His shoulders ached. Half a sack of potatoes weighed more than he had believed possible.

Ahead, the lights of the station glowed. No sounds. No trains, no people. An efficient spy would infiltrate and find out why the town was dead. How? Wake up someone and ask him? That was absurd. His legs were stiff. He saw a shadow that was blacker than the night. A brick wall. He sat and rested against it, holding the sack between his knees, and told himself to think harder while he rested his eyes.

What woke him was the moving of the sack. He grabbed it before it could escape and it was made of skin. He had a man by the throat. The thief squirmed and spluttered and tried to claw at his fingers, but Borodin tightened his grip. The struggle stopped. He stood up and took the man up with him. Took him easily. In the faint light of the moon he saw that the man was a boy. He let go of the throat and held him by the arm. The boy coughed until he was wheezing for breath, and got his breath back and coughed some more.

'Feel better?' Borodin asked. 'I apologize for my behaviour, but you did rather ask for it.'

The boy took a huge breath and slowly released it. He wiped his eyes with his spare hand. 'Feel like shit,' he croaked. The voice was young. Thirteen, maybe fourteen. 'Christ ... look at you. Never saw nobody as tall as you before. Let me sit down. Ain't goin' nowhere.'

They both sat. 'You wanted my potatoes,' Borodin said. The words sounded dishonest. A genuine peasant wouldn't say that. The boy grunted.

260

'You only had to ask,' Borodin said, and fished a big potato from the bag. 'Here.' The boy took it, smelled it, and began eating it. 'It's raw,' Borodin said. 'Got another?' the boy asked. Borodin gave him another potato. He ate with his mouth open. For a while the only sound in the night was the work of teeth and saliva on potato.

Eventually he belched, a long gut-rumbling statement. 'God help your digestive system,' Borodin said. 'What's wrong with this town? Don't they feed you?'

'Got another?' He accepted another potato and put it inside his shirt. 'I saw you sneakin' along the tracks. You don't belong here. You talk like nobody from here. If I told Makhno's men they'd shoot you.'

'Yes. But you wouldn't get any more potatoes.' The boy thought about that. 'You help me,' Borodin said, 'and I'll take you to a place where you'll get three hot meals a day.' More silence. 'Fried eggs for breakfast,' Borodin said. 'Beef stew at midday. Lamb chops for supper. Hot bread with everything.'

The boy was in tears, crying for food. He told Borodin what he wanted to know. Nestor Makhno's men had taken the town, killed half the people, looted everywhere. Vodka, vodka, vodka. They were waiting for a train to rob, and getting angry because no trains arrived, so they went on killing and looting and drinking. They were all drunk now. That's why the town was quiet. They'd drunk themselves stupid. Tomorrow they'd wake up and feel even worse and kill some more.

Borodin asked why they hadn't killed the boy.

261

He said it was because his father was station-master and they needed him to stop the train they wanted to rob. He pointed to the station lights. His father was there, guarded by a Makhno man who was drunk out of his skull, like all the rest.

Borodin had an impossible idea. 'Go and fetch your father,' he said. 'Tell him I am an officer in General Denikin's Volunteer Army. If he comes with me he will be safe and get three hot meals a day, like you.' The boy thought about it. 'And the rest of these potatoes too,' Borodin said.

'Where's your army?'

'Fifteen miles away.' More like twenty.

'Lamb chops. What they taste like?'

'Twice as good as chicken.' The boy's gut rumbled some more. 'Fetch your father. Go now. We can't wait.'

The boy went, as silent as a shadow. He didn't weigh much. It was easy to move like that when you were just skin and bone.

In less than five minutes he was back with his father. The man was thin and not much taller than his son, but Borodin was dismayed to see that he was lame, dragging his left leg. Even walking from the station was an effort. 'We must hurry,' the man said. 'It's dangerous here.'

'Fifteen miles. I can't carry you.'

'Pump trolley.' He pointed into the darkness. 'Please. Hurry.'

The trolley was a small, lightweight truck with a seesaw pump action to make it go. The boy jumped up and worked the pump, and the trolley screamed as if stabbed. 'Get grease, get oil, butter, anything,' Borodin said. The boy jumped down and ran. 'He knows what to get,' his father said. Twenty minutes later they pumped the trolley more or less silently out of town. Borodin felt exhilarated.

'Lamb chops,' the stationmaster said. 'I have never eaten them. Twice as good as chicken, the boy says?'

'Your son is very smart,' Borodin said. 'And the harder we pump, the sooner you can have breakfast.'

6

The first bomb fell in the town square of Warsaw and killed an ox.

The ox was one of six that Makhno's men had looted from different owners. If the owners protested or resisted, Makhno's men shot them, knifed them, clubbed them. Sometimes they murdered them when they didn't resist; such was the appeal of an anarchist movement: total freedom! The oxen were kept in the town square. Nobody fed them. Why bother? Makhno had plans to slaughter them for a grand feast. The bomb was only a 25-pounder, but the unlucky ox just happened to be standing a yard away from the point of impact. The other five oxen panicked and ran. It was a small stampede, but Warsaw was a small town, and five tons of hungry, angry beef make a formidable rampage. A second bomb went through the roof of a large stables where Makhno kept his horses, and started a second stampede. By now, bombs were going off like Chinese firecrackers all over town and everyone panicked. When the Camels came out of nowhere and strafed the mob, they ran. The battle for Warsaw had been fought and won in three minutes.

Hackett went up to five hundred feet and took a long look at the aeroplanes criss-crossing the streaming mob, and he fired a red signal flare. It was the signal to quit. Already the town was emptying. No point in bombing empty buildings. And the panic in the streets was feeding on itself. A few late bombs flowered here and there, and then all the Nines saw his flare and stopped work.

The other Camels came up to join him. He fished out the town plan that the stationmaster had sketched for him, showing the main buildings occupied by Makhno's men. Some were on fire. Or maybe not. The plan was upside-down. He held the joystick between his knees and turned the paper, trying to match it with the streets, and the windstream snatched it from his fingers. Oh well, he thought. *Nichevo.*

There was no ground fire, nobody stood and stared up, everyone was infected by the rush to escape. The bombs alone couldn't explain such panic. It had to be the aeroplanes. They fell on the town like the hounds of hell, raced around at ungodly speed, spat fire and killed. Of course men panicked and ran. Sudden terror knew no other answer.

Hackett fired a green flare and his squadron came together again, Camels leading Nines in the usual arrowheads. They made a leisurely approach, losing height until they roared through the drifting smoke of the town at fifty feet and

264

terrified the anarchists all over again, just as their hangovers were beginning to plead for rest. It was like driving sheep. The squadron circled and did it again, driving them deep into the countryside. Then they flew away. Twenty miles ahead they found a relatively flat stretch of steppe to land on.

'Golly, didn't they run!' Maynard said to Jessop. 'They must be awfully fit.'

'I'll tell you why.' Jessop put his arm around Maynard's shoulders. 'They play a lot of rugger. And cricket in the summer.' Maynard wriggled free. 'That's all tosh,' he said. Jessop looked offended. 'I have it on Borodin's word. He opened the batting for Petrograd Old Boys.' Maynard walked away. 'Average of sixty-nine point four,' Jessop called. 'His straight drive was notorious. He killed three umpires in one match.'

The Pullman trains waited outside the station while the Marines went into the town. Brazier and the Marines were ready to fight but they found silence and smoke and dead men littering the streets. Nobody could tell if they were bandits or townsfolk. Some looked as if they had been trampled to death. The number of half-starved dogs poking their noses into the bodies was impressive.

'Bloody shambles, sir,' the Marine sergeant said.

'Family squabble, sergeant. The Russians can clean it up. They've had plenty of practice. Here...' Brazier gave him a Very pistol. 'You may have the privilege.'

A green flare soared into the sky. The trains pulled into the station and the *plennys* got to work on the coal dump and the water tower. The stationmaster and his son took one look at the town and asked to stay on the train. Lacey made them kitchen hands. They were happiest when close to food.

The pilots lay about, sunbathing. Somebody saw rabbits and everyone went hunting. Revolvers banged; nobody hit anything. 'Elusive is the word,' Tommy Hopton said. 'That's the second thing they taught me at Eton. Rabbits can be jolly elusive.'

'What was the first thing?' Rex Dextry asked.

'Never be rude to the servants.'

They went back to sunbathing. Eventually the trains arrived and the ground crews got to work, dismantling the wings from the aeroplanes. Back to normal.

7

The journey took five days.

Nothing could persuade the locomotive drivers to go faster than twenty miles an hour, and they were more comfortable at fifteen. 'This is in case they have to stop suddenly,' Borodin explained. And they often stopped. Word had spread that the line was safe and expresses thundered past while Merlin Squadron stood in a siding.

The pilots didn't mind. If they could see a farm, they gave a couple of *plennys* a bunch of rouble notes and sent them to buy fresh food: eggs, milk, chickens, dried fruit, potatoes. Once they came back with two fat lambs, very much alive and

266

immediately popular with the squadron. Rex Dextry wanted one to be kept as a mascot. He was arguing with Jessop about which lamb had more charm and friskiness. Jessop pointed to the one he liked and the *plenny* holding it picked up a stone and whacked it on the head, hard. Its legs folded. The other lamb bleated with fright. 'I say, I say!' Jessop cried. The *plenny* misunderstood him and smashed the other lamb's skull. He looked up, expecting approval.

The whole appalling episode spoiled the day. 'It's barbaric,' Dextry said. 'Medieval.'

'My brother farms on the Cotswolds,' Jessop said, 'and all I can say is, it wouldn't happen there. That's all I can say. And another thing—'

'The damn *plenny* smiled at us,' Dextry said. 'Wham. Bam. Smiled.'

'Perfectly normal,' Borodin said. 'He did what he thought you wanted. To him, they were meat, not pets.'

'Well, I don't want any part of it,' Jessop said. 'That's all I can say.'

Lacey made sure the spring lamb ended up in the chef's kitchen. 'I daren't put it on the menu,' he told Borodin.

'Leave it until tomorrow. Make a casserole and call it veal. They'll scoff it down.' He was right. The pilots were young, with little room for gloom. The slaughter of the innocents faded from memory faster than Bellamy's burial. There were more important things to think about. Lacey had found a croquet set in the stores on 'B' Flight's train. It was in a crate stencilled 'War Department – Lightning Conductors One Dozen'.

267

He showed it to the adjutant. 'Nobody ordered lightning conductors,' he said.

Brazier grunted.

Lacey fingered the lettering. 'It's not exactly a military item, is it?'

'That's because you don't know the War Department. Wheels within wheels, my boy. Codenames hide new weapons. "Lightning conductors" could mean, for instance, "Secret Tactical Smokescreen".'

Lacey took a croquet mallet from the crate. 'We could burn this, and see if it smokes.'

'More probably it's a cock-up in Supplies,' Brazier said.

'I'll send a signal to Mission H.Q. Received one crate alleged lightning conductors in fact containing three elephant guns await further orders. That should baffle them.'

Brazier shrugged. 'Just don't involve me. I don't share your taste for confusion.'

'Not confusion. Tactical smokescreen.'

After dinner, he showed the croquet set to the Camel pilots. They were enthusiastic for the game. Practice on the carpet of The Dregs began at once. Mallets swung and balls ricocheted. Nobody's legs were safe. Even Susan Perry – an honorary member of the Mess – took cover behind her chair.

'Let's you and me go and inspect your casualties,' Hackett said to her. 'And leave these maniacs to batter each other.'

They walked and she did not take his arm. He was relieved, he didn't want the squadron watching them stroll like that. Then he began to wonder. Maybe she was being fickle. Women were fickle, well-known fact, everyone said so.

She poked him in the ribs. 'Relax your shoulders,' she said. 'They're up around your ears.'

He let his shoulders slump. 'Now what?'

'Wave your arms. And whistle. Can you sing?'

He whistled the opening bars of 'Waltzing Matilda', and waved an arm in time with it, and sang the next lines: '...*under the shade of a coolibah tree, and he sang as he watched and waited while his billy boiled...*' He stopped. 'Feel free to applaud.'

'You've got a voice like a bucket of frogs,' she said kindly.

'Yes? That's a compliment where I come from. We'd sooner listen to a bucket of frogs than wrestle a mad kangaroo.'

She laughed, and took his arm. 'Give me your hat.' He took off his cap. 'Now you're not the C.O. I'm not going to marry the C.O., but I might just marry you, whatever your name is. What is it?'

'James. Are we going to get married?'

'There's nothing more certain.'

'Good God. Well, I'm glad you told me.'

They talked of other things: his boyhood in Australia, her life at Cambridge. Music, songs, hits from the shows. Lacey's amazing ability to supply the Mess gramophone with records of the hits. 'I asked him how he does it,' she said, 'and he said, "I breathe through the loopholes." What does that mean?'

'It's bullshit,' he said. 'Australian word. It means...' She widened her eyes. It was a look he was learning to recognize. 'Oh. You know what it means. Doesn't matter. Tell me this. Are we really

269

engaged? Or was that just…' He ran out of words.

'Bullshit?'

'No, no. I hope not.' He thought of several answers, some of them romantic, phrases he had never spoken. 'Quite the opposite,' he said.

'Do you want to be engaged?'

'Well, it might settle the minds of the squadron. Stop the gossip.'

'Then let's do it. As long as we both know that it's just for the benefit of the squadron.' That silenced him. 'You may kiss your fiancée,' she said, so he did. That wasn't for the squadron. That quite definitely was not for the squadron. Bloody hell, he thought. This is a girl in a million. They walked on.

A hospital train trundled past, heading for Ekat, and stopped a quarter of a mile from them.

'Casualties from Tsaritsyn, I expect,' Hackett said. 'Do you want a closer look?'

'Not at what's inside,' she said. 'They're all the same. No dressings, no painkillers, no antiseptic, no drugs and one doctor too tired to amputate.'

They watched from a distance. Men were carrying corpses from the train and piling them beside the track as if they were stacking cut timber. Hackett counted thirty bodies and gave up.

'Gangrene,' she said. 'Can you smell it? Like rotten fruit. Slightly sweet but also a yellowy stink. Plenty of dysentery, too. Smells like a broken sewer.' She sniffed the air. 'Malaria, too, probably. That can be the real killer. Dead in a day sometimes.'

The men climbed aboard the train and it pulled away.

'What's the point of a hospital train if they all die?' Hackett said.

'It's a Russian joke,' she said. 'They call it irony.'

Lacey and Borodin sheltered in the kitchen while the passion for indoor croquet burned itself out.

'It will be over in fifteen minutes,' Lacey said. 'Fighter pilots have a low threshold of boredom. Have you seen what they read? Cowboy stories. Penny dreadfuls. Ripping yarns. I speak of those who can read.'

'I was a fighter pilot,' Borodin said. 'I read all of Tolstoy. *War and Peace* twice.'

'Heavens above. Don't tell these hooligans. Your reputation will be in tatters.' Lacey found an apple and began peeling it. 'How can we pass the time?'

'I could teach you more Russian phrases. *Von!* is useful. It means "Get away!" *Poyedz* is train. *Nye refuganski poyedz* might help one day. It means "Not a refugee train". What else? You might hear *Bozhe Tsarya Khrani* at parties. That's "God save the Tsar"'.

'He's dead.'

'I know. Everyone knows. But some people choose not to believe it. *Prazdik* is a good word. It's a celebration. This C.O. should throw a *prazdik*. He's become remote. He makes the squadron nervous.'

'It's the curse of promotion.'

'Time for a *prazdik*, then. It cures all ills.'

They ate the apple. The noise in The Dregs subsided and they went back. The pilots were

271

searching for lost playing cards. 'We've got fifty-two but five are jokers,' Jessop said. 'Can you play poker with five jokers?'

Wragge found the last croquet ball and gave it to Lacey. 'We've formed a team to play the rest,' he said. 'We are the Public School Wanderers and the rest are Serfs.'

'Abolished in 1861.' Lacey said. 'No serfs in Russia.'

'Not that it did them any good,' Borodin said. He was talking to himself as much as to Lacey, but his words were out of character. There was a sudden silence.

'Don't stop there, old chap,' Dextry said.

'It all depends how you define freedom,' Borodin said. 'Yes, the serfs were emancipated, nobody owned them. Good. Now they were peasants, free to survive if they could. Not so good.'

'I bet they got shat upon,' Jessop said.

'They were given land. The Crown had bought it. The peasants, in turn, had to pay back the Crown. Six per cent a year, every year for forty-nine years. Six per cent is a very heavy rate. And the land's value was always calculated above its market value, often twice as much, so the peasants could never earn enough to make their payments, and they fell deeper into debt.'

'I told you they got shat upon,' Jessop said, pleased at his own cleverness.

'Forty-nine years,' Dextry said. 'How many peasants live to be forty-nine?'

'Got it!' Maynard said. He held up the ace of spades. 'Now we can play.'

'Let's leave them to it,' Lacey said. He and

Borodin went out. 'You surprise me,' Lacey said. 'I didn't realize the Russian nobility took such an interest in the soil.'

'We don't. I read about it at Cambridge. People kept asking me what Russia was like, so I looked it up in the *Encyclopaedia Britannica.* The 1911 edition.'

'Ah yes,' Lacey said. 'By far the best. It's very sound on the Tudor Protestant sects. Especially in the north of England.'

CATCH THE WAR WHILE IT'S HOT

1

Hackett awoke suddenly. It was too early, not much more than dawn. He felt tired, and angry because he was tired: what was wrong with his body? Couldn't it give him a decent night's sleep? He had a flickering memory of a dream and then it was lost. It left a taste of a struggle with a great problem. What problem? It had gone. But it had been urgent. How could it vanish so fast when it had mattered so much?

He got out of bed, massaged his eyes and squinted at the steppe. It reminded him of his days in the Navy, being on watch when the dawn came up and painted the ocean. Now it was working the same trick on this prairie and turning it ... not gold. Not yellow either. And blonde was all wrong too. 'Who cares?' he said. He got dressed quickly and pulled on his flying boots and went for a walk in this indescribable landscape while the colours lasted.

The air tasted splendidly fresh. He breathed deeply, felt stronger and stepped out, heading away from the train. The grass was wet and his boots were soon drenched. Songbirds were busy all around him. Well, they would have been busy anyway, but he felt better to know that he had company. When he paused to look back, the trains were just a thin brown strip on the skyline. It was good to be free from all those duties. He turned and walked on, and nearly walked into a goat.

It saw him first and bolted, braying a warning. Other goats answered. He headed for them, out of curiosity, and came across the herd. They crowded together and stared. 'Morning, chaps,' he said. That was when the boy stood up.

Or perhaps he was a girl. He or she was wearing a long robe with a hood that hid the face. A small child, ten or eleven perhaps. The robe had been made for someone much bigger. It brushed the ground and the sleeves were doubled back. Good for sleeping in, probably. 'Hullo,' he said. 'I'm James.' Damnfool thing to say to a Russian kid.

Then the hood got pushed back. Long hair, black and tangled, reached to the shoulders. That proved nothing. Plenty of small boys had long hair. Hackett saw more, and whether it belonged to a boy or a girl didn't matter. The face was severely disfigured. It was as if a child's face had been caught in a trap so that all the features were squashed. One eye was half-shut. The nose was shortened. The mouth was not where it should be, dragged sideways by a twisted chin. Hackett forced a smile. 'These must be your goats,' he said. Gibberish. But he had to say something.

He dropped the smile. The kid's expression hadn't changed. Maybe it couldn't change. 'O.K. if I sit down?' No answer. He sat down. It meant getting his ass wet but a wet ass was nothing when he looked at the wreckage the kid had for a face. 'This is your job, then,' he said. 'I bet you're good at it. I bet you're the best damn goatherd for miles. I wish I'd brought you some food. Bread, cheese, fruit, cold chicken. You look as if a good meal would help.' Help? Nothing could help save this kid. He was born to be pitied. 'What can I do to brighten up your day? There must be something.' Slowly, cautiously, the kid sat down. 'Hey! I can whistle. Used to be good, when I was your age.' You were never his age, you dummy. He whistled. 'What Shall We Do with the Drunken Sailor?' because it was the only tune he could think of. He threw in a lot of trills and swoops, and finished breathless.

'Well, the goats liked it,' he said. And the kid seemed to have relaxed a bit. 'Look, I can't stay. I have all this funny money, roubles, no use to me, I want you to have it.' He reached forward and dropped a handful of notes in the kid's lap.

That hurt. The kid jumped as if stung and the notes went flying. Some fell near a couple of goats, who nosed them and might have started chewing if Hackett hadn't rescued them. 'What's wrong?' he said. 'Take it, kid. You need it more than I do.' He collected the notes and offered them. 'Buy yourself a treat.'

They stood and stared. Then the kid made a decision. He plucked the biggest rouble note from the bunch, went to the goats, found one and dragged it to Hackett. The message was obvious. Hackett had bought a goat.

He laughed and shook his head. The robe had a pocket, so he tucked the rest of the money in there. The kid released the goat. Then something unexpected happened, something that made

Hackett's heart give a little kick of delight. The kid took Hackett's hand.

Now Hackett was led through the herd. The kid named each goat and glanced up to see if this was the one he wanted to buy; until Hackett realized that this was the only way the kid would take the money, so he chose the smallest, probably the youngest goat. The kid picked it up and gave it to him. Honour was satisfied. They shook hands and Hackett was pleased at the firm grip. 'Good luck, chum,' he said, and bent and did something he had never in his life done before to anybody. He kissed the top of the boy's head.

The little goat seemed content to be carried. Hackett, striding away, blinking hard, knew that he had been close to tears. Why? Because a small Russian child had a broken face? What a strange encounter.

When he reached the train he went to Susan Perry's compartment. She was dressed, and brushing her hair.

'I went for a walk and a kid in charge of some goats sold me this one,' he said. 'The kid – he, she, I couldn't tell which, let's say he – he didn't *sell* it, I picked it out. The boy was ... he looked as if a horse had stepped on his face. Two horses.'

She let the goat suck her fingers. 'A mascot. All the best squadrons have a mascot.'

'I had a good idea while I was out. Squadron party tonight. To celebrate our engagement.'

'Yes, certainly.' The goat brayed as if it agreed too, and they laughed. 'Don't make a speech, James. Just bask in their envy.'

'If you say so.' He scratched the goat behind the

277

ears. 'I'd better give this animal to someone.' He didn't want to leave.

'Try the adjutant, he'll know what to do. It's probably somewhere in King's Regs.'

He moved to the door and then turned back. 'I can say anything to you, can't I? Anything at all.'

She looked mildly surprised. 'Yes, you can.'

'I'll get used to it. Never had much practice. But then ... I never knew anyone like you. Pure luck. Luck is everything, isn't it?'

'It helps. I'm glad a horse didn't tread on your face when you were young.'

'An encouraging thought to start the day.'

'I suppose I'm out of practice too. But then, I never had anyone like you to practise on.'

He went to The Dregs, which was busy with breakfast. 'Squadron mascot,' he said. 'And I have an announcement.' He stroked the goat's ears and it brayed happily. 'I'm engaged to be married.' He handed the goat to the adjutant.

'Marriage isn't allowed on active service,' Wragge said. 'Anyway, the goat is far too young.'

'I knew a Canadian in France called Orson,' Dextry said. 'And believe it or not, his surname was Cart.'

'That's nothing,' Jessop said. 'We had an adjutant called Mudd.'

Hackett poured himself some coffee and waited.

'Why shouldn't a Canadian be called Orson?' Maynard said. 'It's not an unusual name over there.'

'He was married,' Dextry said. 'So she'd married an Orson Cart.'

'That alters everything,' Wragge said. 'I

278

withdraw my objection. Goats are in.'

'I know I'm going to regret this,' Brazier said to Jessop, 'but what's the connection with an adjutant called Mudd?'

'Oh ... chaps used to phone him up and say, "Is your name Mudd?" It's a play on words, you see. A sort of pun. They thought it was frightfully clever. They were usually sozzled, of course.'

'Nothing to do with the commanding officer's engagement, then.'

'Um ... on the whole, no.'

'Totally irrelevant, in fact.'

'Don't rub it in, Uncle. I wish I'd never mentioned it.'

Lacey came in. 'Mentioned what?'

Jessop took a large bite of toast. 'Crunch crunch crunch,' he said. 'And don't try to deny it.'

Brazier turned to the C.O. 'The floor is yours, sir.'

'I'm engaged to Flight Lieutenant Perry,' Hackett said. 'We intend to marry as soon as possible. We'll give a celebration party for the squadron tonight.'

Brazier led the applause. 'By a happy coincidence,' Lacey said, 'I found several cases of Russian champagne in the stores.' Much louder applause. 'Ideal for what Count Borodin calls a *prazdik*, which is a Russian beano with all the stops pulled out. Should I invite the whole squadron to the *prazdik*, sir?'

'Of course. We'll have a bloody great *prazdik*.' He relaxed. He was a squadron leader, he was engaged, he was popular. 'Breakfast!' he said.

Lacey waited until the C.O. had finished eating, and then murmured: 'Fresh signals from the Military Mission. Marked confidential.'

Hackett wiped his mouth and gave the napkin to Chef. 'Damn good scoff,' he said. 'More strength to your elbow.' To Lacey: 'Lead on.'

Wragge watched them go. 'Getting engaged has done that man a power of good,' he said. 'He should do it more often. Well, another day of toil awaits us, so we might as well start. Who has the cards?'

Fifteen minutes later he was holding a handsome full house, aces on jacks, when Lacey interrupted the game. Meeting in the C.O's compartment, now. Flight leaders, adjutant and Count Borodin.

'You have just robbed me of enough roubles to stuff an ox,' Wragge said. 'And with what's left over you could have stuffed Daddy Maynard too.'

'I'm unstuffable,' Maynard said. 'I'm a Man of Steel.' But by then, Wragge had left. Still, Maynard was pleased. He wouldn't have said that a month ago.

The C.O. was full of fizz. 'All here?' he said. 'I've spoken to Borodin, he'll be back in a minute. Don't sit down, this won't last that long. The war's on the move at last. Denikin has attacked and his armies have broken the Reds on all fronts. He's advancing like a tidal wave. The British Military Mission has moved out of Ekat. It's now at Taganrog, so that's where we're heading, lickety-split. Our orders are to join Denikin's spearhead and knock hell out of the Bolos. It's our chance to...' He stopped when Borodin came in. 'I asked the count to galvanize the loco-

280

motive crews. I want to see us barrelling down the track to Taganrog, not limping along at twenty miles an hour. Did they agree?'

'Not as such,' Borodin said. 'No.'

'Double pay? You told them?'

'Yes. Their answer was that twenty-five is the absolute safe maximum. They said the locomotives are overdue for servicing. They wouldn't budge.'

'I'll budge them. They're lazy buggers and they want an easy life. Adjutant, put a man with a revolver on the footplate of each locomotive. I'll take charge of the Marines' train. We'll go first. We set the pace. The rest of you – keep up. We're going to catch this war while it's still hot. All clear? Good. Carry on.'

They left, except for Wragge.

'I'm glad to see you firing on all cylinders,' Wragge said. 'You were beginning to look like Griffin Mark Two, eating broken glass for breakfast.'

'Oh...' The idea made Hackett chuckle. 'I wasn't as bad as that, was I? Anyway, I've got a grip on this job now. I'm going to be busy, so can you organize this *prazdik* for me?'

'Of course.'

'Make it memorable. Hackett's *prazdik*. Give the whole damn squadron something to cheer its socks off about. Can you see my revolver? It's lying around here somewhere... Ah. Thanks.'

2

Getting three trains on the move, none crowding

the one in front, none falling far behind, was a process that could not be rushed. Hackett stood behind the driver and the stoker on the Marines' train and urged them to work harder. He found the cord for the whistle and gave a few blasts. It didn't improve the speed but it made him feel better. He was in the lead, where the C.O. should be.

Meanwhile, the rest of the squadron had little to do.

Lacey was in his radio room with Sergeant Stevens, the medic. 'It's none of my business,' Stevens said, 'but that verse which you read so movingly at the funerals of the C.O. and Air Mechanic Henderson. Did you write it for the occasion?'

'A sombre ceremony. I thought something to boost the spirits... Yes, I was responsible. Shall I make some tea?'

'How did it begin? *Now God be thanked...*'

'*From this day to the ending of the world.*' Lacey busied himself with the Primus stove. 'Is Fortnum's Black Blend alright?'

'Yes. You pinched it, didn't you? From Rupert Brooke.' Stevens waited, but Lacey was concentrating hard on getting the stove going. 'And later you had a line, *Was there a man dismayed?* That's definitely Tennyson. "Charge of the Light Brigade".' Still Lacey fussed with the Primus. 'And your splendid ending, *Land of our birth, we pledge to thee,*' Stevens said. 'A masterstroke. Rudyard Kipling must be proud of it.'

At last Lacey turned to him. 'I'm out of milk I'm afraid. War is hell, isn't it?'

'You wouldn't be the first. Every writer steals.

You just did it more thoroughly than most. You pinched bits from all over and tacked them together.'

Lacey screwed up his face and stared at the empty steppe drifting by. 'Not stealing. I adapted. Some of those poets are fairly second-grade, you know. I like to think I enhanced their work.'

Stevens found that funny. 'You certainly enhanced that funeral. Compared with you, the Bible came in a poor second.'

Lacey returned to his Primus. 'Brooke, Tennyson, Kipling' he said. 'Not the reading of the average sergeant in the Medical Corps. Where did you go to school?'

'Winchester. Disgusting food, medieval plumbing, excellent library. And before you ask, I never wanted a commission. For reasons too tedious to explain.'

The kettle began to boil. 'I have a lemon,' Lacey said. 'Lemon is actually better than milk.'

'I may die,' Stevens said. 'The Medical Corps is permanently exposed to disease. If I do, will you enhance my funeral?'

'Child's play,' Lacey sliced the lemon. 'All it takes is a raging talent.'

After about five miles, the locomotive crew had nudged the speed up to twenty-three miles an hour. The gauge was calibrated in kilometres, which meant Hackett had to do some mental arithmetic. Divide by three and multiply by two. The reckoning was a bit rough-and-ready, but it told Hackett they weren't beating twenty-five. Probably not even touching it. This train wasn't running, it was sleepwalking. Its crew needed to be roused. Hackett knew he could do it. He had enough enthusiasm for all of them.

He smiled. He grinned, until it hurt. He rapped the speed gauge and made up! up! up! gestures. He slapped the driver on the back, sang 'Waltzing Matilda,' not that they understood, they could scarcely hear him above the din of the engine. He stood beside the stoker and applauded every shovelful of coal the man threw into the fire. He pointed urgently forward, he grinned and he nodded. They watched him warily. All foreigners were mad. This one acted crazy.

Hackett hid his irritation. He knew they had problems. The driver moved slowly: his right leg was lame. He was old and thin and his hands trembled on the controls. The stoker coughed every few minutes and sometimes brought up blood. An accident had taken two fingers from his left hand. What was left made a hook instead of a grip on the shovel. So – not the best crew in the world. But that was no reason to sleepwalk to Taganrog. 'Faster! Faster!' Hackett roared, with a comradely grin, and rapped the gauge. 'Up, up, up!'

3

Some of the bomber crews had joined the poker school in The Dregs. The game somehow failed to excite anyone. The cards had been given to Tommy Hopton to deal when Chef brought in a fresh pot of coffee. Hopton used the pause to say,

'I'll show you chaps a brilliant trick. This will make your eyes pop out.' He made a fan of the cards, held it face down, and said to Jessop, 'Take a card. Any card at all.' Jessop made a small performance of almost choosing, rejecting, frowning hard, finally picking a card. 'Don't let me see it,' Hopton said. 'It's the eight of spades.' Jessop said. Hopton hurled the pack at his head, missed, and hit Maynard's face just as he picked up the pot, which was very hot, and he sprayed coffee over the table, and especially over the cards. That ended the poker. Jessop got the blame. 'I didn't have the eight of spades at all,' he protested. Hopton scoffed: 'Of course you didn't. I knew that. You had the queen of clubs.' Jessop shrugged. 'Did I? I can't remember.' Dextry stopped picking up sodden cards and said to Hopton, 'If you knew Jessop was lying, why did you chuck the pack at him?' Hopton was defiant. 'It's a matter of the ethos of *léger de main*. You wouldn't understand.'

Now there was nothing to do. Nothing to read. Borodin had the only newspaper, and it was in Russian.

Wragge sprawled in a chair and watched him, and wondered what was so interesting in the dense columns of type. Yards of tripe, probably. Did the Russians eat tripe? Chef would know. Not that it mattered. 'Count,' he said. 'I've been thinking about what you told us. The peasants and taxes and so on. What a rotten life they have.'

'They got shat upon,' Jessop said bitterly. 'From a great height.' He felt badly about being blamed for the hot coffee.

'My point is, it wouldn't happen in England.'

Wragge said. 'They'd kick up a fuss, and Parliament would pass a law, or something. So why do your chaps put up with it?'

'Their toil is appalling, I agree,' Borodin said. 'But look at the holidays. Very generous. Nobody works on the holy days of the church, and they amount to nearly one-third of the year.'

That provoked laughter. 'So they don't mind working like dogs for precious little,' Dextry said, 'because tomorrow's always a day off.'

'It's not as simple as that. You can't understand the peasantry unless you realize how devoted they are to the Church. Russia is not like the West. Our Orthodox Church is the same as the State. The Church is Russia and Russia is the Church.'

'Well, we have the Church of England,' Maynard said. 'It's as English as can be. God Save the King, and all that.'

'Yes. But an Englishman can take it or leave it. A Russian believes that Christ made the Orthodox Church and that's why it's unalterable. And so is Russia, and so is the peasantry, unless the Tsar says otherwise, because the Tsar is God's spokesman. In a sense, he *is* God.'

'Was,' Jessop said.

'And then there's Rasputin,' Wragge said.

'Was,' Jessop said happily. He was doing well. Everyone brightened. They'd heard enough of the Orthodox Church.

'Ah, what a magnificent fraud!' Borodin said. 'I knew him, slightly. The smell was memorable. He never washed and his stench was as foul as his language, but he ravished half the noblewomen in Petersburg. Including the Empress Alexandra.'

'I met a chap in France,' Hopton said. 'He was on the same squadron as a Russian duke who said Rasputin had three balls. Is that right?'

'I never inspected him. It's possible. His stamina was prodigious.'

'A fraud, you said.' Wragge wanted more. They all wanted more. 'A terrific fraud. How so?'

'Oh ... it goes back to the Church, I'm afraid. You see, Rasputin was what we call a *starets*, a holy man sent by God for the salvation of our souls. Surrender your soul to the *starets*, and he will save you. Rasputin preached salvation through sin. How can we repent if we have not first sinned? That's where he started.'

'Not so fast,' Maynard said. He was making notes.

'Rasputin recommended sins of the flesh,' Borodin said. 'Top of the list for winning God's forgiveness.'

'That's jolly clever,' Dextry said.

'And if God sends a temptation, yield at once, so you can be forgiven. That was Rasputin's trump card. The ladies lined up for a chance to sin and repent in his bed.'

'Heavenly humping,' Wragge said. 'Unbeatable.'

'No wonder he was tritesticular,' Hopton said. Maynard looked up from his notes. 'Disease of sheep,' Hopton told him.

There was a silence while they contemplated a stampede of naked noblewomen into a hairy, smelly Russian's bed.

'It's a beautiful swindle,' Wragge said, 'but I can't see it working in the Church of England. Not unless you shave first.'

'I'll shave,' Maynard said.

4

Hackett ran out of enthusiasm. Ran out of encouragement, of urgency, of attack. He gave up. They won. It was their locomotive and they drove it at their speed. Twenty-three miles an hour meant reaching Taganrog the day after tomorrow, maybe even later. Well, this was Russia. They would be shot if they went any faster.

He sat on the coal in the tender and fingered his revolver.

Suppose he fired a couple of shots over their heads. That would make them jump. Would it do any good? The driver looked shaky, gunfire might be more than he could stand. If he collapsed it would make matters worse. The stoker couldn't shovel coal and drive. Forget guns.

In fact Hackett began to feel sorry for them. The driver wasn't strong enough to be on his feet all day behind a roaring, rocking engine. The stoker was younger but gusts of smoke got him coughing painfully and the damage to his left hand meant he could never hold a full shovel.

Hackett couldn't sit and watch him struggle any longer. He got up and took the shovel from his hands.

'I know what I'm doing,' he bawled into the man's ear. 'I did this job in the Australian Navy.' Useless, meaningless; but he felt he had to say something. He set to work, flinging coal into the fire, remembering the easy rhythm, enjoying the exercise. The stoker sat and watched.

Soon, the train picked up speed. Hackett could tell by the change in the engine note, by a difference in the vibration beneath his feet. He took a break and went to look at the gauge. Divide by three, multiply by two. Thirty miles an hour. And climbing. He grinned at the driver and slapped him on the back. The man looked sick. 'Sorry,' he shouted. 'Didn't mean to hurt you.' When he turned around the stoker had gone. Hackett searched and saw the man disappearing over the stack of coal, heading God knew where. 'We don't need him!' Hackett said, and got back to work. The coal burned easily. The fire turned from red-hot to white-hot. Hackett took off his tunic, and then his shirt. The engine had a thundering rumble that was different. He turned to look at the gauge and now the driver had gone too. Over the coal. Who would have thought the old fellow had the agility? He looked at the gauge. Nudging forty. It was vibrating so much that he leaned forward and looked closer. It struck him full in the face as if it had been fired from a gun, which in a sense it had. When the boiler blew, the locomotive shattered and bits rained on the steppe. Only the wheels and the chassis survived. It was almost a mile before the train stopped. Even without an engine, forty miles an hour creates a lot of momentum.

5

At 11.00 a.m., Jonathan Fitzroy met his Working

Party as they arrived at the Royal College of Embroidery. Everyone got into an official car and drove to a side entrance of the Admiralty Building in Whitehall. 'Sorry for the cloak-and-dagger,' he said. 'All will be explained.'

A captain of Marines checked their identities and issued temporary passes. A Marine led them along corridors painted battleship grey, busy with men, some in naval uniform, some not, each carrying a file of documents. 'Navy floats on paper,' General Stattaford said. 'Abolish paper and the Navy would sink like a stone.'

They went down a flight of stairs, along another corridor, down more stairs. 'Must be the crypt,' Stattaford said. 'Where admirals go to die.'

The Marine took them into an outer office, where their passes were examined. They were shown into a large room, with a map table that was brightly lit by hanging lamps. Only one man was present: a naval commander, much decorated, stocky, grey hair cropped short, grey eyes that rarely blinked. Fitzroy took care of the introductions. He was Commander Judd. He shook hands. He had a grip like a blacksmith.

They sat at the table. Fitzroy said, 'Commander Judd has information that the P.M. feels we should know. Something has happened.'

'This is a map of Kronstadt,' Judd said. 'The home of the Russian fleet.' They leaned forward. There was much to see. The map was large, and so was the scale. 'Kronstadt is at the head of the Baltic Sea, where the Gulf of Finland separates Finland from Russia. At its eastern end, the gulf narrows to become the Gulf of Petrograd, and this narrow gulf includes Kotlin Island.' Judd's pointer circled the island. 'Kotlin protects the naval base. Beyond the base, an estuary leads to Petrograd, but what matters to us is Kronstadt.'

'And the damned island,' Stattaford said.

'Yes. Kotlin forms an immense natural defence for the naval base. Ever since Peter the Great, Russia has been enlarging those defences, on land and at sea. Kronstadt has been called the safest, the most protected fleet base in the world.'

'Well, that's act one.' Charles Delahaye said. 'I hope there's act two.' He had left urgent business at the Treasury to be here.

'Patience,' Fitzroy murmured.

'The defences are worth examining,' Judd said. 'Kotlin, of course, is studded with forts covering the approach. On the north side a chain of forts in the sea reaches from Kotlin to the mainland, and each fort is linked to the next by a sub-merged breakwater, making that channel impass-able to a warship of any size. On the south side of Kotlin, several fortresses have been built in the sea. Only one channel exists for vessels leaving or entering the base, and it is here.'

'Not totally safe, then,' Stattaford said. 'I smell a loophole.'

'The channel is narrow,' Judd said. 'It has minefields on either side. Furthermore, here, to the west, outside Kotlin Island, a thick and extensive minefield guards against intruders. And finally, on the mainland, and especially where high land gives advantage, are fortresses carrying very heavy artillery, in some cases 12-inch guns.' He laid down his pointer.

'What you're saying,' James Weatherby said, 'is, take away Kotlin Island, and the northern sea forts and their breakwaters, and the southern sea forts and their minefields, and the huge minefield out to the west, and the land forts with their 12-inch guns, take away all that, and the Russian fleet at Kronstadt is wide open to attack by the Royal Navy.'

'You've forgotten something,' Sir Franklyn Fletcher said. 'Their fleet can see the enemy coming while he's miles away and blow him out of the water.'

'Damn,' Weatherby said. 'And I thought I had the problem solved.'

'Gentlemen, gentlemen,' Fitzroy said. 'The commander is making a very serious point.'

Judd looked at Delahaye. 'Here is act two. The Red Fleet in Kronstadt could indeed blow anything out of the water, considering it has two battleships, both with 12-inch guns, a cruiser with 6-inch guns, a submarine depot ship, seven submarines and a squadron of destroyers, plus several auxiliaries. The Royal Navy's fleet in the Baltic cannot penetrate the Kronstadt defences. At the same time, we cannot stop the Red Fleet coming out and causing havoc.'

'This is a very sad story,' Delahaye said.

'Hang on to your hats, as the Americans say,' Fitzroy told him.

'The Royal Navy sank the Red Fleet,' Judd said. 'The bulk of it. In Kronstadt.'

That had the effect it deserved. Everyone straightened and stared. Most smiled, some applauded. All Judd's careful preparation had paid off: his audience was amazed. Nothing changed in his face or his manner.

'Well done,' Weatherby said. 'You've sawn the woman in half. Now put her together again.'

'The Navy has developed a new type of vessel, called the Coastal Motor Boat, or C.M.B,' Judd said. 'Forty-footers, hydroplane hulls, engines up to 500 h.p., speed over 40 knots. Intended for hit-and-run raids on the German and Belgian coasts, had some success but the war ended too soon. Then two C.M.B.s under Lieutenant Agar R.N. did some Secret Service work, operating out of the coast of Finland, running agents to and from Petrograd.'

'We can't mention that, of course,' Fitzroy said. 'Never happened.'

'What Agar proved was that the C.M.B.'s shallow draught – less than three feet – lets it skim over breakwaters and minefields.'

'Ahah!' Sir Franklyn said. This was rattling good stuff.

'On his own initiative, Agar took a C.M.B. out one night and sank, with a single torpedo, the Red Navy cruiser *Oleg*. His act was contrary to our Rules of Engagement at the time.'

'Can't mention that, either.'

'Do shut up, Fitzroy,' Sir Franklyn said.

'However, it prompted the First Sea Lord to persuade the War Cabinet to give the Navy more freedom of action,' Judd said. 'Agar was sent seven larger C.M.B.s and an R.A.F. squadron, all based on the Finnish coast. The boats penetrated Kronstadt harbour at night while the R.A.F. flew low overhead to drown the noise of the engines.

They torpedoed and sank the battleships *Andrei Pervozvanny* and *Petropavlovsk* and the submarine depot ship *Pamiat Ozova*. Other damage was done. This action effectively removed the Red Navy's threat to our Baltic fleet.'

They pounded the table with their fists. 'Best news since the Armistice,' Stattaford said.

'Inevitably, the defences were aroused,' Judd said. 'We suffered losses. Three C.M.B.s failed to return. Agar won the Victoria Cross.'

'Three C.M.B.s for two battleships and a cruiser,' Weatherby said. 'Not a bad rate of exchange.'

Jonathan Fitzroy proposed a vote of thanks to the Royal Navy in general and to Commander Judd in particular. Oh, and to Lieutenant Agar.'

They left. Sir Franklyn said his club was nearby and invited them to join him for lunch.

His club was the Sheldrake, and as chairman of the wine committee he had no difficulty in getting a private dining room. 'No menu,' he said. 'They know what to bring us. I think champagne while we're waiting, don't you?'

They drank to pluck and courage, dash and daring, and a brace of dreadnoughts at the bottom of the sea. Champagne cleansed the palate wonderfully. 'This opens the way to Petersburg, doesn't it?' Stattaford said. 'Or Petrograd, or whatever it is.'

'Um ... not necessarily,' Fitzroy said.

'What's your problem? The Navy's put the kibosh on Kronstadt. The capital's wide open. Consolidate success. Rule one.'

Fitzroy swirled the remains of his champagne.

'Well ... it's not as simple as that.'

'Judd made it sound simple,' Weatherby said. 'No more Rules of Engagement. We can do what we like. Can't we?'

Fitzroy made sure the door was firmly shut. 'This is a very delicate matter,' he said. 'You must understand that what I'm going to tell you is absolutely secret.'

'Yes, yes,' Sir Franklyn said. 'Do get on.'

'It's true that the Rules of Engagement, for the Navy in the Baltic, are highly flexible. There were losses on both sides at Kronstadt. Weapons were fired in hot blood. It would be hard to deny that a warlike state existed.'

'Not hard. Impossible,' Stattaford said.

'In fact, before our assault was launched, the War Cabinet discussed the matter,' Fitzroy said, 'and the Prime Minister said that we were at war with the Bolsheviks.'

'Hurrah,' Sir Franklyn said. 'Hurrah for honesty.'

'Who's going to pay for it?' Charles Delahaye asked. He was talking to the air.

'*But,*' Fitzroy said, 'and here I must remind you of your pledge of secrecy, the P.M. added that we had decided not to *make* war in Russia.'

'Now what in God's name does that mean?' Weatherby demanded.

'No armies,' Sir Franklyn said. 'That's right, isn't it? A spot of skirmishing at sea is acceptable, but we shan't put an army ashore.' Fitzroy nodded. 'Just words, then,' Sir Franklyn said.

'Good,' Delahaye said. 'Words are cheap.'

'One other thing,' Fitzroy said. 'Well, two

things. First, we keep very quiet about Kronstadt. It's not Trafalgar. Nobody gets excited. And second, we say nothing, nothing at all, about the P.M's words on war.'

'That's absurd,' Stattaford said. 'What the devil is Lloyd George playing at?'

'You should regard this as background briefing,' Fitzroy said. 'Keeping you *au fait* with the *mise en scène,* so to speak.'

'Prime Ministers love secrecy,' Delahaye said. 'It makes them feel in control.'

Weatherby finished his champagne. It was flat, like the general atmosphere. 'Britain's at war, but we can't talk about it,' he said. 'What can we talk about?'

A servant tapped on the door and wheeled in the soup.

'Denikin's broken out of South Russia,' General Stattaford said. 'That should be fairly safe. It was in *The Times* this morning.'

6

They buried Hackett on the steppe.

Sergeant Stevens had been the first to find the body, and after one glance he had covered it and told the adjutant that nobody should come near it. The ground crew made a coffin. Stevens and a mechanic lifted the body and placed it inside and he watched as the lid was nailed down. Then he went in search of Susan Perry.

She was treating Marines for cuts and bruises and a possible dislocated shoulder. 'Instantaneous,' he told her. That was all. He could think of nothing to add; nothing that would help, anyway. She nodded and got on with her job. Her face was as blank as a sheet of paper, and as white.

Brazier was waiting for him. 'Ideally, he should be buried in Taganrog,' he said. 'H.Q. will have a padre. He'll organize the cemetery.'

'Not unless you're ready to ask the doctor to do another embalming.' Brazier rolled his eyes. 'Thought not,' Stevens said. 'Taganrog's two days away, maybe more. The guts are...' He decided not to discuss the guts. 'This heat's getting worse. Inside a boxcar it will be twice as hot.'

'So we do it now.'

The squadron knew the routine. They formed a hollow square around a grave dug by the *plennys*. Susan Perry and Count Borodin stood together. Four officers carried the coffin. Lacey followed. He spoke the familiar words, paused, and uttered his eulogy:

Calm is the morn after direst duress,
For the sword outwears its clasp.
One shade the more, one ray the less,
For the Angel of Death spread his wings
 on the blast.
But trailing clouds of glory do we come.
O fear not the bugle though loudly it blows,
It calls but the warders that guard thy repose.
The meteor flag of England has gloriously flown.
We carved not a line, and we raised not a stone,
But we left him alone with his glory.

The pallbearers did their bit, while Lacey said

297

his final piece. The firing party blazed away. Susan Perry and Borodin walked to the grave and looked down at the box made of packing-case planks. She dropped a handful of earth onto it; so did he. They walked away. 'He was so happy to be engaged,' she said. 'He was like a boy on his first bicycle.'

Colonel Kenny's coffin was intact; it was taken to 'B' Flight's train. But the Marines' train was ruined. Its windows were shattered, its roofs were split, a fire had burnt out the kitchen. Brazier ordered the carriages to be uncoupled and, one by one, they were capsized. So were the remains of the engine. It took every available man, hauling on ropes, but it cleared the line. The Marines found new quarters amongst the ground crews. Merlin Squadron got on the move again. Cautiously.

Borodin took a bottle of brandy and two glasses to Susan Perry's Pullman car.

'I'm told this is traditional after the ... um ... ceremony,' he said.

'Funeral,' she said. 'Burial. We buried him, because he was dead. No euphemisms, please. Nobody passed away. He didn't go to his rest. He died. But the bottle is a kind thought and yes, I'd like a glass of brandy.'

'Good. So would I.' He opened the bottle and poured. 'Sometimes the English are too much for me. Russians let their emotions show at funerals. Men cry when they lose a friend. This English restraint, this silence, is hard to take. I found it ... heartbreaking.'

'You were not alone.' She took a healthy sip of

brandy. 'Daddy Maynard's stiff upper lip began to wobble when Lacey played his ace.' Borodin cocked his head. 'Right at the end,' she said. '"We carved not a line, and we raised not a stone". English understatement. There's no defence against it.'

'Yes.' This was not what Borodin had expected. He had been ready to comfort a grieving fiancée but he wasn't prepared for a candid review of the funeral service. 'What will you do when we get to Taganrog?' he asked. 'Stay in Russia? Go home?'

'I don't know. I'll have to think. I can't just forget James, can I? But what's the point of remembering him? He's the second man I lost almost as soon as I found him. I don't think I was meant to be happy. Being happy is the kiss of death.'

Borodin studied her. If a highly attractive, intelligent woman like this despaired of happiness, something was wrong with the world. Without thinking, he said: 'Marry me. I promise you a long life of gloom and misery.'

She laughed, briefly. Well, that was better. 'You wouldn't survive the honeymoon,' she said. 'You'd be doomed.'

He'd taken one chance. He took another. 'If it happened at the end of the honeymoon, I wouldn't mind. There are worse ways to go.'

She finished her brandy and looked at him, a long look that could have meant anything. 'What became of the gloom and misery you promised?'

'Understatement,' he said. 'I've caught the disease.' She held out her glass and he poured more brandy.

In The Dregs, the adjutant had taken Tusker Oliphant into a quiet corner and was trying, and failing, to persuade him to be the new C.O. Tusker was the most senior officer. He had an unblemished record. *King's Regulations* were very clear.

'It won't work, Uncle.'

'It must work, Tusker. You'll have my full backing.'

'That won't change the chaps. I'm a bomber boy. Fighter boys won't accept me. D'you know what my chaps call them? Camel-drivers. Often worse. And they call us Number Nines. You know what they are?'

'Sick-parade pills. Cure for constipation.'

'Well, then.'

'Schoolboy behaviour. They'll do as they're bloody well told.'

Oliphant rubbed his eyes, and sat with his head in his hands. 'Remember McCudden? James McCudden?'

'Never met him. Different squadron.'

'He shot down fifty-something Huns. Got the V.C., D.S.O. and Bar, etcetera. But first he won an M.M.' Oliphant looked up. 'Not an M.C., Uncle. An M.M.'

'So McCudden rose through the ranks.'

'Started as an air mechanic. Ended as a major. When he got his V.C., the generals offered him command of 85 Squadron. One of the best. They didn't want him. Turned him down.'

'The *pilots* decided?'

'He hadn't been to the right school, Uncle. His father was a sergeant-major. And 85 was stuffed with public-school types.'

Brazier rubbed his chin. He shaved twice a day and it would soon be time. 'You know this for a fact?'

'I know McCudden went to 60 Squadron instead. Everyone believed 85 wouldn't have him because he wasn't one of them. Well, neither am I. But the Camel-drivers are. Eton, Harrow, Rugby, Sherborne, Tonbridge.'

'They accepted Hackett.'

'He frightened them. And he wasn't a Number Nine.'

'You'd get a squadron-leader's pay,' the adjutant said, but he knew from Oliphant's sad smile that money couldn't change anything.

Sergeant Stevens had rescued a percolator from Colonel Kenny's Pullman. Lacey watched him brew coffee. 'I've decided to make you my fag,' he said. 'I take it you served your time as a fag at Winchester.'

'It happened. There was an American boy in my year. He found fagging very amusing. It means something very different in his country.'

'Yes. Did you suffer from homosexuality at Winchester?'

The percolator started to go *bloop-bloop*. 'I don't think anyone actually *suffered*,' Stevens said. *Bloop-bloop* went the coffee. Lacey sprawled, and enjoyed the sound. It domesticated the radio room. 'It hurts me to say so,' Stevens said, 'but I should congratulate you on your poetic tribute to our late leader.'

'Written in haste, I'm afraid.'

'It was a touch too long.'

301

'Perhaps. I didn't have time to write a shorter piece.'

Stevens looked at him sideways. 'Pascal said that first, didn't he?'

'Did he? Quite possibly.'

Bloop-bloop.

'Your first line: 'Calm is the morn...'Tennyson, isn't it? His *In Memoriam*. But...' Stevens hunched his shoulders. 'Not entirely Tennyson.'

'I changed the ending. "Without a sound" is what Tennyson wrote but it sounded flat, so I made it "after direst duress", which also rhymes with line three, "one ray the less" .The chaps like poetry that rhymes.'

'So, not content with pinching bits of Tennyson, you mess them about too.'

'Enhance, Stevens. I enhance them.'

'Who else did you rape?'

'Oh ... Shelley. Line two: "For the sword outwears its sheath". I wasn't convinced by "sheath". Not a very manly word. I changed it to "clasp", which rhymes with "blast" in line four.'

'No, it doesn't.'

'Near enough. And towards the end, I needed a rhyme with "stone". Campbell wrote: 'The meteor flag of England shall yet terrific *burn'*, which is a big disappointment. What he should have said is "has gloriously flown". And now he has.'

'Shameless,' Stevens said. 'At least you didn't fool around with your last lines. The Burial of Sir John Moore, wasn't it? Every schoolboy's read it.'

'It was irresistible. "We carved not a line, and we raised not a stone, so we left him alone with his glory." Perfect bull's-eye. I know two handkerchiefs came out. At least two.'

Stevens lifted the percolator from the Primus and let it rest. 'So what didn't I spot?'

'Bit of Wordsworth, bit of Byron, rather too much Walter Scott.' Lacey, deep in his armchair, fingertips making an arch, looked professorial. 'But you know how Scott burbles on. Hard to stop him.'

They were drinking their coffee when the adjutant came in. 'Oliphant's funked being acting C.O,' he said. 'So I'm in charge until Taganrog. They'll want a report on what happened to Hackett. Give me a copy of your flowery verse. Something to bulk out the sad facts.'

'Oh,' Lacey said. 'Is that absolutely necessary?'

'The curse of genius,' Stevens said. 'The price of a raging talent.'

7

The same amiable, plump captain who, long ago, had been chatting to Maynard at lunch in Novorossisk, was waiting on the platform when the trains pulled into Taganrog and everyone piled out. After five days of trundling across the empty, unchanging steppe, the squadron hoped Taganrog was Paris on the Black Sea. With a slice of Sodom and Gomorrah thrown in.

The captain quickly picked out Brazier as the most responsible man. 'Welcome to Tag,' he said. 'Good journey?'

'Tedious. Got shot at by bandits. One engine exploded.'

'Yes. That's how it is in Russia.'

'The C.O. got killed.'

'My dear chap, what rotten luck. Do you need a C.O.? Yes, of course you do. We can fix you up, I'm sure of it. We've got everything here. Our H.Q. is huge. As soon as Denikin began his Big Push, all the chaps from Novo and Ekat came up here, to be nearer the Front.'

'And where is that?'

'Oh, hundreds of miles away by now. They say Denikin's taken Kharkov. And he may have got Kiev. Come to lunch, somebody will tell you.'

'First things first. You want Colonel Kenny V.C. He's boxed up, ready to go.'

'Of course, of course. Slipped my mind. These chaps will take care of him.' The captain waved to a waiting army lorry. 'Tragic event, truly tragic... About lunch. I've got a car. You'll enjoy Tag; it's like Brighton, bright and breezy. Awfully friendly.'

Brazier pointed at the Camels and Nines lashed to the flatbed trucks. 'We're here to fight.'

'Yes, exactly. No time to waste. Did I say that you leave here tomorrow? Slipped my mind. Who else would you like to bring to lunch? I can get five in the car. Six, at a pinch.'

When the squadron heard that it had only twenty-four hours in Taganrog, nobody wanted to waste any of it on lunch at Mission H.Q.

'Don't worry about us, Uncle,' Junk Jessop said. 'Our behaviour will be in the finest tradition of the Service.'

'That means you'll get blotto and act batty,' Brazier said. He found Wragge. 'For God's sake, Tiger, keep them out of the red light district. Tell

304

them pox is a court-martial offence. Any man gets thrown in jail will stay there and rot. We'll leave without him.'

'Uncle, their conduct will be exemplary. Impeccable.'

'And take Borodin with you. I don't want any stupid misunderstandings.'

'What could possibly go wrong?'

Brazier widened his eyes and stared. 'More things than you could imagine,' he said, 'and worse.'

Wragge got the crews together, and Borodin led them to a line of four-wheeled carriages. 'These are *droshkys*,' he said. 'Russian cabs. I'll tell the drivers to show you the sights. Be kind to them and they will be good to you.'

The *droshkys* set off, four men in each cab. Wragge was in the lead with Borodin and a couple of bomber boys. 'Damn,' he said. 'Forgot to give them Uncle's advice.' Borodin told the driver to slow down until the next *droshky* was almost alongside. Wragge stood up. 'I say, you chaps,' he called. 'Uncle says beware the floozies. And give the jug a miss. Pass it on.' He sat down. His driver shook the reins and they moved ahead again.

'What did he say?' Daddy Maynard asked.

'Sounded like, "See what the floozies are wearing", I think,' Junk Jessop said. 'I wasn't really listening. And don't miss the jug. Funny thing to say.'

'Maybe they serve their tipple by the jug,' Rex Dextry said. 'Saves time.'

'Look,' Tommy Hopton said. 'Floozies! And jolly friendly!' He waved back. 'Tally-ho. This is going to be fun.'

They had entered a wide circus, with heroic statuary in the middle. 'If this was ancient Rome,' Maynard said, 'they'd have chariot races around here.'

'Bloody good idea,' Jessop said. 'A brace of floozies, a jug of wine, and lickety-split around the circus! By golly, that would give the town something to remember us by.'

Lacey had no time for fun. His business partner, Henry, had followed the British Military Mission from Ekat and now he had a penthouse suite at the best place in town, the Hotel Olymp. They met there.

'You'll be gone a long time,' Henry said.

Lacey knew that he was from a New York family of stockbrokers, had been to Yale, served with the American Expeditionary Force in France and left the Force, and France, in something of a hurry. He never explained why and Lacey never asked. They had met in Ekat. Henry's American accent was under control. He spoke quietly, in complete sentences, with no ums or ahs. He knew everyone worth knowing, down to the last rouble in their pockets. He was an instinctive businessman. He did business the way normal men breathed in and out.

'A long time doesn't mean a couple of weeks,' he said. 'It means a month or more. You'll get new high-speed locomotives and you'll have express-train status. Denikin sees your squadron as the spearhead of his advances.'

'How do you know all this? We haven't had our orders from H.Q.'

'Lacey, old pal. You have been away too long from the corridors of power. Staff officers at the British Mission H.Q. are desperate for the essentials of war. I speak of Cooper's Oxford marmalade, hot English mustard, Gentleman's Relish, blades for the Gillette safety razor, the latest novel by Edgar Wallace, Bristol Cream sherry, ten-year-old malt whisky, Edinburgh shortcake, green ink, and many more.'

'Green ink is a red herring, surely.'

'Not a bit. A brigadier at H.Q. was distraught when a servant spilled his only bottle. He always signed orders in green ink. He was famous for it. When I rode to his rescue, we became firm friends. Denikin's advance has given him something to brag about, and he enjoys bragging to me.'

'Express trains,' Lacey said. 'Golly.'

'I took the liberty of doubling the size of your orders,' Henry said. 'It's all in a boxcar that is being hooked right now to the end of your train. H.Q. found replacements for your Camel and DH9. They're on a flatbed car. Fuel and ammo are separate.'

'The green ink still intrigues me. Doesn't Russia make it?'

'No. I got on the radio to our man in Constantinople. He put a bottle on the next British destroyer for Novorossisk, along with other essentials.'

'Cooper's Oxford marmalade,' Lacey said. 'Hot English mustard.'

'Have you got an hour to spare?' Henry said. 'You might be interested in seeing how Denikin finances his war.?'

'Gold from London?'

'This is far better. It amazed me.'

Daddy Maynard had never known a girl whom he could honestly call a close friend. His family lived in a former rectory in a remote corner of Wiltshire, chosen because it was handy for Salisbury Plain where his father, a major, spent much of his time on cavalry manoeuvres. There was an older sister, completely indifferent to her brother. Local girls were farming stock, buxom and ruddy: totally unsuitable. In any case, from the age of six, most of his years were spent at boarding schools where girls were as foreign as unicorns.

He went, almost without pause, from school to the Royal Flying Corps, which was just as masculine as school. On leave, as he passed through London, he was aware that the wings on his tunic excited young women, some of them quite attractive. What to do about it? He had no idea. When he went to Russia, he had never held a girl, let alone kissed one. Now he had two girls, one on each side and they were kissing him. Not continuously, but often enough to make him feel he was a hell of a chap.

They were in a *droshky*, driving along the promenade. 'I say, Rex,' Maynard said. 'I need some advice.'

Dextry detached himself from his girl. 'They're awfully keen, aren't they?' he said. 'Full of beans.'

'Here's a technical question. The one on my right keeps kissing me on the lips.'

'Good for her. And for you, I hope.'

'No complaints. But then she puts her tongue in my mouth. I mean, right in.'

'Does she? Does she, by Jove. Well I never. I must try that.' Dextry turned away.

'I can't talk to her,' Maynard said. 'She talks to me, but I don't understand a word of it.' Dextry wasn't listening. Maynard returned to the kissing business and wondered if he was brave enough to do the mouth–tongue thing. He decided to leave it for a while.

Similar encounters were happening in *droshkys* scattered about Taganrog. Only one thought was cooling the ardour of the air crews. They were hungry. They wanted lunch. Girls were alright, but food and girls would be better. Plus a jug of vodka.

8

Henry had a car. Of course he had a car, a Hispano-Suiza limousine, looted by the Austrian Army in Italy, sold to the German Army, abandoned in the Ukraine, somehow ended up in Taganrog. He drove. They picked up an elderly Russian general who spoke little English and they made their way inland for about five miles. This countryside was not steppe; far from it. There were farms and fields, woods, hills, even a river. The road was cobbled, but at least it was a road. And then, surprisingly, a railway line appeared and ran alongside the road. Both ended when a steep hillside blocked their way.

A guardhouse had been built into the hillside. Armed soldiers stared at the car. The general got out and they saluted him.

'This is the most secret place in Russia,' Henry said. 'The old gentleman will vouch for us.' The general raised a hand. 'We're in,' Henry said. 'Don't smile, and don't touch anything. Fort Knox is Coney Island compared to what's inside.'

They went through the guardhouse. A junior officer opened a pair of gates that belonged to a small castle and they walked into a cavern that was big enough to take the Imperial Coach with outriders. It was a wine cellar, lined on both sides with racks of bottles. It went into the hillside as far as Lacey could see.

The officer had a lantern. They followed him. 'This is all French,' Henry said. 'Burgundies, Beaujolais, Château Lafite, various other Rothschilds. All the great reds.' After a couple of hundred yards they reached a crossroads. 'The French whites are down there,' he said. They walked on. 'I think this is Chianti,' he said. 'I'm not very strong on the Italians.' His voice made a slight echo; the walls of wine bottles absorbed sound. After a while he said, 'This is what I wanted you to see. The great cave.' The tunnel had been made higher and wider. 'Here they keep the champagne. Well, part of the champagne. The good stuff. There's more elsewhere. In the beginning, the cavern was made for the champagne, but it kept growing and growing.' He pointed to the roof. 'Chalk. Temperature and humidity never vary, year round. Have you seen enough?'

'How much more is there?'

'About fifteen miles.'

They walked back to the guardroom, thanked

310

the officer, collected the general, and went and sat in the car.

'Staggering, isn't it?' Henry said.

'Stupefying. And it all belongs to Denikin.'

'It does now. It was the Tsar's private wine cellar for generations. I'm told there are a million bottles of champagne in there.'

'So, when Denikin needs some money...'

'He sells off a few thousand bottles and makes a million roubles, maybe two million. And the war goes on.'

9

The accordion-player had his own sense of time. Usually he played three beats to the bar, sometimes four, occasionally five. He was playing a waltz, and his changes of tempo annoyed the violin and the piano. Often they stopped playing and swore at him until he rediscovered three-quarter time.

Dextry was dancing with his girl and he didn't complain. 'The accordion has some Irish blood in him,' he told her. She smiled and hugged him and the accordion went doolally again.

They were in a big, noisy restaurant-bar dance hall. All the squadron were there, because all the *droshky* drivers had recommended it. 'It's a racket,' Oliphant said. Wragge agreed. 'Still, they seem to want us,' he said. 'The grub's hot, the drinks are big, the waiters are friendly, and my girl likes it. Your Number Nines are enjoying themselves.'

'They're bloody idiots,' Oliphant said.

The bomber crews were competing to see who could get a visible set of footprints on the ceiling. They dragged tables together to make a base for two men to stand on and support a third, whose boot-soles had been blackened with soot. The trick was to turn him upside-down and hoist him. The problem was that they were all drunk, and others were fighting to rock the tables. Those too tired to fight threw things. Fruit, bread rolls, bottles. Two attempts to reach the ceiling failed. The owner looked on as men fell and tables splintered, and he doubled the price of the drinks. The sport lost its novelty. Waiters swept the dance floor clear of debris. The accordion began an eccentric version of 'Alexander's Ragtime Band'. Dancing began again.

Dextry's girl held him tight and they jigged and jogged. He called her Cynthia and told her she was stunning, it meant nothing to her, she had no English, but it made him happy, until an angry Russian got in the way and laid a hand on her. 'Go away,' Dextry told him. 'Private property. Find your own girl.'

That produced a stream of furious Russian. 'You're spitting on her,' Dextry said. 'Have you no manners?' He danced Cynthia away but the man followed. Now he was shouting. His face was twisted and he grabbed the girl's shoulder. Dextry knocked his hand away and the man aimed a fist at his face, missed, and clipped his ear. That stung. Dextry punched him, hard, in the ribs. The Russian kicked him on the shins and was swamped by four fighter pilots. He went down fighting but they dragged him to the door and threw him out.

'What was all that about?' Jessop asked.

'I haven't the faintest,' Dextry said. 'He smelt very strongly of fish. Most unpleasant.'

Twenty minutes later, when a fresh attempt was being made to get footprints on the ceiling, a dozen Russians burst in and the whole squadron was in a brawl. The trio standing on the tables soon crashed, and by luck they knocked down two Russians. The others were young and strong and angry and might have won if the owner and the waiters had not waded in with clubs. Then the police came, with more clubs, and arrested everyone.

They talked to the owner. He estimated the damage and wrote the figure in chalk on the bar.

'We could have bought the whole damn place for that,' Wragge said. The squadron began searching its pockets and filling a bucket. The violin played a wistful Russian tune. Oliphant gave the band twenty roubles. By the time the owner was satisfied, the Russians had gone. They took the girls with them.

The members of the squadron were escorted to police headquarters. Count Borodin was waiting there. 'I was playing billiards at the Literary Club,' he said, 'and doing rather well, until now. You look an unholy shambles.'

'We didn't start it,' Wragge said. 'A gang of local thugs went mad for no reason.'

'Fishermen. You stole their girls. That puts you in the wrong. You're charged with robbery, bodily harm and insulting Russian manhood.'

'I suppose they want money.'

'All you have. Otherwise – jail.'

Lacey and Brazier were outside the train when the squadron straggled back, bloodied, torn, untidy and in many cases still half-drunk. The airmen looked glum. 'I've seen this before,' Brazier said. 'In France. Men came out of the Trenches, got deloused, got paid, got into a big fight with anyone they met, for no reason.'

'We promised them a war,' Lacey said. 'That's a reason.'

'I suppose so. Hullo, Mr Wragge,' Brazier said. 'The chaps are looking very impeccable. Or do I mean exemplary?'

'Bloody town's full of Bolsheviks,' Wragge said.

'I have orders from Mission H.Q. You are promoted to acting squadron leader and commanded to be C.O. of the squadron. The general sends his compliments and wishes you not to die in the near future.'

'It's all a stinking swindle.' Wragge tramped off.

'I think you made his day,' Lacey said.

Lacey's day had not finished. Before he took down the radio aerials, he made a final check in case any incoming messages had arrived. There was one, a signal from Military Mission H.Q.:

Correction stop Your records re boxed item stencilled lightning conductors stop Contents are quantity three trench mortars infantry for the use of stop Delete all reference to elephant guns stop Return mortars to armament stores Taganrog urgently stop Captain Butcher Royal Artillery stop.

Brazier came in and read the signal over

314

Lacey's shoulder.

'Now you're in the soup,' he said.

'I think not.'

Lacey consulted his options, and then sent his reply:

Elephant guns donated to Cossack warlord Reizarb as mark of gratitude stop Reizarb's Cossacks helped repel raid on squadron by Anarchist guerrillas stop Trench mortars invaluable in same action but urgently need barrel locking nuts quantity three stop Commend gallantry Flying Officer Jossip stop J. Hackett Sqdn Ldr OC Merlin Squadron RAF stop

Brazier read the file copy. 'Hackett's gone,' he said. 'And we have nobody called Jossip.'

'We have a Jessop, which is close enough to give Butcher something to ponder.'

'He won't ponder over barrel locking nuts. They're for rifles. Butcher's a gunner, he'll know that.'

'Our mortars are special. They need special barrel locking nuts.'

'And no Cossack ever helped us fight off the bandits. Who is this Reizarb? I've never heard of him.'

'It's a small tribute to yourself,' Lacey said. The adjutant stared down at him. 'I hoped you would decode it,' Lacey said. 'It's Brazier spelt back-wards.'

The adjutant snorted. 'You're playing with fire, Lacey. H.Q. has no sense of humour.'

'Then they'll never guess,' Lacey said. 'It'll be our little secret.'

SUICIDE. THAT'S A BIT STEEP

1

Wragge came out of a bad dream. He was being chased by a mob of Russian thugs and running for his life to catch a *droshky* that was driving away from him, mocking him with its clip-clop of hooves. They never grew fainter, never louder, always just beyond his reach. He awoke, wet with sweat and stiff with effort, and as he relaxed he knew the noise was the click of train wheels on track. The squadron was on the move. His squadron.

He got out of bed and towelled his head dry. His mouth was lined with old sandpaper. He opened a window and poked his head into the stream of cool air. It was dawn, and they were leaving Taganrog. He sucked deep lungfuls of health-giving air and felt his body slowly come alive. The window of the next Pullman car opened and Maynard looked out. 'We're off again,' he said.

'Well done, Daddy,' Wragge said. 'You always were the bright one.' He heard movement behind him and went back inside. It was his *plenny*, Fred. 'Black coffee, Fred. *Beaucoup de* sugar. And get me a new head while you're at it.' His *plenny* blinked. 'Forget the head. Get coffee. Black. Big.' Fred understood that.

Wragge was brushing his teeth when the

adjutant arrived. 'I didn't think you'd want to see this last night,' he said. 'It's your orders from Mission H.Q.' The buff envelope was large and heavy.

'You read them, Uncle. I've been suddenly struck blind.'

'That's not the form, Tiger. The C.O. reads the C.O.'s orders.'

Wragge rinsed his mouth, and spat. 'This train makes a good speed, doesn't it? Hackett would have approved.'

Brazier had nothing to say about that. It was not his job to make small talk with the C.O. in his pyjamas. 'I've cleared all his effects from his Pullman,' he said.

'You must be getting good at that.' Wragge weighed the envelope in his hand. 'I didn't come to Russia to read tons of bumf, Uncle.'

'We must all make the best of a bad job.'

Wragge wondered. Did that mean he was a bad job? His *plenny* arrived with coffee. Brazier left. Wragge opened the envelope. He flicked through the contents fast and made them into three piles: squadron orders; strategic view of the war; and Russian politics. He sent for Count Borodin and Lacey.

'Squadron orders stay with me,' he said. 'You take a look at the rest. Count, you get Russian politics. Lacey has the war strategy stuff. Just skim through it. No hurry. I'll just shave and get dressed.'

After twenty minutes he fixed his collar stud and adjusted his tie. 'Time's up. What's the score, Lacey?'

'Reports on all fronts of the war. About Admiral Kolchak's campaigns in Siberia, it says *results are difficult to estimate,* which means...'

'Nobody knows,' Wragge said. 'And nobody's holding their breath.'

'About the North Army at Murmansk, it says *morale is good,* however *the outcome has yet to be decided,* meaning...'

'Nobody knows,' Wragge said. 'But we're not winning.'

'In Estonia, next to Petrograd, an ugly piece of work called General Yudenitch aims to be a new Ivan the Terrible. The report describes him as *staunch and unswerving,* translated as *brutal and ruthless.* Will he win? H.Q. is observing the situation closely.'

'Because nobody knows. And Estonia can't conquer Russia, so it's Denikin or nothing, isn't it?'

'They're quite candid about Denikin. His goal of a One and Undivided Russia is a brave gamble, they say.'

'He's a reactionary,' Borodin said. 'A good soldier but a woeful politician. Can't administer the territory he captures. Doesn't even try.'

'H.Q. speaks highly of the generals on his flanks,' Lacey said. 'Wrangel on the right and Mai-Mayevski on the left.'

'They hate each other,' Borodin said. 'Mai-Mayevski is useless when drunk, which is often.'

'Nevertheless,' Wragge said, 'Denikin's armies have smashed the Reds and he's off and running for Moscow. Where is his Front?'

'Situation fluid,' Lacey said. 'Opinions vary.'

'What an odd war. Nobody knows anything.

Oh, well. What has H.Q. to say about Russian politics, Count?'

'They copied it from the *Encyclopaedia Britannica*,' Borodin said, 'which has long since been overtaken by events. For instance, the *Britannica* and H.Q. say the peasants are ignorant of Western civilization, hence the power of the nobility. But the peasants have taken their estates and the nobility have no power. Whoever wrote this doesn't understand the Revolution.'

'Too deep for me, old boy,' Wragge said. 'And I don't really give a damn. We get paid to biff the Bolos and that's all that matters. Incidentally, I've decided to make Dextry the new Camel Flight leader. Count, you'll fly the replacement Camel, after you've had a little training.'

'Thanks awfully.'

'Why are we stopping?'

Lacey went to the window. 'We're in a siding. Why, I have no idea.'

The answer soon became obvious. Expresses thundered past, one after another. 'This is absurd,' Wragge said. 'We have priority status. My orders say everything makes way for us. But look!' More high-speed trains sped by.

'The railway authorities make these decisions,' Borodin said. 'I rather think they told your Mission H.Q. what H.Q. wished to hear. It was an untruth, of course.'

Wragge stared. 'That's absolutely bloody ludicrous.'

Borodin nodded. 'Puzzling for strangers, but not at all uncommon in Russia.'

'God speed the plough.' Wragge looked at

Lacey, but Lacey had rolled the Strategic Overview into a tube and was softly blowing into it. 'Thank you,' Wragge said. 'That's all.'

Borodin and Lacey left the train and stood in the sunshine. Half the squadron was out there, kicking a football about. Kid, the mascot, was eating young thistles.

'You hate the Reds,' Lacey said. 'Ghastly lot of murderers.'

'You have no idea just how ghastly. Not yet.'

'Quite. But you despise the White leaders.'

'They want the old days back again. Greedy and stupid.'

'Well, that's what puzzles me. You accept the Revolution, yet fight the Bolsheviks. Why is that?'

'Look at me, Lacey.' Borodin spread his arms. 'The Imperial Empire made me. It was a scarecrow with a crown on its turnip head, but it made me, it raised me, it was all I knew. I am a member of that tribe, and sometimes a man has to fight for his tribe.'

'Even when he fears it won't win?'

'Even when he knows it must lose.' Borodin smoothed his tunic. 'And that is the last we shall ever speak of such things.'

The locomotive whistle gave a warning blast. Men began climbing aboard. 'Off to the wars,' Lacey said. 'Shall we have an *aperitif* before lunch?'

2

The squadron reached the town of Makeyevka

late in the afternoon. They had covered ninety-four miles, much of it spent waiting in sidings. The drivers decided they had done enough.

Wragge asked the adjutant to assemble the whole squadron on the station platform – everyone, including ground crews and Marines. 'We left the Marines at Tag,' Brazier said. 'H.Q. said we shan't need them. Denikin's staff will send an armoured train to protect us. Apparently the main danger is from enemy armoured trains.'

'I see. How do we tell the difference between ours and theirs?'

Brazier looked at his watch. 'Gracious. Is that the time? I'd better get the troops on parade.'

'Not a parade, Uncle. Just assemble them.'

He found a box to stand on. The size of the crowd sobered him. Until Russia, he had risen no higher than flight leader, responsible for half a dozen pilots. Now he was looking at well over a hundred men.

'I'll make this short and sweet,' he said. 'Well, I hope it's sweet. Two things. First is why we're here, and that is to fly aeroplanes. Your job, all of you, is to help us do that. If you're not helping, you're hindering. Do it your way, do it any damned way you like, but keep Merlin Squadron flying. Second: let's enjoy it. Any fool can make war miserable. We're a long way from home, but let's get as much fun as we can out of being in this peculiar country. That's all. Carry on, adjutant.'

Wragge beckoned to the count.

'There's a Russian official watching us,' Wragge said. 'See him? Too fat for his fancy uniform. Could he be the stationmaster?'

'Almost certainly.'

'Ask him what happened to our express-train status.'

The stationmaster saw them coming and his fingers thought about buttoning his coat, fumbled, and gave up. Borodin asked him a question and got a short and surly answer. 'Wrong identification letters on the front of our locomotives,' Borodin reported. 'Nothing he can do.'

'I see. How would General Denikin handle this situation?'

Borodin laughed. 'Hang him.'

'And the Red Army?'

'Torture, and then hang him.'

'Interesting. Would it make the trains run faster? Don't answer that, it was a thingummy question.'

'Rhetorical.'

'If you say so. We'll compromise. We'll tie the bugger to the front of the locomotive and leave him there. He'll make a very good identification. He'll clear the line like a dose of salts. We'll go like a rocket.'

'Yes.' Borodin thought about that. 'And if it fails? We might hit a train in front of us.'

'Then the stationmaster will be the first to know. Tell him.'

Borodin translated. The man seemed baffled by the news. He protested loudly and a gang of *plennys* led him to the locomotive of 'A' Flight's train and roped him to the front. 'He says this is outrageous,' Borodin told Wragge.

'So is hanging about in sidings. We'll leave him there for the night. Give him time to brood.

Russians are good at brooding, aren't they?'

3

Wragge gave all ranks one hour to stretch their legs and see something of Makeyevka. Count Borodin asked the squadron doctor if she would like to go, and if he might escort her. 'I won't suggest that we take the air,' he said. 'In these parts, breathing is something to be avoided.'

They took a *droshky*. Slag heaps and factory chimneys dominated the landscape. Rusting railway tracks wandered off and got lost. The air smelt of burnt carbon and tasted of sulphur. 'If you lived here for fifty years you'd never grow to love it,' she said, 'because you'd be dead by forty.'

'It's horrible. But this is the Donbas, the richest part of all Russia. Almost all our coal comes from here. Masses of steel. If it weren't for the Donbas, there would be no railway lines.'

'Admirable. I hope their chronic lung disease allows them to raise a feeble cheer. Can we go home now?'

'I just want to show you the town. It's not far.'

Makeyevka turned out to be modern and sensibly planned, with wide avenues. There were the usual onion domes, blackened by years of pollution. Everything was smoke-stained: the houses, the trees, the river, the clothes, the people. Borodin pointed to the balcony of a hotel. 'Last year Nestor Makhno made a tremendous speech from there, all about anarchy and what a fine thing it is, and to prove it his army would fight everyone in the name of a free and independent Ukraine. He was very popular. Still is.'

'Are we in the Ukraine?'

'Yes.'

'And do they support General Denikin?'

'Probably not. I expect he'll capture some of it. Everyone does. Then they lose it. Fighting in the Ukraine is like filling a wheelbarrow with frogs. Anyone can do it but nobody can keep the frogs in the wheelbarrow.'

'I need a drink. Let's go home. Top speed.'

They drove back to the squadron trains. He paid off the *droshky* and they walked to The Dregs. 'I'm glad you stayed with us,' he said. 'I feared you might want to escape the sad memories.'

'I reported to Mission H.Q.,' she said, 'and ten minutes of whisky breath and pipe smoke was more than enough, so I scuttled back here, where there's a job for me.'

A flight-sergeant was waiting, and he saluted. 'Beg pardon, ma'm. Aircraftman Simms reported sick. Unfit for duty. Boil on his backside, ma'm.'

She looked at Borodin. 'When all else fails, there are always boils on backsides. Lead on, flight sergeant, before it explodes and kills the onlookers.'

4

At first light next morning, the C.O. met the adjutant and the count on the platform. 'What news?' he asked.

'I set an armed guard, in case his friends came to save him,' the adjutant said. 'If he has friends. A poor specimen. Whimpers a lot. It got very cold.'

'He'll survive. He's fat,' Borodin said. 'Most stationmasters are. Bribes, bribes. I saw him after supper and he told me we could have the correct identification plates for a hundred roubles.'

'Cheeky devil.'

'He was lying. I could tell. His kind always lies.'

'We'll go and see him,' Wragge said.

All the strength had drained from the station-master's limbs. He hung from his ropes like an out-of-work puppet. The colour had gone from his face. His belly slumped: a sack of waste. His eyes were half-shut as he watched them approach.

'Tell him we're leaving in an hour,' Wragge said. 'Tell him we want genuine plates or we'll have a head-on collision and he'll be meat in the sand-wich.'

Borodin told him, and the stationmaster began to sob. He croaked his answer.

'He swears on the soul of his dead mother and various Christian Saints,' Borodin said. 'But he's still lying.'

'Breakfast,' Wragge said.

The Dregs was a subdued place. Camel pilots drifted in, sensed the atmosphere, got on with their eggs and bacon.

'We'll have one more crack at him,' Wragge said. 'Try and terrify the truth out of him.'

'If it doesn't?' the adjutant said.

Wragge sipped his coffee and failed to find an answer. 'We'll never catch Denikin if we keep limping along,' he said. 'He's probably advancing faster than we are.'

The squadron doctor came in, carrying a small box that was heavily sealed and decorated with a large red cross. 'I'm acting on orders from Mission H.Q.,' she said. 'This won't take long.'

Wragge waved a hand.

She cut the seals and opened the box and took out a couple of small glass tubes, closed with corks. 'Morphine. Wonderful painkiller. A few grains of morphine are a godsend when you have typhus. *Tif,* the Russians call it. Also dysentery, which gives you terrible griping pains in the gut. And cholera. Morphine won't save you but you suffer less. Ditto malaria. H.Q. wants every man to have a phial of morphine.' She handed them out.

'Thank you, flight lieutenant,' Wragge said.

'There's more. If you swallow the entire contents of a phial, you will die quickly. You may feel this is preferable to being captured by the enemy. It's the real reason why H.Q. wants everyone to have a phial.'

'Crikey,' Jessop said. 'Crikey Moses.'

'Suicide,' Maynard said. 'That's a bit steep, isn't it? I mean to say, it's asking an awful lot of a chap.'

'It's not compulsory, Daddy,' Wragge said.

Borodin cleared his throat. 'I don't think you can expect to receive prisoner-of-war status. The Bolsheviks kill all captured officers and they are especially hard on foreigners. Invaders, in their view. Torture is normal.'

'They nearly cut off Gerry Pedlow's goolies,' Jessop said.

'That was for religion,' Dextry pointed out.

'Even worse. If the Russian Christians cut off your goolies, what will the Bolos be like?'

'Are you sure H.Q. authorized this?' Maynard asked the doctor. 'I mean, suicide's illegal. Isn't it?'

Wragge signalled Brazier and Borodin. They left, and walked to the locomotive. 'Tell the driver to make a lot of noise,' Wragge said. 'Blow off steam, sound his whistle, ring his bell. Then go fifty yards and stop and come back here.'

The racket was impressive. The bell was above the stationmaster's head and he was in pain every time it clanged. A small crowd of railway workers watched from a distance. They made no move to interfere. 'He has probably been stealing part of their wages,' Borodin said. 'Most stationmasters do.'

The locomotive spun its wheels, shot out sparks, made a scream of steel on steel, and pulled away, clanging non-stop. The station-master shouted but his voice was lost. Some of the pilots looked out from The Dregs and waved goodbye to the C.O. A minute later the train reversed and they waved hello.

Borodin asked the stationmaster a question and got a stammering answer.

'The correct identification plates are in his office,' Borodin said.

'Can you be sure?' Brazier asked.

'He has fouled his breeches,' Borodin said. 'An infallible declaration of honesty.'

A couple of *plennys* cut the man free. He fell on the tracks. They picked him up and carried him, the officers following. He found the identification plates. He had recovered some strength, and he took the plates to the trains and attached them to the locomotives. The *plennys* marched him outside the station and dumped him in a horse trough. 'It's the least we can do for him,' Brazier said. 'Some would say, the least is too much.'

They went back to the trains. The squadron doctor was waiting. 'Your chaps spent all their pay in Taganrog,' she said. 'Now they're playing poker, and they're using the morphine phials as betting chips.'

They laughed. After the saga of the stinking stationmaster, almost anything was funny. Brazier's chuckle was brief. Gambling with property belonging to Mission H.Q. was certainly an offence. But, as Maynard had said, suicide was a crime too. Did two wrongs make a right? He gave up.

They boarded the train, Wragge gallantly allowing Susan Perry to go first. 'I don't think I told you,' he said. 'We're all pleased that you decided to continue as squadron doctor.'

'I had to leave Taganrog,' she said. 'A brigadier was besotted with me.'

'So is half the squadron.'

'It's worse than influenza,' she said. 'And no cure in sight.'

The new identification plates got two cheers. The trains still had to wait in sidings, but less frequently. There were detours around track repairs. Still, their average speed was much better. By nightfall they were in Kupyansk; by noon next day they entered Kharkov. Four hundred kilo-

328

metres from Taganrog, the drivers said. Very good indeed.

Parts of the city were still burning, but Denikin's armies had already gone ahead, advancing fast, aiming for Kursk, only 240 kilometres to the north. Once they took Kursk they would be halfway to Moscow.

Tsaritsyn had been a sideshow; this was the real war. The squadron had been trundling along on these trains for over a week, while the Bolos were going backwards at a rate of knots. Everyone wanted to clobber them while the clobbering was good. Wragge pressed on.

An hour out of Kharkov progress fell to a walking pace. The track had been damaged; repair gangs were at work; all traffic was switched to one line. Even at walking pace the trains swayed and jolted. Soon they had a good view of an armoured train lying drunkenly half off the tracks. The locomotive had one giant rosette of a shell-hole in its boiler and much of the train was burnt-out. No fire could destroy the gun barrels and they made a show of pointing everywhere.

'Ours or theirs?' Brazier asked.

'Probably theirs,' Borodin said. 'I think I see the remains of half a red star.'

'The whole thing took a pounding.'

'My guess is a lucky shot wrecked the engine. They didn't want us to capture the train, so they blew it up. Then they destroyed a length of track to slow down our pursuit. Standard tactics.'

They limped past the end of the wreck. The footnotes of battle lay all around: broken artillery pieces; the mounds of fresh graves, some with makeshift wooden crosses, most without; wagons that had shed their wheels but kept their dead horses between the shafts. There were plenty of dead horses, very visible with their black and bloated bodies. A haze of flies hovered around each horse.

'It's always the same,' Borodin said. 'You can smell a battlefield from miles away by the rotting horseflesh.'

Brazier didn't care. It would take a regiment a month to dig enough holes to bury these horses. What interested him was the why and the how of war. 'This was a minor rearguard action,' he said. 'The Reds tried to make a stand and failed. Not strong enough.'

'That's the curse of being on the retreat. Never enough of anything. Soldiers on the run throw their rifles away. I've seen it happen.'

'Men will stand and fight if you shoot a few. I saw that happen, too.'

Wragge joined them. 'We're being watched,' he said. He handed Brazier a pair of binoculars and pointed overhead. The adjutant opened a window and searched. He grunted and gave them to Borodin. 'Too much dazzle for my old eyes,' he said.

'He's been wandering around up there for fifteen minutes,' Wragge said. 'If he's one of ours, what's his game? And if he's not, it's bad news.'

'Too high to identify,' Borodin said. 'But he's obviously snooping.'

'If we get strafed we could be wiped out. Can you pass word to the driver? First good siding he sees, pull in. Let's get the machines off the trains.

It's time you learned how to fly a Camel. There's a spare you can have. Practise first. It's a tricky little beast.'

'Thanks awfully,' Borodin said.

The battlefield had been left far behind by the time they rolled into a siding. The grassland alongside it was level enough to make an airfield, once a few anthills had been flattened. The ground crews began unloading the aeroplanes. Lacey rigged his aerials. 'Find where Denikin's mob is,' Wragge said. 'Tell them we're here. Where's the war? Find *anything*.'

The watchful high-flying aeroplane had gone. Chef was serving tea. Kid, the mascot, found a patch of giant buttercups and enjoyed some real food at last. The trains would not be moving again today. The afternoon was perfect for a walk, sun sinking, not too hot, and the countryside was inviting. There were gentle hills, patches of woodland, probably a river. The train had passed a meandering stream, just the sort of thing, Dextry said, he had swum in as a boy in County Cork. Maynard said the countryside reminded him of Dorset. Jessop said it resembled parts of Buckinghamshire. Borodin said it looked a lot like Russia. They set off.

'I can see smoke,' Jessop said. 'Smoke means a farm. For a cake of soap they'll give us a pound of butter.'

'Unusual,' Borodin said. 'A farmhouse doesn't need a big fire in this weather.'

'Maybe they're smoking a ham. Butter *and* ham. Yummy.'

Maynard broke into a trot and bowled an

imaginary ball, a good length, just clipping the off stump. 'Run the mower over this lot,' he said. 'Get the heavy roller on the batting strip. You've got a decent cricket pitch.'

'Too decent for Russians, I'm afraid,' Borodin said. 'We like a sport where you can cheat.'

'Decent cricket's had its day,' Jessop said. '*Indecent* cricket, that's the answer. Men and women, stark naked. Mixed teams. Yum-yum.'

'Better yet, forget the cricket altogether,' Dextry said. 'Naked leapfrog.'

Maynard changed the subject. 'I hear you're our new flight leader.'

'Am I?' Dextry said. 'Excellent choice. I'm the best-looking.'

'If you're leading, we're totally lost,' Jessop said.

'Never mind, Junk. It's like Pass The Parcel in this squadron. You're next.'

It was a pleasant stroll. The meadows were lush and sprinkled with wildflowers. They found the river, startled a heron, and watched its heavy wings beat slowly until it curved out of sight behind a tree.

'Reminds me of an FE2b,' Jessop said. 'Pusher propeller, slow as treacle, lovely view of Huns licking their lips.'

'I crashed mine,' Dextry said. 'Best thing I ever did for the Corps.' The conversation developed into a search for the worst aeroplane of the war, on either side. The river turned away and they walked on, aiming for the smoke, and angered a dozen crows, which rose in a black rage. They had been feeding on the carcase of a cow. The horns said it had to be a cow. There was little else left.

'Sloppy farming,' Maynard said. 'Dead stock shouldn't be left lying.'

They moved on, and maddened four more gangs of crows working over four more carcases.

'This is worse than sloppy,' Dextry said. 'It's bizarre.'

By now they were in sight of the smoke, and it wasn't a farm: it was a village. 'I don't recommend going in,' Borodin said. 'There's nothing for us here.'

'We've come this far,' Dextry said. They went on.

It had been a typical Russian village, squat and unexciting, and now most of it was in ruins, destroyed by the fire that was still smoking. The airmen soon stopped looking: one body was much like another, slashed or battered or burnt.

'They're all dead,' Maynard said.

'Not all,' Borodin said. 'Stay here.'

A man was watching them. His skin and clothes were so dirty that he almost blended in with the blackened ruins. He was thin and frightened, ready to run. Borodin stopped when he was twenty feet away; they had a conversation. Borodin came back.

'He was at the river, fishing, when Nestor Makhno's men came and took all the food. That was a week ago, maybe two. He can't be sure. They killed a few old people for no reason. Just practising their anarchy. Later the Red Army came, hungry and angry of course. No food. Killed half the village. Then Denikin's Whites came, like the Reds, looking for food. This chap hid in the woods. They killed the other half and

333

burned the village. Who exactly slaughtered the cattle, nobody knows and it doesn't matter now.'

'Appalling,' Dextry said.

'Multiply by a thousand. Armies live off the land.'

'We should give him some food,' Jessop said. 'All I've got is the soap. Shall I give him that?' But the man had gone.

Nobody had much to say on the way back to the trains.

'How long has this been going on?' Maynard asked Borodin.

'Always. Armies must eat and generals cannot feed them.'

They went into The Dregs. 'Get any butter?' Wragge asked.

'No luck,' Jessop said. 'Early closing on Wednesdays.'

'It's Friday today.'

'It's Wednesday where they are. Also Monday, Tuesday, Thursday and Saturday.' The anger in his voice made Wragge raise an eyebrow. 'Go and see for yourself,' Jessop said. He turned and left.

5

At breakfast next day, the solitary aeroplane was back, and this time much lower. Wragge watched it through binoculars. 'Looks like a Halberstadt. Two-seater, anyway.'

'Probably taking photographs,' Borodin said. 'Red generals like to know if Denikin's being reinforced.'

334

'If he's snapped them, he's snapped us too. Lacey! Any luck with your radio?'

'I raised Mission H.Q. Latest information is the Whites reached Belgorod, twenty or thirty kilometres from here, and might have captured it. Opinions vary.'

Wragge had planned an hour or two of test flights, to make sure the Camels were fit for combat. He scrapped that, he cut breakfast short, he got four Camels in the air, climbing hard. They left Borodin behind to learn how to start the engine, the first thing that Camel beginners cocked up.

It took them seven minutes to climb to five thousand feet. The factory said four minutes, but these were not factory-fresh Camels and Jessop's engine was labouring. They climbed at the speed of the slowest machine and when they got there the Halberstadt had gone. Of course he had gone. Why hang around to let yourself be shot down?

'We put salt on his tail, anyway,' Wragge said aloud. Silly bloody expression. Made no sense. He marshalled his Flight into an echelon to starboard, Dextry, Maynard and Jessop, all widely spaced, with Jessop out where he would hit nobody if his engine suddenly failed, and they cruised north, following the railway.

The Camels rose and fell as gently as boats at sea in a slight swell. A friendly swell, Dextry thought, you can feel it but you can't see it. Sometimes the magic of flying amazed him: the whole business seemed so improbable. Maynard was thinking this was just like one of those rare sunny, cloudless days in England. He looked down and Russia could be a map of Wiltshire: woods, rivers, lots of green, the occasional village. Full of murdered peasants, perhaps. Not so like England after all. He abandoned the map. Jessop was listening to his engine-roar and waiting for the cough. Also, he was hungry. He'd been about to enjoy an omelette when Wragge dragged them out of The Dregs. Chef made a damn good omelette and Jessop salivated at the memory. Wragge was half-thinking of his squadron-leader's pay and half-remembering dancing with Cynthia in Taganrog before that thug had hit him. Nobody was searching the sky above for three chocolate-brown Spads that fell out of the blue. Wragge heard a faint pattering or rattling and saw bullet-strikes chasing across his lower port wing. 'Hell's teeth!' he shouted. Three brown shapes flashed past. By then his Camel was in a vertical bank to the right. Wragge kept turning and searched for fresh attacks. None. Clear blue sky. Empty. Thank you, God. He levelled out, looked down, saw three brown dots getting rapidly smaller. Double thank-you, God.

Dextry and Maynard found him. They had been hit: he saw strips of torn fabric flailing in the wind. No sign of Jessop. They flew home and caught up with him, much lower and slower. He made a forced landing alongside the tracks a mile from the trains, got out and waved.

Wragge let the others land first. Maynard bounced four times and the watching bomber crews all applauded. Dextry didn't like his first approach and went around again. Wragge made a semi-decent job of landing although his rudder pedals felt heavy. He sat in the cockpit and wondered why any of them deserved to be alive.

His fitter arrived and undid his seat belt. 'You've made holes in my nice aeroplane, sir,' the man said.

'Careless,' Wragge said. 'Unforgivably careless.'

Nobody was hurt. Jessop's machine was recoverable. They were all shaken, and disgusted at their folly. The post-mortem was brief. They'd been jumped by three single-seaters, looked like chunky Camels so they were probably Spads. Came and went like the hounds of hell. Didn't want a scrap. Quick blast and gone.

Markings? Roundels? Colours?

Nobody saw. Just a flash of brown. After that ... too busy dodging and weaving.

'They might have been learners,' Jessop said. 'That's why they did a bunk.'

'Might not have been Reds,' Maynard said. 'Made a mistake and scooted.'

'*We* made the mistake,' Dextry said. 'Four pairs of eyes and nobody saw.'

'Enough. Let's learn,' Wragge said. 'Learn what we've forgotten. The sky is one big man-trap. Red, White, striped, makes no difference. Every minute we're flying we search for the bastard who's up there waiting to make us flamers. We find him first, we kill him first. Just because the Bolos are going backwards doesn't make them rabbits.'

'Even rabbits can bite,' Jessop said. 'They've got those big rabbity teeth.'

'Oh, sweet Jesus,' Dextry said wearily. 'Don't you ever engage your brain before you open your mouth?'

'We still have one good Camel,' Maynard said.

337

'Borodin's. Suppose one of us goes up and bags a Bolo? I mean, now. That would show them who's boss, wouldn't it? I volunteer.'

'Not today, Daddy,' Wragge said. 'Today we lick our wounds. Tomorrow we're out for blood.'

There was little for them to do. The Nines had all been test-flown. The Camels were being checked and patched and double-checked by ground crews in case a stray bullet had nicked a control wire. Wragge made his rounds (doctor, Lacey, adjutant, flight sergeants) and all was in order.

Borodin, coached by a fitter, had mastered starting the Le Rhône rotary. It was midday, and hot. The air would be bumpy. Wragge had served, briefly, as an instructor at training fields in England that were rich in graves of Camel pupils who had taken off and failed to react quickly when the engine faltered and the fine-adjustment lever on the throttle demanded instant attention. No dual-control Camels: the pupil went up with only his wits to help him. Stall, spin, crash: a three-step dance of death. Wragge had seen it too often, had paid his half-crowns for too many wreaths and written the same letter to too many parents. Rarely to wives who were widows. Few pupils married at eighteen. So Borodin's first flight could wait.

The Number Nines had found the croquet set. Wragge took leave from the burden of command and challenged Tusker Oliphant to a match, the Toffs, or Camel pilots, versus the Peasants, or bomber louts. 'No offence meant,' he said. Oliphant accepted. 'We'll win,' he said. 'Losers to the guillotine.'

The turf was lumpy and the ground sloped in several directions. The smack of mallet on wooden ball was usually followed by a cry of, 'Bad luck, old man.' Sometimes, 'Jolly hard cheese.'

Lacey, Borodin and the squadron doctor came to watch. They sat in the back of the Chevrolet and drank white wine.

'This is a very old Russian sport,' Borodin said. 'Genghis Khan played it on horseback. Lacking croquet balls, he used the severed heads of captured princes.'

'Not a gentleman,' Lacey said firmly.

'Explain.'

'No restraint. Greedy. Like a child in a sweet-shop, wanting everything. Alexander the Great was another. Also our late C.O., Griffin.'

'Before my time,' Susan Perry said. 'I caught the funeral.'

'He never really approved of me,' Borodin said. 'I was a bloody foreigner.'

'We shouldn't blame him,' Lacey said. 'It's all a matter of breeding. In his case, somewhat lacking.'

'Ah-ah,' she said. 'The precious bloodline. How do you fit in, Lacey?'

'Comfortably. The Laceys go back many centuries.'

'So do I. So do we all.'

Borodin said. 'Last time I looked, my lot went back fifty thousand years.'

'That's not breeding,' Lacey said. 'That's repro-duction.'

'Lacey's a snob,' she said.

He gave her a crooked smile. 'If I made the effort, I could be a clod, like most people,' he

339

said. 'But then, you wouldn't get soft toilet paper, would you? Speaking of which, I had another signal from Mission H.Q. Their information is that Denikin has three squadrons of crack fliers helping his advance. All based on the aerodrome at Belgorod. Just a few miles from here.'

'What does Denikin say?'

'I can't raise his H.Q. Perhaps they're on the move. Perhaps they're too busy fighting.'

'I tried tapping the telegraph line but it's dead,' Borodin said. 'Which makes me wonder: if we can't talk to Denikin's staff, where did the British Mission H.Q. get its information about three squadrons of crack fliers?'

'From Denikin's Chief of Aviation. Colonel Subasnov was on a visit to Taganrog. Mission H.Q. said he was very helpful.'

A croquet ball bounced off a wheel of the car. Wragge strolled over, swinging his mallet at the larger wildflowers. 'Who's winning?' the doctor asked. He kicked his ball into a better position. 'Not us. I think Tusker's team are cheating.' He took a mighty whack and the ball hit one of the Cossack ponies, which had been let out to feed. It shied, and then tried to eat the ball. 'I think I scored a double bogey,' Wragge said. 'Maybe a triple. This pitch is a disgrace.' He walked away. 'Somebody shoot that animal before it ruins the game,' he shouted.

6

In the cool of the morning, Dextry coached

Borodin on the many ways his Camel could kill him.

They stood beside the fighter. A mechanic waited, his hands on the prop.

'Examine the beast,' Dextry said. 'All the heavy stuff, the engine, the guns, the fuel, the pilot, are grouped close together at the front. That's why it's called a Camel – the business end has a hump. Sopwiths can do this because the Le Rhône is a rotary engine, very compact. In a rotary the cylinders whizz round and round and take the prop with them.'

'Air-cooled,' Borodin said. 'Nice idea.'

'Yes. But it has to spin at a hell of a lick in order to fly. If Charlie there were strong enough to hold the prop still so it can't move, then your rotary would try to spin the whole aeroplane.'

'Torque.'

'And torque will try to kill you as soon as you take off. The starboard wing will drop and so will the nose. Correct *immediately*, give a hint more stick, maybe some throttle. If that wingtip touches you'll cartwheel and Charlie will sweep up the bits and put them in a sack.'

Borodin glanced at Charlie. 'That's correct, sir,' Charlie said. 'Every little scrap.'

'Now you're up and you've mastered the torque, the engine has another attempt at murder,' Dextry said. 'Sudden loss of power.'

'I practised that yesterday. On the ground, of course. It's the fine-adjustment, isn't it? Nursing the needle.'

'Be ready. *Expect* to lose power. Just tickle it. A rotary is a woman, it responds to a caress. Grab it and you'll choke it and it'll die and so will you. Which would be a waste, because in combat the Camel is the best there is. A wonderful killer of others. Alright, get in.'

Borodin made himself comfortable, feet on the rudder pedals, stick between legs, and fastened the belt.

'Here's the final way she'll kill you,' Dextry said. 'She can manoeuvre like magic. When in doubt, chuck everything into a right-hand bank and nobody can follow you. You'll turn so tightly it looks like you've gone through a revolving door. *But...*' He prodded Borodin's shoulder. 'It's that bloody torque again. It drags the nose down and before you know it...' He clicked his fingers. '...your Camel's in a power dive. Under a thousand feet, you'll probably make a hole in the ground. The answer is–'

'Opposing rudder,' Borodin said.

'Lots of it, and quick. Don't wait for trouble. Anticipate. Did they tell you about the button on the joystick?'

'Yes. For blipping the engine. Switching it on and off to get the speed right on landing.'

'Learn the art. You have a fine aristocratic nose. Make a crash landing and you'll bash your nose against those gun-butts and spend the rest of your life, if you live, with what we call "Camel Face". Not pretty. Are you ready to taxi? That's what you're going to do now. Simply taxi up and down the field a dozen times. Learn the basics.'

Dextry walked away. He sat on the grass and watched Borodin go through the starting routine with Charlie. The engine roared, belched a smell of castor oil, idled, roared again, settled down to a steady note. The chocks were removed. Borodin taxied away. Within fifty yards his tail was up. Within a hundred, he was flying.

Fifteen minutes later, the C.O. came out and joined the flight leader. They watched the Camel make its approach, shedding height as it blipped its engine, until it seemed to flare its wings, nose up, while the wheels felt for the ground, made the smallest bump, and ran.

'I told the idiot to taxi,' Dextry said. 'Learn how to walk before he runs.'

'Chew him out, if you like,' Wragge said. 'He's a natural. He joins the Flight.'

Dextry walked to the Camel as Borodin was climbing down. 'Nice machine,' Borodin said. 'She wished to fly, so I went along for the ride.'

'Understand this,' Dextry said. 'That's the last order you disobey. Briefing in half an hour.' He walked away. Charlie was waiting. 'Arm and refuel, Charlie,' he told him.

'He seems a nice gentleman, sir.'

'Lovely manners,' Dextry said. 'But can he kill?'

Briefing took less than a minute. The Camels would climb to ten thousand. Form a very loose arrowhead. Count Borodin is in the Flight. We take a look at Belgorod, see what's happening. H.Q. says the Whites have three squadrons based there. Do they know we've arrived? Maybe not. Stay awake. Questions? No? Good.

The Camels were labouring at eight thousand feet, and toiling after another five hundred, so Wragge cut his losses and levelled out. He was gasping for breath, he had sparks before his eyes. Maybe the air was unusually thin today. Anyway, even a new Camel couldn't fight worth a damn much above ten thousand. Huns just ran away from it. And these were not new Camels.

Belgorod was in sight – little more than a small market town, not big enough to be fortified; probably owed its existence to the railway – when Wragge noticed a glitter down there. To get a better view he eased the Flight into a glide, but the glitter vanished. Then it returned. Sunlight off water. He tried to trace the river, but it wandered and he lost it. Then his eye caught another flicker of light, nowhere near the river, and he squinted hard and saw yesterday's Halberstadt two-seater. Sun on its windscreen, probably. The machine was as tiny as a moth, almost camouflaged against the soft green countryside.

Wragge waggled his wings and made sure everyone saw the Halberstadt. He thought about the situation. Assume it was a Red machine, up to no good, maybe reconnaissance, counting the troop trains. Maybe bombing. It must have seen Merlin Squadron being unloaded yesterday, so bombs were likely. But no escort? Already, Wragge was searching the blue immensity above him. Suppose the Halberstadt was bait. Those Spads – if they were Spads – had 200-horsepower Hispano-Suizas, big enough to outclimb any Camel. He had specks of oil on his goggles. What was that up there? A Spad or a speck? A short rattle of gunfire made his pulse jump. Dextry was waving, pointing. Far on the left-hand quarter was a smudge of aircraft, only slightly higher than the Camels.

It matured and separated into a group of six. Three were the brown Spads. The others were a mixture: a Fokker Triplane, an all-red Nieuport, and what might be an Albatros. A mongrel lot. Flown by scruffs or aces? Wragge wondered and waited. His Flight was flying broadside-on to their approach. At four hundred yards all the Spads opened fire. Tracer probed and lost heart and fell below the Camels. 'Optimistic,' he said, counted to three, and banked hard towards the enemy. Now it was a head-on charge.

Jessop crouched and made himself small. Dextry kept his head up and looked for a gap to aim at. Maynard shouted: 'Come to Daddy!' and was glad no-one heard. Borodin murmured a soldier's prayer for a merciful death if death it must be. And the two formations met in a crash of noise and nothing else. They merged and separated in an instant. Nobody had fired. Firing was stupid if you were about to collide and aimless when you were not.

Wragge banked hard right, the Camel's trump card, and the Flight followed him. The Reds had scattered. The Spads climbed in three different directions and he chased the middle one until it was a distant blur in his gunsight. He turned and dived back to the fight, but there was no fight: just a huge and empty sky. No surprise. Air combat was like that. He searched and saw dots swirling with the pointlessness of bugs at dusk. He headed for them. One bug turned a hot red and dropped, trailing smoke. Not so pointless after all.

When Jessop came out of the vertical bank, the

Triplane swam into view, so he turned and fired and his bullet-stream bent as if blown sideways and nearly hit Maynard. Jessop shouted, and reversed bank, which created a huge skid that washed the Triplane out of sight. Not possible, bloody great Tripe couldn't disappear like that. Jessop turned the bank into a roll and made that into a sweet barrel-roll and at the top he looked down at Maynard going the opposite way and firing at something, and simultaneously red and yellow tracer chased itself past Jessop, nibbled at his wingtip, made his Camel twitch, and for an instant Jessop was puzzled, how the devil did Maynard do that? He completed the barrel-roll fast and Good Christ All Bloody Mighty the Tripe was back again. No mistakes this time. He worked to get behind it. Difficult. Damn thing never kept still.

Maynard was looking the other way when Jessop missed him. He didn't know whose guns they were, could have been one of three Bolos, not the Spads, they were gone. He banked and turned, looked left and right, banked again, looked up, looked back, banked again, never flew straight for more than ten seconds, never stopped searching. Maynard knew little about girls and sex but much about how to creep up behind an enemy and blow holes in him. He saw an all-red Nieuport chased by a Camel and an Albatros chasing the Camel, and he joined the hunt. He fired brief bursts at the Albatros, very long range but the Albatros took fright, put its nose down, and the Nieuport blew apart.

Dextry was chasing it and the explosion

amazed him: who did that? Maynard whooped with glee but he knew he hadn't scored. He joined Dextry and they circled the fluttering bits of burning debris, the drifting smoke. Warplanes were dangerous. Sometimes incendiary bullets misfired, touched off a fuel tank, a pilot sat in a wooden frame covered with doped linen and stuffed with explosives behind a red-hot engine, of course some machines blew apart. Nobody said flying was safe.

The flight was over. The Spads were out of sight, the Nieuport no longer existed, and the two survivors had quit in a hurry. Wragge chased them, for sport, and was outpaced. He returned and led the Flight to their landing ground next to the siding. On the way, they met the Halberstadt and shot it down. Its pilot made a brave attempt at a forced landing but the machine was hopelessly lopsided when it touched the ground, and it cartwheeled with surprising ferocity, every impact ripping off a part until there was little left but a trail of wreckage.

7

Lunch was taken. The Dregs was unusually quiet.

When they landed, the C.O. had talked to Dextry. 'We all got back,' he said, 'but that's the best that can be said.'

'Sloppy. Half the time we got in each other's way.'

'We've forgotten what a real scrap is like. I don't count the Halberstadt. To tell the truth, I felt sorry for the bloke.'

'He didn't put up much of a fight,' Dextry said. 'In fact, he didn't put up any fight at all.'

That was one of several things which the pilots did not talk about at lunch. Nobody claimed the Nieuport. Nobody mentioned the near-collisions.

When everyone had finished eating, Wragge said, 'We'll go again. This time I'll take the Nines with us. If there's an aerodrome at Belgorod and it's ours, we'll land there. If the Bolos are there, we'll bomb the stupid place.'

Tusker Oliphant led the Nines at three thousand feet, high enough to escape machine-gun fire from the ground, low enough to make a bombing run. The C.O. was a thousand feet above with the Camels. They followed the railway to Belgorod and nothing happened. No troops, no guns, no burning ruins. Few people in the streets, and nobody ran for shelter. A train stood in the station, the engine making a stick of brown smoke. That was the sum of the action.

The squadron flew a wide circle around Belgorod and did not find an aerodrome. But two miles north of the town, Tiger Wragge saw a racecourse beside the railway line. At first he was surprised. Racing seemed an unlikely luxury, but then why not? All it needed was space and horses, and Russia had plenty of both. He took the Camel Flight right down to a hundred feet and cruised around the course, a simple oval of grass. A three-coach train stood in a siding. A flag as big as a bedsheet waved in the breeze. It had several colours, which was encouraging. A few soldiers came out to watch the aeroplanes.

Wragge signalled to Borodin that he should land, and left Dextry in command. Borodin and the C.O. touched down on a wonderfully wide, flat, smooth stretch of grass, switched off, and got out.

An officer on a horse cantered towards them.

'I'm second fiddle now,' Wragge said. 'This is your show.'

The officer did not dismount. He was an expert horseman and he cut a good figure as he sat and looked down at them. Borodin introduced himself, and the officer dismounted very smartly, and saluted. Wragge strolled up and down while they talked, until Borodin said to him: 'The train belongs to a supporter of Denikin, General Yevgeni Gregorioff. We are safe here. The nearest fighting is at Kursk, a hundred miles north. We are invited to meet General Gregorioff in his salon.'

'Tell this chap I'm going to fire a signal flare,' Wragge said. 'I don't want to frighten his lovely horse.'

He got the Very pistol from his Camel and sent the flare arcing into the sky. He dumped his flying coat and helmet in the cockpit. Now he was recognisably a squadron leader, with a slightly battered but rakish cap. 'Lead on,' he said. Already the squadron was making its descent.

General Gregorioff was a tubby little man, almost bald, with a thick black moustache that reached his chin. He greeted his guests cheerfully, without moving from a cane chair overflowing with pillows. His right leg rested on a stack of blankets. He had no English. He and Borodin exchanged compliments, and the count explained to Wragge that the general had very bad gout and was on medical leave from the Front. That explained the young and attractive nurse.

'Ask him where the three White fighter squadrons are,' Wragge said. 'And the aerodrome?'

Armchairs were brought, and they settled down to a friendly chat. Wragge examined the general's quarters. Bookshelves, a baby grand piano, family photographs, thick carpet, velvet curtains. Not Spartan. Coffee was served. Good coffee, better than The Dregs. The general was an affable man, and whatever Borodin was saying to him, it made him laugh.

Then the audience was over. Everyone smiled happily. An aide opened doors and helped them descend from the train without breaking a leg.

'What did you get out of him?' Wragge asked. 'Apart from merry laughter.'

'For a start, the three squadrons of White fighter aircraft don't exist. Nor does the aerodrome. Denikin has no machines, except us.'

'I see,' Wragge said. 'No, I don't. What about that signal from Mission H.Q? Colonel Somebody. Boss of Aviation.'

'Subasnov. The general was very amused by that story. He knows Subasnov well. The colonel was on Denikin's staff, the biggest chump in the army, couldn't be sacked because of his political connections, so Denikin gave him Aviation and sent him as far away as possible to bother someone else. The general says Subasnov talks magnificently. If talk won wars, we would be in Moscow now.'

'So he lied.'

'Yes and no. To an Anglo-Saxon he lied un-forgivably. To Russians he adjusted the facts to agree with the way the truth ought to be. A great army deserves to have an air force, and of course Mission H.Q. was impressed by what he said.'

'Absurd. He must have known he'd be found out.'

'True. But Russians can't stop themselves. There's a word for that kind of lying. We call it *vranyo*. It satisfies some inner need. Russians lie even when they know the listener knows they're lying. So, *vranyo* does no harm, does it?'

'*Nichevo,*' Wragge said. 'Is that right, *nichevo?*'

'Excellent. You are thinking like a Russian.'

'And the promise of an armoured train. Was that *vranyo?*'

'In its purest form. By the way: Denikin had one aeroplane. The Halberstadt two-seater. He sent it to count his troop trains because the telegraph line was broken.'

'We shot down a friendly machine.'

'General Gregorioff says the telegraph is working now.'

'So ... *nichevo* again.'

'His very word.'

'Mine too. From now on we'll fight like Russians. We'll *vranyo* like fury and if anyone doesn't like it, *nichevo*.' Wragge shouted for Maynard, ordered him to fly back to the trains and tell them to move up to the racetrack sidings. 'Tomorrow we go to Kursk,' he said. 'That's where the fun and games are happening.' He said nothing about the Halberstadt. Fog of war. Forget it.

BIT OF SWAGGER

1

The gardens at 10 Downing Street were neither large nor glorious, but at least the roses were splendid at this time of year. The Prime Minister preferred to hold his garden parties there. It meant he didn't have to trudge around somebody else's pride and joy, shaking hands with strangers until his knuckles ached. It meant that as soon as the party was over, he could get back to his desk. And if it rained, there were always drawing rooms for the guests to shelter in.

He kept the guest list short. Senior Cabinet members, a few ambassadors, some admirals and generals, maybe an artist or a poet, if they were house-trained. No novelists, no playwrights. Drank too much, got into arguments with other guests. Not garden-party material.

The guest list was one of Jonathan Fitzroy's duties, and he quietly added the names of his Ad Hoc Committee on Russia. It was a white-tie occasion, so the garden would look like a penguin colony, and that answered the need for secrecy: his committee would hide in plain sight.

When the P.M. had done enough partying and withdrawn, and the guests were leaving, the committee gathered in a little summerhouse. Fitzroy put a pack of cards on the table. 'A harmless subterfuge,' he said. 'In case anyone looks in.'

Weatherby dealt a few cards. 'I can't play anything except Snap,' he said. 'My children are demons at Snap. I never stand a chance.'

'Mine were like that,' Delahaye said, 'until I began to cheat. That fooled them.'

'You've got to be ruthless with children, in my experience,' General Stattaford said. 'Or they lose all respect. My parents were quite foul to their children, I'm happy to say. It made a man out of me.'

'The modern child is over-educated, in my opinion,' Sir Franklyn said. 'I heard my granddaughter singing "Lloyd George is my father, father is Lloyd George". The child is only nine. I asked her what it meant and she said she didn't know.'

'I bet she did,' Weatherby said. 'They know everything.'

'Perhaps we should ask them to advise us,' Fitzroy said. He was a bachelor; other people's children bored him. 'A little omniscience about Russia might be helpful.'

'Not any more,' the general said. 'The Reds are routed. Denikin's on a charge. In war, momentum is everything. We proved that in France. Once we broke the enemy line, the Huns couldn't stop running. Reds are the same.'

'But not in Siberia,' Sir Franklyn said. 'They seem to have the better of Admiral Kolchak.'

'A sideshow. Denikin's campaign is the key. Poltava has fallen. Kharkov has fallen. Kiev has fallen. Odessa won't hold out much longer. Denikin will take Kursk. Then it's a straight run

353

to Moscow.'

'Napoleon said that too,' Delahaye said. 'Mind you, it probably had more panache in French.'

'His mistake was getting the weather wrong,' Weatherby said. *'Beaucoup de neige.* Dreadfully *froid.* Hadn't done his homework.'

'And no railways. So no return tickets.'

'Denikin has got everything spot-on right,' Stattaford said. 'Summertime, and the railways lead to Moscow. All he needed was a spell of training, courtesy the British Army, to stiffen his ranks. I never doubted it.'

'Excellent. Now, how do we translate this for the P.M.'s benefit?' Fitzroy asked. 'Triumph of right over wrong? Death-blow to Communist world domination? Last battle of the Great War, and Britain helped to win it? What's the message?'

'Well now,' Sir Franklyn said. 'Russia is a very big country. Let us not cheer too soon.'

'The Treasury will cheer if Denikin takes Moscow,' Charles Delahaye said. 'Then we can stop throwing money at Russia with both hands.'

'Penny-pinchers,' the general said. 'We didn't beat the Kaiser by double-entry bookkeeping. Whatever that is.'

'There's a difference. Russia is not about to invade Britain.'

'Undeniable,' Fitzroy said. 'Still, I wonder if there's something in Denikin's success for the P.M. D'you remember that excellent phrase of Sir Franklyn's? "Answering the call of freedom and justice". Well, we've done it, and surely it's earned us the right to ... um ... to reward ourselves. Or words to that effect.'

'What effect?' Stattaford said.

'Reward means only one thing,' Weatherby said. 'Higher wages. And if you want to avoid bloody Bolshevik revolution in Britain, that's what you should do, and do it now.'

'Money.' The general sniffed. 'That's all some people think of.'

'Because prices have gone up much faster than wages.'

'Good point,' Fitzroy said. 'I never thought the police would go on strike last year, but they did. Mind you, that was about recognising their union.'

'Everyone talks of the sanctity of labour,' Delahaye said, 'but what they really want is hard cash.'

Sir Franklyn had begun building a house of cards. 'Look here,' he said. 'This is what we've been doing at these meetings. Trying to create something without foundation. Why are we in Russia? Not to help our gallant allies who fought the Germans. That's ancient history. Not to guarantee a fair fight. We can't. Not to do the decent thing. War isn't about decency, it's about power. Not to answer the call of freedom and justice. In Russia, that's a fantasy. So why are we there?' He looked up. 'What are we trying to achieve?'

'Beat the Bolsheviks,' Fitzroy said. He sounded weary.

Sir Franklyn looked at his creation. 'Who wants to be the one to blow the house down?'

Weatherby filled his lungs and blew the cards across the table.

Fitzroy took a slim gold watch from his waistcoat pocket. 'I have a meeting with the P.M. in five minutes. Unless we have any extenuating thoughts...? No. If you'll excuse me, gentlemen.'

They watched him cross the garden.

'Perhaps we've overlooked the obvious,' Weatherby said. 'Haven't we got a duty to protect the Empire? The damned Russians have always wanted to get their greedy hands on India.'

'The Empire is a heritage,' Sir Franklyn said. 'Future generations won't thank us if we lose it.'

'Future generations don't pay to keep it,' Delahaye said.

'Explain.'

'Riots and rebellions. We're always rushing off to defend bits of Empire. Not cheap.'

'The White Man's burden, I suppose.'

'Not a burden,' Stattaford said. 'Debt of honour. It's why God created the British Army. And, to a lesser extent, the Royal Navy.'

'I sometimes wonder,' Delahaye said. 'I wonder whether we own the British Empire or it owns us.'

'If you don't like it, go and live in Denmark.'

'It has its attractions.'

Time to leave. They walked across the garden. 'This whole Russian affair,' Weatherby said. 'Intervention and so on. It would be interesting to know just what future generations will make of it.'

'Nothing,' Sir Franklyn said. 'We'll file it and forget it. Nobody will ever know it happened.'

2

Kursk was burning.

A strong wind from the west blew the smoke away but it also kept the fires alive and made more smoke. Kursk was an old city. The onion domes were brick but the houses were wood and they burned easily.

The trains stopped in a siding a couple of miles from town, and Borodin talked to the drivers. 'The line runs through the centre of Kursk,' he told the C.O. 'Need I say more?'

Wragge looked at the field alongside the track. 'Pretty flat,' he said. 'If we get rid of those dead horses, and fill in that shell crater, and pull down that fence... What d'you think?'

'The horses can go in the crater.'

'Good thinking. Uncle can organize that. And you and I will take a stroll, and try to find someone on Denikin's staff who speaks English.'

They walked along the track. 'No roads to speak of,' Wragge said. 'Everything is railways in your country, isn't it? Even the rivers dry up in summer. Before the railways came, how did Russians get from here to there?'

'They walked. Rather like most of the English, until quite recently.'

'Slight difference, old chap. Russia's vast. Belgorod to Kursk is, what, a hundred miles? With not much in between. We passed the odd village. Can't image the odd peasant tramping fifty miles to have his appendix removed.'

Borodin was amused. 'A Russian peasant would sooner die than pay a doctor. He dies anyway. Most men are old at thirty-five and lucky to see forty.'

'Good God.' Wragge thought about that. 'How

can you possibly know? You're not a peasant.'

'The *Britannica*. 1911 edition. But you're right about our railways. If Denikin were to march his army from Taganrog to Moscow, it would take six months, his men would be exhausted, the supply columns would be raided by Nestor Makhno and a dozen like him, and we'd be up to the hips in snow. So we fight our battles on the railway. It's easier to advance by train.'

'Unless the enemy rips up the track and blows the bridges,' Wragge said.

'Oh well. Nobody said that war was fair. And unless I'm mistaken we've found Denikin's Staff H.Q.'

The train had once belonged to the Tsar, and the carriages bore the Imperial emblem of the double-headed eagle. Planted alongside the track was the red, green and white flag of Denikin's One Russia, Great and Undivided.

A sentry saluted and they climbed aboard, into a very military setup: maps, typewriters clacking, paperwork, officers with a lot to say to each other. Immediately, Borodin recognized several people and was welcomed with smiles and embraces. He said something about Wragge, and everyone applauded. A servant offered a chair and a glass of tea. For the first time since Tsaritsyn, Wragge's spirits were lifted by the feeling of momentum found in an army that believed itself unstoppable.

Borodin introduced a young colonel whose English was good enough to say that unfortunately Denikin was elsewhere, awarding medals, but undoubtedly the arrival of the R.A.F. would thrill him. Kursk would soon be taken. The enemy was in full retreat. He might attempt a rearguard action. Denikin would wish the squadron to bomb him to... He looked at Borodin.

'Smithereens.' To Wragge, Borodin said, 'When can we start?'

'Tomorrow,' Wragge said. 'Early.'

The colonel embraced him and he spilled his tea, and they all laughed. *'Na Moskvu?'* Wragge said.

'First, *na Orel*,' the colonel said. 'Second, *na Tula*. Then, *na Moskvu*.' He spoke with all the confidence of a man who has added one and two and made three.

'And the Red air force?' Wragge asked.

'N'existe pas,' the colonel said, and everyone laughed again. It was going to be a cakewalk.

3

The wind strengthened. Ground crews turned the aircraft so that they faced into it. They pegged down the wingtips and the tails. They lashed canvas covers over the engines and secured the propellers. The western horizon was as black as spilled ink. They rammed chocks behind the wheels and tied the joystick in a central position.

When the storm came, the wind howled for half an hour and then moved on, leaving the rain to play a drum roll on the carriage roofs all night.

'Listen to it,' Maynard said. 'The cockpits will be full to the brim.' He was playing dominoes with Borodin, Jessop, Dextry and the doctor, in her Pullman.

'Unlikely,' Dextry said. 'Those Camels are pretty moth-eaten specimens. Plenty of drainage holes. If I look down, I can count the daisies between my feet.'

'I wonder if I ought to get married,' Jessop said.

Maynard cleared his throat and nudged him.

'Don't be so damned sensitive, Daddy,' Susan Perry said. 'I'm a war widow. I've seen enough blood to drown you all, and I shan't get a fit of the vapours because someone mentions marriage. You can't play a five,' she told Jessop.

'Yes, I can. Bloody good move.'

'Not against a three. Have you played this game before?'

He took back the domino. 'I could have sworn it was a three. Honestly, the light in here...'

She leant sideways and looked at his pieces and picked out a three and played it. 'Do up your laces and then blow your nose,' she said. 'You're dribbling on my carpet.'

'I say, steady on, doc. Play the white man.'

'Marriage would suit you, Junk,' Borodin said. 'You're ugly and stupid and you talk a lot of bollocks, and somewhere there's a girl, not very bright, just waiting for you to help her make lots of little Jessops.'

'You chaps have minds like sewers. One doesn't want to get married for ... for bedroom reasons.' Jessop rearranged his dominoes.

Maynard, feeling left out, said: 'I was conceived in a hammock. In India.'

'I, on a grand piano,' Borodin said. 'With the top down, of course.'

'In my case it was in a hot-air balloon,' Dextry

said. 'Over Windsor Castle. On a Thursday. Quarter to three. They rang all the church bells.'

They looked at Jessop. 'I have nothing to add,' he said.

'Do you understand how the human plumbing arrangement works, Junk?' she asked. 'See me tomorrow and I'll draw you a picture.'

'That sounds fun,' Dextry said. 'Can we all come?'

She played her last domino. 'I win,' she said. 'And heaven help the poor girls who marry you lot.'

The rain stopped as suddenly as it began. It woke the C.O., and he lay in bed wondering how soggy the airfield would be. But when he walked its length with his flight leaders, the turf was wet but firm. 'Chalky soil,' Tusker Oliphant said. 'Drains well. Last night's rain was probably the first for ages. Ground just sucked it up.'

'Good,' the C.O. said. 'Test flights. Then we'll all go and find some Bolos to biff.'

The fires of Kursk had been doused, and the squadron flew low around its onion domes. There were five, clustered together, each topped by a cross. The domes were of different heights and styles: the tallest and biggest was gilded; some were sky-blue with gold stars; others were ribbed in blue and white, or cross-hatched like pineapples, or swirled upwards in bands of yellow and green. Dextry liked their cheerful splendour. He had seen too many grey Irish churches, hunched defensively against the rain, with nothing outside or inside to warm his heart except the threat of eternal fire and brimstone. The Russian God did not object to brightly striped onion domes. He seemed like a friendly God. Made you wonder why Russians had to be so bloody to each other all the time. Never smiled. Or, if they did, they made it look as if it was coming out of their wages. Oh, well. *Nichevo.*

Nobody in Kursk fired at the squadron, so Wragge turned north and followed the line.

After the storm came a battalion of small clouds. Showers fell from a few. Rainbows formed and glowed and faded and appeared elsewhere. The morning sun made shafts between the clouds that increased the theatrical effect, and the C.O. gave everyone a little innocent fun by climbing towards the biggest rainbow and swerving around the clouds. It made for good practice in formation-keeping. He was leading them down a shaft of sunlight when dirty brown blots of shellfire stained the sky. Some came so close that he could smell the cordite.

He grabbed the Very pistol and fired a red flare: the signal for the Nines to operate independently. The Camels broke to the right and the Nines banked sharp left, out of the spotlight. The C.O. hid his Flight above a cloud until he was sure the formation was intact. Then he sideslipped and they fell through the cloud and emerged, fast and getting faster. The gunners on the ground were slow to find them and their fire was wild, not helped by the fact that they were shooting from an armoured train moving at speed.

It was a power dive, a new experience in a Camel for Borodin, and he was conscious of the frantic flapping of a piece of loose fabric in the wing near his head. If the whole wing got stripped, half the controls would be lost and he would have about ten seconds to live. Maybe fifteen. Then Wragge pulled out of the dive and chased the train, and Borodin followed. Not dead yet, Wragge thought. Thank you, God.

He was below treetop level, where the big guns couldn't reach him, but the train had machine guns. Borodin could see the muzzle-flash and the streaks of tracer. If there is a God, Wragge thought. And then the Camels were strafing the train from left and right. He saw it shake in his sights as the twin Vickers pounded away but he knew the tremors came from his Camel. His bullets wouldn't dent armour plating. Only a very lucky shot would find a machine-gunner. The Camels climbed and banked and fled to safety. Let the bombers do their worst.

The strafe gave Tusker Oliphant time to get his Flight lined up behind him. He aimed to fly down the length of the train, where the bombs stood a better chance of hitting something. They went in at three hundred feet, high enough to escape their own bomb-blasts. The machine-gunners on the train had not been killed. Their tracers swam up, searching.

Oliphant's approach seemed horribly slow to him, but that was because the train kept speeding away. And the Nine felt horribly vulnerable. That wide wingspan was easy to hit. So was he. Tracer flicked by and he remembered butterfly collections pinned through the body and the thought made his testicles try to crawl inside themselves.

Then he reached the train, stuck his head into the thundering gale and tried to line up the target. It looked very narrow. He pulled the bomb toggles and hoped, gave the engine full throttle and banked so as to let his gunner vent his spleen on the Bolos. He'd survived. Full marks. Vent his spleen, he thought. Odd expression. How do you vent a spleen?

The others followed. Some Nines missed and the bombs threw up fountains of dirt. Some hit, but their bombs bounced off the armour. Some bombs found chinks in the armour and the explosions shook the train. But it charged on.

The last Nine was flown by Douglas Gunning and Michael Lowe. This was the most thrilling test they had faced since they came to Russia, a high-speed duel against a deadly enemy.

Gunning made his approach from wide of the right of the track to give Lowe freedom to rake the machine-gunners, who seemed to have multiplied. He saw the bombs that missed. Sometimes their blast rocked the train. 'Blast!' he shouted. An extreme swear word in his home, rarely used. 'Blast blast!' This wasn't good enough. 'Can do better. Must try harder.' He lost a hundred feet as he banked towards the train. Now the target was bigger, and right under him. Tough luck on poor old Lowe, unable to fire straight down.

Gunning had a brilliant idea. Bomb the engine. Lay his eggs in the firebox and blow the vitals to kingdom come! He went down another fifty feet and crept forward. More tracer zipped by. 'Can't catch me!' he shouted. Lowe got shot twice in the right thigh and felt as if he'd fallen into a fire and couldn't get out. Gunning guessed his Nine was perfectly placed. Now or never. He dropped his bombs and they overshot his target by forty yards. Most of them killed a lot of wildflowers but one jammed itself under the steel track and blew it apart. The wheels of the engine charged into the gap and the rest of the armoured train followed it, capsizing as it charged into a ditch and disaster.

Gunning soared and swung into a wide half-circle to enjoy the spectacle of the wreck. 'Did you see that, Michael?' he shouted, and looked back to exchange grins and saw instead a face full of pain. The most that Lowe could do was raise a gloved hand and the tearing wind blew streaks of blood from it. Gunning gave the engine full throttle and flew home. But Michael Lowe was dead when the ground crew lifted him from his cockpit.

The adjutant met the C.O. when he landed and told him the news. 'And Lacey received this signal,' he said. It was from their new English-speaking liaison on Denikin's staff. Red strongpoint resisting White advance. Please assist. The C.O. looked around, saw Dextry, and waved the signal. 'We're off again, Rex,' he shouted. 'Refuel, rearm and bomb up. Just time for a wash and a bowl of soup.' To Dextry he said: 'Where is he now?'

'The doctor's got him. Cleaning him up. He bled to death. Bit of a mess.'

'Alright. Look, keep it under your hat. The boys will find out soon enough. Kursk isn't far, there's bound to be a church with a graveyard. Scout about. Lowe, did you say? Which one was he?'

'Shortish, curly hair, smiled a lot. Looked like his pilot, Gunning. Could have been twins.'

Wragge worried about it, couldn't remember the face, gave up. A late Nine sailed in, its engine sounding like a bag of rusty nails and the exhausts burping smoke. More bad news. Lowe could wait.

They took off, one bomber short, flew over the wrecked train and, twenty miles north, saw the Red strongpoint long before they reached it: a brisk exchange of artillery fire flashed and flickered. Tusker Oliphant's Flight climbed hard to four thousand feet, where broken cloud would trouble the anti-aircraft guns. The Camels climbed higher, to give the Nines cover, and patrolled the twisting avenues of sky. As they cruised into a suddenly enormous space, a Red flight arrived by a side entrance. Three Sopwith Pups, each glowing with dazzle camouflage, and three brown Spads. For a moment both formations kept their shape and looked at each other across an empty quarter of a mile.

Pups, Wragge thought. Good in their day. Camels eat them for breakfast. And Spads are cads. Usually.

He had a couple of hundred feet advantage of height. The enemy cruised on. Maybe it was a trap. Or maybe they suspected the same. He led the Flight in a climbing turn, away from the Reds, and went circling up until he was six hundred feet higher and the enemy were further away than ever. But at least the Camels were above them.

It took five minutes of full-throttle flying to catch up. If there was a trap it was lost in the clouds. Wragge made a last scan above and behind, and pushed the stick forward. The whistle of wind in the wires built to its usual scream. Still the enemy flew straight and level in two arrow-heads, Pups leading Spads. Wragge found a Spad growing big in his telescopic sight and his fingers were tightening on the trigger when the Spad vanished.

Borodin, arriving last, saw it all. The Pups banked hard left, the Spads went hard right, and the Camels plunged through the hole. Someone had watched, had known just when to scatter. Now the Reds had height advantage. The machines might be old but the pilots could fly. They could fight.

Wragge pulled out as hard as he dared and used the power of the dive to climb, which brought the familiar grey mist to his eyeballs and a deadening to his fingers on the stick. His heart pumped more blood, the mist faded and he saw two Pups drifting towards him in perfect formation, wing-tips almost touching, even the jazzy camouflage was identical, look, they fired at exactly the same instant. Something kicked his Camel so violently that the stick jumped in his hands. He lost control and the sky turned sideways. His brain got to work. Double vision. Thanks very much, brain. One single Pup flashed overhead, so close that he could see its ailerons working. But by then the Camel was in a sideslip that became a spin and Wragge had his hands full.

The others saw none of this. Dextry was in a tail-chasing duel with a Spad whose turning circle was inferior to a Camel's but the pilot didn't know this and Dextry was trapped in the chase. If he straightened up and banked hard the Red pilot would get a chance of a clear shot. Maynard was chased by two Spads. He worked the rudder pedals and stick and swore without stopping until he found a cloud to hide in. The Spads prowled and searched but he escaped from cloud to cloud until they got bored. Borodin and Jessop scrapped with two Pups until one of the enemy had serious engine failure and glided out of the action, leaving a black scarf of smoke across the sky to mark its going. They shot it down. The other Pup vanished.

That was pretty much the end of the fight. Dextry's tail-chasing Spad tried to frighten him with bursts of bullets behind his tail, ran out of ammunition and abruptly dived away. The others followed: he was evidently their leader. The C.O. toiled up from his spin and assembled the Flight. They flew home, all except Maynard. He was totally lost.

All that dodging and swerving had bewildered his compass. He had no idea where the railway was. The sun was no help: it was overhead and half the time it was behind cloud. He found a little river and followed it, for no good reason but he couldn't think of anything better. It was a placid river and its meanderings told him nothing at all. Not very clever. He abandoned the river and decided to go to the other extreme. Climb high. Better view. He began spiralling up and got a view so frightening that he clenched his toes and his stomach muscles. His fuel gauge was a shocking sight. The needle was bouncing on empty.

That simplified the problem.

Maynard stopped climbing and throttled back and began a long glide that must end somewhere down there, preferably not a bog or a forest or a rocky hillside. Or, God help us, a Red Army camp. His phial of morphine was on the train. Unthinkable that he'd ever need it. Forget it. Look harder.

In the end the Camel decided. It skimmed a few birch trees, coughing its final warning, died and settled on whatever came next, which turned out to be a hayfield. The wheels found hard land deep in the grass and ran. The stems brushed the wings, but grass was no match for a Camel, and it mowed down the hay and came to a halt.

He closed his eyes. The sun was warm and the cockpit was wonderfully comfortable, so he rested his tired body and enjoyed being alive. When he opened his eyes, a man on a horse was looking at him. 'I don't suppose, by any amazingly good luck, that you speak English?' Maynard said.

'Not a bloody word. I'm from Wales. I don't suppose you speak Russian. Is this your Camel? I don't suppose it speaks Arabic.'

The more he thought about that, the funnier it got. Maynard laughed, and knew that what he was really laughing at was his amazingly good luck in not killing himself. Rocky ground would have thrown the Camel ass over tit and broken his neck.

He unclipped the pocket watch from the dashboard, undid his seat belt and climbed down. 'Flying Officer Maynard,' he said.

'Major Edwardes, Royal Artillery. I'm an adviser to Denikin's guns. I saw you looking lost, so

I breezed over to pick up the pieces. You could probably do with a cup of tea. It's a long walk. Jump up.'

He kicked one foot out of a stirrup. Maynard poked his boot into it and swung up, behind Edwardes. They trotted away. 'Pleasant countryside,' the major said. 'Reminds me of Suffolk. Where are you from?'

'Wiltshire. Went to school in Dorset. Sherborne.'

'I was at Gresham's. Norfolk. Never learned a damn thing except sums. Won prizes for sums. So the army put me in guns.'

'Very far-sighted.'

'Perhaps. Also short-sighted. This was '16; lots of gunners had kicked the bucket. Clobbered by Boche counter-battery fire. War Office was desperate. I was perfect. Clever enough to calculate range, stupid enough not to work out the chances of survival.'

Maynard realized that Edwardes was only a year or two older than himself. Maybe twenty-three or twenty-four. Probably only a captain raised to major for service in Russia. So he'd been rescued by a man more or less his equal. 'Can you get a message to my squadron?' he said.

'We'll try. Things are a bit fluid around here.'

Maynard's legs were feeling the strain of being stretched across the broad hindquarters when they reached Edwardes' unit. It was six field guns, horse-drawn, and four tents. Meals were being cooked on an open fire. Maynard slid off the rump and massaged his thighs. 'I don't suppose you brought your toothbrush,' Edwardes said. 'Never mind. You can use mine.'

4

The C.O. called a meeting with the flight leaders and Borodin. 'That was a rough scrap,' he said. 'Where's Daddy Maynard?'

'Nobody knows,' Dextry said. 'Last seen chased by the Spads into cloud. We tumbled one Red bus. Most of the Camels took some punishment. I got peppered. They knew their stuff, didn't they? Pretty hot.'

'How did you get on?' Wragge asked Oliphant.

'Well, we lost Lowe this morning. You know all about that. Otherwise we bombed the target. Might have hit some artillery pieces, might not. Gave them something to think about, anyway. Last time I looked, the Bolos seemed to be retreating.'

'Good.'

'It was a bit messy. Bombs got sprayed all over the scenery. I hope we didn't hit anybody on our side.'

'Fortunes of war, Tusker. *Nichevo.*' Wragge looked at Borodin. 'Your man on Denikin's staff said the Red air force *n'existe pas.*'

'*Vranyo.* Like the armoured train.'

The C.O. briefly explained *vranyo* to his flight leaders. 'Two can play at that game,' he said. 'I'm going to signal Mission H.Q. that we shot down half the Bolos and silenced their artillery. And I'd be obliged, Count, if you would tell Denikin the same.'

'Nothing simpler.'

'That might win a few medals,' Dextry said, 'but it won't win the war.'

'*Nichevo*,' the C.O. said. '*Nichevo* in spades. Any problems?' They had no problems. 'Uncle has found a church within walking distance. Lowe's funeral will be at six p.m. Spread the word.'

The squadron filled the church. It was a small building, dedicated to St Erasmus. 'A very minor saint,' Borodin murmured to the C.O. 'Supposedly the protector of sailors. How he washed up in Kursk is anybody's guess.'

'They don't believe in pews.'

'Congregations stand in Russia. Sitting in church is bad form. Decadent.'

The priest arrived. He was old, and so bent that his beard seemed to weigh him down; but he was well organized. The packing-case planks of the coffin were covered with a large Russian flag. Lowe's cap was on top, and there were flowers. The priest had assistants to ring bells and hand him incense and holy water for sprinkling. Altar boys held weighty prayer books for him, and turned the pages. All told, it was an impressive performance. The squadron didn't understand the words, but they had the good manners to shut up and listen, and bow their heads when the altar boys and the acolytes did. The general meaning was obvious. Farewell to Michael Lowe.

The priest said something to Borodin. Four strong airmen lifted the coffin to their shoulders and carried it out, blessed on its way by the priest. He was mercifully brief at the graveside:

he had already said what mattered most. He looked at Borodin. Borodin looked at Lacey. Lacey cleared his throat, and let everyone hear his words.

And think, this heart, all evil shed away,
A pulse in the eternal mind, no less,
Gives somewhere back the thoughts by
 England given;
Her sights and sounds; dreams happy as her day;
And laughter, learnt of friends; and gentleness,
In hearts at peace, under an English heaven.

The cap was removed, and the flowers. The flag was folded. The burial was signalled by the rifle volleys, echoing off the church and scattering a flock of birds. Everyone knew the shots were coming but even so, many heads flinched, and the event was too much for Douglas Gunning. Grief overwhelmed him. His throat choked on suppressed sobs. The squadron parted to let him stumble away.

Lacey sent the C.O's report to Mission H.Q. and turned to the really rewarding work.

A signal had arrived from Captain Butcher at H.Q., and Lacey showed it to the adjutant. 'You said I was in the soup over the elephant guns in the croquet box. Alas, it is poor Butcher who is bamboozled.'

Brazier read:

Re your request barrel locking nuts stop local trans-
lator suggests mistranslation from Russian of barrel

373

elevation locknut stop no replacements available stop weapon is highly dangerous without this item stop am sending urgently quantity three Maxim machine guns and ammunition stop officer commanding Mission requests congratulate Cossack leader Reizarb stop provide further details gallantry flying officer Jossip for information War Office London stop Captain Butcher Royal Artillery stop.

'This is an elephant trap, Lacey, and you are digging it deeper and deeper.'

'You really think so? You know the Cossack Reizarb better than anyone. Could you send him H.Q's warmest thanks?'

'Twaddle.'

'Reizarb could become a footnote in history. He's worth watching.'

'I know nothing of this humbuggery. Thank God.'

Lacey sharpened a pencil and got to work. Brazier sat at his desk and browsed his *British Army Pocket Book, 1917.* 'Characteristics of an Arab Raiding Party' caught his eye. May consist of anything from two thousand to five thousand men. If Bedouin, on camels. If semi-nomads, on horses. If many sheep are present, signifies loot. Before action, banners will be unfurled.

Interesting. Worth remembering.

'This should occupy his mind for a while,' Lacey said.

The adjutant read his draft:

Regret report mortars on loan to Cossack Reizarb for training purposes exploded stop result death of Reizarb

374

and ten Cossacks stop new leader is Georgi Godunov stop claims is rightful heir to Boris Godunov Tsar 1598–1605 stop Georgi Godunov unreliable stop has deserted White cause and now campaigns as warlord stop squadron highly successful Bolsheviks in full retreat Russian civilians applaud ground crew jazz band stop request urgently quantity one each trombone trumpet clarinet E flat banjo stop Squadron Leader T. Wragge Officer Commanding.

'We haven't got a jazz band,' Brazier said.

'We shall if he helps. I am no slouch on the banjo, of which, as you know, an E flat version doesn't exist, but we'll let Butcher worry about that.'

'Not we, Lacey. I never saw this. Incidentally, your contribution at the funeral was feeble. You cobbled it together in a very slapdash way. Rubbish.'

'That's rich.' Lacey clapped his hands. 'I didn't have time to cobble anything. That wasn't me, it was pure Rupert Brooke.'

'It was gibberish,' Brazier said. 'If anyone wants me, I shall be in The Dregs.'

There was still an hour before sunset. The C.O. sent Dextry to look at the land beyond Kursk and find new landing fields, preferably this side of the Red lines. If they had any lines.

The squadron doctor watched him take off and climb away. She turned and saw Borodin looking at her. 'My apologies,' he said. 'Dreadful manners.'

'Doesn't worry me. I'll worry when men don't

look at me.' She gave a last glance at the disappearing Camel. 'It must be wonderful to fly. That speed, that height. Just you and the birds.'

'The birds fly better. But one can't help feeling a little godlike sometimes. Up there with the gods. And the view is spectacular.'

'I can climb a mountain for that, but mountains don't fly.'

'It's not all fun. It gets very cold, and very noisy, and on a long flight the aeroplane seems to hang in the air and go nowhere. Manoeuvres are fun. Bank and dive and roll and so on. Look: I'm going riding for half an hour. Do you ride?'

'Yes. Not sidesaddle. Will that scandalize the squadron?'

They rode across the airfield, followed a wandering track in a birch spinney, galloped across a meadow and walked into a stream. The ponies enjoyed that, so their riders let them splash up and down, making a great froth and soaking the riders' legs until the water deepened and the ponies stood belly-deep and drank.

'This is yummy,' she said. 'Good idea.'

'You looked a bit forlorn, so I took a risk.'

'Risk.' She stroked her pony's ears. 'Some of the pilots shy away. Don't want to be alone with a widow. Get too close, I might infect them. Look what I did to poor James.'

'They think they're giving you time to grieve.'

'No, they want me to look heartbroken. Losing a man is a cardinal sin in their club.'

The ponies drank their fill and turned and waded back to the shallows.

'What is man's cardinal sin?' he said. 'According to the women's club.'

'Expecting praise. Men want sex, meals and praise, endless praise for being so wonderful.'

They looked at each other. 'What if I were to say that I'll forfeit the praise and do the cooking if you will marry me?'

'I'd say you don't know me, and I don't know you, and I need a long holiday from matrimony. But I'll bear it in mind.'

They walked the ponies home.

'When I said flying makes us feel godlike, I wasn't being completely truthful,' Borodin said. 'It makes us feel remote and privileged. Earth is far below, sometimes a mile or even two miles, and therefore nothing to do with us. We can bomb it and strafe it and never feel the pain. We might kill the enemy, we might kill our own troops, it's all the same to us. We live in a different world.'

'And nothing really matters because *nichevo*.'

'Ah. You know about that.'

'I hear it from the pilots. *Nichevo* suits their style. Another thing: they walk differently.'

'Really? How?'

'Never in step. Put two soldiers together, they always march in step. Pilots never do. Hands in pockets. Bit of slouch, bit of swagger.'

'Not me. I don't walk like that.'

'Then you're a freak.'

'And you're a cruel and heartless woman. And I don't want to marry you.'

'Yes, you do. Tell me one thing. What are the chances you'll get shot down and killed?' He was silent. 'Fifty-fifty?' she said. 'Or worse? Quick

377

death for you. Long gloomy life for me. Is that fair?' No answer.

Dextry returned, having seen no Bolos and found a suitable landing field, thirty miles to the north. The C.O. decided that was good enough. Tomorrow, the squadron would fly and the trains would move.

5

Maynard politely declined the offer of Edwardes' toothbrush. The man had been with his field-gun unit for a long time, and Maynard suspected he had gone native. He hadn't shaved today, and perhaps not yesterday, and to judge by his hands and arms, washing wasn't a priority either. What Maynard, when he had ridden behind him, assumed was the smell of the horse, turned out to be the smell of Edwardes too. At Sherborne, Maynard had been taught to take a cold bath every morning; it kept a boy pure in body and in thought. Edwardes could do with a bath.

But he had undoubtedly saved Maynard from a spot of bother, and it would be fun to tell The Dregs about being rescued by a sort of robber baron and his gang. Maynard knew that rubbing his teeth with a finger dipped in salt was as good as a toothbrush. And the Camel wasn't broken, so he wouldn't be here for long.

He knew what was for supper. The cook made no secret of slaughtering a sheep, skinning it, and hacking it into chunks with a bayonet. They sizzled as they went onto an iron grid over the fire.

'Nice to know that the meat is fresh,' Maynard said.

'It always is, old boy. Russians don't have the luxury of quartermasters. They live off the land.'

'I see.' Maynard had an image of the little village with its sole survivor in the ruins and dead cattle in the fields, and knew at once that Edwardes would not be interested. 'There are advantages in travelling light,' he said. 'My squadron can pack up and be off in half an hour.'

'These lads do it in five minutes.'

'I say! Good egg.' That had been the highest praise at Sherborne, but Edwardes merely raised an eyebrow. 'Which reminds me,' Maynard said. 'The question of moving. Really, all I need is a few gallons of petrol and I can be on my way.'

'Petrol, petrol. God knows where you'll find that. It's not a thing that Russian gunners have much use for. Horsepower gets us from A to B.'

'The squadron has plenty.'

'Then that's your best bet. It's too late today. Tomorrow I'll send a man to the nearest railway station. Maybe they can send a wire. You're not in a hurry, are you? Good. Relax. See how the poor live.'

The roast mutton turned out to be excellent. It would have been even better with a little red-currant jelly, but to say so would be bad form. For the first time since he joined the R.F.C., he was not eating in an Officers' Mess. They sat, men and officers alike, around the fire. There were no plates; either you ate with your fingers or you went hungry. There was black bread, and a bottle of vodka circulated. After his adventure in the

Cossack camp long ago vodka did not frighten Maynard, and he was pleased to see that the men approved when he took a swig. He passed the bottle to Edwardes and said, 'Not a drop is sold till it's seven days old.' Edwardes grinned. 'Seven-day vodka is vintage stuff. A bit like crusted port.'

There was only one course but there was plenty of it. Maynard ate his fill and was gazing into the glow of the fire when he felt the habits of a life-time assert themselves. 'Awfully sorry to be a damn nuisance,' he said, 'but I'm afraid I need the latrines.'

Edwardes said something in Russian and a man got up and fetched a spade.

'Normally we don't aspire to such luxury,' Edwardes said. 'But as you're a guest...'

Maynard took the spade. 'Where?' he said.

Edwardes made a generous, sweeping gesture. 'You have all of Russia,' he said.

Maynard walked deep into the dusk, and dug and squatted. 'This isn't why I came to Russia,' he whispered, 'but no doubt about it, the roast mutton was utterly delicious.'

Edwardes had his own tent but no bed. 'Camp bed broke long ago,' he said. He gave Maynard some blankets. 'Find a small hole that fits your hip. After that, it's like a featherbed.' He was right.

Breakfast was a black-bread mutton sandwich and a glass of Russian tea, brought to him in the tent. Another treat for the guest. He sat in the sunshine and watched the gun crews doing chores. He had a nagging feeling that he should be busy, but there was nothing he could do.

Edwardes wasn't there. He folded his blankets. He got his hands wet with dew and washed his face. He walked to a tall tree and emptied his bladder against it. What now? He went back to his tent and sat in the sun.

About an hour later, Edwardes came back on the same big horse.

'Meeting with the Russian commander,' he said. 'Denikin's advance is still advancing, and we've got orders to go with it. Pockets of Red resistance to be snuffed out. It's up to you, but I don't recommend staying here. An unarmed Englishman on his own is asking for trouble.'

'You were going to send a message to my squadron.'

'I told a bloke on the staff about you. He promised to do something. Don't bet on it. They're big on promises.' Maynard turned away. He had heard a faint growl, no louder than the drone of bees but deeper. He searched the sky and found a distant speckle of dots, quite high. 'That's the squadron,' he said.

Edwardes gave him some binoculars. Nine aircraft, flying high in the east. He followed them until they were lost behind cloud.

'Forget about the message,' he said. 'I think they're on the move again.'

'Doesn't surprise me. Everyone's chasing the Bolos now.'

Already the tents were down and dumped in a big farm cart. Everything went into the cart: cooking pots, a few rifles, some sacks of stuff, shells, a bundle of firewood, and Maynard. The horses were harnessed. The field guns rolled. Maynard's

381

cart followed. Some men rode. Most walked.

It was pleasant countryside, all woods and meadows, occasional valleys and hills. After an hour or two its pleasantness wore thin and Maynard would have swapped it for a good straight road. The cart had no springs. Farm tracks were tolerable but they were rare and mostly the cart bumped and jolted. He made himself as comfortable as possible on the tents and blankets and watched the sky go by. He'd give a year's pay to be up there in a Camel.

They didn't stop to eat. He found some stale bread in a sack and chewed on that. The sun was burning his face so he covered it with a handkerchief. He had no idea where he was going and he didn't want to ask Edwardes for fear the man would tell him and it would be really remote. He might end up living with this gang for a week. Or more. He itched and scratched. There was something in this bloody cart that was biting him. He opened his shirt and smelled himself, and got a sour whiff of old, dried sweat. Horrid.

The sun was going down when the gun team plodded over a rise and the ground exploded in front. Several explosions: high fountains of brown earth and blast that ruffled Maynard's hair. Everyone was shouting. Men were releasing the horses and dragging the guns into position to fire. Maynard stood and watched them load and was shaken by the savage crack of their detonations. He had never been near artillery before. He had no idea how loud it was. How harsh. Someone kicked his leg.

It was Edwardes. 'Get down, you bloody fool!

Get out of here! Run, run!' He went back to his guns. Maynard ran as fast and as far as his flying boots would let him. He stopped and looked back. The guns were doing very well without him. Edwardes was using the binoculars, shouting, pointing, and then in a blink they were all gone, swamped by pounding, furious shell bursts which swallowed the gun team and when the smoke drifted away, only a little tangled wreckage was left. Maynard could not believe it. The phrase 'wiped out' presented itself. Men said the enemy had been wiped out and that was just what had happened here. Guns and gunners, wiped out, vanished. As if they'd never been.

Maynard walked away. After a while he found a hollow in the grass, so he curled up in it. Nothing made sense to him and he stopped thinking. He fell asleep. That was where the Red soldiers found him.

He was a rarity, a curiosity. They knocked him about a bit, just enough to realize that he wasn't Russian, and gave him to an officer who, mysteriously, was riding in an open horse-drawn coach, rather like the *droshkys* of Taganrog. More questioning. 'Angliski,' he said through a split lip. He was blindfolded and seemed to spend several hours in a series of vehicles. The blindfold came off and he was in the boxcar of a railway train. A very young soldier with a very old rifle was guarding him. Outside it was night. The train started.

Maynard felt rotten. His head hurt, one eye was swollen shut, he could taste blood from his lip, and his tongue found gaps where teeth had been. His body ached from the impact of soldiers' boots.

The guard looked to be about sixteen, and not very bright. Maynard pointed forward, the way they were going. *'Na Moskvu?'* he said. The guard thought about it. *'Na Moskvu,'* he said.

That decided Maynard. He was damned if he was going to Moscow. He was damned if he could see how to avoid it, but he sat still and behaved nicely. His chance came when the guard slid open the boxcar door and prepared to urinate into the night. Both hands were needed to brace himself. Maynard dived past him and hoped for a soft landing. Instead he dived into the stone wall of a cutting and broke his neck.

The guard fired his rifle three times and the train stopped. An officer and five men walked along the track and found Maynard. He looked very dead indeed, but the officer shot him to make sure. Then the men shot the guard. They threw the bodies in the boxcar.

TUMULT IN THE CLOUDS

1

'Chef says we're out of mustard,' Tusker Oliphant said. 'We're one hell of a long way from Taganrog.' He was looking at a map. 'Not much hope of getting supplies sent up here.'

'The further from England, the closer in to France,' Wragge said. 'As my dear old dad used to say. We'll be in Moscow soon, at this rate. Lots of mustard in Moscow. Famous for it.'

They were in the C.O.'s Pullman, with Rex Dextry, drinking coffee.

'I can live without mustard,' Dextry said. 'As long as we don't run out of cheese. That's unthinkable.'

Oliphant was estimating distances on the map, using hand spans. 'Supposing we're halfway between Kursk and Orel... That makes another sixty, seventy miles to Orel. Then Orel to Tula, say a hundred, and Tula to Moscow, hundred and fifty. All told, three hundred miles or more.' He looked up. 'Can Denikin do it?'

'Why not?' Wragge said. 'He's already captured half of Russia. Not Siberia, but who cares about Siberia, they've all got icicles on their testicles, while we've got the best airfield since Tsaritsyn, so well done, Rex.'

'We strive to please,' Dextry said.

He had found a short spur of railway that forked away from the main line and gave up after a mile. An engineer's mistake, evidently. The rails were rusted and grass grew high between them. Everything was blessedly quiet. The loudest sound was the bleating of lambs in a meadow as big and smooth as Lord's cricket ground.

'Down to business,' the C.O. said. 'First point is, are the machines all operational? Yes? Good. Right, the Nines can get on with their knitting while the Camels go and find the Bolos.' A tap on the door. Lacey came in, handed him a paper, said: 'From Mission H.Q.,' and went out. As Wragge read it, his eyebrows rose. 'Goolie Chit,' he said. 'Anyone heard of it?'

'Yes,' Oliphant said. 'My brother's with a squadron in India, on the North-West Frontier. He mentioned it in a letter.'

'Did he, by Jove? Well, according to H.Q., it's a linen envelope attached to the fuselage. On the outside, it says in the local lingo that this is a British officer, help him and you shall be rewarded. Inside are twenty gold sovereigns.'

'That's right. If it works, you get to keep your goolies. My brother says the natives are a bit ferocious and the women are even worse. Afghans and so on.'

'Bless my soul.'

'Famous last words, if you get engine failure over the Khyber Pass.'

'Mmm. It's marked "For Information Only". H.Q. thinks only of our welfare.' Wragge stuffed it in a pocket. 'I'll ask Borodin what he thinks.'

They went out and enjoyed the sunshine.

Wragge breathed the sweet smell of lush countryside at the height of summer. 'Reminds me of the Scottish Borders,' he said. 'I wonder if there's any trout fishing near here?'

'About Daddy Maynard,' Dextry said. 'When should we count him as lost? Uncle was asking.'

'Give him a day or two,' the C.O. said. 'You never know. Daddy's no fool. Not like that clown who got lost at Butler's Farm. Silly ass was only three miles from the field. Barnett? Burnett? No.' He clicked his fingers. 'Bennett. Got it.'

'Never knew him,' Dextry said.

The four Camels followed the railway north. It was stocked with troop trains. Few were moving and the rest had emptied their troops into the fields beside them. They sat or lay in the sun, doing what all soldiers do well, which is wait. Cook fires were everywhere. Soldiers learn to eat whenever possible, in the certain knowledge that they'll go hungry soon. Some waved at the aircraft. Others saved their energy.

A few miles further on, Wragge found the reason for all this nothing-doing. Lengths of track had been torn up and squads of engineers were restoring them. Presumably the Bolos did it. Some holes were big enough for shell craters. Or perhaps dynamite.

The Camels climbed to three thousand feet and spread out, four hundred yards between each, the better to search the land. They saw nothing to defend, no towns, no rivers except the one the railroad followed. It looked half-dried-up and no obstacle to anyone.

They cruised on for ten, twenty miles, looking down at empty countryside and up at empty sky, down again, up again. 'Christ!' Dextry said aloud. 'This is boring bloody country. Where's the damn war?' Borodin was not bored. This was his Russia and he was proud of its enormous spaces, there was room to breathe in Russia, more than anywhere in the world. Except perhaps China, but China was full of Chinese who, let's face it, can't write *War and Peace* or paint anything except urns and vases and couldn't spell Tchaikovsky let alone play him. Jessop was getting a sore neck and wondering what it would be like to be stripped naked for an examination by Flight Lieutenant Perry. Would she have warm fingers? Strong warm fingers? His stomach muscles tightened. Wragge worried what he would do if someone's engine went on the fritz now. He kept looking for landmarks, something a search party could find. That was when he saw the tents. Brown bell tents, sixty, seventy, maybe more.

He waggled his wings and waved, and as the Flight came together he searched below for a marker. He saw a wood shaped like a broken star: that would do.

He got the Flight between the sun and the camp, and dived. Nobody fired up at them. A handful of men ran. He got a clear view of rows of tents with well-trodden paths between them. The Camels buzzed the camp, low enough to wake the dead. Still no gunfire. As the C.O. pulled out and climbed away he glimpsed stampeding horses, scared by the racket. But no men.

The Camels flew a mile-wide circle around the tents and found nothing. Wragge's fuel gauge read less than half-full, and it was unreliable. This was not the time or place to meet the Red air force. Combat drank petrol. Nobody wanted that. They headed south.

The landing ground was easy to find: Just follow the rail line and find the rusty spur. The field looked wonderfully green, and the C.O. knew that something was badly wrong when he saw a Nine lying flat on its belly and another with its tail high and its nose buried in the grass. He landed, saw Oliphant waiting, taxied towards him, climbed out.

'We got strafed,' Oliphant said. 'Ten minutes after you left. Three Spads, not the same bunch you saw, these were black. Caught us on the hop. My chaps did their best to get off the ground, but that one lost its wheels and looks like a pregnant duck, and that one overcooked his throttle so his tail came up too soon and he snapped his prop. Then the troops got the Lewis guns going and scared the Spads away, thank Christ.'

Wragge did some counting. 'You're one short, Tusker.'

'Ah ... now for the bad news. Tommy Hopton did manage to get airborne. With Mickey Blythe. Naturally the Spads went for him and there was a hell of a scrap. We watched it all. They got him in the end. Three to one: pretty lousy odds. He was a flamer, Tiger. They both jumped.' He pointed to a distant wood. 'Somewhere over there, probably. I've got search parties out.'

'Jesus Christ Almighty.'

'They did the right thing, Tiger. Taking off, I mean. Better to be up there than strafed down here. If you'd seen–'

'Yes, of course they did. No question about that. Absolutely the right thing. Tommy Hopton and Mickey Blythe ... God help us. If only we'd been here.'

'Then maybe the Spads wouldn't have come.'

'How did they know?'

Oliphant shrugged. 'Spies? Or perhaps just chance.'

Wragge sat on the grass, and so did Oliphant. 'I feel knackered, Tusker. And we didn't find a damn thing except empty tents. We're losing good men too fast. First Lowe, then Maynard, and now your two chaps do the right thing and...' He couldn't find words, and gave up.

Already the ground crews were working on the Nines. It would be another long night for them. At dusk the search parties came back, empty-handed. There were tens of thousands of trees, they said, all in full leaf. Maybe they got caught in the branches, maybe not. Who could say?

It was a quiet evening in The Dregs, briefly enlivened when the C.O. came in with Borodin and a smart young Russian officer, heavy with gold braid.

'Gentlemen, this is General Polakov,' he said.

'Pokalov,' Borodin murmured.

'Well, I was close. He has ridden here post-haste with good news. He wishes to address you.'

Pokalov spoke for three minutes. He was brimful of energy and excitement, but it was still a long three minutes. They understood nothing until his final words: *'Na Moskvu!'* Borodin led the applause. Pokalov smiled and joined in.

'Please,' Wragge said to Borodin.

'The general congratulates the squadron on its stunning victories, and is proud to announce that the Bolsheviks have retreated to Orel, which with your help General Denikin will now take on his glorious way to Moscow.'

They waited. 'Is that all?' Dextry said.

'What he failed to say is that three battalions of the enemy have shot their officers and deserted to join our ranks, and one Cossack cavalry brigade has tired of retreating and gone home. There are indications of a Bolo collapse.'

'Are there?' Jessop said. 'Tell that to Tommy Hopton and Mickey Blythe.'

'We must expect casualties,' the C.O. said. 'It's the price we pay for victory.' Nobody applauded that. It had been a hard day and Wragge wanted to put it behind him. 'What are Denikin's plans?' he said to Borodin. 'What does he want of us?'

'Ground-strafing at Orel.'

'Sweet blind O'Reilly,' Jessop said. 'Haven't we done our share of that? Strafing fixed defences is bloody dangerous.'

'Look at it this way,' the C.O. said. 'One last Big Push and the enemy's done for.'

'They told us that in France,' Dextry said. 'Told us over and over again.'

'And we won in the end.' Wragge cranked up a smile and shook the general's hand. 'I think champagne is called for, don't you?'

2

The search parties went out again next morning. The C.O. told the adjutant that he was damned if he would walk away and leave two dead men as if they didn't matter. The adjutant agreed but, he said, the hard facts had to be faced. 'I know, I know,' Wragge said. 'A lot of good men vanished in France. Took off, never seen again. Lost. I know that, Uncle. Look, we'll hold a memorial service of some kind. Get Lacey to sort something out. Noon today.'

The squadron doctor left the train after the morning sick parade and found Borodin waiting in the Chevrolet. 'I asked the troops to unload it,' he said. 'We could drive around. Might see something.'

'Rubbish. You just want to take me for a ride.'

'I was thinking of the search parties. They might need your professional advice.'

'About what? Two men jumped out of an aeroplane. They're dead. What else?' She got in the car. 'I don't mind if you lie, all men lie, but don't fudge the facts.'

He started the engine and they drove away. 'You sound as if you've had a rough morning.'

'I look at hairy, sweaty, male bodies every day, Borodin. How d'you think I feel?'

'Ah, but the men love you, Mrs Perry.'

'Some of them love themselves. There's a mechanic who keeps coming back because he's sure he's ruptured himself, and you know where that usually happens.'

'Lower stomach?'

'Groin. I examine him, he lets out a long groan. He hasn't got a hernia, but he's proud of his pathetic manhood.'

'Let me guess. Abnormal.'

'Who cares? Size is an accident of birth. In France, in Forward Casualty Clearing, I saw a hundred naked men a day. Some wanted me to hold their hand, usually the ones who were dying, but nobody ever asked me to measure their genitalia, which was just as well because sometimes there was nothing left to measure.'

That silenced him. They had crossed the field and now he was driving carefully between Scots pines. 'Where are we going?' she said.

'Anywhere. I too get tired of the company of men. Especially Englishmen.'

'What's wrong with them? Apart from phantom hernias.'

'They thought they came to save Russia. Actually they came for the fun of flying aeroplanes at someone else's expense. Now it's not such fun and they're turning sour. Russia's fault, of course.'

'You sound a little sour yourself.'

He stopped the car beside a huge cypress. It had split down the middle and some branches almost touched the ground. 'Do you like climbing trees?'

'Did once.'

'I climbed them with the Tsar. He enjoyed playing hide-and-seek, and he was happiest hiding up a tree. Come on.'

The branches were thick and horizontal and easy to climb. Squirrels fled and poked their heads out to watch the invaders. The doctor and the count found a comfortable perch thirty feet up. 'This was a good idea,' she said. 'I feel deliciously free. What did you and the Tsar talk about when you were hiding?'

'He told jokes. He wasn't the Tsar then, only the heir. Nobody laughed in the Imperial court. Too stuffy. I was just a boy, he made me laugh.'

'What sort of jokes?'

'Oh ... silly riddles.' He thought. 'What do you get when you cross a crocodile with a parrot?'

'Give up.'

'A big surprise when it bites your leg off and says, "Who's a pretty boy, then?" He found that hilarious. Sometimes he laughed so much that I had to finish telling the joke. Then he'd laugh even more.'

'He sounds like a cheerful chap.'

'He was cheerful when he was hiding. The rotten thing is he couldn't hide forever, could he?'

'Nobody can. We all have to grow up.' She stroked his jaw. 'You know, you're not bad-looking, for a decadent bastard aristocrat. Have you another name? Apart from...'

'Pierre Alexander Porphyrevich. The last two are after my father. He was also a brilliant chemist. He taught at the St Petersburg School of Medicine for Women. Music and chemistry. Both a complete mystery to me.'

'You have an open mind, Pierre Alexander Thingummy, even if it is absolutely empty.'

'We should be getting back,' he said. 'Susan Perry.' They climbed down.

Lacey welcomed the challenge.

His big problem was the absence of coffins and graves. A service needed a focus, a visible memorial. He talked to a flight sergeant and they sketched a wooden plaque, nailed to an upright. 'Make it a bit wider,' the flight sergeant said, 'and it looks sort of like a cross.'

'Excellent.' Lacey gave him the inscription.

He went to his Pullman, shut his eyes and put himself in the C.O's shoes. Then he wrote the eulogy. It took ten minutes: Lacey was fluent under pressure. That left him time to concentrate on the tricky bit, his own poetic contribution. The squadron expected verbal fireworks, and he'd exhausted Rupert Brooke. Lacey reached for his small library of British verse and got down to some serious larceny.

With half an hour to go, the flight sergeant brought him an armourer with a bugle. 'The Marines left it behind, sir,' he said. 'Miller here says he used to be in a Salvation Army band.' Lacey auditioned him on the spot. 'Good enough,' he said. 'You'll close the show. After the rifles.' He inspected the plaque for spelling mistakes and found none, checked the depth of the hole dug by the *plennys* in the field, and told Wragge the order of battle.

At twelve noon the hollow square had formed. The flight sergeant held the post in its hole, not touching the plaque where the paint was still tacky. Brazier handed Wragge a spade and he shovelled some earth into the hole and gave the spade to an aircrew member who did his bit and passed it on until all the officers had helped erect the sign. Oliphant was last. He tramped the soil down firmly and stood back.

Wragge read aloud the inscription: In Memoriam, Thomas Hopton and Michael Blythe, Merlin Squadron, Royal Air Force, and the date. It was a calm morning, soft sunshine, good hay-making weather back in England. He spoke the lines Lacey had written, about how often in war the phrase *Lost in action* was used but never more tragically, and splendidly, than in this case. He said that Hopton and Blythe had died fighting and that they had known exactly what they were doing at the end, and it was an ending of great courage. He talked of their pluck and devotion to duty and huge strength of character. 'Let this memorial, and this raw earth, be their burial ground,' he said.

Lacey allowed a long pause for the words to fade, and stepped forward and did his best to improve the tone of the occasion.

In our hearts believing
Victory crowns the just,
And that braggarts must
Surely bite the dust.
So bear the brunt and pay glad life's arrears
Of pain, darkness and fears,
For sudden the worst turns the best to the brave,
The blackest minute lies in its grave.
Happy is England in the brave that die
For wrongs not hers and rights that loudly cry;
Happy in those that give, give and endure
The pain that never the new years may cure.
Nor law, nor duty bade them fight,

Nor public men, nor cheering crowds.
A lonely impulse of delight
Drove to this tumult in the clouds.

He took a pace back. Three rifle volleys echoed back from the trees. The bugler sounded the 'Last Post'. He cracked a couple of notes but nobody remembered that when he held the last, saddest note so sweetly that even Brazier gave a slight nod of approval. That was as good as a standing ovation. Lacey almost smiled.

3

The Camel Flight was getting smaller, so a few bomber crews had been invited to join The Dregs: Tusker Oliphant, Douglas Gunning, Prod Pedlow, Joe Duncan. They were expected to contribute to the conversation. At lunch, after the ceremony, Gunning broke the silence. 'Ah, soup,' he said. 'I like a drop of soup.'

Nobody added to that.

'Summer's going fast,' Oliphant said.

'Not in Australia,' Jessop said. 'Summer hasn't begun there.'

'How did you get in the Corps, Junk?' Pedlow asked. 'Who did you bribe? I ask because my mentally defective cousin wants a commission.'

'Is he any good at ground-strafing?' Dextry said. 'He can have mine.'

'It's true, about Australia,' Joe Duncan said. 'They count backwards, they stand on their heads, and they have very hairy feet. To keep the sun off.'

'How did you get a commission?' Jessop said. 'Find it in a Christmas cracker?'

'The thing about summer,' the C.O. said, 'it's getting to the end of the county cricket season, and cricket, I think you'll agree, is what made Britain great. Any cricket news on your magic box, Lacey?'

'Alas, no.'

'Cricket. Is that the game they play with racquets?' Dextry said.

'You're thinking of the University Boat Race,' Gunning said. 'Who won that, Lacey?'

'Oxford. Or perhaps Cambridge. There was some dispute.'

'I joined a boat club once,' Jessop said, 'but it fell apart when we put it in the water.'

'There's a pint of arsenic in your soup, Junk,' Dextry said. 'Drink up while it's hot.'

'Used the wrong type of glue, you see,' Jessop said. 'I joined it but... Never mind.' He stirred his soup. 'Where can you get arsenic in Russia?'

'Drink up and I'll tell you.'

'Nip in the air this morning,' Oliphant said. 'Soon be autumn. Rugger season.'

'Not the same as cricket, is it?' Wragge said.

'Flannelled fools or muddied oafs,' Dextry said. 'Take your pick.'

Merlin Squadron's gypsy existence continued. Borodin heard from Denikin's staff of an abandoned Red air force field about five miles this side of Orel. Wragge got the flights in the air and in tidy formation, and they circled the woods where Hopton and Blythe probably lay: a fare-well gesture. They followed the railway north and, surprisingly, Denikin's staff had forgotten their *vranyo* because the field was just where they said. Well, even staff officers tripped up occasionally.

The Nines landed. Wragge took the Camels onward to have a squint at Orel. They flew over great numbers of troops, guns, cavalry. Nobody was on the move. The railway was clogged with trains. None had steam up. Orel was safe for today.

The Camels took a good look at it from a thousand feet. Compared with Kharkov and Kursk, this was a small town with pretty little onion domes. The biggest building was the railway station. Orel was a quiet, civilized place where the citizens were too polite to fire guns at visiting aeroplanes.

The C.O. waved the other Camels away and dived hard, pulled out at little more than rooftop height and zigzagged across town, showed off with a vertical banking turn around the onion domes and made his exit on the other side. Some women shook their fists at him. He'd probably woken their sleeping infants. He climbed and picked up the Flight and they cruised home. No trade today. Maybe the Bolos had given up. What a swindle.

The train was on the move.

The adjutant, the doctor, Stevens and Lacey were playing whist in The Dregs. The track was in bad shape, and as the train swayed, it jolted the needle back to the start of the gramophone record. 'What is that curious music?' Brazier said.

'American ragtime,' Lacey said. 'Henry sent it. It's by a man called Scott Joplin. The tune is "The Entertainer". Joplin has been called the J.S. Bach of our time, but you don't think much of Bach, so you won't like Joplin.'

'On the contrary. His ragtime would make a good regimental march. Stick to ordering groceries, lad. That's your level.' He played his card and took the trick.

'Chef says we're nearly out of cheese,' Susan Perry said. 'Can't you order some more?'

'I can order whatever you like,' Lacey said. 'But will it arrive? We're five hundred miles from Taganrog. Any train not guarded by British troops is bound to be looted, probably by our allies.' He took the trick, and played a low club. 'I can see your cards, Stevens.'

'They're dreadful, aren't they? I was hoping you'd feel sorry for me.'

'Play your six of clubs,' Brazier suggested.

'That card? It's got jack of hearts written on it.'

'So who has the real six of clubs?' Susan Perry asked. Nobody had. 'What d'you want it to be?'

'Ideally, the ace of diamonds,' Stevens said.

She plucked out the card and played it for him. 'Ace of diamonds, by majority vote.' The train jolted, and the needle jumped back to the start of 'The Entertainer'.

'Maybe we can buy some Russian cheese,' Lacey said.

'It's foul.' Brazier trumped Stevens' ace with the two of spades and won the trick. 'Inedible.'

'That's the second time you've played the two

400

of spades,' she said. 'This is my idea of purgatory – playing whist with a crooked pack and a batty gramophone record.'

'And to complete your suffering,' Brazier said as he tore up his two of spades, 'Lacey reciting his poetry.'

'The C.O. thanked me for it,' Lacey said. 'He told me the last four lines really hit the bullseye.'

'Remind us,' she said.

Lacey quoted: *'Nor law, nor duty bade them fight, Nor public men, nor cheering crowds. A lonely impulse of delight, Drove to this tumult in the clouds.'*

'W.B. Yeats,' Stevens said.

'One of my contributors. It sums up the squadron, according to the C.O.'

'Good for him,' she said. 'I hope we never hear it again. But I fear we shall.'

Stevens played the four of diamonds, Lacey played the five. 'Bloody officers,' Stevens said. 'There's no justice.'

4

Count Borodin awoke to the sound of rifle fire. The noise came in irregular bursts, like the faraway crackle of burning stubble. Experience told him that the firing was more than a mile away, probably two miles, and the blackness said it was the middle of the night. He closed his eyes and guessed how many men were fighting. Perhaps two battalions. A small battle. The firing grew more intense and then faded and died. He went back to sleep.

At breakfast, the talk was all guesswork. 'What d'you think happened, Count?' Jessop said.

'I think you have egg on your chin.'

'I know. I keep it there in case I get peckish later.'

Borodin ordered a pony to be saddled. He visited the staff train, came back and joined a meeting of the C.O. and the flight leaders. 'There was a small Red attack during the night,' he said. 'Several, simultaneously. All beaten off.'

'Where did they spring from?' Wragge said. 'There were no Reds in Orel when we looked. Nobody fired a shot at us.'

'Wise restraint. If they fire at us, we bomb them. So they don't fire, and we go away.'

'The Huns learned that trick,' Oliphant said. 'We bombed their cities at night and at first they were easy to find because when they heard us coming they turned on their searchlights, but then they realized they were advertising themselves so they stopped. Hid in the darkness. Not easy to find a blacked-out town in the middle of Germany. If we found it, of course, their searchlights came on and they chucked all kinds of filth at us.'

'Cunning buggers, Huns,' Dextry said.

'What are you saying?' the C.O. asked. 'Orel's full of Bolos, hiding in back alleys, waiting to do their worst?'

'Maybe. Maybe not.'

'Moscow by Christmas,' Borodin said. 'That's all everyone thinks of. Some of Denikin's people have even picked out the white horses for their triumphant entry.'

'Why not?' Oliphant said. 'Denikin's made mincemeat of the Bolos.'

'Mincemeat, you say. Russians prepare many a hearty meal from mincemeat.'

'So what was last night's nonsense all about?' Dextry said. 'The Bolos made a nuisance of themselves and then went home. Not very heroic.'

'Delaying tactics,' Borodin said. 'Spoiled our troops' sleep.'

'Or maybe it was a last gasp.'

'We're guessing,' the C.O. said. 'What does Denikin want us to do?'

'Ground-strafing,' Borodin said. 'Targets of opportunity.'

'So he's guessing too. Well, let's get in the air. With any luck, someone will try to kill us.'

Wragge took the whole squadron, four Camels and four Nines.

From two thousand feet, Orel still looked peaceful. Still no burning buildings, no heavy machine guns chucking filth at the sky. No point in strafing something that might be a barracks but was more likely to be a hospital. Proves nothing, Wragge thought, even a hospital might be a hiding place full of Bolos. Or it might be an orphanage, and we'd end up strafing a hundred blond-haired blue-eyed boys and girls. Hard cheese. Teach them not to grow up to be ruthless Bolsheviks. And anyway they're orphans, nobody would miss them, so *nichevo*. And we'd *vranyo* Mission H.Q. and Denikin and say the Camels were returning enemy fire.

But Orel remained a picture of a market town drowsing in the midday sun, and the squadron cruised on, and soon Wragge's humane and civilized conduct was rewarded by the sight of two armoured trains, north of the town, not moving. Almost at once, the old familiar ink-blots decorated the sky ahead. One burst was close, and he felt rather than heard the rattle of shrapnel pocking his wings as he bucked through the broken air. He looked back and pointed at Oliphant, the Flights separated, and he led the Camels away in a long, shallow sideslip.

We have been here before, Oliphant thought. The Nines had moved wide apart as soon as the shelling began. From this height the armoured trains were very thin, no wider than strips of ribbon. The C.O. would want him to go in low, very low, to improve his bombing chances. That was how the Bolos got Michael Lowe. Oliphant searched the sky, half-hoping for three Spads to appear and give his Nines an excuse to dive hard towards home. No Spads. Black shell bursts marched towards him and forced a decision. A compromise.

He took his Flight down to a thousand feet and put them in line astern. A strong wind kept nudging him to the right. He crabbed to the left and hoped the correction would let his bombs drift onto the target. The old familiar tracer, red and yellow, was pulsing up, searching, racing past. Oh yes, we have been here before.

He bombed the first train, then banked hard to give his gunner a clear shot, and watched his explosions chase each other through the grass. He circled and watched the rest of his Flight have the same bad luck. Well, we tried. Oliphant looked up and saw three Spads arriving from the north. You're late. What kept you? Pink, with yellow flashes. Did the Reds repaint them every night? Or was there an endless supply? The Nines formed up and made haste for home. Slow haste. The bomber flown by Prod Pedlow and Joe Duncan had been hit. Their machine had lost a wheel, the last three feet of its lower port wing was gone, the rudder was trailing yards of fabric and the engine was streaming black smoke. Pedlow and Duncan waved to show that they were unhurt, but they were losing height and their speed was not much above stalling. The other Nines stayed with them, watched the Spads with one eye, and hoped the C.O. would keep the enemy busy.

Wragge did his best. His plan – to strafe the trains when the last bomb exploded – got scrapped. The Camels climbed hard. The Spads, very cavalier in their bright décor, had seen the Nines and were in a long dive to cut them off. By great good luck, Wragge's course would meet the Spads halfway. It would be a perfect interception: hammer the enemy broadside while he couldn't bring his guns to bear. The Spads saw it coming.

When the Camels were just out of gun-range, the enemy suddenly turned away and climbed, turned even more and came at them as nicely as a display at an airshow.

The Camels scattered. The usual madhouse began.

Dextry never flew straight. He saw flashing glimpses of a gaudy fuselage, got few chances to fire and by then he was looking at blue sky until a Spad wandered so close to him that he could smell the stink of its exhausts, and he fired one long burst at the cockpit, one single glorious battering burst and the Spad reared so that he saw the pilot's arms thrown up as if in surrender. Dextry used the Camel's escape, a hard right bank, and it was too slow. He flew into the Spad and buried his engine into its cockpit. Now the two aeroplanes were welded into one. The control column impaled itself in his stomach and the gun butts flattened his nose. Dextry knew nothing of this. In the instant when he went from a hundred miles an hour to nothing, the fuel tank behind him tore loose, smashed through his seat and crushed his spine.

The wreckage fell, slowly and awkwardly spinning. It did not burn until it struck the ground. The impact burst the tanks and the flames roared.

The scrap had ended. The other two Spads had gone back where they came from and the three Camel pilots had no appetite for pursuit. They went down and circled the crash until the big guns of the armoured trains chased them away.

They caught up with the Nines, by now down to a few hundred feet. They kept clear and tried to guess whether the broken bomber had enough speed to reach the airfield, and if it had, what sort of landing Pedlow would make on one wheel. They watched it tip sideways, at first gently, as if testing the manoeuvre, and then more boldly, until the wings were vertical and the aeroplane sideslipped hard.

From height, say from fifteen hundred or better yet two thousand feet, with ample space to pull out, the move would have looked smooth, even slick. From a few hundred feet, the best that could be said is that it was a quick death. The force of the crash crumpled the Nine as if it had been made of paper. It burned like paper.

Nobody hung about. Once you've seen one crash site, you've seen them all. And no amount of looking would improve this one.

5

Orel fell, without being pushed.

The town sent spokesmen, under large white flags, to say that the Red Army had all gone, were probably halfway to Tula by now, and Orel was glad to offer every assistance to the splendid White armies, including a gala banquet in the town hall that very night.

An invitation to Merlin Squadron was politely declined. 'Nobody feels like getting hilariously drunk,' the C.O. told the adjutant, 'and we're not going to sing funny songs for the benefit of a lot of fat, over-decorated...' He couldn't find the right insult. 'Fiascos,' he said.

They were in the Orderly Room. Lacey was filing his radio reports. 'Strictly speaking, a fiasco is a total failure,' he said. 'Originally a term used by Venetian glassblowers. If one of them blundered, he turned it into a flask, a *fiasco*. Perhaps the word you seek is *farrago*, which means—'

Wragge punched him. Lacey saw it coming and swayed. The blow skidded off the side of his head. Brazier was between them at once. 'Out, out, out!' he roared. Lacey ran.

Wragge sucked his knuckles. 'Sorry about that, Uncle,' he said.

'I'm not. Lacey needs to be struck often and hard. Like insolent children.'

'Blame it on the war. It's not panning out the way we all thought, is it? If we carry on like this, the whole squadron will be wiped out before we get anywhere near Moscow. I need a drink. What's wrong with us, Uncle? What's wrong with me? I've lost six men in four days. Three today. Griffin led the squadron all through the Tsaritsyn show and lost no-one.'

Brazier opened a desk drawer and took out a bottle of whisky and two glasses: essential equipment for any adjutant. He poured, they clinked glasses and drank. 'Griffin killed himself,' he said. 'He didn't do it for the good of the squadron. Or maybe he did it to teach you a lesson.'

Wragge thought about that. 'Nobody liked him, but so what? Not the C.O.'s job to be liked.'

Brazier settled his meaty backside in Lacey's chair. 'He told me he was disappointed in you. All of you. He said Russia wasn't like France. He felt badly let down.'

Wragge tried to work that out. 'He blamed *us* because Russia isn't like France? That's cuckoo.'

'Well, all pilots are slightly cuckoo. You wouldn't fly if you were completely sane. He said he'd lived the life of Reilly in France. Every day in the air, getting paid to fly top-notch fighters and chase Huns. Marvellous. Time of his life.'

'Griffin told you all this? Extraordinary. Not his style. Was he blotto?'

'Slightly drunk. We were at that big Russian

banquet and the vodka made him open his soul. Said he didn't believe in God until the Royal Flying Corps showed him the heavens, but the war ended and dumped him in the mud. Said he felt worthless. Worse than worthless.'

'That's ridiculous. You can't be worse than worthless. It's like…' Wragge was struggling. 'Forget it. Anyway, they gave him another squadron. The Camel's a decent enough bus. What's he got to complain about?'

'Russia's not France.'

Wragge booted the waste-paper basket and scattered Lacey's rubbish. 'I think I'm beginning to understand that, Uncle. It's not Mexico, either. Or Portugal. Nobody promised the silly bastard it would be France. Why blame us?'

Brazier spread his arms in defeat. 'Maybe every C.O. needs somebody to blame.'

'Too deep for me. And I don't give a toss why Griffin picked a fight with all those Bolos. Who cares, anyway? I want to see the chief mechanic. Anderson. Peterson.'

'Patterson. Very good man. I'll get him.'

'Now.'

Patterson arrived, very grimy. He was twice Wragge's age and his grey hair was stained with oil. Wragge told him to take a seat, offered him a whisky which he readily accepted, and asked him for a frank account of the condition of the aeroplanes.

Patterson gave it to him: engines, guns, gauges, pumps, airframes, control wires, wing structures, struts, rudder units, wheels, fabric. He didn't waste any words – he was from Glasgow and he knew that you had to keep it simple when you talked to the English – but it took him ten minutes. The whisky was a lubricant. Brazier topped it up.

'It comes down to this,' Wragge said. 'If it were up to you, they would all be scrapped.'

Patterson had been in the Service too long to be tricked into saying that. 'Complete overhaul, sir. Everything stripped and tested. Everything.'

'Do it, Patterson. And thank you.'

Patterson finished his whisky, every last drop stripped and tested, and left.

'All operations are cancelled for a week,' Wragge told Brazier. 'This isn't France. The bloody silly war can wait.'

'I hope your decision has nothing to do with what I said about Griffin.'

'Certainly not. Griffin was crackers. I may be batty but I'm not crackers. Big difference. That was the first thing they taught me at Eton.'

Sergeant Stevens had taken the Chevrolet ambulance to the crash sites and shovelled as much as he could find into canvas sacks. He was always guessing. Was that half a shinbone or a bit of broken strut? Never mind, shovel it in. Extra weight would be useful. He worked fast at Dextry's wreck. The Red armoured trains had gone but they might come back.

So there were three coffins and nobody had any illusions about what might be in them. Some of it could be Prod Pedlow and some of it Joe Duncan, but which was in whose coffin would never be known, just as half of Rex Dextry's remains could easily be those of the Bolo pilot he crashed into.

Oliphant went to the C.O. 'No speeches. No Lacey. No heroics. And no God stuff,' he said. 'That's what my bomber boys want. A few words from me about Pedlow and Duncan will do, and you should say something about Dextry, and then the coffins go down. Rifles, bugle. Dismiss.'

'Alright. Actually, I think we're all getting a bit sick of Lacey's poetry.'

'Tumult in the clouds,' Oliphant said, and they both laughed. 'In the clouds is where we go to get away from the damn tumult. Lacey's a penguin. He calls himself a pilot officer but he flies a desk.'

The service lasted ten minutes. The rifle volley was crisp and the bugler did not sound any false notes. They were getting better with practice.

THE JOLT OF BULLETS

1

The ground crews worked. The air crews had a holiday.

Lacey paid everyone, which made them feel better, and he took the Chevrolet to go shopping in Orel. Borodin drove. The doctor and Jessop came along for the ride.

The car bumped across fields which were now empty of the White armies. Denikin was advancing again, northwards, ever northwards, to Tula, to Moscow. As the car drove into Orel, the doctor said, 'Everything is untouched. Pleasant surprise.'

'Maybe the Bolos just did a bunk,' Jessop said.

'They could have smashed it up. Like Kursk.'

'Perhaps the Bolsheviks expect to recapture it,' Borodin said. 'Or perhaps they laid the dynamite but nobody could find the matches.'

He parked the car and they strolled the streets. In fifteen minutes they had seen the sights, which were a railway station, two onion domes and the town hall, which was shut. Borodin translated the sign hanging on the door: *Open tomorrow.* 'They never change it because it's always true,' he said. There were no unburied corpses in the street and nobody begged them for food; equally, nobody smiled.

Lacey found what he was looking for: an open-air market. Not big but better than nothing. He left the others and went to see what he could buy.

Borodin stood and sniffed the air. 'Follow me,' he said, and quickly tracked down a house with no sign but an open front door. 'This is either the Café Royale of Orel,' he said, 'or someone has thrown his breakfast on the fire.'

It was a large room, very dark, with half a dozen tables and a bar. Tiny shells crunched under their feet. 'Sunflower seeds,' Borodin said. 'Everyone chews them.' The aroma of fried onions fought with the stale smell of tobacco smoke.

'It's not the Café Royale,' Jessop said. 'You get white tablecloths at the Café Royale.' A woman appeared. 'This must be the *chanteuse*,' he said. 'Past her prime, I'm afraid.'

Borodin had a brief conversation.

'It's a bar,' he told them. 'There are no restaurants in Orel. People eat at home. Mainly she sells vodka. As a favour to us, she can make omelettes.'

'Omelettes are good,' the doctor said. 'Ask her if we may eat outside, where the stench is tolerable.'

They carried out a table and two benches. The woman brought chipped glass tumblers and a jug of red wine.

'She speaks highly of the wine,' Borodin said. 'She trod the grapes with her own bare feet.'

The doctor took a sip. 'That was last week,' she said. 'The bacteria are dead by now.' She poured, and they drank to each other's health.

'I was hoping to find a gentleman's outfitters,' Jessop said. 'My underwear is in absolute tatters.'

'I don't think they have that sort of shop here,' Borodin said.

'Then where do they buy their underwear?'

'I rather think they don't. Some member of the family knits it. In winter they sew themselves into a complete set, head to foot, and coat it with bear fat. They wear it until spring. The Russian winter can be brutal.'

'I can't imagine you coated in bear fat,' Susan Perry said.

'Heavens, no. I speak of peasants. My English nanny took care of my underwear. Silk, usually... Hullo, what can we do for you?'

A man had stopped at their table. Everything about him was ruined. His hair was tangled, his face was bruised and blackened by dried blood, his clothes were torn and stained. His army tunic lacked sleeves and his breeches had split at the seams. He had no shoes. He was trembling. His left arm hung at his side. In his right hand he held a pistol. He made a hoarse and angry statement.

'He wants our money, or he will shoot us,' Borodin said. 'He was wounded fighting the Reds and now nobody cares, he hasn't eaten in a week, he says give him money or he fires.' He said a few words in Russian and got a grunt for an answer.

Jessop was suddenly furious. 'Listen, you squalid little peasant. I've had enough of you ungrateful Russians.' Jessop's forefinger had been pounding the table. Now he thrust it at the robber. 'We came ten thousand miles to risk our lives day in day out so you can live a decent civilized life and Russian rotters like you think you can wave a gun and get

414

what you want. This table isn't Russia, my friend. This is part of Britain. Put your stupid gun away and clear off!'

The flood of words made the robber gape. Borodin translated, very briefly.

'I said a damn sight more than that,' Jessop said.

'I told him you thought he was an utter cad.'

The robber mumbled something, and waved his pistol.

'You have insulted him,' Borodin said, 'and he will shoot you first.'

'I don't like the way his hand is twitching,' Susan Perry said. At that point the cook appeared with three plates of hot omelettes. The robber salivated so much that he dribbled down his chin. 'Tell him to sit down and eat,' she said. Borodin did. The man sat and ate and drank from her glass. His left arm hung uselessly and he ate with his right hand, which meant he had to put down the pistol. Jessop's hand sneaked across the table and stole it. His caution was wasted. The man had no time for anything but food. The cook watched with interest. Even in vodka dens like hers, customers rarely waved pistols. 'More omelettes,' Borodin told her. 'More wine.' She went. As the man finished one omelette, Jessop slid another in front of him.

'He has a very bad abscess on his left arm,' the doctor said. 'Unless it's treated the whole arm could become infected, possibly gangrenous. He must come with us so I can treat it.'

Borodin translated, and the man cried, although he did not stop eating and drinking. 'I think that means he agrees,' Borodin said.

Ten minutes later, Lacey arrived. 'They didn't have what I wanted, but I drew pictures and they're getting it for me, later today. What's wrong with him?' The man was asleep with his head on an empty plate.

'He held us up.' Jessop waved the pistol. 'But I read the riot act to him and he realized the folly of his ways.'

'He was starving,' Susan Perry said. 'We filled him up with omelettes and he conked out. He's a wounded veteran.'

'Probably a deserter,' Borodin said. 'Who can blame him? Badly armed, badly led, badly fed. But deep down he's got a heart of gold.'

'He'll need a jolly good scrub before you can find it,' Lacey said.

They drove the man back to the trains. Chef made a platter of sandwiches and he wolfed them while she washed his arm and examined the abscess, swollen red and hard, blue in the centre, where the skin was so thin that she could see the yellow pus beneath, clearly ready to rupture; so she opened it and let the pus escape. This was painful but he didn't flinch. The sandwiches took his full attention. She finished the treatment, covered the injury with lint soaked in boric-acid solution, bandaged the arm, and told him, through Borodin, to keep the bandages on for a week.

Borodin gave him back the pistol – Jessop said it was broken anyway and wouldn't fire – and he drove the patient and Lacey back to Orel. 'It was a lot of needless fuss,' he told Lacey. 'He waved his gun, and I said we'd give him fifty roubles if

416

he'd stop being a nuisance, and he was happy with that. But Jessop had a fit of indignation and nearly picked a fight.'

'Pilots,' Lacey said. 'Excitable folk. Not you, Count.'

'No, of course. I have your famous British stiff upper lip. I keep it in an old cigar box.'

The week passed quickly. The air crews played their own version of polo, riding the ponies and swinging the croquet mallets at croquet balls. There were no rules, and nobody kept score. Perhaps there was no score.

Wragge and Borodin watched. 'We are a sporting nation,' Wragge said. 'Reminds me.' He felt in his pockets for a piece of paper. 'Meant to ask you. Goolie Chits. Worth doing?'

Borodin read H.Q's signal. 'This assumes the finder can read,' he said. 'Odds are ten to one against. If he reads, will he understand? Fifty to one. If he understands, will he trust us? A thousand to one.' He folded the paper and gave it back. 'This is Russia, Tiger.'

'Oh, well. We haven't any gold sovereigns, anyway.'

The poker school reopened. It had closed when Dextry cleaned everyone else out and said he was keeping the money to show people the folly of gambling and besides, he needed it for his pension. After his crash, Uncle refused to release the money, even for I.O.U.s. Now there was pay to gamble with.

Lacey bought many sacks of potatoes in Orel market; also eggs, milk, radishes and loaves of

417

black bread as hard as wood. The value of the rouble was tumbling daily and he spent lavishly.

He stayed in contact with the outside world. Signals from the British Military Mission H.Q. informed him that Captain Butcher had been transferred and that Captain Stokes, Grenadier Guards, would assume his duties.

'Stokes is a fool,' the adjutant said. 'I knew him in France. Wears a hairnet in bed.'

'He says he needs a complete audit of squadron stores.'

Brazier grunted. 'Stop the war, H.Q. wants to count the bullets.'

'The impertinence of it. I shall put Master Stokes in his place.'

While Lacey wrote, Brazier wound up the gramophone and played Scott Joplin records. 'Fig Leaf Rag' was good. Sprightly was the word for it. He liked 'Magnetic Rag' too, you could imagine the regiment stepping out in style behind a smart band doing its best with 'Magnetic Rag'. He wasn't so keen on 'Gladiolus Rag'. Didn't have the same pep. Might make a slow march.

Lacey stopped tinkering with his first draft, made a clean copy and showed it to him.

Squadron is fighting for its life against Bolsheviks by day and tribal warriors of Georgi Godunov by night stop Inflicting heavy casualties stop Instances of gallantry too frequent to mention stop Morale holding good but where is trombone trumpet E flat banjo requested in last signal query stop Regret audit squadron stores impossible while under fire stop Suspect Red high command are intercepting signals stop If so suggest communicate in Welsh Gaelic Portuguese

Cherokee stop Squadron Leader T. Wragge Officer Commanding.

Brazier read it. 'The C.O. is losing his wits.'

'The strain of battle.'

'If Stokes comes here to see for himself you're skewered.'

'We're hundreds of miles by rail from H.Q. Two days' travel, at least. Stokes won't leave Taganrog.'

Brazier yawned, and returned the paper, holding it by a corner between finger and thumb. 'I've seen officers court-martialled for less than this. The war isn't made so that you can write your *Comic Cuts*.' He put on his cap and picked up his blackthorn stick.

'You may be right, Uncle,' Lacey said. 'But if not for *Comic Cuts*, then what is it for?' Brazier didn't stay to argue.

2

The C.O. sat in his Pullman and wondered how to improve the success of his Camels.

Height and surprise were always a good start. If the Camel Flight could claw its way up to, say, eleven thousand, and place itself between the sun and the enemy, there was a good chance of surprising a formation at, say, eight thousand. The Camel was a small aeroplane. Even four might well get lost in the dazzle. But when the Camels dived for a great distance, they built up a great speed, at least a hundred and fifty miles an hour

419

or more. Some said two hundred.

That's where the trouble began.

Controlling the plunge became progressively harder. If the airflow started to spin the propeller faster than the power of the engine to turn it, the entire Le Rhône rotary might fail, might even blow up. Or the propeller might fly off and shatter. So – no long, full-blooded dive. It must be held in check.

Even so, the guns were aimed by aiming the aircraft, and the Camels would reach the enemy at a speed that gave their pilots only brief seconds to fire before they must alter course. What's more, their targets would not be steady as a rock, they would be swerving and sliding out of the gunsights. Next, their dive would put the Camels below the target. Now the enemy had the advantage of height.

Wragge drew sketches of an interception. He closed his eyes and imagined the sequence of events, again and again. Always the Camels were too fast, always they had too little time. An idea presented itself so clearly that it had obviously been waiting patiently to be summoned from a corner of his brain.

He sent for Jessop and Borodin.

'See what you think of this,' he said. He had a sharp pencil and a fresh sheet of paper. 'Here we are, high, lurking in the sun. Some Bolo machines appear below us, here. We let them fly on, and then we follow after them and dive, not *at* the enemy but *behind* him. Two or three hundred yards behind, where he's still unlikely to see us. We continue with the dive until we're below them and

420

going in the same direction, and we pull out, use our speed to climb hard, bloody hard, almost vertically, so we're pointing at their bellies. As we stall, we fire. Or, if you prefer, we fire as we stall. And keep firing as they fly through our bullet-stream. Then we fall out of the stall and the enemy, we hope, falls to pieces.'

'And he never even saw us,' Borodin said. 'In theory.'

Jessop traced with his finger the final part of the Camels' dive and their climb into a stall. 'That's the trick,' he said. 'Getting that bit right.'

'Distances are crucial,' Borodin said. 'If we dive too far behind the target we might not catch it because it's flying away. Dive too near and we might climb and overshoot it. This distance...' He took the pencil and drew a line from the start of the climb to the stall. 'That must be exactly right.'

'We'll practise,' the C.O. said. 'The Nines can be Bolos.'

It took a long day's work to find the right formula.

The Nines cruised at four thousand and the Camels attacked from five thousand, sometimes more. Wragge experimented with angles and speeds of dive and distances of climb. Sometimes the Camels stalled too soon. Sometimes they stalled at the right height but the Nines were no longer there.

They landed, ate lunch, and went up again, this time to eight thousand for the Nines and nearly ten for the Camels. Here the air was thinner and every action had to be adjusted. But at 3.45 p.m.

421

they made the perfect, speedy, unseen interception and all three Camels hung in the air, aiming at the silhouettes of the Nines close above them, and then fell away. Everyone landed. Wragge had his formula in his head.

He knew it wouldn't last. Combat without violence was a nonsense, and violence had a way of making fools of planners. And the enemy wouldn't cruise up and down as placidly as Tusker Oliphant's Nines. But Merlin Squadron had not performed well lately, indeed not since Griffin vanished in a fit of futility; and Wragge wanted to do something they could all feel proud of.

They had tea. Chef had baked muffins, which were ideal with the Gentleman's Relish that Lacey had found in the bottom of a crate of tinned marmalade.

A locomotive arrived, pulling nothing but carrying a lieutenant from Denikin's staff. The squadron's aid was requested. The White advance had been checked at a river between Orel and Tula, where the Red Army presented an unusually strong defence. Denikin's armies would attack, of course, and scatter the enemy, an excellent opportunity for ground-strafing and bombing. A suitable landing field had been identified, six miles behind the lines. It was unmistakeable: three large flags had been erected in the middle of the field.

Wragge thanked the lieutenant, asked him to have the flags re-erected at the edge of the field, and said he hoped to arrive before sunset. The locomotive carried the lieutenant back to the battle.

Next morning it rained, the first interference with Wragge's formula. Cloud, as grey and woolly as an old blanket, didn't help either: it shut out the sky at two thousand feet.

The ground crews tested the engines, mopped out the cockpits, kept the bombs and bullets in the dry until ordered to arm. Everyone could hear the battle, rumbling away, six miles to the north. The adjutant listened. 'Heavy artillery,' he said. 'Red or White, impossible to say. Maybe both. God help the Poor Bloody Infantry.'

Wragge and Oliphant sat over a pot of coffee in The Dregs. 'This muck isn't going to clear,' Wragge said. 'Even if it does, your target must be the Red big guns.'

'They'll chuck all kinds of filth at us, there's no escaping that. I mean, I hope to hell we do escape. Where will you be?'

'Upstairs as usual. On guard duty.'

Oliphant looked at the raindrops hurrying down the window. 'We'll make one run and hare for home,' he said. 'And if any Nine gets shot down by Denikin's idiots I shall be very cross.'

An hour later they were all in the air, the Nines leading the Camels, everyone just skimming the cloud base. The battle lines were obvious, despite the rain: the flash and smoke of many artillery pieces, the massing of troops behind what were probably fords in the river, cavalry lurking, shell craters appearing in a burst of smoke: it was the same on either side of the river. This was the biggest clash of arms the squadron had seen since Tsaritsyn. As the Nines crossed the river, Oliphant took his Flight up into the cloud.

Wragge cruised on. The cloud base was far more ragged than it seemed from the ground, and the Camels buffeted through these thick tatters. Ground fire contributed a scattering of hopeful ink-blots but the guns couldn't find the height and they soon gave up. Windscreens were opaque with rain and the pilots didn't even bother with goggles. All that mattered was the steady, friendly roar of a Le Rhóne rotary.

Wragge kept an eye on the time. After two minutes, as planned, the Nines reappeared, widely scattered as he knew they must be. They flew a wide half-circle while they formed up in line astern. Oliphant began the long dive towards the Red positions. The Nine was a heavy biplane and heavily loaded with bombs. Weight and height combined to build speed to its maximum. Oliphant hoped it would see his Flight safely home.

The Camels watched. No Red aircraft were in sight. Not surprising. How could the enemy know exactly when the Nines would raid? But gunners on the ground, heavy-machine-gunners, light artillery, had ample time to see the line of Nines, flying fast but getting lower, and just as Oliphant knew they would, they chucked all kinds of filth at him.

His head was out in the stinging gale of rain, his eyes clenched to slits, trying not to blink as he searched for big guns worth bombing. He saw a battery off to his left just as it fired, and he jinked the Nines to correct their approach. He dropped his whole load in one thankful happy high-explosive goodbye and enjoyed his bomber's little leap of relief, and zigzagged out of this madhouse.

Wragge waited until all the Nines had bombed and he climbed into the cloud.

It was mysterious stuff, grey and gloomy, seemingly shapeless but populated with swirls and gusts that made an aeroplane drop or bounce or swerve. Some pilots hated cloud, refused to believe their instruments, feared that the cloud would never end, panicked and dived to escape. Sometimes they fell into clean air upside-down and hit a hilltop before they could recover their wits. Wragge knew that trust was the only way to beat cloud. Trust the instruments, trust the altimeter, trust the fact that he'd done it before and it worked. He ignored his senses and his Camel burst into a dazzling world of sun and an outrageous amount of blue sky.

Jessop and Borodin followed, nowhere near him. They came together and searched the sky. Empty. They were at three thousand five hundred. Wragge took them up until he knew their propellers were clawing at the air, just short of ten thousand feet above an earth lost below cloud so white and so widespread that it defeated the eyes.

They settled down to watch and to wait. They flew around a large invisible box: every five minutes Wragge turned them ninety degrees to the left, which meant that every twenty minutes they ended where they had begun, two miles high and alone in an immensity of air.

Jessop didn't like it. He was cold, his neck ached, he got bored easily even on patrols where you could see the ground, so this nothingness in every direction made time pass awfully slowly. He made a bored face at Borodin, and Borodin smiled back and gave a jolly wave. Jessop scowled. What had bloody Borodin got to be so bloody happy about?

Borodin asked himself that question. It was a very long time since he had experienced happiness. Now, out of the blue – literally so, he was surrounded by the blue – a small rush of happiness had surprised him. Perhaps it was caused by a sense of escape. When he was on earth, nothing raised his spirits. His country was tearing itself apart, and both sides deserved to lose. Up here he was free from Russia and its suicidal folly. Not for long. Enjoy it while you can.

Wragge changed course. Five minutes. Changed course. Five minutes. He began to worry about fuel. Also about winds. Impossible to know whether there was a wind at this height and if so, where was it blowing them? Over Bolshevik territory? They might face a long slog home. Run out of fuel, forced landing, captured by Reds, no morphine phial, no goolie chit, prospects grim. He checked his fuel gauge again and when he looked up Jessop had closed in and was pointing down.

Wragge searched and found nothing and searched again and saw a tiny pencilled mark on the cloud. It moved. It wasn't one mark, it was three. He used his binoculars. Three hulking great machines, twin-engined, must be bombers, could it be true? Why not, Britain had them, Germany bombed London with them, why shouldn't the Reds have a few? What a gift. What a bonanza. What a jamboree.

The Camels lost height, spiralling down, checking their speed, keeping themselves between the sun and the target. It was still a fast descent: five thousand feet in as many minutes. The air was thicker, breathing was easier, the rotaries had more oxygen and made more power. And now Wragge saw four bombers, not three, each looking twice as big as a Nine. They flew in pairs, one behind the other. Monsters. Juggernauts. Twin streams of exhaust smoke were pumped out by their twin engines. How big a crew could a beast like this carry? How many guns? Wragge had a sudden fear that his clever plan might not work. Too late now. Should have thought of that earlier.

The bombers had ploughed on. He led the Camels in a dive, full power, if the wings fell off that was tough luck, and they burst through the broken air left behind by all those twin engines. Wragge held the dive and the shapes of the bombers were shrinking. The moment Wragge pulled out, Jessop and Borodin pulled out too, climbed as he climbed. They were clamped in their seats by centrifugal force, vision slightly grey but that passed as the climb became vertical and Holy Moses, the trick worked. The Camel pilots were looking at the shapes, black against the sun, of four Bolo bombers marching to their doom.

Or perhaps not.

Three Camels at the point of stall could hit only what they aimed at. Changing direction to find a new target was not possible. And the bombers were widespread.

Jessop saw an engine and he fired his twin Vickers into it until flame and smoke blotted everything. Borodin saw a tail unit, wide, with double rudders, and he pounded it until it fell to pieces. Wragge was the lucky one. A nose slid into his view and he fired and kept firing as the rest of the fuselage followed and he stopped only when his Camel fell off its stall. By then enemy gunners in the fourth bomber had found the Camels, highly vulnerable as they hung in the sky. Wragge felt the jolt of bullets ripping into his machine. That had not been part of his plan.

In seconds the firing ended, the bombers moved on, the Camels fell towards cloud and safety. They came out of the cloud base and saw three bombers crash and burn and make spectacular explosions. All had fallen on the White side of the river. Wragge wondered whether that was good or not. To be a soldier in the winning army and have an enemy bomber drop on you would be a rotten way to die.

Oh, well. *Nichevo.* The Camels flew home.

3

All the aircraft needed to be worked on. Holes patched, spars replaced. A Nine needed a new oil pump, a Camel had a wonky wheel. Wragge gave his crews the rest of the day off. It was still only mid-morning.

The rain had passed and the countryside looked fresh. 'I'm going fishing,' Borodin said to Susan Perry. 'It's rather a long way. We could take a couple of ponies.' She was helping Sergeant Stevens clean up after the morning sick parade.

'When he talks of pony rides, that means he

wants to propose to me,' she told Stevens.

'I'd marry him, like a flash,' Stevens said. 'I've always fancied being a countess.'

'Last time I was cruelly rebuffed,' Borodin told him. 'She doesn't deserve me. But it's too good a day to be stuck in a train. Nature calls.'

'Bugger nature,' she said. 'I've just treated a case of piles, a blood-shot eye and a dislocated finger, so nature doesn't impress me.'

'In case you were wondering,' Stevens said to him, 'those three medical conditions were in no way related.'

'If it's rather a long way,' she said, 'what exactly are your plans for lunch?'

'Chef's picnic basket. Caesar salad. Ripe melon. Cold beer.'

'You're in charge here,' she said to Stevens. 'Feel free to amputate anything below the rank of flight sergeant.'

'The iron grip of privilege. Bloody officers.'

Borodin was right: it was a perfect summer's morning. The cloud had gone, and the air had the extra clarity that comes with sunshine after rain has washed the colours brighter. At first the ponies galloped just for the fun of it. When they slowed to a walk, she said, 'It's quiet. All the guns have stopped.'

'Yes.'

'Does that mean we won the battle?'

'No. The Red Army didn't win, either.'

'So it's a draw.'

'Probably both sides simply ran out of shells. It often happens. There will now be an interval for refreshments.'

'Oh.' She thought about that. 'Suddenly Moscow seems rather a long way away.'

'Look,' he said. 'A green woodpecker.' It flew, and made a good show of green plumage and red head. 'Not to be confused with the black, grey-headed or great spotted woodpecker. Russia has them all.'

'I don't care. I cruelly rebuff them all.' She clapped her heels and the pony galloped through the long grass.

They rode through woods and meadows and parkland and reached the river. The ponies splashed into the water and drank. 'I have a sense of *déjà vu*,' she said. 'So let me make it clear that I wouldn't marry you if you were Adam and apples were sixpence a pound. That's a split-cane fly rod by Hardy's of Alnwick, isn't it? Where did you get it?'

'Uncle let me borrow it. Belonged to Gerard Pedlow.' He sat on the bank and assembled it. 'Do you fish?'

'Never. But Father had fly rods all over the house. Very boring man. Look: you fish away. I'm going for a walk.'

Half an hour later he walked upstream and found her sitting next to a waterfall. 'Lunch,' he said. He put down the picnic basket.

'I've been studying this waterfall. It seems to me that it was made for sitting under.'

'Don't think so much. Go and do it.'

'I will if you will.'

She took off her uniform until she was wearing only her shift. He stripped until he wore only his shirt. He followed her. The river fell onto a shelf

430

that made a conveniently smooth seat. The first impact of the water was a shock; then it became silkily smooth.

'I don't know why we're being so coy,' she said. 'Coy people make me want to hit them.'

'Leave it on, it's far more revealing. I think you wear it as an armour against my tremendous appeal. You don't like to admit that we are destined for each other.'

'There you go again. Romantic novelettes. All jam and no bread.'

After a while they climbed out and sat in the sun. He opened the basket. They ate the melon and the Caesar salad and drank the beer. She said, 'The truth of the matter is you're not in love with me, Peter Borodin. A man like you, good looks, charm, nobility, you're always in love with someone. Here, with me, you're just marking time because there's nobody else within reach.'

'Oh dear.' He was startled. 'Am I such a bounder? I had no idea...'

'I don't blame you. It's how you are. You can't help bounding.' She began sorting out her clothes.

They rode home, and as the trains came in sight she said, 'I'm glad I met you, and I wish I knew why. No, I don't. I don't give a damn why. But we don't have to marry everybody we're glad to meet, do we?'

'That depends on the degree of gladness.'

'No, it doesn't. And for God's sake stop bounding.'

Next day the aircraft were repaired and ready for operations again. Wragge had them test-flown

431

and waited for orders. In mid-afternoon a solitary locomotive brought Denikin's liaison officer. He strolled with the C.O. on the landing ground and explained that his orders were that there were no orders at present. Denikin wished the squadron to remain at full strength and to conserve ammunition and bomb stocks until they were needed for another assault.

And when would that be?

As soon as the losses in the first assault could be made good.

A week?

Almost certainly in a week. Perhaps ten days. Supply trains were on their way. Every urgency was being applied. The Red Army had withdrawn with heavy losses. Definitely in ten days the attack would begin. Success was inevitable.

Wragge took him to The Dregs for tea. He asked him if Denikin had been impressed by the destruction of three large enemy bomber aircraft, and the officer smiled and said it reflected much credit on the White artillery units which had shot them down. He ate two toasted muffins with Gentleman's Relish, and shook hands, and the locomotive carried him away. Wragge watched it get smaller. 'Stinking fish,' he said. 'What a swindle.' The words did not express his feelings. 'Great masses of truly stinking fish,' he said. Still not enough.

A BIG, BUCCANEERING ACTION

1

Usually the ground crews complained because they were overworked, although secretly they enjoyed the pressure, the sense of achievement. Now they had nothing to do and that was not what they wanted either. The squadron quickly became slack and sluggish. Ball games were tedious. Everyone had his pay and there was nothing to spend it on except poker, and even poker became dull. Wragge worried, but he could think of no solution.

He discussed the problem with Oliphant and Borodin.

'We can't just sit here for ten days,' he said. 'I mean, look around. There's nothing. We're fifty miles from Orel, and God knows that was a dump.'

'This ceasefire, or stalemate, or whatever it is,' Oliphant said. 'Not good for morale. We came hotfoot from Taganrog, jumping from one landing field to another, the chaps quite liked that, it appealed to their sense of adventure. Now this. And The Dregs has run out of cheese and bacon.'

'Russians don't eat bacon,' Borodin said. 'Ham, sometimes.'

'Can't have eggs and bacon without bacon.'

'Lacey can get us bacon, I expect,' Wragge said.

'Anyway, bacon's not crucial. But Uncle tells me he's had some applications for leave from amongst the ground crews. *Leave,* for God's sake.'

'Well, they're bored,' Oliphant said. 'We've lost half the squadron. They're kicking their heels. Cheesed off.'

'Sometimes I wish those idiot bandits would attack us again,' Wragge said. 'Give the troops something to do.'

'Beware of wishes for they may be granted,' Borodin said.

'I'll tell you what part of the trouble is,' Oliphant said. 'This country's too damn big for us. The chaps have begun to feel lost. Maybe it suits the Russians, that's fine, good luck to them. Not us. People can cope as long as they're on the move. Once they stop, have time to think, look around, see thousands of miles of bugger-all in all directions – no offence, Count – they ask themselves, what in God's name am I doing here?'

'We're making a difference,' Wragge said automatically.

'With three clapped-out Camels and three patched-up Nines?'

Wragge felt his temper rising. 'We do our best with what we've got. If you can come up with an alternative, tell me. That's all.'

Nobody could. Time dragged.

Wragge was sitting in The Dregs on a hot and sultry afternoon, alone, with all the windows open, thinking it was a lot more fun to command a squadron in action than one that was killing time, when he heard a conversation outside. Two men, perhaps three, were sitting in the shadow of

434

the train, a favourite spot. He thought he recognized the voices: bomber boys. They were talking about war. It was lazy, jokey talk, just chewing the fat. Wragge moved closer to the window. The topic was mutiny.

– That was after Verdun, a voice said. Remember Verdun? Grim business. French Army ran out of coffins, I was told. Anyway, Verdun was what caused the mutiny. Frog troops had had enough.
– Didn't last long, did it? a different voice said. They shot a few and the rest went back to the Trenches.
– Yes, bleating. Baa-baa, like sheep. Just to let everyone know. Laughter.
– Say what you like, the Frogs weren't as bad as these Russkies. Didn't shoot their officers.
– Be fair. Russians only do that when they're losing.
– Somebody has to lose.
– I wish they'd all lose, and be damn quick about it. I'd like to bomb H.Q. at Taganrog and get the next boat home.
– Moscow's nearer.
– Alright, bomb Moscow. What's the difference?
– You get the V.C.
– Posthumously.
Laughter.
Wragge stood up, stretched, walked to his Pullman, lay on his bed for five minutes, got up, went in search of Tusker Oliphant. He found him talking to Patterson. 'A word in your ear, Tusk,' he said, and Patterson saluted and went away. 'What's the endurance of a Nine? How long can

you stay in the air?'

'Depends. The book says four and a half hours, but De Havillands wrote the book for new Nines, straight from the factory. Would one of our Nines stay up that long? Very doubtful.'

'And speed? How fast?'

'Well, again you can forget the book. Level flight, carrying a pair of big bombs, our absolute maximum, say a hundred, maybe hundred and a bit. But our Nines won't keep that up. Cruising, let's say ninety.'

Wragge did the sum in his head. 'Four and a half by ninety is just over four hundred miles.'

'Assuming nothing breaks.'

'Four hundred is roughly the distance from here to Moscow and back.'

'Seems right.' Oliphant caught up with Wragge's meaning. 'Oh, sweet Jesus. Excuse me while I fall down and faint.'

'It's just an idea. Thinking aloud, so to speak. Testing the technicalities. Can it be done? Don't answer that, give it some thought, work out the practical side.'

'You are talking about Moscow? Russian capital?'

'Forget that. Treat this as a tactical exercise. And don't tell anyone. Total secrecy. That's an order.'

'Tactical exercise,' Oliphant said. 'Moscow. I don't think that's quite how the rest of the world would see it. Don't worry, I shan't breathe a word. Of course I may babble in my sleep.'

'Stuff a sock in your mouth,' the C.O. said.

The idea was fixed in his mind. For the next twenty-four hours, when he wasn't asleep he studied it from every angle, and the more he looked at it, the better it seemed.

There was the excitement of attacking the enemy deep behind his lines, something only an R.A.F. squadron could attempt. There was the satisfaction of surprising the Bolsheviks, hitting them where they least expected it. And the raid would add a new battle honour to the squadron's flag, if it ever got a flag. They came to Russia to make a difference, and by Harry, what a shining difference this would be! The squadron had fought hard and achieved depressingly little so far; even the glory of tumbling three twin-engined bombers had been stolen by Denikin's guns. Now was the time to make a big score. It was the sort of big, buccaneering action that other squadrons would talk about for years to come.

He sent for Oliphant and they walked around the airfield.

'Is it on?' Wragge asked.

'It's *just* on. What I mean is it's right on the extreme edge of these Nines' performance. And that's assuming a lot of things. It assumes that the weather doesn't turn lousy, on the way there or back. If we hit a northerly wind and we have to slog through it, then all bets are off. We'd burn up so much fuel we'd never get back here.'

'A northerly wind might blow you home.'

'Might. Or it might drop, and drop us in the manure. And what if the wind comes out of the west? We'd have to crab to Moscow. That's like putting an extra fifty, sixty, seventy miles on the trip, depending on the strength of the blow.'

'Here's a thought,' the C.O. said. 'Do without

an observer-gunner in your back seat. Carry his weight in cans of petrol. For any emergency. You run low, you find a field, land, top up, Bob's your uncle.'

They stopped, and Oliphant screwed up his face while he pictured the situation.

'This field,' he said. 'It's going to be in Red territory, isn't it?'

'The Bolos can't be everywhere, Tusker. And it wouldn't take long, would it?'

'I'm thinking of this bloody awful engine in the Nine. You do know that it takes two men to start a Puma? One to turn the prop, one to sit in the office and play with the knobs and switches. Unless you were thinking of leaving the engine running while the driver gets out and opens the cans and pours the precious fluid into the tanks, taking care not to spill any on the red-hot exhausts.'

'To be honest, Tusk, I hadn't worked out the details.'

'Another detail might be the bullets from the nasty Red infantry buzzing about his ears.'

'I suppose I thought that both Nines would land and sort of help each other.' They began walking.

'Ah. That alters everything,' Oliphant said. 'The other pilot would hold off the Red Army with his trusty Service revolver while I poured. Then vice versa. That should be worth a double D.F.C.'

'Look: don't tell me about the problems. Any fool can find a hundred ways of not doing something different. Find some solutions.'

'Well, it would help if your Camels gave us

cover on the way out and back.'

'We can do that,' the C.O. said. 'Halfway to Moscow is about as far as we can cruise. Yes, we can cover you.'

'Navigation's no problem. Just follow the railway line.'

They strolled on, Wragge kicking the heads off dandelions, Oliphant's heels scuffing the turf.

'I don't suppose you'd rather bomb Kaganovich?' Oliphant said. 'Vital rail junction. Very Bolshy. Only fifty miles away.'

'And nobody's ever heard of it. Moscow's worth a hundred Kaganoviches. I take it you'll be leading? With who else?'

'Douglas Gunning. He feels very badly about losing Michael Lowe. Give him the chance to biff the Bolos and he'll fly to the pit of hell.'

At sunset, before supper, the C.O. called a meeting of all aircrews and ground crews of the surviving machines. They gathered in the open and formed a half-circle. The air was still, and the last rays of the sun caught heads and shoulders and cast long shadows.

'Your squadron has not had a long existence,' Wragge said, 'but we have accomplished much. I have no hesitation in saying that we now have an opportunity to crown these achievements with a bold stroke that will secure the reputation of this squadron wherever men fly. Gentlemen, I plan to bomb Moscow.'

It had the impact he expected. When they were quiet again he told them the details of the raid. Wragge was not a sentimental man, but he thought that the gilded faces, alive with excitement, were appropriate to the occasion.

2

After breakfast, the adjutant came into his Orderly Room, and found Lacey with his headphones slung around his neck. He was sorting out several pieces of paper. Brazier sat down with a thud that made his inkwell jump. 'I expect you heard the rumour,' Brazier said.

'I'm impervious to gossip.' Lacey didn't look up. 'Gossip butters no parsnips, as we grocers like to say.'

'This does. I asked Oliphant and he confirmed it.'

'Stout fellow.' Lacey turned over a page. 'Listen: this will interest you. Our man in Taganrog, the inimitable Henry, has found a fellow in Orel with a supply of genuine English mustard. In Orel, of all places.'

'The C.O. plans to send aircraft to bomb Moscow.'

Lacey looked up. 'Moscow. Well, they can't miss, can they? Very big town. What's interesting is this man in Orel has a brother in Taganrog. Henry does business with one brother, and he tells the other to supply us. Clever, eh?'

Brazier stared at Lacey as if he had appeared on parade with his buttons undone. 'Do you know what orders this squadron was given when it came to Russia?'

'Show the flag.' Lacey went back to his notes. 'That's what Griffin kept bellowing, anyway... If he can get mustard I bet he can get marmalade too. And sugar. We're low on sugar.'

'I'll tell you the orders,' Brazier said. 'We are part of the British Military Mission and its role is purely and simply advisory. Our orders were that we instruct and advise Denikin's Russians. Instruct and advise. Nothing more.'

'Well, that's a fairy tale, isn't it? You don't believe it, Uncle. Nobody does. But I'll tell you what's very real: toilet paper. People on this train are self-indulgent. We'll have to ration it.'

'Bombing Moscow is different, Lacey. A blind man can see that. It's an act of war.'

'You may be right.' Lacey picked out a piece of paper and held it up. He was smiling. 'You won't believe what that fool Stokes has done. He's referred our request for jazz band kit to the Director of Military Music in London. The man's a poltroon. I've trumped his ace. Listen to this—'

'No.' Brazier stood up, suddenly, knocked his desk, sent pens and pencils flying. 'I've worn the King's uniform since before you could walk, and one thing I know. When the limits of command are in doubt, always Refer to a Higher Authority. Always.'

'Oh dear,' Lacey said. 'I suppose you're right. We'll just have to see what the Director of Military Music says. But this man in Orel—'

'No.' Brazier took two strides and swept all the papers from Lacey's desk with one angry hand. 'No. You will send an urgent signal to Mission H.Q. now. To the General Commanding.'

Lacey stared. He was a small boy below a large and domineering schoolmaster. 'You just had to

441

ask,' he said. 'After all, you were the one who wanted mustard.'

'To the General Commanding, British Military Mission H.Q. Urgent. Merlin Squadron R.A.F. requests permission to bomb Moscow. Signed, Brazier, captain, adjutant.'

'Simple.' Lacey put on his headphones. 'Neat but not gaudy. I think I can manage that.'

3

The C.O. and Tusker Oliphant reached a compromise. Each bomber would carry an observer-gunner, but they would be the smallest, lightest men in the Flight. Cans of petrol, equivalent to the savings in weight, would be packed into their cockpits. There would be a trial flight and landing to see how the refuelling worked.

'Just to make it more realistic,' the C.O. said, 'and seeing that we have so many ground crews doing nothing, they can be the Red Army.'

'Firing realistic rifles?' Oliphant said. 'I hope not.'

'Blank rounds. And your gunners can have blanks in their Lewis guns. Don't worry. I'll stage-manage it.'

The Nines, loaded to the maximum with fuel and bombs, laboured into the air and made two careful circuits. They landed into the wind, turned, taxied to the other end, turned again and killed their engines. Oliphant and Gunning scrambled out and stood on the lower wings. Their observers heaved up cans.

'Heavy weather,' Jessop said. He was watching from a distance. 'No handles on those cans. Petrol's heavy. And you need a big funnel to get it into the tank.'

'They forgot the funnels,' Wragge said. 'Lesson one.'

'Where's the Red Army? Honestly, the Bolos are a disgrace.'

'Hiding in the woods.'

When the first can was empty and flung aside, and the pilots and observers were struggling with the second, the C.O. fired a red signal flare. The attack began. The ground crews came from many different points. Their rifles made noise and smoke. They shouted profane abuse. They enjoyed themselves enormously. The observers' Lewis guns doubled the uproar. The pilots emptied the second can and shouted for a third, but the observers could not fire the Lewis and hoist another can.

There was no option but to escape. The pilots got into their cockpits and the observers got out to swing the propellers. All this took time. The Lewis guns were silent. The ground crews raced across the field and captured the Nines. They took pleasure in marching the crews to the C.O.

'Lessons to be learned,' Wragge said.

'Yes,' Oliphant said. His trousers were soaked. 'Forget refuelling.'

'Well, there was only one way to find out. Frankly, I never had much faith in it. And it doesn't affect the basis of the operation, does it?' He saw the adjutant watching him. 'Hullo, Uncle. The Army trounced us today, didn't it? Only a

443

little experiment. Nothing serious.'

Brazier held up a piece of paper. 'This calls for your attention, sir.' The *sir* surprised Wragge. Only the Other Ranks called him sir. He and Brazier walked away from the crowd. Brazier gave him the paper. It was a signal from the General Commanding at Mission H.Q. *Permission denied,* it said. *No aircraft is permitted to bomb Moscow under any circumstances whatever.*

'This can't be right,' Wragge said. 'Only a fool would throw away an opportunity like this. A fool and a coward.' He thrust the signal at Brazier. 'Reply immediately. Request clarification. Now.' His brain caught up with events. 'Who did this? Somebody told him. Who told him?'

'I did.' Brazier folded the signal and tucked it into a tunic pocket. 'You could put me under close arrest for exceeding my authority, sir. Or you could bomb Moscow without permission and face court martial yourself. I chose the lesser offence. For the good of the squadron.' Wragge was silent.

Brazier walked back to his Orderly Room. Within the hour, the C.O. got his reply. The General Commanding in H.Q. also believed in Referring to a Higher Authority. Air Ministry in London categorically refused permission for any R.A.F. unit to bomb Moscow. In the interests of clarity, this meant Merlin Squadron R.A.F. must not repeat not bomb Moscow.

Wragge turned the signal into a paper glider and made it fly. 'Sometimes it's a privilege to be court-martialled, Uncle. Did you ever think of that?' Brazier said nothing, and Wragge walked away. He

444

went to his Camel. 'Full tanks?' he asked his fitter.

'Half-full, sir.'

'Good enough. I'll take her up.' He got in.

He climbed until the airfield was out of sight. All he had for company were some fluffy clouds. He tested the Camel with every aerobatic trick he knew. If his ground crew had done their job, nothing would break. On the other hand, they couldn't see inside every spar and wire and yard of fabric. Nothing broke. Some parts creaked and the wings flexed more than usual, but nothing actually snapped. He ended the flight at slightly. above ground level, vaulting over trees, sometimes squeezing between trees, and landed as delicately as a dancer.

Oliphant met him. 'Alright?' he said.

'Perfectly.'

'We thought you might have gone off and done a Griffin.'

'Not me. Anyway, I couldn't find anyone to fight.'

'Bloody Bolos. Let you down every time. I heard the news.'

'It's a stupid war, Tusker. H.Q. doesn't know whether it's fighting or farting. Well, to hell with Taganrog. To hell with London. And to hell with Moscow. Tonight we'll throw the biggest party this unlucky squadron has ever had.'

'First sensible order you've given,' Oliphant said.

NICHEVO

1

Three days later, the Red Army launched a surprise assault, with fresh troops, and crossed the river at a rush.

By midday the squadron's trains were rolling south while the aircraft flew on ahead of them. The pilots were waiting, on the beautiful green field as big as Lord's cricket ground, when the trains pulled into the rusty spur line. It was dusk. Travel had been painfully slow. The tracks were crowded with trains – troop trains, hospital trains, refugee trains – all going south. That was to be the story of Merlin Squadron for the next month.

Lacey strung his aerials and failed to make contact with Denikin's staff but a signal from Mission H.Q. referred to 'a temporary reverse'. He tried again next day and told the C.O. that reportedly the White armies were making a strategic withdrawal to strong defensive positions. 'The Red Army claims to have captured Orel,' he said.

Borodin walked to the main line and talked to some staff officers whose train was waiting for signals to change. He came back to The Dregs. 'They say that the Reds are fighting like dervishes, not that they know what a dervish fights like. What really depressed them was the new Red uniform. All their troops have it. Even boots.

And good food too. Some of Denikin's units mutinied so they could join the Reds and eat.'

'But we had them beaten,' Jessop said. 'What happened?'

'Russia is a big country. And now their supply lines are very short while ours are very long.'

'Uncle,' Wragge said. 'Kindly ask the *plennys* to dig up that memorial to Hopton and Blythe. We're not leaving it here.'

He waited. On the third day the traffic on the main line thinned to a trickle, which was a bad sign. The squadron trains moved south again, sluggishly, passing the capsized ruin of the Bolo armoured train. Smoke was still drifting over Kursk, but there was little left to burn. The machines had already landed at the field where the dead horses had been piled into the shell crater.

The squadron ran out of tinned fruit, oatmeal, butter and dried peas.

During the night, all the *plennys* except Chef deserted.

Sounds of battle could be heard, probably in Kursk. No orders from Denikin's staff reached the squadron. Wragge decided to get out before he was overrun. The aircraft flew south, to the racetrack. General Gregorioff and his gout had left. The squadron trains did not arrive for three days. The pilots and observers lived on roast rabbit (shot with Service revolvers), mushrooms, wild strawberries, and a fat pheasant which had been too slow to avoid Jessop's Camel as he landed. They slept badly: the nights were cold.

The squadron ran out of eggs, onions, marmalade, Gentleman's Relish, tinned green beans, and pepper.

Lacey led a group into Belgorod and managed to buy twelve cabbages and two dead sheep. It was not easy: inflation was raging, the value of the rouble had slumped. There was no enthusiasm for Denikin's currency. 'He prints it like a newspaper,' Borodin explained. 'Fresh every day.'

The C.O. decided to dismantle the aircraft and stow them on the flatbed trucks. While this was being done, the adjutant discovered that the driver and stoker of Oliphant's train had gone. Decamped. Left for good. Worse still, there was little coal in their tender. 'We don't need two trains,' Wragge said. 'Shift everything onto ours. Including the coal.' News arrived: Denikin had lost Kursk.

It took a slow, depressing week to get near Kharkov. Refugee trains often broke down. It was dangerous to stop because refugees mobbed the squadron train, forcing it to travel with locked doors and drawn blinds. There were fewer troop trains, perhaps because the countryside was thick with deserters. Often at night they tried to break in. The adjutant posted riflemen on the roof.

The sheep Lacey bought made mutton stew. Kid, the squadron mascot, disappeared at the same time. Nobody commented.

Kharkov was full of tired soldiers and rumours. The Red Army was carving up Denikin's flanks, it was said. Tsaritsyn might fall, or had fallen, anyway it was finished. So was Voronezh. And the Ukraine, well, if the Reds don't get there first the Poles will have it. Heard about Admiral Kolchak? As good as dead. He's made Denikin the

Supreme Ruler. What a joke.

The C.O. stocked the locomotive with coal and water, taken at the point of a gun, and moved south.

Kharkov fell.

A hundred men take a lot of feeding. The Cossack ponies were slaughtered. The squadron ate the last of the black bread.

Summer ends quickly in Russia, and autumn is brief. Greatcoats were being worn when the squadron train rolled into Taganrog. Lacey went to see Henry at the Hotel Olymp and found he had checked out a week ago. The C.O. and the adjutant went to Mission H.Q. A sergeant was in the garden, burning files. He was in his shirt sleeves: there were many files and they generated great heat. 'Everybody's gone to Rostov,' he said. 'Me too, as soon as I get through this heap of shit.'

H.Q. had left two sacks of potatoes in its kitchens. Wragge and Brazier carried them back to the train. All Ranks were on a diet of bully beef and biscuit. The stationmaster at Rostov told Borodin that the Red Army would soon take the city and that British Mission H.Q. had gone to Ekaterinodar, where Denikin was rumoured to be making a last stand. The stationmaster's advice was to make for Novorossisk.

2

Lloyd George was sitting in an armchair next to a window when Jonathan Fitzroy tapped on the door and came in. 'Good afternoon, sir,' he said.

'Take a seat, Jonathan. I don't want you to collapse with shock.'

I'm not going to get the sack, Fitzroy thought. He'd keep me standing for that.

The P.M. was polishing his spectacles with the end of his silk tie. 'I wonder if too much reading weakens the eyes,' he said. 'Perhaps it actually strengthens them. That would be good. But it hasn't worked for me... The Services send me monthly bulletins about how things are going in Russia. Their last reports coincided happily with the leaps and bounds made by Denikin's advance. The soldiers, of course, put that down to their training of his armies. No doubt the War Office is now thinking up excuses for his headlong retreat. The weather is probably to blame. In France the generals always blamed the weather when the war didn't go quite right. The Navy reported that it was still master of the Baltic, where the hulks of Soviet warships continue to rust. And the Royal Air Force... Well, I have their bulletin here. Read it for yourself.'

Fitzroy undid the ribbon on the folder and flicked through the pages. 'Blessedly brief,' he said.

'Well, they haven't many aeroplanes.'

Fitzroy began reading. Lloyd George turned and looked at the typically grey London weather. Wintry, very wintry. He got up and went to his desk and checked his diary. No surprises there. Fitzroy turned a page. Lloyd George read three letters and signed them. Fitzroy turned another page. Lloyd George picked up the telephone and asked for some tea, if you please, thank you.

Fitzroy said, 'Oh, damn.'

'Ah, you've found it,' the P.M. said.

'Damn and double-damn.' Fitzroy looked up. 'The man must have been a maniac. The commander of this squadron, that is. He's a lunatic. How could he even contemplate... Good God, the consequences would have been immense. And unforgivable. Bombing Moscow would have been like ... like the Zeppelins bombing London. Worse!' He stood up and slapped the report against his thigh. 'An act of madness.'

'I thought it might excite you.' The P.M. examined his fingernails and found them all present and correct. 'I didn't expect you to be quite so hysterically indignant.'

Fitzroy had held his job long enough to know when to say nothing.

'Your problem, Jonathan, is that you read too many newspapers and not enough history. History teaches us that war does not travel in a straight line. Obstacles spring up that never before existed, and so armies ricochet, and leaders must duck and dodge or they suffer. Last year we nearly joined forces with the Bolsheviks. Even Winston was for it. He wanted to offer them a formula that would protect their revolution and consolidate their power, if only they would restart their war against Germany. We desperately needed someone to fight for the Allies in the east, and the Bolsheviks seemed the most warlike. But, alas, not for long. Then the Huns collapsed, a very large surprise indeed, since most of us expected the war to go on for another five or ten years. Now we no longer needed an eastern front. But – a

451

little ricochet – Bolshevik revolutions began breaking out in Europe like chicken pox, so we put our money on the anti-Red forces in Russia. Worth a gamble. Nearly paid off. How far from Moscow was this R.A.F. bombing squadron?'

Fitzroy looked in the report. 'Two hundred miles.'

'Only two hundred?' The P.M. stretched his arms out sideways. 'More or less from here to Manchester. If only Denikin could have kept going, he might have taken Moscow.'

'That was what we had all hoped, sir.'

'And a few bombs on the capital might have been just what was needed to panic the enemy.'

Fitzroy sat down and fanned himself with the report. 'Now I'm thoroughly confused. Do you approve of the bombing plan?'

'No, of course not. Lenin would never have forgiven us. He's prepared to overlook the Intervention. He won't forget it, but he'll overlook it if we sign a few lucrative trade agreements with his government. They're stony-broke, and he has quantities of timber and furs and caviare to sell. The Soviet government is the de facto state, Jonathan. Pity about Denikin. When he was two hundred miles from Moscow he was, alas, at the end of his tether. He tried awfully hard, but second-best in that strange country is ... well, they don't have a second-best. Either you win or you go to the knacker's yard. Ah, tea. Just what you need to restore your shattered nerves.'

Fitzroy sipped his tea and put the mystery of the non-bombing of Moscow aside. 'That would seem to be the end of the matter,' he said. 'Air

452

Ministry shows no sign of wishing to court-martial...' He checked the report. '...Acting Squadron Leader Wragge.'

'Very wise. He obeyed orders, he did no wrong. On the contrary, he would claim that bombing Moscow was just what he had been sent to do. His squadron was Denikin's spearhead. Perhaps if he had bombed Moscow a little sooner, when the Navy was sinking Soviet battleships in the Baltic, we might have given Mr Wragge a V.C., like Lieutenant Agar. Wragge got everything right except his timing. Timing is everything in war. Should we suggest to Air Ministry that Wragge be retired and given a gold watch?' The P.M. smiled. 'Joke,' he said.

Fitzroy nibbled a digestive biscuit. 'All the same, it would be disastrous if the newspapers were to get hold of the story. Imagine what the *Daily Express* would do with it. "R.A.F. Bombers had Moscow in Their Sights." That's what they'd say.'

Lloyd George slammed his fist on the desk. 'Official Secrets Act. Send a large Air Vice-Marshal to lecture the entire squadron. Not a word to anyone about anything. Or they'll be prosecuted, convicted, jailed. Not a syllable.'

'It shall be done,' Fitzroy said. 'Intervention? What Intervention?'

'Have some more tea, Jonathan. And another biscuit. You worry too much.'

3

For the last few miles into Novorossisk the train

moved at walking pace. Even this was faster than the stumbling mass of humanity spread widely on either side of the tracks. Some were peasants in the usual shapeless sheepskin clothing. Some were soldiers, often bandaged, wearing tattered uniforms, many of them barefoot. A few might have been from the moneyed class: sometimes fur coats could be seen. There were even men in business suits. Nobody looked up at the train. They plodded on in their thousands, hugging whatever mattered most to them: a sack, a suitcase, a child.

'Not a happy sight,' Lacey said to Borodin.

'No. War is not all bright uniforms and dashing cavalry. The newspapers never show the misery, do they?'

'That chap...' Lacey pointed. 'He looks rich enough to take the train. Rich enough to buy the train, in fact.'

'Money is meaningless now. You've seen the trains that we passed, broken down, abandoned. A lot of these people were on those trains. Look at the corpses. Almost certainly typhus. It's a plague here. Everyone's desperate to escape.'

'Escape where?'

'Anywhere. All they know is that if they stay, the Red cavalry will kill them.'

'But if they crowd together, the typhus will get them.'

Borodin turned away from the window. 'Not all problems have solutions,' he said.

The train crawled into town. It was a grey, cold day with spatters of rain being flung by a bitter wind. 'Same as ever,' Jessop said. 'Nothing

454

changes in gay Novo.' The tracks terminated at the docks, and the train had to nudge its way through the mob of people. Most looked as if they were hungry or sick or both. The dead lay where they had fallen and were trampled upon. When the train stopped, the people nearest tried to rush it and break in. Brazier was on a flatcar with a Lewis gun and he fired a burst in the air. The crowd fell back. 'Not so gay after all,' Jessop said.

Wragge and Borodin got off the train. 'God help us,' the C.O. said. 'There must be five thousand civilians here.'

'More,' Borodin said. 'And more arriving every minute. All desperate for one thing.' He pointed to ships anchored in the bay. 'Escape.'

'It's a madhouse.'

'It's worse than that. It's a nightmare.'

A warship produced flame and smoke, followed by the deep boom of a salvo. 'Hell's teeth,' Wragge said. 'Don't tell me we're being shelled.' They waited, and counted the seconds, and heard the crash of explosions far inland.

'They're shelling the approaches to the town,' Borodin said. 'Discouraging the Bolshevik advance. So it must be a British ship.'

'Bully for them,' Wragge relaxed. 'Hullo, I think I see a small sign of discipline and order.'

Six Royal Marines with fixed bayonets jabbed and kicked their way through the mob, escorting a cavalry colonel who looked as if he hadn't slept for a week. 'You can't stay here,' he said. 'We'll get you onto a ship. For Christ's sake don't touch anyone, there's typhus and worse everywhere. First, you must empty your train of everything of

455

military value. I'm leaving nothing for the Bolsheviks.'

The Marines helped the squadron to unload the bombs and the bullets, the grenades and the Lewis guns. All got dumped in the Black Sea. They scoured the rest of the train and threw out Lacey's radio equipment and his files, Brazier's *King's Regulations,* tins of oil and drums of petrol, ground crews' toolkits and spares, Susan Perry's medical supplies, the Cossack saddles, even the croquet set and Pedlow's fly rod. They all went into the sea.

The colonel's orders were that each man could take one kitbag or suitcase. The ground crews were also allowed to carry their rifles. 'If you have bayonets, fix them,' he said. 'You'll need them to keep these animals at bay.' He took Wragge aside. 'I'll get your men ferried out to one of our big ships as soon as I can. Might take time. You're not the only British personnel in this chaos.'

'We have a squadron doctor, sir. Female but very experienced. If she can help you in any way...'

The colonel shuddered. 'Look around you. A battalion of doctors wouldn't make a dent in this catastrophe. For Christ's sake don't let her out of your sight. You must hold your ground here.' He left with his escort.

The C.O. told the adjutant to carry out a roll-call, just to make sure everyone was present. The check was made, was repeated, and Brazier reported one man missing.

'Aircraftman Simm,' he said. 'Not on the train, not off it. One man says he saw Simm go behind those trucks.' A row of empty cattle-trucks stood

456

nearby. 'Thought he'd gone to relieve himself.'

'What a damn nuisance. Well, we can't leave him here. Take six men with rifles, Uncle, and find the silly bastard.'

Brazier's men rapidly searched the area and found Simm with a tubby middle-aged man in an astrakhan overcoat. The man held an expensive leather suitcase and his other hand kept a firm grip of Simm's arm. A young woman, clearly frightened, clung to his shoulder. Brazier seized all three and marched them back to the C.O.

'He's Russian, and so is she, and they're up to no good,' he said. 'Exactly what, I don't know.'

'Explain yourself,' Wragge told Simm.

'Well, sir, this Russki feller comes up to me, wants me to take all his money. In that suitcase, sir. Got a fortune in there, sir.'

Brazier prised the man's fingers from the handle and opened the suitcase. It was packed with bundles of hundred-rouble notes, all new.

'Wouldn't let me go, sir,' Simm said. 'Kept gabbling at me. I tried to get away, sir, but he wouldn't let me.'

'And it's a lot of money,' Wragge said.

'I think he wanted me to sign a receipt or something, sir. Kept pushing a pen into my hand, sir. Fountain pen, sir. I didn't want to break it, sir.'

'And it's still a lot of money,' Wragge said. 'Search the Russian.'

The search produced a printed document, stamped and sealed and signed. 'Could be a diploma for tap-dancing.' Wragge beckoned to Borodin. 'Translate, please.'

A quick glance was enough. 'It's a marriage

457

certificate,' Borodin said. 'That's the mayor's signature. He performed the marriage. This is the lady's name. The bridegroom's name is left blank. My guess is the girl is his daughter.'

'He was selling you his daughter,' Wragge told Simm. 'If you signed this paper, you got the girl and the money.'

'Crikey,' Simm said. His eyes flickered from the open suitcase to the daughter and back. It was a colossal amount of money, and she was young and not unpretty, if tear-stained and dishevelled. 'I mean to say, sir. Bloody hell.'

'He was selling his daughter in order to get her out of the country. To escape.'

Aircraftman Simm was still looking at the money. 'Never saw that much before, sir.' He took a packet of notes from the top. 'Is it real, sir?'

Borodin turned to Wragge. 'With your permission.'

'Do, do,' Wragge said. 'Whatever it is.'

'Please bring everyone with me,' Borodin said to the adjutant. 'The father, the daughter, the money, Aircraftman Simm.' He led them to the dockside. Wragge followed. 'Throw that money in the sea,' Borodin told Simm.

Simm had a tight hold of the packet, and he hesitated.

'Do as you're bloody well ordered,' Brazier said in his ear, 'or I'll throw you in with it, you tiny streak of shit.' The notes vanished over the edge.

'Now throw the rest in.' Borodin gave Simm the suitcase. 'Just the money. Not the case.'

Simm got to work. Packets of hundred-rouble notes went flying into the Black Sea. Everyone watched. It was rare that Simm was the focus of anyone's attention. He worked hard, and he was gasping for breath when he straightened up.

Borodin closed the suitcase and gave it to the father. 'They were worthless,' he told Simm. 'Denikin roubles. He's been printing money at top speed but his roubles collapsed even faster. Now they're worth nothing. Waste paper.' He looked at Wragge. 'You can let the Russians go.'

'Go,' Wragge said. They left. The girl was in tears, and so was the father.

'Let me speak to the squadron,' the adjutant said. Wragge nodded. They walked back. Brazier assembled everyone in a half-circle.

'This man...' Brazier held Simm by the ear. 'He disobeyed an order while on Active Service. Told to remain here, he absented himself without permission. That is conduct prejudicial to good order and discipline. The maximum punishment is two years' imprisonment.'

Simm wriggled. His ear hurt. Brazier tightened his grip. Now the ear hurt even more. Simm stopped wriggling and shut his eyes to the pain, but his ear was still on fire.

'Furthermore,' the adjutant said, 'this man was apprehended in the act of taking a large bribe in exchange for going through a form of marriage to a young Russian woman with the purpose of getting her out of the country.'

That information impressed the squadron, but not by its criminal nature. Fancy old Simmy, trying to pull off a trick like that. Old Simmy, ugly as sin, thick as two short planks, gets a headache just tying his shoelaces. Old Simmy wanders off

459

to have a slash and someone tries to give him a place to dip his wick twice nightly plus a load of loot! God looks after fools and idiots, that's all you can say.

'The marriage would not have been legal,' Brazier said. 'An act of fraud. The maximum punishment for fraud is penal servitude. The money was in worthless roubles. They have now been dumped in the sea. The girl was almost certainly riddled with disease. If he married her, this man would have been infected with incurable types of pox that would rapidly deprive him of what little manhood he has.'

He let that sink in. Old Simmy didn't look so clever now.

'Think of this. Our sole task is to get this squadron off these docks and onto a British warship. Ignore the civilians. They are not your concern. Irrelevant. Only the squadron matters. Nothing else. Dismissed.'

'Well said, Uncle,' Wragge murmured. He took Oliphant's arm and said, 'Come with me, Tusker. I have a great wish to rise to great heights and get above this squalor.'

They climbed the ladder on a boxcar and sat on the roof.

'Did you ever see such a miserable crew?' Wragge said. 'Dregs of a nation. Not their fault, I suppose. No food, no shelter, winter coming on, and they're trapped in this godawful dead-end.' From time to time the warships boomed out another heavy echoing salvo but nobody paid them any attention. 'Is it my imagination,' Wragge said, 'or is there a strange smell in the air?'

Oliphant sniffed. 'Five thousand armpits.'

'More like ten thousand. Could be twenty.'

'You can't count the blighters. They keep moving.'

'Going everywhere and nowhere. I'm as humane as the next man, Tusker, but I can't feel sorry for them. I can feel a sort of pity for one man, or his family, maybe his village. But this lot are just an enormous nuisance.'

'It's not why we came to Russia, is it?' Oliphant asked.

'They cheered us when we arrived. Seems a long time ago.'

'They liked to cheer. Cheer and say *Na Moskvu*. Usually when they were sozzled.'

'I say. Look over there.' They stood up. 'Isn't that the Russian father and his daughter? The one he tried to sell? See? On the dockside. Right on the edge.'

Oliphant saw them. 'He's holding her hand. That's a damn dangerous place to stand. Oh, my Christ.' The father and daughter had jumped. Vanished from sight.

Wragge turned away. 'Sweet sodding buggeration in spades,' he said.

'The water must be freezing cold. I don't suppose they can swim. Most Russians can't, according to Borodin.'

Wragge walked to the end of the boxcar, stared at the sky, and walked back. 'Well, she wanted to escape,' he said. 'That was some kind of escape.'

After that there was nothing to say. Time passed. They grew bored, and stiff and cold; then a Royal Marine arrived and they climbed down from the roof. 'Colonel's compliments, Sir,' the Marine said. 'Please unload all aircraft without delay.' He saluted and left. Oliphant went to tell the ground crews.

'They jumped,' Wragge said to Borodin. 'The father and his daughter jumped in the sea.'

'Yes. A lot of people are doing that.'

Amazingly, a small British tank appeared, and it rumbled up and down, emptying a space alongside the train.

'If he could give us a good fifty yards of clearance,' Wragge said, 'I bet we could take off. Maximum revs. No problem.'

'What then?' Borodin asked.

'Dunno. The Navy has aircraft carriers. There might be one out there. Or we could fly to Turkey.'

The ground crews set about offloading the Nines and the Camels. They were quick; it was an old routine for them. They had assembled the final aircraft when the colonel and his escort arrived. 'Fine machines. You must be proud,' he said to Wragge. 'You do realize that we have no choice. Nothing must be left for the enemy. Not a thing.'

The tank's engine roared and pumped smoke from its exhausts. Its tracks climbed over the tail unit of a Camel and crunched along the fuselage until the undercarriage collapsed and the tank crushed the cockpit, the twin Vickers guns, the radial engine, the propeller.

The C.O. watched his ground crews and saw them standing quite still, all the fitters and the riggers and the armourers. Some had looked away.

One or two seemed to be in tears. As the tank moved forward, a young mechanic made a move towards it as if he could save the next Camel. The adjutant and a flight sergeant grabbed him. 'Discipline, lad, discipline,' Brazier said, and the airman went back to his place. The tank climbed on top of the aeroplane and collapsed it. Tank-tracks made sparks on paving stones as the Camel got chewed up and shattered. Then the next Camel, and finally the Nines.

The C.O. sought out Patterson, the chief mechanic. 'I'm terribly sorry about this,' he said. 'Your chaps must feel very let-down.'

'They put heart and soul into their work, sir. Toiled night and day. Owned those aeroplanes. You borrowed them, sir, but they belonged to us. Mind your back, sir.'

They moved away from the tank. It swung around until it was facing the Black Sea. It roared and rolled forward. The driver came out of the turret hatch in a hurry and jumped clear. The tank picked up speed and went over the edge and made a splash that reached up and soaked the dockside. The ground crews gave an ironic cheer.

'Get your men lined up,' the colonel told Wragge. 'They must follow me to the embarkation point. Only your squadron. No refugees. Use your bayonets, if you have to. No civilians! The women are the worst. They'll bribe you with the family jewels, if you let them.'

As they formed up, the train reversed and slowly vanished into the crowd. Wragge realized that he had completely forgotten about Chef and the engine crew. Well, they had whatever food was left in The Dregs, which was something. Where would they go? Nowhere good.

The squadron marched through the wretched crowd. It watched them go, silently and sullenly. They went down some harbour steps and into a boat. Nobody in the boat looked back as it bucketed across the bay. Everyone looked at the British cruiser waiting for them. It was big and clean-cut and reassuringly safe.

The cruiser sailed two hours later. Oliphant and Brazier stood at the rail, watching Novo fade away. 'Well, Uncle, that was an utter shambles,' Oliphant said. 'I can't see that we did the slightest bit of good to anyone. If anything, we just helped to make a total balls-up of their whole stupid war.'

'There's a useful lesson to be learned,' Brazier said. 'Interfere in someone else's family quarrel and you'll always end up with a bloody nose. And you'll get no thanks.'

'I'll try to remember that, Uncle.'

'Nobody else will, Tusker. The interfering will go on. And so will the bloody noses. You watch.'

4

It was raining in London; had been raining all day. Outside 10 Downing Street the policemen's capes shone like polished lead. Lloyd George was in Geneva, lucky chap, putting in an appearance at talks about the League of Nations. Jonathan Fitzroy took the opportunity to hold a small sherry party at Number 10. It was an occasion to convey the P.M's gratitude to the Sub-Committee on Russia. Former Sub-Committee. It had ceased to be, through force of circumstances. But Fitzroy had a tidy mind, and a word of thanks cost nothing.

'Never knew such a summer,' Sir Franklyn said; 'I felt sorry for the county cricketers. Season's been a washout.'

'*The Times* says there are floods in America,' Fitzroy said. 'Of course, there are always floods somewhere in America.'

'One place you don't want to be is Russia,' General Stattaford said. 'Freezing snow from now until spring.' Silence. Nobody wanted to talk about Russian weather. 'All our troops got out before winter,' he said. 'British Army knows how to extricate its men. Point of pride.'

'Not all,' Charles Delahaye said.

'Brace yourselves,' Weatherby said. 'The Treasury is going to bombard us with statistics.'

'And money,' Delahaye said. 'Widows' pensions, for example. Maintenance of military cemeteries. The Army left 526 men buried in North Russia alone. I can give you the figures for the other campaigns, the Caspian area for instance, and the men we sent to aid Denikin, and the Siberian wars...'

'Some other time, perhaps,' Fitzroy said.

'Then there's the Royal Navy,' Delahaye said. 'The Treasury takes a keen interest in sailors. Warships are costly to replace.'

'Undoubtedly,' Fitzroy said. 'But we reviewed that very carefully, didn't we? The Kronstadt affair, Lieutenant Agar V.C., splendid stuff. We lost a few motor boats, am I right?'

'Not entirely. By July of 1919 the Royal Navy

had an average of eighty-eight warships and auxiliaries in the Baltic, at no little cost. They lost
seventeen ships, including a cruiser, two destroyers and a submarine. Thirty-five officers and
128 men were killed.'

'What's your point?' Stattaford said, sharply.

'Simply that our Intervention in the internal
affairs of another nation came at a price.'

'We were never publicly at war,' Sir Franklyn
said. 'Now we are very publicly at peace with the
Soviets. Lloyd George deserves a little credit for
his secrecy.'

'Denikin might have won,' Stattaford said stub-
bornly.

'So what?' Weatherby said. 'The Kaiser might
have won. That's not what the history books will
say, is it?'

'Gentlemen, gentlemen,' Fitzroy said. 'Please.
Let us not bicker. The matter is over and done
with. General, let me give you more sherry.'

There was silence while he topped up their
glasses.

'Now we have nothing to talk about,' Weatherby
said. 'Except the bloody awful weather, and we've
done that.'

'Perhaps the matter is not yet quite finished,'
Sir Franklyn said. 'Who will write the Official
History of the Intervention?' He looked hard at
Fitzroy. 'Surely the question has arisen.'

'I'm not at liberty to say.'

'And is that because you don't know, or
because you've been told to stonewall?'

Fitzroy spread his hands. 'I'm not at liberty to
say that either.' They laughed, except for Sir

Franklyn, who gave a wintry smile.

'There won't be an Official History, will there?' he said. 'You needn't answer that. You already have.'

Weatherby looked at his watch. 'I have a train to catch.'

Delahaye shared a taxi with him. General Stattaford chose to walk.

Fitzroy was helping Sir Franklyn into his greatcoat, and finding his umbrella, when Sir Franklyn said: 'Just imagine that Russia, France, America, Czechoslovakia, Japan, and a few more – Canadians, Serbs, Chinese – imagine that they all sent armed forces into Britain at different points, in order to decide our form of government. Can you imagine that?'

'Scarcely.'

'And if they did what I've said, and if we defeated them, how long would it take the British people to forget this?'

'Oh ... generations. Perhaps never.'

'Just a thought. Goodnight, Mr Fitzroy.' He put on his hat, stepped outside and opened his umbrella, and walked into the night.

AFTERWARDS

Every record of Merlin Squadron's operations in Russia was burnt when the British Military Mission left Taganrog. All of Lacey's signals, including his exchanges with Captain Butcher about elephant guns and with Captain Stokes about jazz-band instruments, were lost. He kept copies of his fabricated verse eulogies, thinking that they might, one day, be useful for his memoirs.

The squadron disembarked the cruiser at Portsmouth. Most of the ground crew, with their valuable skills, stayed in the R.A.F. Brazier returned to his old regiment, soon grew dissatisfied with peacetime soldiering, and applied for a posting to Palestine, which was now a British Protectorate. He became expert at leading small groups of soldiers in night-time raids on Arab terrorists. In 1935 he was shot dead in one such raid, and was awarded a posthumous Bar to his Military Cross.

Tusker Oliphant left the R.A.F. and worked as a flying instructor at a civil aerodrome. His patience and his calm authority made him popular with students. For many years he organized an annual reunion of members of Merlin Squadron.

Tiger Wragge was offered a job as an R.A.F. test pilot, and took it, on the understanding that he would be free to fly in international air races.

His successes in these events won him some public fame. In 1931 he was testing the prototype of a new fighter aircraft when it disintegrated at low level and he was killed.

Junk Jessop left the service and sold Ford cars in London. Later he grew a moustache in the style made fashionable by Douglas Fairbanks Jr (he slightly resembled the actor) and moved up to selling Bentleys. His ghosted memoirs of the Russian war were a minor success, but when the Special Branch questioned him about a breach of the Official Secrets Act he moved to Australia.

The R.A.F. had no use for Borodin, and Susan Perry made it clear that they could never be more than friends. She went back to nursing at Guy's Hospital and let him stay in her flat until he found a job. Within weeks he married an American film actress who was in London recovering from a divorce. He went with her to Hollywood. When she divorced him he made a career in movies, playing supporting roles as a suave but dangerous Englishman. Susan Perry qualified as a doctor, married a farmer and never regretted it.

Air Ministry terminated Lacey's commission as an acting pilot officer, so he left the Services. He enjoyed the period of freedom, then became bored and invested his savings in a series of high-risk ventures – night clubs, films, new plays. All failed. In 1923 he re-joined the Army and served in the Pay Corps. In 1925 he vanished, together with a large amount of the Army's money. He was never arrested. In 1933, ex-Sergeant Stevens met him on a train in France. 'He asked me if I thought there would be another war,' Stevens recalled. 'I told him it looked likely. He sounded rather nostalgic.'

AUTHOR'S NOTE

A Splendid Little War is fiction based on fact. The reader is entitled to know which is which.

In brief: the characters are invented but the broad sweep of events is true.

In 1919, Britain did indeed send military forces from all three Services to support the White armies of General Denikin and Admiral Kolchak against the Bolshevik armies led by Lenin and Trotsky. General Wrangel commanded the White Army in the battle for Tsaritsyn (soon to be re-named Stalingrad, and to be fought over in another war) but in this narrative his remarks are invented.

In 1919, Lloyd George was the British Prime Minister and Winston Churchill was his Minister of War. Churchill was obsessed with destroying Bolshevism; Lloyd George was willing to back Denikin and Kolchak while claiming, piously, not to interfere in Russia's right to decide its own government, a piece of double-think that fooled nobody.

Jonathan Fitzroy's Advisory Committee on the Intervention in Russia is invented, as are its members: Charles Delahaye, General Stattaford, James Weatherby and Sir Franklyn Fletcher. However, the events that they discuss are true. For example, when Weatherby speaks of mutinies by British Army units in Luton, London and Calais, he is referring to actual events. Similarly, discussion of the Irish problem, or the Royal Navy's successes at Kronstadt, or the campaign to hang the Kaiser, and many more, are all based on fact.

The Royal Air Force raised new squadrons as part of the Intervention. These flew Camels, DH9s and other aircraft, left over from World War One and showing their age. My accounts of their performance in combat are as accurate as I could make them. An R.A.F. squadron fought in the battle for Tsaritsyn, and it made the long journey – first westward, to Taganrog, and then north for some eight hundred kilometres, to Orel – in support of Denikin's fast-moving assault, before retreating an even greater distance, to Novorossisk and evacuation by the Royal Navy. However, Merlin Squadron is my invention and none of its officers and men is based on actual R.A.F. personnel. The same applies to Count Borodin and to other Russian officers.

Some incidents in the narrative may seem bizarre or improbable. Was there a Russian religious cult, known as the Skoptsi, whose members self-mutilated in accordance with the teaching in Matthew, chapter 19? There was indeed. And it is true that the British Military Mission H.Q. in Russia issued each aircrew officer with a phial of morphine, both for medical treatment and as a last resort if captured; similarly; 'Goolie Chits' were attached to aircraft in India. Both Red and White armies routinely shot any enemy officers they captured, just as units that mutinied or deserted usually shot their own officers. Details of the elaborate banquet to mark the fall of Tsaritsyn are typical of Russian celebrations in those days.

The part played by the London Scottish Regiment in the Somme offensive is based on fact but Colonel Kenny V.C. is fiction. On the other hand, Lieutenant Agar V.C. did indeed lead the M.T.B.s that destroyed the Soviet fleet in Kronstadt; similarly, Lieutenant Colonel Johnson did command a battalion of the Hampshire Regiment in Siberia, where he came to regard the situation as 'pretty hopeless' and led a dozen soldiers in the extraordinary journey to Archangel, which I have described.

My accounts of Nicholas II – first as a happy youth, then a reluctant Tsar, lastly as a disastrous Commander-in-Chief – follow the facts, as does Rasputin's success with ladies of the nobility. Nestor Makhno's Anarchist Brigade was a brutal reality in 1919, and the sad inadequacies of Russian hospital trains were all too true: disease, especially typhus, was rife. The vast wine cellars, used by Denikin to fund his treasury, existed, although not exactly where I located them. Another detail: the idea of decorating a ceiling with black footprints was not invented by aircrew in World War Two; it began a generation earlier.

The Royal Navy kept a large fleet in the Baltic, enjoyed victories and suffered casualties, mainly from mines; and Lloyd George did indeed – briefly and secretly – declare war on Soviet Russia. At the other extreme, Susan Perry's pragmatic embalming technique reflects the methods of the time. The scale of official corruption at all levels, and especially the theft of British aid to Denikin, was as great as I indicate, and possibly greater; it was a large reason for his ultimate failure.

I have tried to do justice to the qualities of the Russian armies, both White and Red. The truth was enormously complicated. This book is primarily about the experiences of an R.A.F. squadron, living in trains and often isolated from the population, and so the picture of the wider campaigns must be sketchy, and – for purposes of narrative convenience – somewhat telescoped.

What they discovered about the Russian military – that it could be both brave and incompetent, resolute and corrupt, loyal and treacherous, long-suffering and thoughtless – left the R.A.F. officers baffled and bewildered. Atrocities were committed by both sides. *Nichevo* and *vranyo* played a real part in Russian life, and for all I know they still do. In the end, my reported comment of the bomber pilot who wished that both sides would lose reflected the views of many who served in the Intervention.

Life on an R.A.F. squadron in the Intervention was a strange mixture of bloody combat and a summer holiday in the countryside. They travelled by train, in some comfort, with *plennys* acting as batmen. Often the surroundings were pleasant, and an officer might take his horse and go shooting or fishing. They were nominally part of a White army, but in fact they were largely independent and a long way from British Mission H.Q. In those circumstances, it is not altogether surprising that a squadron might realize that Moscow was within range and plan to bomb it.

This plan did, in fact, take shape. It seemed an obvious and desirable step to take in a war. Moscow had been the goal all along. It was the enemy's H.Q. If it could be hit, why not hit it? When Mission H.Q., and then London, firmly refused permission, this must have seemed to the squadron a foolish decision. In London's eyes, it was a wise precaution. The Russian Civil War was not yet won and lost. There was no merit in impetuous gestures.

There can be no doubt that the Intervention left Russia feeling threatened on all sides. After World War Two – when 1919 was only a generation ago – the Iron Curtain had one great merit from the Soviet point of view: it defended Russia's borders against attack. In 1957 Nikita Khrushchev, on a visit to the United States, declared: 'All the capitalist countries of Europe and America marched on our country to strangle the new revolution... Never have any of our soldiers been on American soil, but your soldiers were on Russian soil. Those are the facts.' The Intervention of 1919 cast a long shadow.

None of this can be confirmed or refuted by reading an Official History of the Intervention, because that work was never written (or, if written, was never published). No doubt Lloyd George's government saw nothing but embarrassment in detailing the decision-making behind a venture that was costly in blood and money at a time when Britain could afford neither, and which ended in total failure. Compared with other campaigns, few first-hand accounts of the Intervention survive. *The Day We Almost Bombed Moscow*, by Christopher Dobson and John Miller (Hodder & Stoughton, 1986) tells the story of that incident and of many other facets of the Intervention. Two sets of memoirs by serving officers are very revealing. *Farewell to the Don* (Collins, 1970) is the journal of Brigadier H.N.H. Williamson, an artilleryman whose task was to advise and instruct Denikin's armies. He travelled widely and saw both the best and the worst of the Russian soldier. *Last Train Over Rostov Bridge* (Cassell, 1962) is by Captain Marion Aten D.F.C., whose squadron flew Camels in many combats against the Red air force. They arrived in Russia full of enthusiasm and left it, months later, a lot wiser and not sorry to get out. The immediacy of their experience makes their accounts invaluable reading. Of other books on the subject, *The Victors' Dilemma: Allied Intervention in the Russian Civil War*, by John Silverlight (Barrie & Jenkins, 1970) is scholarly and invaluable.

Any factual errors, of course, are down to me.

D.R.

The publishers hope that this book has given you enjoyable reading. Large Print Books are especially designed to be as easy to see and hold as possible. If you wish a complete list of our books please ask at your local library or write directly to:

Magna Large Print Books
Magna House, Long Preston,
Skipton, North Yorkshire.
BD23 4ND

This Large Print Book for the partially sighted, who cannot read normal print, is published under the auspices of

THE ULVERSCROFT FOUNDATION

THE ULVERSCROFT FOUNDATION

... we hope that you have enjoyed this Large Print Book. Please think for a moment about those people who have worse eyesight problems than you ... and are unable to even read or enjoy Large Print, without great difficulty.

You can help them by sending a donation, large or small to:

**The Ulverscroft Foundation,
1, The Green, Bradgate Road,
Anstey, Leicestershire, LE7 7FU,
England.**
or request a copy of our brochure for more details.

The Foundation will use all your help to assist those people who are handicapped by various sight problems and need special attention.

Thank you very much for your help.